THE DEPARTMENT OF SUPERNATURAL RESOURCES

KYRA FULLAM

Copyright © 2023 Kyra Fullam All rights reserved

The characters and events portrayed in this book are fictitious. Any similarity to real persons, living or dead, is coincidental and not intended by the author.

No part of this book may be reproduced, or stored in a retrieval system, or transmitted in any form or by any means, electronic, mechanical, photocopying, recording, or otherwise, without express written permission of the publisher.

Cover design by: Kyra Fullam
Printed in the United States of America
ISBN: 979-8-218-31517-7
Imprint: Independently published

To my family, friends, and, most importantly, my mom and dad — thank you for reading and re-reading every rough draft. I love you.

Chapter One
Cracked

With my eyes glued to the rearview mirror; I flung my phone out of the window like a frisbee. I wanted to see it smash into a million pieces as it hit the pavement. I laughed as a distant crunch sounded over the rushing wind. That felt even better than I'd expected. I didn't care how insane I probably looked right now. Enough was enough. I'd gotten twenty-seven texts since leaving the police station. Twenty-seven in less than fifteen minutes. It might sound normal if they were from a big group message with all my besties, but no. Abso-fucking-lutely not. If I had more than one friend to speak of, I'd be sitting here crying tears of joy — not throwing my phone into the Wyoming wilderness like some melodramatic tween girl. Instead, the rapid-fire, digital ass-chewing was from none other than Chief Garcia — my overbearing and clearly batshit boss. What the hell was he thinking blowing me up like that? I'd already sat through his stupid lecture in person this morning!

Don't fuck this up, Georgia.
This Josh Peters thing is our TOP priority right now.
Think logically!!!
We can't afford to lose his donations just because you have "issues" with him.

His texts went on and on. Like... *Okay?* I get it. What was I even supposed to say to all that? I knew what he *wanted* me to say. He wanted some long-winded kiss-ass apology or promise that I would make everything better, but I wouldn't give that to him. If he was looking for that, he was talking to the *wrong* girl. I shouldn't even be surprised by now. I dealt with this kind of bullshit on a daily basis. Everyone loved to pretend I was invisible until they needed something from me.

Today, that "something" was helping Switchback PD finally solve the Josh Peters' case. It had been open for months now, but no one had been able to come up with any real leads. When he came into the station to raise hell again this morning, I thought he was just pissed about our progress and looking to big-dick my boss into getting it solved. I would've sold my soul to see how *that* little conversation would've played out. Unfortunately, the actual reason behind his visit was far less exciting. Someone had vandalized his new construction site again. It's happened twice before, but today was different. Today, he had come to *my* office first. Considering how his other visits had gone, it was a shock. He'd always dismissed my help — brushing me off as some "wanna-be police officer" who "couldn't solve a case if the answer smacked me right in the face". His words, not mine. I don't care what he says, I know how good I am at my job. In fact, I was *happy* not being assigned the case until now. If he didn't want help from the best damned detective in the state, that was on him.

How he'd expected anyone else to solve it before was beyond me, though. I suppose it was par for the course for him. He was your typical rich white dude with too much free time and too little common sense. The only suspect he had was his older than dirt neighbor, Mrs. Jessops. It was pathetic. He was clearly targeting her. Sure, she'd protested his build at a few Switchback city council meetings, but that didn't make her a criminal. It felt like no one else could see that besides me. I mean, the theory was *so* bizarre, I thought no one would ever take him seriously, but… I was obviously wrong, because here I was now — headed to interrogate the poor woman.

The only reason Josh had finally come crawling to me for help was because he couldn't afford to keep fixing his new site. Everything always came down to money and I was his last hope. Chief Garcia couldn't have made it any clearer for me. Josh Peters' donations to the department were just too important. If Josh was losing money, so were we. In return, he'd gotten special privileges like never getting dismissed for anything — even if it was something as outrageous as this. But if Josh says someone did it, you can bet your ass the Chief is going to listen. I, on the other hand, nearly pissed my pants when Josh told me why he thought Mrs. Jessops had done it. She lived next to the construction site, and she didn't like him. That was all the evidence Josh had. *That was it!* Well, *that* and he claimed she looked "spry enough to do it", but that part of the argument was so flimsy even Chief Garcia had laughed.

I glanced back at the dirt road to see where my phone had landed.

Shit.

It had felt pretty damn good to throw it out in the moment, but I was starting to regret it now. I'd have to go back for it eventually. I chewed on my lip. It could wait until I was done with this godforsaken interrogation, right? *Ugh, the interrogation.* I didn't want to do that either. Like... really, *really* badly. I sighed and slowly turned my car around. It was the most appealing option I had right now. Anything to delay the inevitable. A tight knot of dread flared up in the pit of my stomach. I was late, and I knew I was making everything worse by procrastinating, but I couldn't help it. I wished I could skip town. Run away. Disappear. Literally *vanish* off the face of the earth rather than go to Mrs. Jessops' house and accuse her of a stupid crime I *knew* she didn't do. *Jesus H. Christ.* That's exactly what I had to do, though! There was no getting around it if I wanted to keep my job... Which I very much did, despite my helicopter boss situation. It wasn't like anyone was lining up to hand *me* a job — the town freak.

From a very early age, I'd learned the ability to smell lies wasn't normal. I'd never understood it, but when someone lied to me, it stunk. The odor was a mix between sweaty gym socks and gasoline. Beyond my immediate family and my best friend Charlie, everyone thinks I'm just abnormally perceptive — like how Sherlock Holmes can look at a crime scene for five seconds to know who did it and how. It's not like that, though. Not even close. A lie always has to be clear and direct for me to smell it, so yes or no questions are the easiest. The smell of a lie always seems to get lost somewhere along the way if someone starts ranting. By then, it's impossible to separate fact from fiction. It's pretty lame as far as hidden talents go. Sure, I was a great consultant on tough-to-crack police cases, but when it came to making friends? Not such a cool party trick anymore. Who wants to be friends with someone who knows for a fact that you're lying when you say you can't make it to dinner because you've got "work stuff" to catch up on? *Nobody,* that's who. Well, except for Charlie. But he's so blunt that lying has probably never even crossed his mind.

After a few minutes of scratching around in the dried-up brush, I retrieved my now cracked-to-hell phone and headed back towards Adelaide Road. Although the tree-lined trident was on the outskirts of town, I arrived much faster than I was prepared for. The branch to the left led to the McKinney's property, the one in the middle to Mrs. Jessops', and the freshly carved one on the right was to Josh Peters' latest construction site — or the "scene of the crime" as he was calling it. I crept down the middle lane, my foot feather-light on the gas pedal, until I finally found myself in Mrs. Jessops' circular driveway. I wasn't ready for this. My anxiety was off the charts. I was just thankful I'd worn a black sweater today because it was doing a good job hiding my sweat-soaked underarms. I stepped out of the car and surveyed the familiar house.

Although Mrs. Jessops had been a widow for at least twenty years now, she'd always insisted on the "Mrs." part of her name staying. I'd never understood why people thought it was weird. Her soft yellow cottage was practically a time-capsule full of those moments she'd shared with her husband. He'd built the wobbly fountain in the drive that still worked, even after all these years. He'd planted the ivy that crawled across the rickety trellis entryway, and the tall hydrangeas that brushed against the tin roof. Every single part of it had Mr. Jessops' fingerprints all over it. Why should she forget him when he was practically still here?

The cold fall air bit at my bare fingertips as I rapped out three sharp knocks on her door. I hopped from foot to foot, trying to stay warm as I listened to the telltale scuttling of Mrs. Jessops making her way to me.

"Georgia!" she exclaimed.

Despite Mrs. Jessops' age, which was crawling up to eighty, the woman seemed barely older than my mother. Her dark skin was smooth as glass, and the way her black hair fell in thick, long waves would make any supermodel jealous. Her youthful appearance might be a red flag to Josh Peters but... *Come on.* It's the twenty-first century, there *are* things you can do to stay looking good. I knew Josh was well-versed in some of those tactics himself. From what I recall, his teeth were not that perfect and white in high school. I remember because me and Charlie used to call him "Piano keys Peters" behind his back. It was *that* bad. I mean, I'm talking buck-toothed beaver status. When I saw his new face plastered on every billboard in town a few years after graduation, I almost crashed my car. He'd gotten some *major* work done since then, not just the teeth. If his name hadn't been on the ad, I probably wouldn't have even recognized him. People say he's *so* handsome now, but to me, Josh Peters is just a human Ken doll with dentures and a nasty attitude.

"Come in, come in! You'll catch a chill standing out here in the cold!" Mrs. Jessops was saying.

God, what was going on with me? My nervousness was making it *impossible* to focus on the real reason I was here.

I gave her an awkward grin as she ushered me in through the stone foyer to the cozy sitting room where a fire was blazing in the hearth. She had already set two teacups out on the table next to an assortment of finger sandwiches and fall-themed cookies on tiered trays.

I sank into a chair across from her. "Sorry, I should've called first. Were you expecting someone?"

Laughing, Mrs. Jessops waved a gnarled hand in front of her. The crooked fingers and knobby knuckles seemed to be the only part of her that truly showed her age.

"I was expecting *you*, Georgia."

Even though I could tell it looked strained, I smiled again. I wished I could've been there for a simple cup of tea, but I was on business today and this whole polite charade was feeling very slimy. Clearly, someone had already phoned to tell her I'd be coming around to ask some questions. That damned Chief Garcia. I wanted to wring his fat neck. She'd probably seen right through me as soon as I'd stepped in the door.

Stop that, I silently chastised myself. *You haven't done anything wrong. It's not like you came in here all fake, then sprung it on her that she was being investigated.*

The zesty scent of oranges and earthy sage filled the air as she poured our tea. "I always know when you're wrestling with yourself, Georgia. You give yourself away by fiddling with that bracelet of yours. You know, your Grams used to do the same thing."

I let out a strangled laugh as I tried to hide my bandaged wrist.

"She did that, too." She pursed her lips. "When she was anxious. A terrible habit, really. You've got blood on your jeans, dear. You won't have any clothes left if you keep ruining them like that."

Okay, fine sue me. I had trouble managing my anxiety. My old therapist would call the bracelet thing a *coping mechanism*. I'd twist it around to find the sharp edges, where the stones had fallen out, and dig them into my wrist. Depending on how bad I was feeling, sometimes I even drew blood. This morning when Garcia was screaming at me about this stupid case, there *was*. Hence the bandage. I'd be the first to admit it wasn't the healthiest thing in the world, but I couldn't stop. No matter how bad it looked, it was the only thing that worked for me. During a panic attack, it brought me back to reality — helped me breathe again. If I *could* stop, I would.

I stared at the hardened patch of blood on my thigh. The woman had eyes like a hawk. I'd thought the stain was invisible against my black jeans. I might've been shocked, but then again, she *was* Mrs. Jessops. Nothing got past her.

She clasped her hands together in lap and straightened. "Those bracelets she gave you kids are different from the one she wore, though. The stones are *very* curious. Did you know that she—"

"I'm sorry, Mrs. Jessops. It's just that I'm not here for tea today. Josh Peters' construction site was vandalized again, and — Well, stuff was stolen — Copper. And he thinks it was you. *Again*."

Mrs. Jessops froze in her seat like she was waiting for a painter to capture her portrait. My heartbeat thudded in my ears. I tried to focus on arranging my expression into something more pleasant, but my hand ached to twist my bracelet around my wrist. She blinked. Once. *Twice*.

"Everything about you is like your Grams," Mrs. Jessops answered. "That fire — that passion you have. It's always bittersweet to see you, Georgia. You remind me so much of her when we were girls — especially that long, black hair and proud nose of yours. All of you Beretta's have that same intensity about you."

I pressed a palm over my heart to quell the ache there. Being compared to my Grams was the best compliment anyone could've given me — even if it wasn't completely true. She had been beautiful in a way I'd never be. The nose that looked too large on my face worked great on my Grams', and even my brothers. They all had the carved, robust features for it. But mine... "*Intense*" was definitely a word for it. We all looked like Roman statues, but in my case, not the good kind. As much shit as I talked about Josh Peters, sometimes I wished he would stop being an ass long enough to tell me who his plastic surgeon was. They'd done a damn good job considering how busted he looked before.

I shook my head. Although I welcomed the distraction, we weren't here to reminisce on the Beretta family's Mediterranean features today.

"I'm sorry. It's just a formality. I know there's no way you could've done it, but Josh was so persistent and—"

Her eyes fixed on the crackling fire as she brushed her fingers through her hair. "Never mind all of that, Georgia dear. I've always been outspoken about the construction site, and I wish I could say it *was* me who sabotaged Josh, but... I don't have the guts or even the physical strength to pull that off. Not anymore." Her face was full of warmth and honesty when she looked at me again.

The expression made me relax. The part of me that could sniff out a lie was silent. She was telling the truth. She had to be. I was almost never wrong. I retrieved a triangle of cucumber sandwich and slumped back into my seat.

"Maybe when I was younger, I would've done something like that," she said. A faraway look had entered her chocolate eyes, as if she was imagining herself, maybe around my age, going and doing exactly what Josh had accused her of. "He was a rotten little boy, and I'm afraid to say he's grown into an even more rotten man."

"I'm not afraid to say it. He's an asshole."

"That site is on protected land, Georgia. That's why I've always been so against it, but it truly couldn't have been me. Although, when you find the culprit, I'd like to thank them. They finally put that little bastard in his place."

I smiled through the fresh, creamy bites of my sandwich. I'd always had a certain bond with Mrs. Jessops. Even if she hadn't been my Grams' best friend, and my surrogate grandmother since her death, I'd always loved her because she had the courage to say what everyone else was thinking. Or, at least, what *I* was thinking.

"I tried to tell him that! Ugh, this is so frustrating. It could be anyone. Like, for example, Josh basically pays his workers peanuts. Some of his boys are bound to be pissed with the amount of money he has." I paused, thinking about my other theory. "Or *women*, considering the last gift he received."

Mrs. Jessops nodded, as if she'd heard the same thing. At the thought, though, I dug through my bag for the photos Josh had given me and extended them to her. A smug smile crept across her lips as she sorted through them, and I couldn't help but laugh at her reaction. I'd like to thank whoever did it, too.

The photos showed men's brief-cut underwear, size extra-large, with a skid-mark stain all the way up the back to the tag which was monogrammed with the initials "J.P.". The shit-stained panties hung on a sharpened stick in the dead center of his new construction site, waving in the fall breeze like the white flag of defeat. If the embarrassing message hadn't been clear enough, another was scrawled in the mud below to drive home the sender's point.

"Don't shit where you eat."

The lettering was unhurried, deliberate, precise. The vandal had taken their time.

Mrs. Jessops' eyes were mischievous as ever when she passed the pictures back. "Can I have copies? I think they'd look perfect in frames on my mantle."

"Hmm… I think I could make that happen, but it would have to be our little secret."

I smoothed my rumpled sweater and picked a few crumbs from my pants as I made to leave but stopped as I remembered one last thing. I still needed an alibi from her. Even though I'd been forced to do this, to interrogate her and see if she was lying, I knew my word alone still wouldn't be enough for Josh. He was almost as vindictive as I was, and without solid proof Mrs. Jessops hadn't defiled his new refinery… Well, there was just no way he'd ever stop hounding her.

"Mrs. Jessops? I have to ask, um — What *were* you doing last night? Josh said his cameras cut out between eleven and twelve, and… I sort of need an alibi if I'm ever going to make him drop this."

"I was in the woods, of course," she explained, as if the answer was the most obvious thing in the world.

"In the woods? *At night?*"

Her nose wrinkled. "In the woods, yes. I was out there until early this morning. I had to go around my property to perform a hearth and home ceremony."

"I'm not following," I squinted at her, now moving to sit again.

"Why, it was Mabon last night, dear," she chided, as if it was some major holiday I should've been aware of. "The autumnal equinox?"

My lips spluttered. "But that's a Witch holiday, Mrs. Jessops. We're not supposed to be—"

A shrill alert siren blasted out from the radio on the mantle. "In other news, the Triad makes continued success at lobbying Washington for the expanded bill of Supernatural rights," the bland newswoman droned. "Here today in Switchback, Wyoming at the Supernatural's home base, known as the Citadel, to speak about their progress is Triad spokeswoman Celine Bissonnette."

Mrs. Jessops moved to cut it off, muttering something to herself about "divine timing".

"You're a supporter, aren't you?" she asked after returning to her seat.

"Sure, but we're still not supposed to be—"

"To hell with what we're *supposed* to do and not do, Georgia. I'm too old to care what people think of me. I've practiced Wicca for years, and just because it's not "proper" now since the Supernatural's came out from the shadows doesn't mean I'm going to give that up."

I was too stunned to speak.

"Look at me, Georgia," she commanded. "Look at my eyes. Everyone can see I'm not a Witch. I know exactly what you're thinking, but why would it even matter if I was? They're people, too. People with feelings and jobs and kids. People that we humans could all learn a thing or two from."

I agreed with everything she was saying, of course. Ever since the Supernatural's government, the Triad, had taken up residence in our hometown almost ten years ago, they'd barely even shown their faces. The reaction from us humans had been so bad, they were probably scared we'd go feral, even now. Sure, I *was* a supporter, but I also knew better than to advertise that fact about myself. People already thought I was weird enough. I didn't need to give them any more reasons to make me the town pariah.

Around here, it wasn't just the Witches that were taboo. It was *all* Supernatural's. Which also made pretty much *everything* that had to do with the occult forbidden, too. Even Halloween got canceled. At best, the Supernatural's were openly discriminated against. At worst, they were attacked on sight. Not that humans stood any real chance against them anyway, but it had definitely been enough to set their Great Integration plan back a few years. Honestly, I was pretty sure I'd be hard-pressed to find *anybody* in Switchback who supported the Triad besides me and a few other weirdos. It was a strange thing to live near the capital of the Supernatural world in a town where everyone wanted them dead. The old military test site they'd taken over with its isolated location was certainly a plus for the Triad's home base, but I wasn't sure why they hadn't opted for somewhere like New York or California. Surely, they'd be more welcome there.

"It's just, well..." I paused, having trouble getting the words out. "It's just that, if people ever knew you were doing something like that Mrs. Jessops... If Josh ever knew..."

"He'd burn me at the stake?" She deadpanned.

I nodded.

"That's precisely why I've never told anyone before now, my dear."

Shifting into full detective mode, I decided to set my personal feelings aside for now. The lecture could wait until after I'd put all the pieces together. "So, you were out in the woods performing this... Mabon ceremony?"

"Mabon, yes."

"And what did this ceremony entail?"

"I was creating a protective boundary around my home for harmony and protection last night, and when I'd finished, I set up an altar of fire to show my gratitude and celebrate the full harvest moon. It's still outside if you'd like to see it." She stood suddenly, much faster than I thought her capable, and threw out a hand to indicate the door.

Again, I was reminded of Josh Peters' insistence that she wasn't as frail as she seemed. Either the old woman had just gotten a sugar rush from those fall-themed cookies, or I was starting to see things.

I stayed seated. "Maybe later, Mrs. Jessops."

I still had questions for her. *Lots of them.*

She sat back down with a huff.

"Did Grams know about these ceremonies, too?" I asked. The question had nothing to do with my investigation, but I needed to know the answer for selfish reasons.

"Of course not! We were best friends, but she didn't know everything I did. People don't like different, Georgia," she tapped a crooked finger against her temple. "Especially the close-minded people around here. If word got out, and people believed I was a Witch, or, Goddess forbid, suspected *your Grams* had been just for being associated with me, well... I'm afraid there would've been a Witch hunt for the both of us — even without the Marking. I would never put your Grams or your family in danger like that. It was just easier to keep it all a secret."

The Marking. The creepy glowing eyes I'd only ever seen glimpses of on television. That was how everyone knew who was a Witch and who wasn't. All those crazy conspiracy theory people said that all the other Supernatural races had obvious physical tells like the Witches, but who really knew? They may come out of the shadows, but that didn't mean they'd stepped into the spotlight. In fact, their spokeswoman, Celine Bissonnette, was the only Supernatural who made regular public appearances. She was a Vampire, but with all the TV lighting and makeup, she didn't seem that much different from me or any other human.

I thrust my flattened palm towards her. "Grams wouldn't have cared, you know. She *wasn't* close-minded. She would've loved you no matter what."

"I know that, Georgia. Your Grams was the most accepting woman I've ever met, but surely even you can see why I had to keep that from her."

It felt like a struggle to see straight. I couldn't believe she'd *lied* to Grams for so long. I thought about my friendship with Charlie. Did he have a secret like this, too? I hoped not. I hoped that *my* best friend would never keep anything like this from me. Hell, even Charlie knew the truth about my whole "lie-sniffing" ability, so why couldn't Mrs. Jessops tell her own best friend something like this? She was wrong. I *didn't* understand how she could hide such an important part of herself from the one person who was supposed to know her best.

Instead of saying all the things my angry tongue begged me to say, I took a shaky breath and asked, "Did anyone else see you performing this ceremony, Mrs. Jessops?"

"I'm very careful, so I really don't think anyone did."

Everything I'd ever known about Mrs. Jessops had changed in a matter of minutes. I didn't care if she was a Witch, or practiced Wicca, or whatever, but... *A liar?* There was nothing worse than being a liar.

My anger finally won out. "Grams *always* defended you, you know. She made herself look like a fool for defending you every time someone would call you a Witch."

Mrs. Jessops gave me a small, sad smile. "She didn't look like a fool, Georgia. I'm not *really* a Witch, after all. Besides, Wicca and real Witchcraft are two completely different things," she laughed to herself. "You can't *imagine* how excited I was when I found out about the *real* thing, though. The *real* Witches. I—"

"Why tell me? Why now, after all these years? After the lengths you went to, hiding this... this *secret* from my Grams?"

"Because you asked. And we both know I can't lie to you, Georgia Beretta."

I gnashed my teeth together, feeling... I don't know what I was feeling. Second-hand betrayal? *Yes.* Anger? *Absolutely.* I knew the point she was trying to make, but I couldn't help but feel furious that she wasn't exactly the person my Grams had thought she was. Best friends weren't supposed to have secrets. *Ever.* As childish as I knew it was... What was the point of even being best friends if you had to hide parts of yourself?

She reached across the table to clasp my hands. "In the end, we're the same you and I. Deep-down, I know you understand *why* I had to hide this from your Grams. I was protecting her, Georgia. If I was lying about *that*, you'd know. Even best friends have *some* secrets. Please don't think of me or my relationship with your Grams any differently, dear."

I didn't know if I could, though. I'd obviously known Mrs. Jessops was an odd bird, but *this*? She'd never even *hinted* at something like *this*. It made me furious! I still remember the days Grams was alive and someone would mention Mrs. Jessops being just a *little* off to her — she would lose her mind. Hell, *I* did the same thing! Sure, my family was known for having a short temper, the "Beretta bomb", but we protected those we loved.

Fiercely. And we all loved Mrs. Jessops. She knew that! She had *used* it to her advantage. Why else would she let her best friend do something like that when she *was sort-of* a Witch? She had *used* Grams' love and trust to keep her secret for all those years. And... I'd never even suspected it myself. *How had I never suspected it?*

As much as I didn't want to accept it, I knew that Mrs. Jessops wasn't lying when she said she'd done it to protect Grams and our family, but... she was also protecting herself.

Even though I was hurt and upset now, I knew I couldn't stay that way for long. Despite everything, I loved Mrs. Jessops like I'd loved my own grandmother, and nothing could ever stand in the way of that. Still, that didn't mean that I wouldn't be doing some serious self-reflection later about how she'd hidden that part of herself all these years — and how I'd missed it. Until now, I'd never *directly* asked her about being a Witch, but still... I couldn't shake the feeling that I'd overestimated my abilities after all.

Chapter Two
Bling

I'd always thought that Nostra Casa was the perfect name for my family's restaurant in town. It meant "our home", and my parents had always taken the name quite literally. There wasn't a single day in my entire childhood I could remember not being at the restaurant. From birthdays, to holidays, and everything in between — we always spent our time together right inside those walls.

I'd always enjoyed being there, too... Right up until the day my parents had sat me down and explained that *I* was supposed to be the one taking it over when they were gone. It wasn't like I didn't love the place, I did, but... I wanted *more* than the restaurant. I wanted *out* of Switchback. Eventually, when I'd saved up enough money, I wanted my own life where people didn't know me *or* my reputation. I hoped they might understand that. It seemed like such a simple request, seeing as I had two older brothers who could've easily taken it over, but... When I tried to explain it to my parents, well... Let's just say their reaction was *anything* but simple.

Charlie was already waiting for me outside the restaurant in his huge, shiny red truck. *His latest toy.* And I'll be damned. It was even *bigger* than the last one he'd had. I was willing to bet my entire life savings that he had to scale the tires like some circus performer to even get inside it.

Compared to the wide-open spaces of farms and fields surrounding Switchback, our downtown area was practically an oasis. It was a miniature replica of a European city with gray stone buildings, cobblestone roads, and old-timey black lamp posts. The shops, bakeries, loft-style apartments, and antique malls were all squashed in beside each other to make a perfect walking district for residents and tourists alike. I shook off a chill as I stepped into the preemptively salted street and tucked my coat tighter around me. Even though it was only the end of September, it seemed like everyone was already expecting an early winter this year.

As Charlie clambered from his truck, I had to turn my eyes towards the mountain range beyond the city to contain my laughter. I'd been right after all. The slick bottoms of his cowboy boots slipped on his person-sized tires at least twice before he actually made it down.

Ridiculous.

Nostra Casa was the largest building on Main Street. Its two imposing stories commanded nearly an entire block. If I was looking at it through a tourist's eyes, I might've even thought it was the town's courthouse or a museum of sorts. Warm air and soft light spilled out onto the pavement invitingly despite the cold, carved shell the restaurant stood in. Like a moth to a flame, I hovered near the entrance as Charlie got his bearings.

"Finally made it out of your tank?" I laughed.

He rolled his eyes and sent a right-hook towards the back of my shoulder. "Oh, shut up, G! Once I take you for a spin in the monster, I'm sure you'll be changin' your tune."

"What do you get like… Two, maybe three miles to the gallon in that thing?" I scoffed, sending my own punch of greeting straight into the center of his puffy jacket.

Charlie laughed as he held open the foyer's heavy door for me. *God, it smells fantastic in here.* My stomach rumbled at the scents of roasted garlic, butter-slathered bread fresh from the oven, sweet, caramelized onions, and some sort of succulent meat that must've been today's special.

The restaurant was sectioned off into three parts. The more casual bar area was in the front where patrons could have a drink while taking in the downtown scenery, the formal dining area in the back with its white tablecloths and rich decor, and the top floor where the bakery was located beyond a lavish set of red-carpeted stairs. Most days, I would've made a beeline for the kitchen to see my family, but today, I needed a stiff drink to chase away the chill and the conversation I'd had with Mrs. Jessops.

"I need alcohol. *Immediately*, if not sooner." I announced as I made my way to the polished curve of the bar.

Charlie snickered again as he followed and pulled up one of the leather stools. My hands pushed into my hair as I stared at the counter and tried to think of anything else but the terrible day I'd had. Mrs. Jessops was innocent, that much I knew. But what I couldn't figure out was how to get her off the hook. No one had seen her perform her little "Mabon" ritual — meaning she had no alibi and no way to protect herself against the wrath of Josh Peters. I just hoped that the police wouldn't be able to find any of her DNA at the scene. That would be her only saving grace now.

On top of all that mess, I was now trying to come to terms with the fact that my grandmother's best friend, a woman I thought I knew even better than myself, had secretly practiced Wicca for years. It didn't seem *that* bad to me, but... *Why hadn't I known?* Why was it some big thing she'd wanted to keep from us? Was it really *that* dangerous of a secret? The worst part was that I didn't have answers to *any* of my questions. I felt helpless, and helpless was something that I *never* wanted to be.

A firm hand gripped my shoulder, causing my muscles to go as taut as a bowstring.

"What's wrong, G?" Charlie was asking.

The warbly tunes of Frank Sinatra filled the bar above the loud chatter of tipsy guests seated around us. Nostra Casa was *never* empty. For whatever reason, it had always served as that *one place* in Switchback where everyone gathered. Our guests ranged from teenagers to folks at the retirement home. No matter who you were, it was just *that* spot to be.

I blinked at my friend, at his tanned fingers gripping the shearling coat that I'd been too distracted to take off. I quickly threw the jacket by our feet as I tried to think of where to even start.

"Wanna go riding tonight?" He asked. "You could tell me then, if you want."

He knew better than to push when I was in a mood. It had to be one of my favorite things about him. We were so similar in that way — moody and stubborn until we had time to cool off. Riding around his dad's farm was our cure-all for practically anything we were going through.

After this, though, I was positive my social battery would be drained. What I really needed was an extra-strength melatonin and a twelve-hour hibernation in my own bed.

I rubbed my forehead. "Can't tonight."

"Well, tell me what's up then, G. I hate to see you all stressed out like this."

I instantly melted beneath the hopeful look on his boyishly handsome face. "Okay, fine. But it's a lot, so you better strap in."

He flashed me a megawatt grin as he pretended to find a seat belt and buckle up.

Although Josh Peters was considered the most eligible bachelor in Switchback, it was Charlie Fairburn who had graciously let him have that title. Not even Josh's wealth could compare to Charlie's estate — let alone his good looks and decidedly more pleasant personality. Though, it was Charlie's reputation of being a flaky "one-night stand" kind of guy that mostly kept the Switchback girls at bay. *Mostly* because he'd already been with everyone in town besides me. If we hadn't grown up together, I might've even found myself under his spell, too. As his oldest and best friend, I'd be lying if I said I couldn't see it. That whole scruffy, half-country, half-city boy thing he had going on, combined with his brown curls and sapphire-blue eyes, was, *admittedly*, swoon-worthy. If you were into that sort of thing.

I steeled myself before launching into a full run-down of my day — Josh Peters' accusations against Mrs. Jessops, her lack of an alibi, the pressure I felt from Garcia to solve the case and identify someone to arrest, the horrible, lost feeling I'd gotten when Mrs. Jessops told me she was a sort-of Witch. I told Charlie *everything*. He nodded along — his expression staying neutral until I'd mentioned the last part.

"A w-what?"

I stared at the floor, unable to offer any kind of further explanation. How could I explain that? How could anyone?

"A Witch... Like a Supernatural Witch?" He clarified.

I shook my head.

"What other kind of Witch is there?"

I shrugged as my fingers found each other in my lap — rubbing and worrying over every knuckle like they were trying to wash away the idea that I hadn't known Mrs. Jessops as well as I thought I did. After a long moment, Charlie's rough hand joined mine — his skin settling over me like a soothing blanket.

"If Mrs. Jessops didn't want your Grams to know something, Georgia... There was a damn good reason for it. She's a smart woman — a *good,* kind woman who loves you more than anything in this world. Hell, even before your Grams passed, she treated you like blood. Don't beat yourself up about this, okay? You know her, *I* know her, and being a *"Witch"* or whatever the hell she is in her free time shouldn't matter."

I cursed as a hot needle of pain pierced through my vision. I grabbed my hand back and pressed a sleeve against the corners of my eyes before the tears could fall. If they fell now, there would be no stopping them.

"I just wish —" I stopped short, not knowing *what* I wished.

That she hadn't kept this from Grams? For me to have maybe picked up on this sooner? For my Grams to still be around so I could talk to her about this? I wanted that more than anything in the entire world. But, as far as I knew, not even the best Supernatural Witches possessed enough power to reverse death... So now, all I had were questions, and this ache in my bones that only served as a constant reminder that I'd probably *never* know all the answers.

"I know," Charlie said firmly. "That it might seem like a betrayal of trust to you, but some things are just better left alone, G. At least she told you now, right?"

I nodded; the motion as empty as I felt inside.

"What about her alibi, though?" He changed the subject, clearly sensing we needed to shift gears before I full-on snot-cried at the bar.

"Have any ideas?"

"Well, what about that ritual thing? She couldn't have been at the construction site when all that happened, right?"

"Right"

"And she didn't lie — as far as you could tell?"

"No."

"But, with Josh Peters out for blood, and the lack of someone to corroborate her story... That's just not enough, is it?"

"What do I do, Char? He's going to want her arrested no matter what I say, even if they *don't* find her DNA! They'll do it, too. You know they will. Josh has way too much power."

Charlie bit into his bottom lip. I would've offered solutions myself, but I'd run through it all so many times that it felt like everything had turned into a stew of random facts and ideas.

"Mrs. Jessops said she was performing a ritual around the time of the vandalism, right? Didn't you say she made some kind of fire?"

I scowled. "Charlie, I already told you, she was *positive* no one else saw her. And, even if someone *had* seen the fire, I know Josh will say there's still the possibility she could've made it as a distraction when she snuck over to his property."

Charlie shook his head so hard that his brown curls swooped into a comb-over. I almost let myself laugh at the wild state of his hair before he started speaking again — his serious expression dragging me back to the gravity of the situation.

"No, G, I think you're wrong! You know Dale and Tommy-Lee McKinney?"

How could I forget *them*? The only two brothers in Switchback who'd wreaked more havoc than my own — although they'd done it with a lot less charm and finesse.

"Trash."

"True, *but* they're trash who work for *my* father."

I gave Charlie a pinched look that said, "*And?*"

I didn't give a flying fuck who they worked for. In my book, they were at the very bottom, sandwiched right between Josh Peters and my ex-boyfriends. Before I was a police consultant, I'd been Switchback's one and *only* social worker. I honestly couldn't count the times I'd gone out to their decrepit old trailer. They could just never seem to remember that their brood of kids needed to have a clean house and at least three full meals a day if they wanted to keep them in their custody.

"I'm the supervisor at the ranch, G!"

"Jesus, get to the point already, Charlie!" I groaned, unable to control my frustration any longer. He really *was* an awful storyteller.

"Well, when I'm there, I have to walk around and make sure everything is running smoothly, which also means that I basically have to listen to everyone's conversations all day."

Yes, the key point being "*when*" he was there. I didn't want to be the one to point out the fact that I *also* knew that Charlie was *rarely* out there doing his "supervisor" duties in the first place —

maybe one week out of the month if he was feeling generous, and only then to appease his father, and keep his bank account full.

"Dale and Tommy-Lee live on Adelaide, too. The road to the left of Mrs. Jessops. There are some woods between them, but I've heard them talking, G. I'm pretty sure I remember them saying something about how there's a clear shot between their backyard and her house."

"And, what? You think they spy on her for fun or something?"

"No, I *know* they spy on her for fun."

I stiffened, suddenly much more interested in what he had to say. *He might be onto something…*

"They've said that?"

"Yeah! They watch her whenever she's in her yard doing stuff. It's like some drinking game to them or something."

Of course, it was. Those two could make anything into a drinking game.

"So, you think since Mrs. Jessops was out in her yard that night, Dale and Tommy-Lee were watching?"

"Exactly."

I practically flew off my stool, arms outstretched, as I caught Charlie in a tight hug. Amber, pine, and the sharp scent of outdoors filled my nostrils as I nuzzled against him.

"You're a goddamn genius, Charlie Fairburn!"

Charlie was wagging his eyebrows when I finally pulled back, reminding me of just *why* I had to be so sparing with the compliments — he clearly didn't need any further reinforcement to know that he truly was "the man".

"Sometimes," I corrected myself with a smirk that earned me a punch in the shoulder.

"Whatever, G. I know you think I'm great. You don't have to be embarrassed to admit it."

I rolled my eyes, catching sight of the clock on the wall and finally realizing how long we'd been sitting there.

"Wait… What the hell is taking so long?" I complained, raising my voice loud enough so that even the people sitting at the very back of the bar could hear me.

Anyone else would've been embarrassed by the outburst, but not Charlie. He just laughed, slammed his fist on the bar, and yelled, "Yeah! Whose dick do I have to suck to get some service around here?"

"If I would've known it was like *that*, Char, I would've told you to meet me around back," a deep voice dripping with sarcasm purred behind us.

I twisted on my stool to find Nico with a tray full of yellow shots in his hand. He grinned and waggled his brows seductively at Charlie.

"Please tell me those are for us?" I begged, ignoring Charlie and Nico's shared laughter and "bro" handshake as I licked my lips. For a moment, all my worries vanished at the sight of the glass's sugar-coated rims.

Limoncello, my favorite.

"Of course, they're for you." Nico placed three shots before me and another three before Charlie. "But hurry up and finish them, alright? That nasty attitude you brought in here is ruining everybody's vibe."

"Shut up, Nico," Charlie and I both griped in unison as we downed our drinks.

Nico tucked the empty tray beneath his arm and raised his hands in innocence. "Honestly, that's no way to talk to your *sweet* brother, who just gave you free shots."

"Where have *you* been?" I asked, wiping sugar from my lips with the back of my hand. "You can't just run off and leave the bar empty for so long. Dad would be pissed."

Nico rolled his eyes and ran a hand through his black hair. He'd recently gotten it cut, shaved on the sides and longer on the top. I made a side note to tell him it suited him much better than the nearly shoulder-length bob he'd been rocking for the past few years.

"Oh, uh, I, uh... had to get some more glasses from the back. We're really busy tonight, and our dishwashers are too swamped to keep up. Besides, what's with the attitude?" He asked, clearly trying to change the subject.

"Nothing, it's stupid. Where's your little girlfriend, um—" I looked up to the ceiling for help as if the name would magically fall from the sky.

"Laura," Nico supplied with a toothy grin.

"Laura," I repeated. It was so hard to keep up, considering Nico was just as much of a ladies' man as Charlie. In fact, I was almost positive that Charlie had hooked up with Laura a few years back himself. "Isn't she supposed to be working the bar with you tonight?"

"She's... *Busy*. Powdering her nose or something."

I squished my face up in disgust, silently wishing I had another one of those limoncellos to wash away the sudden bad taste in my mouth. "Ew, Nico, you're gross."

Nico winked at Charlie, who was now giving him a solid nod of approval.

"Well, if it isn't Switchback's finest football champ," a horribly familiar voice sang out from the foyer.

Shit. Shit. Shit. What the *hell* was he doing here? I scrunched down in my seat and hoped that my long hair would be enough to hide me. This day really couldn't get any worse.

"Class of 2023 forever!" Harrison Howard shouted with all the gusto of someone who was clearly still living out their high school glory days.

"Hey, hey, hey, man!" Nico cheered as he crossed the bar and jumped, actually *jumped,* into the air to chest-bump the man.

Unbelievable.

Charlie let out a low whistle and leaned in close to me. "What's his deal? I thought you banned him for life?"

Still trying to be invisible, I cupped a palm around my mouth and whispered back, "He's not actually banned for real. I just thought we had this... I don't know, *mutual understanding* that he would never come in here. This is my territory."

"That's what I meant." He sucked in a sharp breath. "Don't look now, but he's headed this way."

My neck nearly snapped from the force of me whipping it around just in time to see Harrison's long legs crossing the bar. Yep, he was heading straight for us.

"Ugh! I said don't look!" Charlie hissed.

Well, I'd been wrong about this day getting any worse because there he was... And there *she* was with him — the girl he'd not so secretly cheated on me with after our two-year relationship.

"Long time no see, G!" Harrison smirked as casually as if we were old teammates like him and my brothers, and not exes with a horrible, messy past. "I know I never come in here, but me and Jessica just got engaged, so I thought — *what the hell!* We deserve a nice dinner to celebrate."

His poreless skin, warm and chocolaty, seemed to glow as he reveled in his small victory. He'd come here to gloat. He'd come here to say, "Look at me! I'm getting married and you're still pathetically single." I didn't think I could hate him any more until now.

I grinned back, just as big and bright — the same fake smile I always wore when I talked to basically everyone outside of my immediate circle. "That's amazing! Congratulations!"

His satisfied expression faltered as he reached for Jessica's hand to show off the large glittering diamond on her pale finger.

"Isn't it *beautiful*?" Jessica gushed — completely unaware of the little power-struggle happening between me and her new fiancé.

She'd grown up a few towns over and was therefore blissfully unaware of the entire cheating scandal that had brought her and Harrison together. Although I probably would've smelled the lie on Harrison after the incident, it was Charlie who'd discovered his little secret first. After a trip to the drive-in movies in Battenburg with one of his many flings, Charlie had seen that my boyfriend was getting a little action on the side, too. Needless to say, Charlie hated Harrison almost as much as I did.

"Seems like Josh Peters is finally paying you boys for all your hard work, Harry-boy," Nico said as he eyed the ring Jessica was now wiggling about.

Well, I had to give him that. It *was* bigger than I'd expected Harrison could afford. Especially seeing as how he was employed by Switchback's very own Scrooge. Unless he'd been saving since the day he was born, I was positive he'd racked up a pretty hefty debt with that purchase.

"Yeah right! That bastard is about as worthless as the mud on my boots!"

Something about what Harrison had said smelled like a lie, but I shrugged it off. As fascinated as I was to hear them talk more shit about Josh Peters (fake or not), I figured it was about time to assert my dominance. Harrison Howard would *not* win this round; I would make damn sure of that. I cleared my throat loudly as I placed a palm across Charlie's forearm. Thank God, he'd taken off his marshmallow jacket, because the muscles straining beneath his flannel were now on full display.

"What a happy coincidence!" I cried, making sure I seemed every bit as delighted as Jessica had been.

Harrison faltered — the chiseled planes of his face going taut. "What's the coincidence?"

"Just that," I broke off emotionally to look deeply into Charlie's eyes. "Charlie proposed to me, too! *Today*, in fact!"

Charlie's arm snaked out around my shoulders as he pulled me into his chest — the familiar woodsy scent of him making me feel a bit more grounded. His legs straddled my barstool, creating the least amount of space between us possible.

Charlie's thumb flicked over my nose playfully. "It's true!"

I didn't dare look at Nico. His stupid laugh was about to burst out and ruin our whole charade. I might've hated lying, but I hated Harrison Howard more.

Jessica hopped in place and clapped her hands. "Oh my gosh! Can I see your ring?"

Shit. My spine snapped straight as I suddenly became *very* aware of the *very* empty spot on my left finger.

As quick as ever, Charlie's hands moved up to massage the back of my shoulders. "Oh, we haven't gotten the ring yet."

Jessica instantly deflated — her mouth tugging down at the corners. Harrison's grin was bigger than ever, though. He'd seen straight through our lie.

Charlie nuzzled a kiss against my hair, but I could feel the smile he was hiding beneath it. His face remained pressed into the side of my own as he crossed his arms back over my chest and continued, "Yeah, well, I couldn't wait to make G my wife, but… There weren't any rings at James & Company that were big enough to show Georgia just *how much* I love her. So, I figured we'd wait and go to Tiffany's in New York. Surely, they'll have some big rocks there!" He chuckled — an arrogant, awful noise that reminded me of just how filthy rich he was, and how he could actually make good on a promise as insane as that one.

"What were we thinking, baby?" Charlie asked, sounding as snotty as ever. "Nine, maybe *ten* carats?"

Jessica nearly fainted. "Oh, wow! Well, I can't wait to see it! I'm sure it'll be absolutely to die for."

Harrison pressed a palm on Jessica's back. "Let's go, babe. I don't think I'm in the *mood* for Italian anymore."

As soon as they left, Charlie and Nico rolled to the floor, dying in laughter. In all honesty, it was kind of annoying to see how hilarious they thought the idea of Charlie marrying me was. Of course, I'd never seen him in *that* way, but still... Was it really *so* crazy to imagine me as someone's wife someday?

"Hey, G," Nico said after finally recovering enough to straighten out his bow tie and black uniform. "We need to talk later, okay? Before you leave." A rare seriousness marred his smooth brow.

I nodded stiffly.

Nico and my other brother, his twin Lucky, were known around town as Switchback's golden boys — the polar opposite of their weird outcast of a sister. They were too handsome, and talented, and charming to be held accountable for any of the reckless, wild things they did. Everybody loved them, which meant Nico and Lucky never really had to be serious about anything. It scared me to see my brother wearing such a grave expression. It could only mean bad things.

I had been so wrong.

This day *could* get worse.

Chapter Three
Fault

After a strained dinner with my parents, Charlie helped clean up the table while I grabbed Nico from behind the bar. All they'd wanted to talk about was the news and how the Supernatural bill of rights would allow all those "freaks" to work and own property. I probably should've kept my mouth shut, but I couldn't help it sometimes. I'd known exactly how that conversation was going to go, and I still did it, anyway. Maybe I was a masochist.

Unlike me, my parents were fully against the Triad's plan for integration with us humans. They claimed they would never even serve a Supernatural in our restaurant, let alone *hire* one. Of course, that one got me going. A few choice words later, all I'd done was make my mother cry about how college had made me a liberal. She could cry all she wanted. I wouldn't budge. My father was beyond mad at the exchange. He had leveled me with a look so humbling that I'd re-opened the cut on my wrist with my bracelet and had two more gemstones pop loose as a result. Mrs. Jessops was right. I really needed to stop doing that. I was going to ruin the bracelet and all my good clothes if I kept on. It was getting harder and harder for me to control the impulse, though. It was getting to the point where it wasn't even an anxiety thing anymore. I was starting to use it to control my temper, too.

I patted down the edges of my fresh bandage as I watched Nico take care of the last few guests. We headed straight for our usual meeting spot when he was done — the walk-in fridge.

"I'm worried about Lucky," Nico said flatly. "Something's been up with him lately."

I pressed myself into the cool racks for support. I was grateful that our spot was refrigerated because the news had given me hot flashes.

"Worried as in, *"he's been busy lately,"* worried, or worried, *"he's on drugs again,"* worried?" I clarified, hoping beyond hope that this was just another one of their twin problems.

They had *lots* of those — like if Nico and Lucky didn't hang out at least three times a week outside of work, one of them would panic. I didn't understand their weird, codependent bond, but I was really praying it had something to do with that.

"The drugs one."

"Why do you think that?"

"I just *know*, okay? He's my twin."

"So, what are we going to do? Have you tried talking to Olivia yet?"

"No, G. I haven't talked to *Olivia* about this yet."

"Why? She's his girlfriend. She might be able to help if there's really something wrong."

"Not if *she's* the problem."

I pressed the heels of my palms into my eyes. "Listen, if you actually wanna talk to me about this, you're going to have to give me a little more to work with, Nic."

"Fine. You're right. He's been super flaky with me recently, and he's been coming into work all wired, and I don't know, G. He's been working overtime here, *and* at the garage. He's there tonight, actually. I just don't know why he's so desperate to make money like that. He was doing pretty well already, but… You know how he acted the last time he was —" Nico broke off, unable to even say the words aloud.

"I know. And you still think it's *Olivia* who's the bad influence?"

Nico gave a half-hearted shrug, like he might be reconsidering his theory. After all, it *was* Lucky who'd been to rehab all those times. Unfortunately, he was the common denominator in every single problem he'd ever had.

"Should we tell Mom and Dad?"

Nico's hands splayed out before him. "No! We can't do that, G. They'll just send him right back to treatment."

I tried to grab Nico's shoulder, but he brushed me off and skirted back further into the fridge.

"He might *need* to go, Nic. I know you missed him when he was gone, but if he's as bad as you say, he might really need the help."

"I should've never told you. Whatever, I'll handle this myself," he spat, now turning to leave.

I sagged against one of the ice-cold racks again, hoping the burning, chilled sensation could soothe me.

"Nico, I need you to promise me something." I said, much louder and stronger than I felt.

I didn't wait for Nico to turn around or give me any sign that he was listening. As pissed off as he was, I still knew he wanted my help, so I continued, "I need you to promise me that if you can't handle this, and *soon*, that we tell Mom and Dad. They *need* to know if Lucky needs help."

"Fine. Promise."

I met Charlie in the foyer a few moments later. After that conversation, I was ready to sleep for twelve *years*, instead of hours.

"Nico thinks Lucky is in trouble," I blurted before I could talk myself out of it.

Charlie's smile of greeting disappeared. "Drugs?"

"Apparently. Nico said that he thinks Olivia's involved in it somehow."

"You don't believe that, do you?"

Even though I loved my brother and always wanted to give him the benefit of the doubt, I couldn't deny the truth — especially not when it had become this constant pattern of destruction in all our lives.

"No... No, I don't think that it's Olivia. He's been doing so well ever since—"

"Ever since the last time. When they first got together, right?"

"Yeah. After Nico left treatment last year, he met Olivia, and I thought—" I stopped, unable to finish the sentence without wanting to cry again. Everything about to today made me want to cry.

"What *exactly* did Nico say? Are you going to tell your parents?"

"I want to, but Nico said he wanted to see if he can handle it first. He doesn't want to get them involved yet, but I'm just so, *so* scared that something bad will happen again." The words tumbled out so fast that I hadn't realized I'd let the tears fall out along with them until they rolled down my cheeks.

I was crying, not only for Lucky, but for myself — for my family. I wasn't sure if we could survive another one of Lucky's drug-fueled spirals. The last one had almost broken us entirely. Like most things, our family had always been divided when it came to Lucky's addiction problems. He would seem fine at first, maybe a little strange, but fine... Almost like he had everything under control. But then, it would turn ugly — and fast. He would lie, and steal, and do whatever it took to get his hands on his next fix. Nico and my father were always in denial, saying that Lucky was stronger than we thought. Afterall, he was a Beretta man. He could work through his problems without some expensive shrink telling him what to do. And every time, after their tough-love approach failed, me and Mom had always been there to pick up the pieces and send him to treatment. It always felt like a point of no return by then — a point where he'd *really* hit rock bottom, and we were scared there would be no coming back.

The last time had been the worst, though. It had been scary enough that there had been no disagreements between the rest of us that he truly had a problem — a problem that would never be solved, only treated through therapy and support groups for the rest of his life. Of course, that hadn't stopped Lucky from creating lies and trying to turn all of us against each other. With my ability, that obviously hadn't worked very well, but still... I didn't want this to get out of hand again. I couldn't *let* this get out of hand again.

"Give him a week," Charlie said at last. "A week, and if nothing's changed, you go to your parents about it."

I didn't even bother to brush the tears away this time. "What if a week is too long, though?"

"Just give him a week, G. It'll be fine."

A week, then. I would give Nico one single week, and if things hadn't gotten better by then, I would intervene. Until then, I would at least have enough time to sort out the Mrs. Jessops' situation. Despite my feelings towards her right now, I needed to make sure she wouldn't go to jail for somebody else's crimes.

The next morning, I found myself rumbling back down Adelaide Road before the sun had even peeked above the horizon. Instead of taking my usual route straight through the center, I made a hard left turn. I needed to catch the McKinney brothers before they left for their shift. For my plan to work, it needed to be done in privacy.

It physically pained me to see the sorry state of the brothers' property. Even the trees and brush on the sides of their dirt path was different from Mrs. Jessops'. Where hers was neat and well-kept, the McKinney's side was absolutely littered with trash and beer cans that had probably been tossed there before I'd even been born. Their front yard was no better than the drive leading up to it. Although I tried not to judge where someone came from, or how they lived, it was as clear as day that the McKinney's didn't care about *anyone* or *anything*. Even if they hadn't been poor, I was almost positive that if they'd lived in a mansion like Charlie's, they probably would've trashed it, too.

Their shared double-wide trailer was completely overgrown by weeds and thick vines that threatened to swallow it whole. To make it worse, chopped-up cars and rotted boards of lumber were haphazardly strewn about the property like their own personal junkyard. If I hadn't known that someone really did live there, I probably would've thought the place was abandoned. My heart ached for the McKinney children — ached for the fact they'd never know what it was like to have a normal home, and a normal yard that they could play in without accidentally contracting tetanus or something worse. I wasn't here for them today, though. As bad as I thought the McKinney's were, it still hadn't been enough for the *state* to justify taking their children away, so I reminded myself to focus on one thing at a time. I took a deep breath before stepping out of my car and walking up the wobbly front steps to their door — knocking loud and hard enough to wake up the dead.

I took a generous step back as the sound of angry footsteps clomped out from inside. A moment later, the rawboned, vulture-like face of Tommy-Lee McKinney appeared from behind the slashed edges of the screen door.

"What do *you* want?" Tommy-Lee asked. There was enough venom in his gravelly voice to kill the entire population of Switchback.

Fair enough, considering I'd been a constant nuisance in their life during my old social work days. Who was in my place to bother them now?

"We need to talk," I said as I tried, and failed, to muster up a pleasant smile.

"What about?"

I raised a pointed brow at the battered door still between us — the same door he'd not even bothered to open. Not that I wanted to come inside or anything, but... With the screen in the way, I couldn't be sure if it would be that much harder to get a whiff of his lies.

"I need Dale out here, too." I grimaced as if the next word was going to stab me in the gut. "*Please.*"

Tommy-Lee scowled before he muttered some inaudible insult and trudged back into the trailer. I took his sullen look as a sign of defeat and smiled a small secret smile to myself before he came back with his considerably younger and larger brother in tow. The two of them standing side-by-side was the dictionary definition of the word opposite. Where Tommy-Lee was tall, bald, and thin like a Chinese crested dog, Dale was short, hairy, and stocky like a troll. There was no denying the two were related, though. They both wore that same leery expression that spoke of low intelligence and a taste for violence.

"Well? He's here now. Say what you've gotta say and get the fuck off my property, Beretta," Tommy-Lee snarled.

Reflexively, I attempted a polite smile again, but caught myself. These men didn't deserve pleasantries. They certainly weren't giving them to me, so why *should* I smile?

"What were you two doing between the hours of eleven and twelve on Wednesday night?"

Dale narrowed his pig-like eyes. "Is you tryna arrest us, or somethin'?"

"Yeah, you don't have the power to do that, do ya, girlie?" Tommy-Lee chimed in.

"No. No, I'm just trying to get an alibi worked out for someone. You two aren't in any kind of trouble." I tried to use the most soothing tone I could manage — almost as if I were trying to calm a pack of wild dogs like that animal-whisperer, Cesar Millan.

The brothers exchanged a suspicious look.

"I promise I'm not trying to get you in any trouble."

Tommy-Lee nodded, and then their ruddy faces simultaneously screwed up as they tried to remember through the booze-filled haze of the past forty-eight hours.

Dale's eyes lit up first, but he kept his mouth shut — waiting for Tommy-Lee's approval before speaking. Tommy was the clear leader between the two, but if I had to take a guess, it was Dale who was the real brains — well, whatever the McKinney version of "brains" was, anyway. Tommy-Lee gave his brother a little grunt as if to say, *"Go on."*

"That ol' Witch bitch was castin' spells in her yard again, 'member Tommy-Lee? We was watchin' her like usual," Dale drawled.

Tommy-Lee pursed his lips — finally remembering. "Yeah, she had a great big fire out there, and we was watchin' her dance 'round it 'til real late."

I tried to suppress my excitement as I pulled out the recorder I'd stashed in my bag. "Do you mind if I get that on tape? Just repeat what you said, and make sure you're specific about the timeline, okay?"

As if on cue, the brothers both narrowed their eyes, but it was Tommy-Lee who took the lead again. "Supposin' we do what you ask, what's in it for us, huh?"

A ragged groan of frustration rose in my throat, but I quickly disguised it with a cough in case they got the idea I was trying to make fun of them somehow.

"Do you need groceries?"

I'd known the answer before I even asked. Was this considered a bribe? I didn't care if it was. I didn't have time to go the traditional route of having an officer bring them in to make statements. *Mrs. Jessops* didn't *have* that kind of time. As pissed as Josh had been, I knew she would be arrested by lunchtime if I didn't get this done right here, *right now*.

After a bit of stiff bargaining with the brothers, I was back on their doorstep in a few hours, loaded down with the essentials. Canned goods, fresh fruit, meat, vegetables, snacks, and enough Natural Light beer to last them at least a week — which meant it was enough beer to last any normal human being about two or three months. Thankfully, the sight of the beer had loosened their lips just enough to get their statements on tape and get the fuck back off their property as Tommy-Lee had so politely suggested I do earlier. Not that I needed any more encouragement. Now that I had a solid alibi for Mrs. Jessops, the only thing I wanted to do was get the hell out of there and back to the station.

Nico called me before I could even reach town. I watched his name flash on my cracked screen for a moment. I wasn't in the mood to talk, but I was too afraid to ignore it. *It might be something important about Lucky*, I reminded myself before answering.

"G, Hey!" He was panting hard, like he'd just been on a run, but... There was something else in his voice, something horribly familiar.

"What's wrong?"

"Come to the hospital. There's been... There's—" Nico sniffled before holding the phone away to sob.

"I'm on the way."

Even though the hospital was only twenty minutes away from Adelaide Road, each second felt like an eternity. Hearing Nico cry had ripped open a gulf of unbearable pain and sadness in my chest. Every minute, every *second* I wasn't at the hospital only seemed to deepen that hollow, bottomless trench within me. This was bad. I knew this was bad. Nico never cried. I slammed my car into the center of two parking spots and blindly raced for the entrance. I couldn't even remember if I'd turned my car off or not — it didn't matter. Nothing mattered but getting there. Nico and my parents were all in the lobby, huddled together in the hard plastic chairs — eyes cast to the laminate floor. I was sprinting now, hurdling straight towards them. The squeaking sound of my boots made them all look up in unison. My mother instantly burst into tears and hid beneath my father's shoulder. I crashed into them with my arms outstretched, trying to scoop them all into a hug.

"He overdosed," my father spoke first.

I knew what he was going to say before he'd said it. I'd been so fucking foolish for not telling my parents as soon as I'd found out Lucky was having problems again. The tears fell over my purple sweater before I even registered that I was crying. I was frozen, only able to stare at the vibrant fabric as the wetness from my eyes turned it black. I felt Nico's long fingers dig into my shoulders. He was shaking me. I looked up at him, feeling utterly broken. Nico's eyes told me everything I needed to know. We were responsible for this. *I* was responsible for this. If I had trusted my instincts... If I hadn't let Nico talk me out of telling our parents... None of this would've ever happened. *My fault.* I saw the same awful guilt flash on my brother's expression.

Our fault.

I felt like I was falling into a pit so big and dark that I'd never find my way out.

My fault. Our fault. My fault.

The words played on a hellish endless loop in my head.

"Is he going to be okay?" I rasped, my voice sounding like bone on sandpaper. The words didn't sound right, like I hadn't been the one speaking them. The way they scratched against my throat made me never want to speak again. Why should I when I couldn't even be bothered to say something that would've helped Lucky? The realization hit home again and the world around me suddenly went quiet and still. It felt like one of those moments where you were totally disconnected from reality, but somehow still there — forced to watch as every single one of your nightmares came true. *My fault.* This was all happening because of me. Because I'd been too damned scared of going behind Nico's back.

There was no one to blame but me. I made this happen, and I hated myself for it.

Lucky wasn't okay. And neither was his girlfriend Olivia. She'd overdosed with him, too. They were kept in a coma for two days while they ran toxicology screenings, stabilized their vitals, and monitored brain activity, but only Lucky woke up when they brought him out of it. The overdose had been too much for Olivia. Her body was too weak to recover from the damage, and the only choice left was to take her off life support. The toxicology only raised more questions, though. Questions that Lucky was not yet prepared to answer. Perhaps he'd never be ready to answer them at all. Although traces of cocaine and ecstasy had been found in their systems, the overdose had been caused by something else entirely. Something even more dangerous, even *more* lethal — *Vampire blood.* With no puncture wounds present, it had been clear to the doctors that this was no attack either.

They'd injected it themselves.

Chapter Four
Saph

Olivia's funeral was tomorrow. Since the toxicology report had come back, Lucky had refused to speak to our parents, the cops, or anyone else for that matter. Not that it would've made a difference, though. The police had already decided that Vampires were responsible for this — "Tainting the drug supply so they could kill us off one by one."

Since Lucky hadn't said otherwise, that was their number one guess for now. It sounded like a load of conspiracy theory bullshit to me. Nothing about it made sense. Why would they taint the drug supply when they could eat us just as easily? There was no evidence to support it, but I guess no one really cared about that. It seemed like everyone, police included, had latched on to the most obscene theory possible and run with it — just because it was scandalous and exciting.

We decided as a family that it would be best if Lucky came and stayed with me for a while. Me, Nico, and Charlie would all take shifts watching him to make sure he didn't do anything stupid. If he'd been going through it before, well... He was *really* going through it now, and we didn't know how he would handle his already volatile emotions after Olivia's death.

Lucky was the type of person who'd always felt things *more* than other people. Officially, his therapists at the rehabilitation centers he'd gone to said that his substance abuse problems resulted from his "maladaptive coping mechanisms". I supposed it ran in the family. Basically, when Lucky's emotions got out of control, he turned to drugs as a way of dealing with them — just like how I dealt with my own emotions with my bad bracelet habit.

The sun was already setting by the time we got back to Grams' house. She'd left the place to me after she died. Probably a smart choice, seeing as how my brothers had never seen the magic that I had in the old house. It was a fifteen-minute drive from the city, but not quite far enough out to be considered the boonies like Charlie's ranch or Mrs. Jessops' place, even though it certainly felt like it.

The entire property was surrounded by a forest of white-barked aspen trees and the occasional Douglas fir. The trees provided enough privacy to feel as if the house were on an island of its own. Despite Gram's insistence on calling it a "cottage", it was undoubtedly too much house for only one person. It was an old Victorian-style home with sage green siding, diamond-paned bay windows, stacked turrets, and hand-carved trim. My brothers had always compared it to one of those houses in a scary movie that the family buys for like a dollar and then gets surprised when it turns out to be haunted. I'd never seen it like that, though. I thought it was perfect.

Nico had gone to grab a few of Lucky's things at the garage while Charlie and I had taken him to the house. Lucky had bought the old warehouse a few years back after saving up enough money to turn it into an auto repair center. The garage was his safe space. It was somewhere that he could live and work on the one thing he was truly passionate about — unlike me, who'd always gotten shit for wanting a different life for myself.

I found myself obsessively checking my rearview mirror to look at my brother. His tall slim frame was laid out in my backseat beneath a quilt. Lucky had always had a gaunter set to his features, but now, after this overdose… He was painful to see. The dark shadows below his brown eyes were like bruises, his cheekbones like razor blades, and even his olive skin was so pale it verged on translucent. I'd never seen him so fragile before, not even at his worst.

After we'd rolled up the drive, Charlie and I helped Lucky from my car and set him on the floral sofa next to the fireplace. He fell asleep almost immediately, and I felt a twinge of guilt for being grateful that he had. It was unbearable to see him like this. He was a shell of the man my brother used to be. Physically he was there, but everything else, everything inside him that mattered, had just... *Disappeared*.

I didn't know how much time had passed before I realized Charlie was trying to get my attention.

"Earth to G," Charlie hissed, waving his hands in front of me.

I'd been staring at Lucky for so long, watching the rise and fall of his every breath, that my eyes had gone dry from not blinking. I rubbed at them and jerked my chin towards the kitchen. I didn't want to risk waking Lucky up. He needed to rest.

We rose in unison from the matching sofa across from Lucky — both crossing the floorboards in a familiar zigzag pattern to avoid the creaky ones until we'd made it to the kitchen. Besides my bedroom, the kitchen was by far my favorite room in the house. Although there had been a few renovations, Grams had tried to preserve the originality of the house as best she could. Painted a sage green like the outside, the kitchen was spacious enough to have a six-seat dining table *and* an island. The tall cabinets reached up to the ceiling, with the highest ones made of stained glass that matched the window above the deep farmhouse sink. Of course, the appliances had to be updated over the years and were now stainless steel, but the yellow and green-tiled floor was the same one that four generations of Berettas had once walked over.

I plopped down at the table and silently watched as Charlie expertly navigated through the cabinets. Once he'd retrieved a bottle of whiskey and two carved tumblers, he came back to sit beside me.

I eyed the generous pour in my glass. "Do you really think we should be drinking, Char?"

"Yes, I really think we should be drinking."

"What about Lucky?"

"What about him?"

"We're supposed to be watching him, remember?"

Charlie suppressed a grimace as he downed his glass and set it back on the table to pour another.

"Nico will be here soon, and he's asleep. He'll be fine until then."

I tipped the glass back between my lips. "Fucking Vampire blood."

"Fucking Vampire blood," Charlie repeated.

"I don't get it. What did they even think that would do to them? Not kill them, I guess..." My hands wound up into my inky hair.

Charlie's rough fingers wrapped around my wrist. "Don't say that, G. I'm sure they had no idea what they were getting into."

I stared at the table again. "Do you think they *knew* it was in there... Like they were trying to turn themselves or something? Is that even possible? I thought the Triad said ingesting Supernatural blood or tissue is deadly."

During the early days, after they'd officially come out to the public, some people had thought that killing and eating a Supernatural would somehow give you their powers. It was barbaric. I almost couldn't believe that the Triad had even had to make a statement to discredit the insane theory, but... They *did* because crazy ass people really *did* believe it.

Charlie didn't say anything.

We both knew my mother was right about this one. She always loved to remind me that even though the Supernatural's had gone public nearly ten years ago, practically no one knew how they worked or how they came to *be*... Well, Supernatural. They said it was a genetic defect, that they'd all been born that way, but... It was sort of hard to believe, considering all the fairy tales and legends we'd all grown up with. Still, if it was a lie, I couldn't tell. My ability didn't work unless I was face-to-face with someone.

Although the Triad had explicitly said it themselves, it took our own government spreading it all over the media that Supernatural's were "assumed" to carry over four hundred blood-borne pathogens that would "most likely" kill you if ingested. If that wasn't a big, fat stop sign to anyone who was stupid enough to put it to the test, I didn't know what was. I supposed the terms "assumed" and "most likely" were more like a yellow light to some people, though. The Triad had never allowed proper scientific testing to be done on them by humans. In fact, during the initial phase of the Great Integration, the Triad had made it their first law — no scientific or medical testing on any Supernatural's ever. *Period*. They were born, and that was the end of the story.

Even if it wasn't true, which I doubted, it was most likely a safety precaution to keep those cannibal crazies away. Though, I couldn't help but wonder now if there was another reason behind all the secrecy. What if they really *were* made somehow and not born? Did Olivia and Lucky know something that we didn't? I'd already discredited the police's theory, but I wasn't even going to entertain the other possibility... That maybe they'd taken the blood in some strung-out Romeo and Juliet suicide pact.

Whatever reasons they'd had, I guess they had their answer now. Supernatural blood, Vampire blood, *was* lethal. Olivia *had* died, and Lucky hadn't been far behind her. I just couldn't fathom what the hell they were thinking when they tried to test the theory. Was my own brother one of those whacked-out cannibal conspiracy theory people? Or were they really trying to kill themselves?

"Since when did everything go to shit, huh?" I chuckled.

"Everything hasn't gone to shit, G."

I was about to make some snappy retort when his steady gaze made the words dry up.

"We can research it, if you want? See what people think it's *actually* supposed to do to you? It might make you feel better just to know what was going through their heads. I'm almost positive Lucky would ever do something so dangerous on purpose."

I wasn't so sure about the last part, but I was still grateful for the kindness. After all, wasn't cocaine and ecstasy just as bad? I knew he'd at least done *that* on purpose. Still, it was hard to believe that Lucky would *knowingly* take Vampire blood after hearing all those awful stories on the news. After all, he'd seemed happy. He'd given no indication that he was trying to end it all anytime soon. I shook my head to get rid of the idea. No, I wasn't even going to go there. I'd rather believe that Vampires were tainting drugs than believe that Lucky had been feeling that way. I'd be completely swallowed up by the guilt that I was still drowning in.

"I'm gonna look it up, 'kay?" Charlie nudged my knee with his and I nodded.

Sometimes, it still surprised me how well Charlie knew me. No matter how dumb my brother could be, or how sick, he knew I'd never give up hope. And he knew I'd never stop until I had answers, and Lucky clearly wasn't going to give them to me anytime in the foreseeable future. I doubted he'd find anything useful, probably just the same theories or guesses, but still... Any bit of insight I could get into *why* Lucky had done this would be better than what I had right now... Which was basically nothing. I drank while Charlie googled, feeling more relaxed with every sip.

"I went to the McKinney's the other day," I announced, breaking the easy silence that had settled between us.

"Oh, yeah?"

The trip felt like it had been a thousand years ago. "I got an alibi for Mrs. Jessops. They said they saw her out in her yard doing some Witchy-woo-woo right around the time of the vandalism, so she couldn't have possibly done it. Just like I said to begin with."

I was faintly aware that I should've been happier about the news, but... I just couldn't be happy about anything right now.

"That's really great, G. I told you not everything has gone to shit."

"Yeah, I guess. I haven't even had time to tell anyone about it, though. I've been so busy with all of this..." I trailed off — too embarrassed to admit that I'd nearly forgotten the whole thing with the McKinney's because I'd been so wrapped up in all this awful mess.

"Don't beat yourself up about it, G."

It was hard not to, though. I was basically controlling Mrs. Jessops' fate now. She was relying on me to help clear her name, and I felt like I'd let her down. All it would've taken was a quick call to the station to let the Chief know what I'd found, and I hadn't even been able to manage that. Jesus, I was such a disappointment.

"Hey, look what I found," he gasped.

I immediately clamored over the table, trying to paw at the phone to see what Charlie was looking at so intensely, but he just slapped my hands away like I was some big, annoying gnat.

"Chill, I'll read it out loud."

I scowled at him.

"I found this Triad conspiracy theory thread. They're saying that the government has been forced by the Triad to come out with lies about Supernatural blood, so humans won't go looking for it... Like to protect the Supernatural's from harm, I guess."

Just like I'd already thought.

I slapped my palms to my cheeks and slowly raked them down to my neck. "Another half-baked government conspiracy theory?

Honestly, some people will believe *anything* is part of a secret cover-up."

Charlie waved me off. "It says here that some people still believe that Supernatural blood *can* give you powers, but especially Vampire blood. I guess its street-name is "*Saph*". The blood won't turn you into one by itself, though, so there goes that idea. Nobody on here seems to know how *that* whole thing works still, but... From what I'm seeing, it *is* supposed to be like the best drug ever. Huh, that's so weird. Apparently, the stuff is super hard to come by, too."

I bit at the already ragged stubs of my fingernails as I waited for him to go on. Although it was easy for me to condemn the tin-foil hat, internet trolls and bloodthirsty cannibals... It was even easier to believe them when their lies fit the narrative I was looking for. I guess I really wasn't any better than those crazies, after all.

"It's supposed to be like a mixture of cocaine, heroin, and one of those mind-expansion pills from that old movie... Ugh, what's it called again?" He smacked his forehead. "*Limitless!*"

My phone buzzed in my pocket, but I ignored it — still too focused on what Charlie had discovered to care.

"What's *Limitless*?"

"It's this movie about a guy that takes some pill that lets you have access to one hundred percent of your brain. According to this blog, that's what Saph is supposed to do to you, too."

"Why would you want that?"

"I don't know, it says that it helps you learn things fast... Like *really fast* and be able to retain all the information even when you're off of it. The comments on here say that it's mostly used by like... Kids in Ivy League schools or those people on Wall Street working the stock market. Some people are even saying pro athletes take it because no one tests for it yet and it can make you strong for a while, like a Vampire."

"Are you even listening to yourself right now? You think Lucky and Olivia took Vampire blood so that they could... What? Study for their big test at Harvard?" I shook my head. "No, that couldn't be it. Lucky hates schoolwork. Maybe they just wanted to act like Hulk for a few hours and smash some stuff up!"

Even saying the sentence out loud felt ridiculous.

"Damn, I don't know. Maybe. Or just because it feels great. You didn't even let me finish what I was going to say. Besides all of that, I think it's just supposed to make you feel like... *Really, really good.* Euphoric or something. We already know they like drugs, so it wouldn't be *that* far off-base to think they'd be chasing after a new high, right?"

Charlie set his phone down and rested both palms on the back of his head to stare up the ceiling. We sat like that for a long time; him looking at the ceiling, and me looking at him. Figuring that the conversation was probably done, I retrieved my phone from my pocket and checked the text I'd received earlier.

Nico: Police still investigating at Lucky's. Don't know how long they'll be there. Went home to get some rest. Coming by in the morning with some of my clothes.

I tucked the phone back into my jeans with a sigh before informing Charlie of the news.

His brows threaded together. "Why are they still there? Did he say?"

I tried to nod but my limbs felt like they weighed a thousand pounds. "I don't know. Probably trying to find more evidence that Vampires are lacing drugs."

It had been days since the overdose, and I couldn't think of a single reason they would still be poking around there. They should've been able to turn the whole place upside down in a few hours. It wasn't *that* big. Besides, they already *had* their theory, didn't they?

"You should go get some rest, G. I'll take the first shift."

After a yawn escaped my lips, I decided I would just take his advice. I was too exhausted to even argue. I stood from the table and playfully ruffled his curls.

"Thank you, Charlie."

I wasn't sure what time it was when I woke back up. A muffled, scraping sort of noise coming from downstairs had made my eyes snap open in the darkness.

Scrape, thump.

Scrape, thump.

A sickly sweat had settled over my skin despite the chilled air floating in from my bedroom window. I wanted so badly for the noise to be Charlie, stumbling around in a drunken hunt for a snack, but the hard pit in my stomach told me otherwise. Sure,

Grams' house was old and sometimes made creepy noises when it was settling, but this was different. I knew every knock and creak this house made by heart. Something was *wrong*. And, oh God! Why did it have to sound like someone dragging around a dead body? That's the *last* noise anyone wants to hear in the middle of the night. The *very* last. I swung my shaky legs from beneath the comforter and hissed as my toes hit the icy floor. The noise stopped then, and my mouth went dry. Was I being too loud? I prayed I was wrong about the dead body thing. I shouldn't have even had that thought! I'd probably fucking manifested it somehow. If there was a killer in the house, he probably knew exactly where I was now! Everything went sharp around me, like even the air would shred me to pieces if I breathed wrong. I wanted to crawl back in bed and hide — to pull the covers over my head like I did when I was a child. I glanced back at it for a long moment. Somehow, my bed was the only thing that seemed all warm and fuzzy amidst the bleakness of this situation. As I took in the fluffy blanket and soft, familiar pillows my panic began to die down until it was little more than a faint whimper in the back of my mind. There weren't any more noises. There hadn't been for a couple minutes now. Should I even still be worried?

You're just being paranoid, Georgia. You've always had an overactive imagination!

I crept back towards my bed, about to hike my knee up and get back in when the noise rang out once more. Alarm bells cracked through my body like lightening. The sweat that had dampened my pajamas during the night kicked back into overdrive — sliding down the nape of my neck in fat, salty rivulets. No, this couldn't be happening right now! Why the hell did these kinds of things happen to *me?* I couldn't catch a fucking break! But it wasn't *just* me this was happening to. My self-pitying dried up as Charlie and Lucky's face swam through my vision. This was happening to them, too. I had to act, but I needed a plan first. I couldn't just charge in unprepared if there really *was* a murderer downstairs. I looked around my room for a weapon as I tried to come up with something, but the combination of fear and anxiety had scrambled my brain into mush. All I could think about were the possible outcomes to this mess.

Someone did break in and kill everyone in the house or was in the process of doing so right now.

I was just hearing things and I would go downstairs, guns-blazing to find nothing amiss.

I squeezed my eyes shut and tried to ground myself. I needed to be strong. I needed to figure out what the hell was going on so I could protect the boys — especially my brother. Lucky needed me more than ever now. He was *so* heartbreakingly frail. If someone had gotten into the house and done something to him and Charlie, I was the last one left. *Wait, yes that's it!* I was alone, so that meant I needed… *Backup!* I had to call for backup. Maybe Nico would still be awake…

Temporarily giving up on my search for a weapon, I checked my phone — biting my tongue hard as I held back a curse. It was dead. How the hell had that happened? I could've sworn I'd plugged it in. I'd been so out of it, though. And kind of tipsy… Shit, I was an idiot. I should've never let Charlie convince me that drinking was a good idea.

Breathe, Georgia. Breathe.

I tamped my fear down once more as I forced myself to think logically. How many home invasions happened in Switchback, anyway? Maybe one, *two* max, in the past few years. Switchback was boring, and boring meant safe. Yeah, option one was worst-case scenario, but option two wasn't so bad. *Right?* I had a fifty-fifty chance of coming out of this with nothing more than a little humiliation.

By the time I slung on one of my robes, grabbed the lamp on my bedside table for protection, and carefully made my way towards the stairs, every hair on my body was standing on end again. The motivational speech I'd given myself a few minutes ago had shrunken into a distant memory that now held no comfort at all. I looked down the shadowy stairs and tried to remember why the hell I'd been so positive that the noise was nothing more than my imagination. Even though it had stopped again, seemingly for good this time, that nasty feeling in my stomach remained. I grabbed the edges of the robe with my free hand and held them tight against my throat. My heart hammered against my fingertips. If I hadn't alerted the intruder before, my thundering heartbeat was sure to give me away now. I peeked over the banister into the living room. The fire had died down, leaving the wood-paneled room bathed in a buttery light. I had conflicting feelings about what I saw next. There was some relief, but a whole lot more terror. Charlie had his feet propped up on the coffee table, and his head was thrown back over the sofa. He was safe, but God dammit, he was *asleep*! I watched in silent horror as his throat bobbed ever so slightly.

He was snoring.

Shit, shit, shit. This wasn't just an accidental catnap; he was *really* asleep.

Intruder be damned, my feet smashed down the stairs as I raced to where I hoped Lucky would still be passed out on the couch. I threw the blanket back to find a carefully arranged lump of pillows. The lamp I'd had wrapped in a chokehold slipped from my fingers — clattering to the floor with a metallic screech.

Bastard.

There wasn't an intruder! He'd escaped.

My fear morphed into a hot knife of anger that cut me straight to the core. I had to find him. I shouted something desperate and unintelligible at Charlie's sleeping body as I ran towards the foyer. I just hoped he would wake up from all the noise I was making, because I didn't have time to do it myself. He was the *worst* at waking up. It usually took his housekeepers having to bang pots and pans next to his head to get him to even crack an eye in the morning. I yanked the front door open, nearly slamming face-first into the screen as I sprinted down the porch steps and into the front yard. My panting breath was visible in the chilled night air, the frozen grass hard and crunchy beneath my feet. I frantically whipped my head around, trying to determine which way Lucky would've gone. My car was still here, a good sign. Charlie's truck was here too, an even better sign. Blood thrummed in my ears like the beat of a war drum. I silently cursed myself as I tried to think. *How could I have let this happen?* My parents were trusting me. *Nico* was trusting me… And now I'd gone and fucked it all up.

A soft breeze swept over the yard, making the branches of the nearby trees scrape against each other in the pale moonlight.

Yes, they seemed to agree. *Yes, you fucked up. You always do.*

My ears strained as I tried to find the source of that scrape-thump sound from earlier. Had it been Lucky? Or was it my imagination? No, it couldn't have been. Lucky was gone, but this didn't feel like your average runaway situation. Something was weird about all of this — *that noise*. It had been so oddly distinct, like a shovel striking hard earth. Still, it had to be him making that sound... Or someone else. I shuddered to think about who it could be. Did one of Lucky's drug dealers come to make sure he never breathed a word about where he'd gotten the Saph? What if they were burying his body right now? What if that's what I'd heard? A chill that had nothing to do with the cold spider-walked down my spine again.

Without thinking, I slapped my face — hard enough to taste blood. I couldn't be doing this. I couldn't get distracted. If I thought about all the "what-ifs" now, I'd lose my courage. I *had* to find Lucky. He could've died because of my stupidity before, and I couldn't bear the idea of that happening all over again — this time for real. I furiously swatted at my eyes as I felt the hot tears slipping down my cheeks.

Not the time, Georgia. This is really not the time.

I tried hard to listen again, searching for any sounds of life. It was silent now, though — the rustling trees my only companion beneath the blanket of snow-white stars above. A faint scraping noise sounded from behind the house again. Yes, there it was. That was the same noise I'd heard before! My feet were moving before my brain could catch up. My arms and legs pumped with a vicious strength and speed I hadn't known I possessed until now. I was too worried about getting Lucky back to think about the very real possibility that the noise could be some bat-shit murdering drug dealer. I rounded the corner of the house, only realizing then that I'd been too stupid to grab my makeshift weapon. My eyes honed in on a hooded figure across the clearing. They wore an onyx cape so dark it nearly melted into the night, and so long that it brushed the ground like some train on an extravagant wedding dress. *What the absolute fuck?* It was the most stereotypical villain outfit I'd ever seen, but I wasn't scared. I knew that outline.

"Hey!" I screamed, still hurtling at breakneck speed towards the figure. "Lucky!"

It had to be him. That tall, slender frame was unmistakable. Even the dense cloak he'd draped over it couldn't hide that. Yes, it was Lucky. Oh, thank God it was him. My heart soared as a delicious wave of relief washed over me. Where the hell had he gotten that ridiculous outfit from, anyways? I didn't think Grams had anything like it. He cocked his head ever so slightly in a deliberate attempt to keep his face hidden from me. Something about the gesture threw me off. My feet slowed as if they were trudging through quicksand — like the way I ran in one of my nightmares. The jerk of his head, the odd tilt it had made... Needles of dread jabbed into my flesh. With his head at that angle, I couldn't tell if he was looking at me or towards the tree line. Whatever he was doing, it was hard not to feel like I was being assessed by a pair of inhuman, obsidian eyes lost between the matching shades of his hood. I tried to shrug off his strange gaze as my own paranoia, but I could still feel it burning straight into my marrow. I shouldn't be scared. This was Lucky! There was nothing to be afraid of. I mentally grasped onto the tendrils of my earlier joy before they could fade completely.

Nothing to be afraid of here, Georgia. The only thing scary about this is Lucky's bad fashion choices.

The joke relaxed me enough to where I could choke out the first letters of my brother's name before he jolted and *ran*. I wasn't even sure it could be called that — *running*. The movement was so sudden, so inexplicably fast, that my eyes almost didn't catch it. My stomach twisted as the realization finally dawned on me. It wasn't him. That person, that *thing*, wasn't my brother. I should've trusted my instincts. I found my voice again, screaming for the person to wait, but they were already gone. *Vanished*, just like that. My lungs seared with a fiery pain as I finally made it to the spot where they'd been standing. The wave of relief I'd been riding suddenly crashed into nothingness — lost forever. I dropped to my knees and screamed, louder this time. The howl sounded raw and primal even to my own ears — a scream of pure agony and frustration at myself, at my brother, at the world. I faintly got the feeling I should be terrified of whatever the hell I'd just witnessed, but the ache in my chest was too much. It was the only thing I could feel right now. A deep, overwhelming misery that clawed me open inside and out. My fists slammed into the grass over and over, each time coming up with fistfuls of weeds and dirt until I could no longer feel the pain of slamming into the frozen earth. That thing wasn't Lucky. It wasn't him. I'd lost him. *Where was he?* I still hadn't found him.

That last truth was sobering, and in my blurry haze of snot and tears, I finally raked a bloodied palm across my eyes to see where I'd crumbled. My grandmother's grave. Her tombstone was simple, elegant even. Before she died, she'd insisted on being buried on our land — on Beretta land, where she belonged. I couldn't remember the last time I'd come out here. The pain of even seeing her grave still felt as fresh as the day she'd been put in it. The screams dried up in the back of my throat then. I suddenly got the feeling I'd been trapped in a piece of amber. This was my breaking point. I couldn't move or call for help as the seconds or minutes ticked by. I wasn't even sure how long I'd been sitting there. All I could think about was how I'd failed Lucky. How I'd continued to fail him even after the universe had given me a second chance. I wanted to sink into the frozen earth and lie next to my Grams for eternity. It was probably what I deserved. Who else could lose their brother like this? He was half-dead already. I might as well have pushed him in his grave myself. Who else would be so selfish and careless? I'd been a coward — waiting in my room for so long and even contemplating going back to sleep. I felt disgusted by myself. How could I even look anyone in the eyes anymore? My parents? Nico? They would never speak to me again, and I wouldn't blame them.

I'm pathetic. Useless. I deserve to feel like this.

A rough palm jerked on the collar of my robe and wrenched me up to my feet — effectively snapping me out of my self-pitying. I tried to scream, but my voice was still gone. Acting on pure instinct, my fists flung out and connected with hard muscle and bone. I was a wild animal seized in a trap. My legs kicked and flailed, but it was no use. I'd been caught. *But… Caught by who?* Did it even matter anymore? Hadn't I wished for death only a moment ago? Perhaps this was karma already coming to get me. *Damn, that was quick.*

"Calm down!" He bellowed, wrapping one strong arm around both of mine and using the other to lift me up and lock my legs into place against his chest.

I was utterly defenseless now. All I could do was accept it. I jerked my chin back and forth as I tried to see through the river of tears and tangled hair that blocked my vision. Was this really how I was going to die? At least I'd gotten my wish — to die on top of Grams' grave. I tensed up — bracing for whatever was coming to me. I just hoped it would be quick. I couldn't stand to suffer like this for one more minute.

"It's me. It's *me*. You're safe!" Charlie gently brushed the hair away from my face. "It's me."

At the sound of his voice, my body instantly turned to gelatin. Even though I'd been fully prepared to cross the rainbow bridge a second ago, I felt relief flood through me. Maybe I'd been a little dramatic earlier. Even though I truly hated myself right now, I didn't want to die just yet. I buried myself into his chest, taking in the familiar smell of him, as I tried to catch my hitching breath. We stayed there for a long moment, panting and wrapped in each other's arms, while I mustered up the strength to tell him that Lucky was gone. But I supposed he already knew that, seeing as how he'd woken up to the empty sofa across from him.

Failure, failure, failure.

The word beat against the back of my skull until I was sure I was going to be sick.

"I'm so sorry," Charlie blurted.

"What am I going to do?" I pulled back. He looked about as tired as I felt. His blue eyes were bloodshot, and his tan skin wan.

His face screwed up. "What?"

Now it was my turn to be confused. His words, his expression… Everything was off. I pushed against him hard, and he set me back down. Once I was standing on my own, I took a step back out of his reach so I could get a good look at him.

"Lucky's gone," I said, right at the same time he said, "I found Lucky in the front yard."

My stomach dropped to my toes. What was he talking about? I'd been in the front yard myself, and I hadn't seen Lucky anywhere. If Lucky had been in the front, then… *Who the hell had I seen out here?* In my heart, I had known it couldn't have been my brother. But, somehow hearing my suspicions confirmed made who, or *what*, I'd seen that much more terrifying. With my luck, I was probably being haunted by some menacing, cloak-wearing, ghost who was an Olympic track star in his past life. It would make perfect sense with the way my life was panning out these days.

"Is he okay?" I asked, brushing the image aside. Nothing else mattered. Not even the ghost of Lightening McQueen.

"He's fine now, but G…"

"What?"

His lips flapped, seemingly unable to find the right words.

"I don't know. He was acting *really* weird when I found him."

I didn't wait for an explanation. I bolted to the house, only aware that Charlie had followed me when I heard his heavy footsteps thumping up the porch behind me. His long fingers caught my arm and yanked me back before I could reach the door handle. I yelped in pain and began winding back to sock him in the face before I caught the panic in his eyes.

Charlie's hands flailed out before him, waving in a wild motion that clearly said, *"Just wait"*. So, I did — allowing him to catch his breath again before he gave me a proper explanation.

"He's in the bath right now," Charlie wheezed. "I put him in the bath. He was all covered in mud — like head to toe, G. He was out here rolling around in the yard and acting all hysterical when I found him."

My eyebrows shot skyward as he continued. *How long had I been out here screaming?* Time felt like a completely foreign concept to me right now.

"And sweating and saying all this weird shit—"

"What weird shit? What was he saying, Charlie?"

"He just kept repeating things. A lot of it was him saying that it wasn't his fault, but then when I took him to the bath, he, like… *Grabbed* me, *really hard,* and asked me if I understood why."

Thinking of the memory, Charlie's hand reached up to rub at a spot on his bicep — as if he could still feel the crush of my brother's fingertips.

"Why what?"

My eyes ping-ponged back and forth between Charlie and the door. My body felt like it was being torn in half. I knew Lucky was safe now, but I needed to have my own eyes on him to make sure. Sensing my anxiety, Charlie nodded once, and I took that as my sign. I burst through the doors, nearly tripping over my own feet as I raced up the stairs and into the bathroom. Lucky was hunched over with his knees tucked into his chest as he stared into the milky bathwater. I flung myself to the floor beside him, bracing one hand on the tub so that I didn't go flying straight into the wall.

My abrupt entrance hadn't startled him in the slightest. He didn't even bother to look up as I cautiously placed one of my dirty hands on his damp back.

"Lucky?" I asked, barely more than a whisper.

Only the faucet dripped in response.

I cast a glance over my shoulder to find Charlie leaning against the doorframe. Deep lines of worry crisscrossed his forehead and tugged on the corners of his mouth.

"Lucky?"

As slowly as one of those haunted dolls in a scary movie, Lucky swiveled his head towards me. His eyes weren't hollow anymore. They seemed to bulge from the sockets, nearly bursting with a delirious sort of fear behind them. His expression was terrifying, and yet still so full of despair. Whatever emotions I'd been feeling before were *nothing* compared to what I saw on his face now. *What the hell happened to him?*

His lips trembled with words he seemed unable to speak, so I spoke for him. I had to be strong for him. It was nothing short of a *miracle* that I'd gotten a third chance with him tonight. I wasn't going to waste it.

"It's okay, Luck. You're okay now."

The dark tendrils of Lucky's hair were plastered to the sides of his cheekbones, reminding me of our childhood summer's when we'd all go to the pool and swim until dark. Unlike Nico, he still wore his hair long like he had back then. It felt like I was face-to-face with that little boy once more. The one who was innocent and scared of the "sharks" that lived in the deep end.

Lucky's lips wobbled a bit more, followed by his chin. His tanned skin still seemed *so* pale in the bathroom light I was again struck by how utterly fragile he looked. Even when they were scared of imaginary sharks, Lucky and Nico had never seemed weak to me. They were my big brothers, the stars of the football team, the party animals, my fiercest protectors. Seeing Lucky like this was nearly enough to break me all over again. My chest ached with renewed sorrow. A sorrow that was becoming all-too commonplace these days. Even though I'd felt it for what seemed like a hundred times now, it never got any better.

Lucky didn't speak again for the rest of the night. After getting him out of the bath and back into some clean clothes, courtesy of the late grandfather I'd never met, I stayed up and watched him — all the while, being plagued by the image of the cloaked figure I'd seen standing above Grams' grave.

Chapter Five
The Department

Nico came by the house the next morning with both arms loaded down by breakfast and a trash bag full of clothes for Lucky. I'd heard his truck pull up on the gravel before he'd even gotten out. I hadn't been able to sleep for the rest of the night, not that I'd even felt tired after everything that had happened, though.

I pushed open the doors to let Nico through. "Hey."

"Hey, G. Mom sent breakfast."

I followed him to the kitchen, trying to decide on whether I should tell him what happened. Nico already had so much on his plate; I didn't even want to bother him with it. *No.* No, I decided I couldn't. Besides, it's not like anything had *really* happened, anyway. Lucky was safe now, and that's all that mattered. Nico didn't need to be any more worried than he already was. I could practically feel his anxiety in the air.

"How was he last night?" Nico asked as he wiggled out one of the Styrofoam cups and slid it towards me. "He give you any trouble?"

I wrapped my hands around it, soaking in its warmth as I breathed in the rich smell of coffee.

"Fine."

"Fine?"

Unable to meet his questioning gaze, I nodded and looked away.

"So then why did I find your bracelet on the front porch, G?"

The color drained from my face as my eyes flashed to my bare wrist. I hadn't even known I'd lost it. I snatched it from him, and fumbled with clasp as I tried to come up with an answer.

"Hey man!" Charlie crowed as he stumbled into the kitchen with a lazy grin.

Thank God for Charlie Fairburn.

"Mom sent some breakfast sandwiches for you guys," Nico replied.

"So, what was up with the cops last night?" Charlie asked through big, greedy bites of sausage and egg.

Nico slung his thumbs through his belt loops. "Not sure, the whole place was still taped off when I got there. Have you talked to any of them, G?"

"Not yet."

"I don't know what they could even be looking for at this point," Nico said.

I blew on the steam rising from my cup. "Was Garcia there?"

Nico's head bobbed. "He was the one who told me I couldn't come in."

"Well, did you even ask *why*?"

"*Obviously*, but he said that he couldn't say yet — just that they were being forced to wait for another division to come in and check it out," Nico clucked his tongue. "He seemed about as annoyed about it as I did, though."

"Another division?" Charlie repeated, now moving on to his second sandwich. "Who could that be, G?"

I leaned back in my chair, feeling my eyes go in and out of focus as I tried to think about who the hell Garcia could even be referring to. Switchback was small, so our police department didn't have the resources to deal with a crime of this magnitude. Maybe it could be Elkheart's homicide division? I wasn't sure what the protocol was for dealing with an overdose "tainted" by Vampire blood... Or, I supposed, an overdose tainted by "Saph", as all the kids were calling it.

I pushed the hair away from my face with both hands, cringing internally as I felt how greasy it was. "Will you two be okay getting Luck ready today? I'll meet you guys at the funeral home later. There's something I have to do really quick." It was a lie, but I knew they'd try to stop me if I told them the truth.

After taking a quick shower and sweeping up my still-damp locks into a bun, I wiped the fog from the mirror and took a cautious peek at myself. The lack of sleep I'd gotten last night had definitely taken its toll. My wide mouth looked like it had been stuck in a permanent frown. I smoothed a generous amount of lotion over my cheeks, glancing away from the mirror as I caught my own bloodshot eyes staring back at me. The rest of my routine seemed pointless in my current state. Makeup would probably help, but just thinking about the entire application process was enough to make me want to crawl back in bed. *No use polishing a turd, right?* With that done, I settled on a pair of dark wash jeans, combat boots that had seen better days, and an oversized black sweater that nearly swallowed up my compact frame.

Before leaving, I double-checked that my trusty leather backpack held all the essentials, then headed straight for Lucky's Garage. No thanks to my brother, we still had no idea about what the hell the police were still searching for. Although I'd only met her a few times, I still felt bad that I'd be missing Olivia's funeral. I wanted to be there for Lucky, but I needed to see what was going on before all my useless wondering drove me crazy.

Lucky's Garage wasn't far from Nostra Casa, only about half a mile down the road at a spot where Main Street ended. The area wasn't as clean or pretty there, but it wasn't exactly a dump either. Settled between a gas station and an empty lot that was merely a flat expanse of rocks and dirt, Lucky's Garage looked about the same as any other auto repair shop in America. The three street-facing garage bays were attached to a slightly taller building that housed the main office and, atop that, Lucky's loft-style apartment. The candy-apple red shade of the shop's tin siding made it hard to miss. If there was any confusion though, a large sign that said "Lucky's Garage" was perched on the roof below a checkered racing flag that had taken Nico and Lucky *months* to weld together and paint.

Yellow and black police tape crisscrossed the garage like spiderwebs. My eyes bulged as I saw that nearly every Switchback police cruiser had been parked out front. I rolled to a stop next to a shiny white van that read "Channel 4 News" on the side and felt my stomach immediately do backflips. *Why would the news be here? I couldn't believe* they could be broadcasting their crackpot Vampire theory so soon. Had they somehow found real evidence to support it?

I dug through my bag and hurriedly slung the badge over my head as I jogged up to the first strand of tape where my hardass co-worker, Officer Stevens, was holding the line. Her dark eyes narrowed as I came up, her hands finding a firm hold on her curvy hips.

"What are you doing here, Beretta?" She grumbled — briefly glancing at me, then past my shoulders as if she was already too busy to chat.

Even though I knew she'd seen it, I flashed my badge at her. "Police business."

"You mean *consultant* business?"

"Sure," I said, reaching forward to step beneath the tape. "Whatever makes you happy, Stevens."

Her hand lashed out in an instant, grabbing my shoulder, and pushing me back so hard I stumbled over the uneven sidewalk.

"Hey!"

She pursed her lips at me and resumed scanning the distance for some invisible threat. "Sorry, Beretta. This is *strictly* police business."

I stamped my booted foot on the ground like a whiny little kid. "So what? I have clearance, don't I? I demand to be let through. *Immediately.*"

"I don't care what you *demand*, Beretta. You're not—" Stevens broke off, swearing beneath her breath as her eyes went round with shock.

Seizing my opportunity, I skirted beneath the tape and made a beeline for one of the half-opened garage doors. I didn't dare look back at what she'd seen. At this point, I really didn't care. I needed to get inside and see what the hell was going on in there.

I was halfway through laughing like I'd just pulled off some high stakes bank heist when I ducked beneath the door and slammed straight into the barreled chest of Chief Garcia. We both stepped back in a daze as we tried to see who we'd run into.

Garcia's reaction was quick, though. Much quicker than mine, damn him. His steel-gray eyes turned to slits as he pounced for my elbow. "*Beretta.* I should've known you'd come here sooner or later."

I tried to wriggle out of his grasp, but he was too strong. His meaty hand was like a vice as he began to half-walk, half-drag me back out of the garage.

"Tell me what the hell is going on here!"

He only ignored me and kept hauling me out — stopping short before the garage doors as he caught sight of something outside. With the metal half of the doors lifted, my eyesight was completely blocked. In his shock, the firm grip locked around my elbow had loosened just enough for me to get free. I took a step forward and leaned in on my tiptoes, balancing my weight on the pull handle as I peered out to get a better look. A Rolls-Royce Phantom had hopped the curb and nosed its way through all the patrol cars and news vans to steal a front-row spot. Built more like a brick than a car, the angry-eyed automobile was painted a shade so black it seemed to swallow up every ounce of color around it. As its doors were thrown open, I could make out the slender leg of a woman in a snow-white pantsuit and towering pumps exiting the vehicle. A flash of gold on her lapel caught my eye. A broach, about the size of my palm, was pinned there — three thick interlocking triangles.

Garcia gulped hard beside me.

"Who is that?" I breathed, knowing good and damn well that it wasn't the Elkheart homicide division.

"The Department of Supernatural Resources."

I turned my head toward him so fast it made my vision blurry. Though the woman's broach had given me all the answers I needed, I asked anyway, "From the Citadel? Like, the *Triad*?"

Even from where we stood behind a wall of glass and metal, I could feel the ancient power rolling off the woman in waves. Her mere presence seemed to crush the life out of everything that stood in her way. It was both terrifying and magnificent to behold. She was a woman of all vertical lines with a thin, lithe body, pointed features and a beaklike nose that gave her the overall air of indifference. Her pale-yellow hair was styled in a bob so sharp it looked like it could cut somebody.

I struggled to remember where I'd seen her before. Everything about her seemed so unique, so unforgettable, that it was a wonder I was having trouble coming up with a name.

"That's Celine Bissonnette," Garcia murmured the answer to my unasked question.

Of course, it was. Celine Bissonnette was the face of the Triad. Every time anything about the Supernatural's came up, she was there. She was their spokeswoman, the striking Vampire I'd seen on all the news stations ever since I was a teenager. Jesus, she looked *way* different in person.

"What's the Department of…"

"The Department of Supernatural Resources," Garcia finished. "Is the Triad's version of a police department. It's new."

Celine's back was toward us now. More news crews had pulled up with an army of eager reporters — all of them locked in a bitter fight to see who could shove their microphone the closest to her. A younger man in his late twenties, with the impressive height of some NBA basketball player, was watching Celine from a few paces away. He surveyed the scene with a lazy, heavy-lidded gaze that almost seemed like a ruse to make any potential attacker think he wasn't paying attention. His tawny skin was faintly ashen against the dark jeans and sweater he wore, and had it not been for the same triangular pin fastened over his heart, I might've attributed the odd pallor to the overcast sky above. All the Supernatural's wore those pins now. It was supposed to be like an identification thing, although they certainly didn't need it. Anyone with working eyes could see what they were from a mile away. Those conspiracy theory people had been on to something. You really *could* tell they were different.

Vampires. They're real-life Vampires.

Without a second thought, I swooped beneath the door and edged in closer to hear what Celine was about to say. Another crowd, small but growing quickly, had started to form beyond the newscasters. A few people in the crowd held messy cardboard signs that read, "*Nothin' natural 'bout being Supernatural*" and, "*America is doomed*" in dripping red paint. My personal favorite had to be the signs from the obviously more prepared protesters who carried printed versions reading, "GOD HATES FANGS" in black lettering so big it could probably be seen from space. I recognized *those* signs as being from the Switchback Baptist Church.

They'd had them posted up around town ever since the first phase of the Great Integration began, but their slogan never got any less funny to me. I still wasn't sure why the Witches and Fae weren't the primary targets of their hatred, but I'd given up on understanding those prejudiced bible-thumpers a long time ago. The Triad's announcement of the Great Integration ten years ago had been the most mind-blowing moment in my life, but I was getting the feeling that *this* was somehow going to be even better.

Celine paced in front of the cameras like she was making sure that they were all turned on and ready to capture the very second she started speaking. If her ashen skin and triangular pin hadn't been enough, there was something about the way her willowy frame moved too slowly, too gracefully to ever be mistaken as human. A line of police officers had rushed out from the garage to hold back the crowd as she moved again to assess their furious faces. Finding nothing of interest, she turned on one towering stiletto with her nose to the air and stalked back to center-stage. Her arrogance only seemed to piss off the crowd even more. Their feverish skin and bulging eyes blended into one another as they howled, spit, and threw out every curse they could think of.

Honestly, it was a real turn of events to see people finally caring about substance-abuse — and, to think, it had only taken a few drops of Saph to do it. Hell, if the human government had gone with these tactics right from the start, the war on drugs probably would've been won decades ago.

Despite how skittish the angry mob was making me feel, I found myself rooted to the spot — unable to look away from Celine's sheer perfection. I'd never seen a Vampire in real life. It was unlike anything I ever could've imagined. I was star-struck, plain and simple.

"As you all know, phase one of the Great Integration has brought our community together for the first time in history," Celine began in a lilting, musical voice that had the power to silence even the most passionate of her protestors. "Vampires, Witches, and Fae are now united as one under the Triad's rule."

The way she spoke was slow and clear, like someone who'd never been interrupted before. The sheer confidence she possessed made my mouth pop open. I'd never had an idol before. It had never made sense to me how people could be *so* obsessed with someone who didn't even know they existed, but... There was just *something* about her that made me *want* to become one of those overzealous fangirls.

"Phase two has been focused on obtaining more rights and protections for our people—" She tilted her chin towards the now speechless mob. "*And yours.*"

Garcia's thick fingers gripped my chin to put my mouth back in place. "You're gonna catch flies."

I was so distracted by Celine that I hadn't even realized he was standing right next to me. I didn't reply. I was too afraid to miss even a single word she was saying.

"The Triad has been in the process of establishing community supports for quite some time now. One of those supports being our new Department of Supernatural Resources, modeled after the police force you humans possess. Our new department will help us transition even more smoothly into this integration process, while simultaneously working to resolve any unfortunate incidents like the recent tragedy that has occurred here." She clapped her pale hands together so hard I almost thought someone had fired off a bullet.

"I'm sure that, *by now*, many of you have heard the malicious and spurious accusations being spread by *your* law enforcement. They believe that Vampires have been lacing illegal drugs with our blood in an attempt to kill humans."

I raised a brow. Wow, okay. She was cutting right through all the bullshit, then.

"As a representative of the Department of Supernatural Resources, I'm here today to tell you that what you've heard is *false*. In light of recent events here, involving a *gross* exploitation of Vampires for their blood that has resulted in nothing but the expected consequences, the Triad has assigned a special task force to this case so that we may identify the perpetrator and restore safety to both of our communities."

She leveled the crowd with a stern gaze. "As one last reminder to the public, or anyone that wishes to copy the acts of the victims, obtaining or consuming Supernatural blood, bodily fluid, or tissue of *any* kind is *lethal* and illegal. The Triad begs you to heed this warning and learn from the mistakes of your community members. Thank you."

"Holy," Garcia rasped, seemingly too stunned to finish the sentence.

"Shit," I supplied, just as blown away as he was.

Chapter Six
Discovery

Tear gas and pepper-spray was Switchback PD's not-so-gentle way of encouraging the angry mob at Lucky's to disperse and go back to whatever Hellmouth they'd crawled out from. Amid all that chaos, I found my way to a semi-circle of folding metal chairs, staring directly into Celine Bissonnette's black, orb-like eyes.

"It's *not* happening," Garcia was raving. He seemed like he was about to have a stroke and fall out onto the oil-stained concrete.

Across from me, Celine's expression remained cool despite the fact she also seemed like she was having a hard time trying not to vomit. I didn't even think she was being dramatic. Compared to her magnificence, the garage suddenly looked absolutely disgusting. I wouldn't even be shocked if she told us she was scheduled for tea with the Queen after this. It was hard to imagine *her* ever stepping foot in a place with so much dirt and grease, but there she was — the ice queen herself, here in my brother's shop.

"It *is* happening," Celine purred.

"On whose authority?"

"The United States Government. As per the new Bill of Supernatural Rights, *passed this morning*, when there is *any* crime involving *any* element of the Supernatural, we are given full authority to conduct an independent investigation into the matter."

Celine's intense gaze honed in on Garcia like a laser-beam. A single bead of sweat dripped from his triangular hairline, the only outward sign of his distress. They stared at each other for a long, tense moment. The other officers who had gathered around for the meeting shifted uncomfortably.

Garcia broke first — his gaze snapping towards Officer Stevens in a silent plea for help.

"This case involves elements of the Supernatural, does it not?" Celine drawled, now looking to her own companion for confirmation.

"I believe it does, mistress," the man chimed in. He was watching our meeting from a spot in the room that I knew had to be calculated. He hid in a shadowy corner with his back towards one of the furthest walls. From that vantage point, he could surely keep his eyes on every other person in the room all at once.

"Our report stated that Vampire blood was present at the scene of the crime." He spoke with an accent so slight that it was nearly undetectable. *Maybe Russian?* I couldn't place it.

Garcia jerked out of his seat and leveled a finger at Celine. "You're not getting access to this crime scene unless you provide a warrant signed by Governor Ivey."

Celine merely grinned, revealing the ultra-white tips of her pointed incisors. Like her companion's accent, her animalistic teeth had been nearly undetectable until she'd bared them. They seemed to be only slightly longer than an average human's, not at all like the big garish ones from the movies I'd seen. Still, the thought of them sinking into someone's flesh (probably Garcia's) instantly sent a chill running through me.

"We're not leaving until you allow us to investigate," she countered. The subtle power behind her voice was as unyielding as her horrible black eyes. "It's unfortunate that you've spread these lies, because now you have to clean up the mess you've made."

"We have to let them, Chief," I let the words spill out before I lost my nerve. "It's the law now. Isn't it your sworn duty to uphold the law as a police officer?"

Celine's attention shifted to me now, burning a hole through every fiber of my being.

I didn't think I'd ever known what true rage was until I saw it behind Garcia's steel-gray eyes. Not even the protestors had looked *this* furious. If Celine's gaze was hot, well... Garcia's was pure magma. A hard lump formed in my throat, but my mouth had gone too dry to swallow it.

"They'll get the warrant, and that's final," Garcia gnashed his teeth so hard they sounded like they'd cracked to pieces.

Celine stood then, erupting in a tinkling fit of laughter as she exited the garage with her bodyguard trailing close behind. "No need to worry about that. We'll be back."

"What the *hell* is wrong with you?" Garcia demanded once they'd rumbled off in their extravagant ride.

Feeling like I was stuck in some kind of trance, I shook out my limbs and looked up. Garcia was towering over me with his hands balled up at his sides. When he raised a bushy brow, I realized it was my turn to say something.

"What do you mean?"

He was sweating profusely. Dark, wet stains dribbled from his armpits and along his broad chest.

"Why would you even say that? There's no way in hell I'm gonna let them have access to this crime scene, Beretta. This is *our* jurisdiction, *our* case. They have no right sticking their fangs into *our* business."

I really didn't like the way he kept saying "*our*". In fact, it annoyed me so much that I began to fantasize about throttling him right then and there. One good punch to his meaty face and he'd be down… He wouldn't even be expecting it. I twisted my fingers around my bracelet as I tried to brush away the thought of his bones cracking beneath my flesh.

"It's the law, Chief. Just trying to uphold the law."

Garcia's fists splayed out beside him and curled back together. Clearly at a loss for words, he repeated the motion again and again until he could think of something else to yell at me about. He knew what I'd said was the truth. There was no other way around it.

"Why are you even here?" He finally bit out.

"To find out what the hell is going on. It's been days since the…"

I wasn't sure what to call it. The accident? No, they hadn't *accidentally* injected themselves with drugs. But maybe they *had* accidentally injected themselves with Saph. The incident, then? *Ugh, whatever.*

"Anyway, I'm here for answers," I finished.

If it had truly been on purpose, I needed to know. And, if there really was some Vampire out there trying to kill Olivia and Lucky like they were saying... Well, I needed to know *that*, too. Hell, *any* scrap of information would help me ease all the worry I'd been feeling these past few days. I was drowning in all this uncertainty.

Garcia rifled through his pockets for a dirty tissue and absentmindedly patted his slick forehead. "Well, you're out of luck, too. This is official police business."

I wanted to scream. What the hell did I have to do to get some credit around here? I mean, I *was* just a consultant, but... They still had me running around interrogating suspects, for God's sake! Didn't that count for something? *Wait...*

I sprung out of my chair so quick my knees popped. Immediately going on the defense, Garcia took a step back and reached for his gun belt.

I snorted at him. "Relax, I just remembered something I had to tell you."

Garcia dropped his hands, but the leery look in his eyes stayed firmly in place.

"I spoke to Mrs. Jessops about the Josh Peters case like you told me to. She wasn't lying when she told me she didn't have anything to do with it, but she also didn't have a solid alibi, either."

A smug grin replaced the worry on Garcia's face, but I continued on. He hadn't won yet.

"So then, I went to the McKinney's. Mrs. Jessops claimed she'd been, uhh..." I paused to think of the right word. "Having a bonfire in her yard between eleven and twelve — which, *as you know*, was the time of the crime. When I asked the McKinney's about their whereabouts, they admitted to spying on Mrs. Jessops at that *exact* same time. I got it all on tape. Anyway, like I said before, there was *no way* she could've done it."

Garcia's face fell.

"What is it?"

His eyes darted back and forth between his bare wrists. "What time is it?"

"Three-thirty, why?"

Garcia grabbed the chunky radio clipped at his shoulder and barked out, "Victor twenty-seven, what's your twenty?"

The radio made a garbled beep as the officer on the other end clipped out, "Twenty-seven — code eleven, go ahead."

Code eleven... I tried to remember what that meant. I hadn't been trained on the radio like the other cops had, but I'd picked up a lot since I'd started working at the station. A code eleven meant the officer had just arrived on the scene. Was the "scene" he was referring to Mrs. Jessops' place? Christ, they couldn't be going to arrest her already, could they?

"Victor twenty-seven — Ten-nineteen to command," Garcia continued, now pacing in a tight, little circle. Ten-nineteen to command, I'd heard this one often enough to know he was telling him to abort the mission and head back to the station.

"Twenty-seven, we've got a ten-fifty-four at three-eight-seven Adelaide," the officer shot back. "Calling all units, ten-five-four at three-eight-seven Adelaide, requesting back-up."

Three-eight-seven Adelaide. Shit, shit, shit. It *was* Mrs. Jessops' place. But...

I latched onto Garcia's burly arm. "What's a ten-fifty-four?"

When he looked at me, his terra-cotta skin had turned as ashen as the Vampires.

"Possible dead body."

I gripped the steering wheel tight as I tried to remember one of those calming techniques I'd learned in therapy. Tense up for five seconds and then relax? Or was it supposed to be longer than that? And how many times was I supposed to repeat it? I sank back into my seat and pressed the gas pedal down even harder as I flew towards Adelaide Road. Why did I even bother? Those stupid tricks had never worked for me. Jesus, my anxiety was giving me anxiety now.

Snow poured from the gray sky above, coating the tree-lined road with fresh powder. Although my mind was racing with a million other thoughts, I briefly wondered if it would stick. My phone buzzed in my lap, but I made no attempt to reach for it. I figured it would probably be an annoyed call from Nico for missing Olivia's funeral... Or worse, my parents.

As I came to the trident-shaped branch in the road, an overwhelming sense of dread came over me. The awful, stomach-churning sensation in my belly only grew worse and worse as I got closer. Seconds later, I found myself at her cheery yellow cottage alongside a squadron of police cars and ambulances who'd somehow managed to beat me there.

Possible dead body. Garcia's empty words ran through my head over and over until it was all I could think. *Possible dead body.* Something *felt* wrong. I'd known it even before I'd pulled the key from my ignition. I knew it couldn't be just *"possible"*. No, this feeling in my stomach, my flesh, and my bones was too great — too overwhelming for that to be right. *Dead body*, a nasty part of me thought. *She's dead.*

The sickness in my stomach was quickly replaced by a hollowness, leaving my insides feeling like they'd been scooped out like a pumpkin on Halloween. I stepped out of the car, immediately taken aback by the heavy silence that pressed down on my ears. The quiet was suffocating, stealing the air from my lungs.

It shouldn't be this quiet with so many officers on the scene.

Why was it so damned quiet?

I rolled my shoulders back and shook out my limbs like an athlete warming up for a race. I was being stupid. It had to be my mind playing tricks on me. I walked past the empty patrol cars and ambulances. The sirens were off, but their emergency lights were still on — bathing the cottage in shades of red and blue.

Everything was probably fine, right? The officer had said *possible*, and there were ambulances here. They wouldn't send out *this* many ambulances for a dead body, *right?*

"You're being dumb, G," I whispered to myself.

I kept trying to convince myself of that as I treaded up the neat path towards her home and beneath the ivy-covered trellis that led to the front porch. I still couldn't hear any sounds coming from inside.

I wiped a hand over my sweaty neck and took another step forward. The door was open, but only slightly — a crack barely large enough to let a sliver of afternoon air past. My fist trembled as I knocked on the door. No footsteps, no reply. Where were the other officers? Should I just go in? For some reason, I got the feeling that I would be intruding.

I knocked again, more urgently this time. The force of my fist bashed against the door so hard it flew open and slammed back into the wall with a violent thud. Worse than the bubble of silence around the cottage, an alarmingly frigid air poured out from within. The air carried with it a sharp, metallic stench that nearly made me gag. There was no mistaking the foul, almost sweet odor. It was a smell that was permanently ingrained in my mind — the repulsive, rotting stench of a dead body. I'd smelled it only once before, when my Grams had died.

I shouted Mrs. Jessops' name, and then the names of the officers I knew through the opened door frame. Again and again, I called out with no reply before I finally mustered up enough courage to step inside the house. *Where the hell was everybody?*

I made my way through the halls carefully — once familiar, and warm, and cozy, but now alien, and icy, and evil. Even though I knew it was utterly crazy, I suddenly wished I'd brought a weapon with me. With everything going on in my life lately, I *really* needed to start packing heat. The fading light of the afternoon sky threw dark shadows across the gray stones lining the hallway. The house itself seemed to grin at me with sharp, eerie teeth — like it had become a wide, salivating mouth, licking its lips as it prepared to swallow me whole. I gripped my keys between my fingers, making sure the ends pointed out of my fist like a cat's claws. *Voilà, a weapon.*

Again, I was all too aware of the silence. Every step I took, every heartbeat that thundered in my chest, was like the ear-splitting ricochet of a gunshot. The blue-shirted backs of the officers were facing me as I stepped into the living room. The smell had grown almost unbearable now, clearly indicating that *this* room was its source.

Dark, congealed blood was splashed across every surface, even the walls were coated. Strangely enough, though, there seemed to be no signs of forced entry. No broken furniture or misplaced piece of decor that would show a struggle. Still, I knew that there was no life here. I knew she was dead even before I saw her. There was too much blood. None of the officers or paramedics were speaking. They stood there, frozen like statues in the Chinese terracotta army. I was able to push my way through the crowd easily. Everyone was so dazed that they barely even acknowledged my presence. When I saw what they were staring at, though, it became all too clear why.

Mrs. Jessops' body seemed like it had been arranged like a life-sized doll. Her knees were on the floor, the side of her face and palms pressed down — almost as if she'd dropped something and was now searching beneath the sofa for it. The cocoa-colored skin of her neck looked as if it had been ripped wide open by some sharp-toothed animal. Blood had pooled onto the stone floor. It spilled across the handwoven carpet and soaked into the bright silk muumuu she wore. The backs of her legs were clearly exposed by the way her body had been positioned, like it had been done on purpose for whoever found her. My trembling hand flew up to my mouth to stifle a scream. Impossibly deep gashes, like claw marks, were ripped down both of her thighs. Exposed muscle, and sinew, and bone spilled out of her legs like ribbons. I pushed my way out of the silent officers as I sprinted outside and threw up in Mrs. Jessops' favorite bushes.

Within an hour, nearly every cop in Switchback had descended on the house. I thought about Lucky's Garage. It was probably long forgotten by now — completely abandoned as the police jumped on the even hotter mystery in town. I couldn't remember the last time we'd had an *actual* murder around here. That's what they were calling it now — a murder. It had to be, though; I didn't think any of the wildlife around here would have attacked her in her house without at least breaking a few things first.

It only took another hour for the news crews, protestors, and even officers and residents from the neighboring city of Elkhart to reassemble and gawk on the edge of the property. I'd taken up a spot on the porch, leaning against the trellis, dead-eyed and trying not to vomit again. I watched as the morbidly curious spectators craned to get a view of the house from behind the freshly placed police tape. The officers had finally started to move again — buzzing around the house and property like angry hornets as they searched for evidence. All I could do was watch, though. Watch as the reporters in the drive straightened their suits and checked their teeth in compact mirrors as they waited for more information. Watch as those nasty signs with "GOD HATES FANGS", and new ones saying "REJOICE, GOD KILLED THE HERETIC", were thrust into the air with a chorus of hateful jeers and shouts. Mrs. Jessops' only crime against them had been the fact she'd never gone to their church. Now they were celebrating her death. Her murder. I wanted to scream at them, to knock down all their signs, and spit in their disgusting faces... Even so, all I could do was watch. I had nothing left inside me to give. No strength, or nerve, or fear. I had nothing. I *was* nothing.

The coroner said that her body had been there for at least twenty-four hours, and along with the horrible wounds on her neck and legs, there were two puncture marks on the *inside* of her left thigh. The lacerations coupled with the puncture marks had been enough to completely drain her body of blood. That was when the preening homicide division from Elkheart had announced that it wasn't a regular murder anymore, but the definitive work of a Vampire. And this time, I knew that Celine Bissonnette wouldn't be able to explain it away so easily.

There was a rogue Vampire on the loose, and he was coming after us all.

Chapter Seven
Warrant

Switchback exploded. Ever since we'd become the official center of the modern Supernatural world, and subsequently thrust to center-stage in the public eye, our small town had become a common household name. But now, with the first ever reported instance of a Vampire-related homicide, we were all anyone could talk about.

Mrs. Jessops' body was plastered over every newspaper, magazine, and website in the world. Photos of the grisly attack had been leaked by the press and splashed across every media outlet thinkable. If the memory hadn't been seared into my brain enough, I could just as easily relive the horrific day with two taps of my finger. It was inescapable. Every time I closed my eyes, I saw her — the sadistic pose of her ruined body. All the blood, *so much blood*, painted across the living room. I couldn't get away from it.

Despite my protests, Garcia had forced me to go on administrative leave after the incident. I didn't want to be at home, though. I couldn't stand being left there alone with Lucky, who still hadn't spoken. He floated around the house like a ghost, only waking to eat and use the restroom before drifting back to sleep. Charlie had been busy with his father's ranch (as per his half-hearted monthly obligations) and with the new influx of visitors Switchback had received over the past week, even Nico and my parents had become too busy running the restaurant to check-in. It was torture. I was alone. Completely alone, with nothing but my thoughts and a great, big, empty house.

After a few days of binging season upon season of television shows and stuffing my face with anything I could get my hands on, I decided I couldn't sit still anymore. The snow *had* stuck around after all, and now coated everything in sight with at least three solid inches of ice. I'd barely slept since the murder, so I was up early that morning. I tugged on my disheveled work boots and padded over the squeaky snow to the greenhouse behind my house. A blast of sweet air greeted me as I entered and reveled in that sense of calm that I'd always gotten there.

When I was younger, my Grams had introduced me to the world of essential oils. At first, I'd used them in a diffuser for a happier mood, or relaxation, or focus, but... As I'd delved deeper, I found the world of perfume making. It had become a hobby of mine when I could find the time. I think I loved it so much because of my weird relationship with smell. Charlie had always pushed me to sell my creations, but everything I'd ever made seemed too personal. Perhaps, in another life, I could've even become a "*Nez*" or master perfumer, but for now, it was just something fun and relaxing I could do to get my mind off things.

My favorite part about it was feeling like I could recreate and bottle memories. I had perfumes that reminded me of Christmas when Grams would make frosted sugar cookies and macchiatos to dunk them in. There were some that reminded me of going on midnight drives with Charlie. I had ones for nearly every special moment in my life that I didn't want to forget. The perfumes *always* had a way of bringing me back to those moments like a time-machine.

I flicked on my space heater and stood before my workbench to study the tiered shelves above it. They housed nearly two-hundred miniature glass bottles that were labeled according to their particular scent. *The sickly sweet, rotted scent of...* A wave of nausea came over me as the intrusive thought popped into my mind.

I leaned forward to unscrew the cap of the lavender bottle and breathed in deep, trying to banish the memory. A mellow feeling instantly replaced the nasty image as I inhaled the soothing scent. I replaced the vial and stooped below my desk to paw through the collection of empty perfume vessels. I never quite knew what I would make until I'd found the right one. One of the empty vessels would speak to me and the recipe would follow. My fingers finally wrapped around a bottle, and I set it on my desk to examine it. It was an opalescent amber color, with gently curved slopes that fell from the mouth and ended in a flat, linear base. The stopper was tall and proud, carved from the same honey-colored glass and fashioned with natural-looking ridges like a crystal. Immediately, I knew what scents I needed to use. My recipe for perfume was stronger than most of the recipes I'd studied online, but I preferred it that way. I liked a scent that would last all day and not have to be reapplied.

I chose black truffle and pink pepper as my top notes, the spicy punch of fragrance that would be the first scent to hit the nose. I followed those with a mixture of seductive ylang-ylang, bitter orange, and a dewy sweet peony. These would be the heart notes of my perfume, the scent that stuck around longer, an hour or so, before the base notes took hold. For those, I finished the perfume off with a woodsy patchouli followed by a sugary vanilla and a few drops of a boozy black plum. The whole concoction was rich and powerful — brimming with sexy magnetism and an intoxicating mystery that quietly demanded attention. The slick sides of the bottle nearly slipped from my grasp as I finally realized what I'd made... Or, rather, *who* I'd made. Without a doubt, the perfume was my rendition of Celine Bissonnette. I'd been put on leave to forget about all this mess and here I was, *clearly* still obsessing over this case.

As if on cue, my phone buzzed on the desk. I quickly corked the perfume and answered. I was so startled that I hadn't even bothered to check who it was.

"We need you back at the station. We have a problem," Garcia said, then abruptly hung up.

Not wasting any time, I ran back to the house with my perfume in tow. I showered quickly and threw on a pair of red plaid slacks, my combat boots, a black turtleneck, and a matching oversized blazer. I eyed the perfume bottle as I threw my work stuff into my backpack, shrugged to myself, and splashed on my new creation. So what if I was obsessed? I wasn't going to let my embarrassment stand in the way of making my delicious new perfume go to waste.

Before bolting out of the door, I wrote a quick note to Lucky, telling him where I'd gone and how to heat the lasagna in the fridge. I hoped he would be okay by himself. He hadn't done any more running away since that first night, but I still couldn't seem to stop worrying about him. Every time I saw him, I was reminded of the fact that he was ten times more breakable than even I felt inside. Despite how guilty I was about leaving him, I *had* to. I was all out of options at this point.

The station was absolutely crawling with protestors and news vans who'd all gathered there ever since the story of Mrs. Jessops' murder had broken. I waited as a car pulled out of the only spot left — pressing my cheek against the icy glass and watching as my rapid breaths fogged up the window. The slushy parking lot around me was as busy as Time's Square. It was chaos — completely packed with the gentle purrs of car engines and yellow-hued headlights as more and more people arrived to find the already too full lot.

"What the hell is going on *now?*"

Switchback PD looked more like a high school than a police station. Its imposing red brick façade was perched atop a series of concrete stairs that led to the grand marble entryway. Climb-resistant barricades had been set up halfway between the stairs and the rotating glass doors that led inside. A line of officers stood in full riot gear beyond the walls of metallic black mesh, facing the screaming crowd as they clawed and scratched to get past. I locked my car twice just to be safe.

Christ, it was insane out here! It felt like I was witnessing the start of some zombie apocalypse or something. I wasn't sure how Garcia had expected me to navigate my way through the mob and into the station. A makeshift podium of wooden pallets had been erected near the back edge of the crowd, where a fully robed priest was shouting some fire-and-brimstone sermon through a megaphone. As I edged in closer, I saw it wasn't just *any* doomsday priest. No, of course not. It was the infamous spiritual leader of the Switchback Baptist Church himself — Leslie Rathmore. *The bastard.* He'd been the man who'd given his church the whole idea of coming to Mrs. Jessops' house with those awful signs. I wanted to wring his neck — to take back some of the power that those signs had stolen from me that day. I hated him, and I hated his stupid fucking cult.

I glared at him, imagining for a moment that my stare was as menacing and powerful as Celine's. Although Leslie Rathmore was a stiff man, his stark white robes fluttered around him in the icy breeze like a dove's wings. His deep, powerful voice could've cut over the deafening roar of the crowd even without the use of a speaker. Like Josh Peters, Leslie's pale face was blandly handsome and nearly unremarkable except for the elegant horn-rimmed glasses he wore. He seemed like someone you could look up to — a man that was old enough to be knowledgeable about the ways of the world, yet still young enough to be in the know. I'd only seen him in person once before, but now, I was reminded of how such an awful man like him could capture the hearts and minds of so many. It made me hate him that much more.

As if he'd sensed my presence, Leslie turned towards me. His glassy eyes locked with mine. The front of his robes had been splashed with a deep reddish-brown fluid that was clearly supposed to look like blood. Maybe it was even actual blood, I wouldn't put it past him. An appalling silicone wound, like the ones you could purchase on Halloween, had been pasted onto the right side of his neck — a sickening mockery of the one Mrs. Jessops had died from. Rage began sparking up at my fingertips, twisting up my arms and chest until my entire body was filled with an electric fury. *How dare he!* He was *disgusting*. I felt close to bursting, to releasing that current of anger on anyone who stood in my way. I would have his fucking head for making this some kind of joke! He couldn't get away with this! He couldn't turn this into some twisted propaganda. I would —

My next thought was cut short as I saw Leslie move once more. He had leveled a finger at me with such conviction, I almost thought flames would shoot out of it. I guess our feelings about each other were mutual, then. "Here comes a sinner now! You'll be next unless you repent! God killed the Heretic, but he's not done yet, folks! He'll kill everyone else who stands by and suffers these Supernatural abominations to live!"

At his words, the entire crowd shifted their attention away from the barriers to turn on me. Their signs were hoisted into the chilled air, their noses pink and frozen from the light snowfall. A few began stalking forward, encouraged by their leader's accusations. A terrible shudder rippled over my skin as I grasped what was happening. *Oh, shit.* I backed up a few steps as I fumbled for the canister of pepper-spray attached to my keyring. What the hell was I going to do? There was no way I could take *all* of them on by myself! I wanted to look for a way out, but I was too worried about taking my eyes off the mob. They were unhinged. I couldn't let my guard down. They looked like they wanted to eat me alive.

"Repent sinner!" One particularly burly man howled above the crowd.

Yep, that was *definitely* murder I saw on all their faces. *What the hell?* For whatever reason, I'd somehow become the latest sacrificial lamb to their cause. *Shit!* I should've kept my head down. Ugh, I just *had* to go and provoke the psychopath, didn't I? My gloved fingers finally caught hold of the pepper spray can, but it was too late. The entire horde of protestors were already gunning for me. Pure adrenaline raced through my veins. I screamed as I turned to run away, but it was cut short as I felt my boots catch on a slick patch of ice behind me. Blue and green stars burst behind my eyelids as my skull slammed against the concrete. My head hurt like hell, but I didn't have time to nurse my wounds. *Get away, get away, get away.* The frantic mantra played on repeat in my mind. My feet couldn't seem to find purchase on the ground, though. I scrambled like a newborn deer on a frozen lake — desperate to get my legs back under me. I was terrified. Even with the adrenaline now coursing through me, I felt my limbs growing heavier as they became paralyzed by this fear. It was overwhelming. It didn't even feel like I was myself anymore. My whole being was just one big ball of shivering panic.

"Kill the heretic!" The burly man yelled as he barreled his way to the forefront of the mob.

"Kill the ally!" All of them were screaming in unison now, chanting the words over and over as they grabbed for me. They wanted to rip me to shreds. They were *going* to rip me to shreds. Oh my God. What a pathetic way to go. Right in front of the police station, too! This was bullshit! Why was nobody helping me? Wasn't that what those pathetic excuses for cops were literally *paid* to do?

Because no one likes you, the dark intrusive thought hissed in my mind. *No one cares what happens to you. You're nothing. No one.*

A strange sense of clarity finally dawned on me. I was on my own. I was *really* on my own. No one was going to save me. My fear wrestled with my animal instincts as they tried to grab the reigns tight. Everything suddenly seemed too sharp, too real. My scalp was full of hot prickles that made me want to grab fistfuls of my hair and tug until they went away. It was always hard for me to describe anxiety to someone who has never experienced it. I'm sure that it's different for everyone, but for me, it felt like time would slow down and speed up all at once. It felt like I was the only person in the world who realized that we were all going to die. I would ask myself why no one else was freaking out — why did no one else care? Everyone always talks about the physical effects of anxiety, but no one ever tells you how lonely it is. It's absolute hell feeling like you're the only person on the planet that's worried about this big, scary thing that everyone should be losing their shit over. It makes you feel like either everyone else is stupid, or they all know something that you don't. Shoving those feelings down, using pain to bring myself back to my body... Anything was better than feeling like that. *Anything.*

   Instead of running away from that anxiety, or trying to smother it with all my stupid tricks... This time, I leaned into it. I wouldn't allow my terror to struggle with that fight-or-flight impulse anymore. I needed to use it — needed to let it work alongside those survival instincts instead of battling inside me. Fear wouldn't paralyze me this time. It would *save* me. That was the only way I would have any chance of getting out of here — no matter how slim that possibility was becoming by the second. I couldn't allow those feelings to rage some internal war with each other while I did nothing. I was *more* than my anxiety. I could overcome this. I *would*. I let myself hear every deafening beat of my jackhammer heart, feel every gasping breath, and see every possible outcome to this grim situation. If I really had to die today, I was going to give it a damn good fight first.

   I'd managed to get into a crouch before I felt fat fingers crunch into the bones of my ankle. My chin hit the ground so hard this time that my mouth instantly filled with the sharp tang of blood. The pepper-spray rolled from my grip as I clawed against the slippery concrete to get away, but they were too strong. No matter how determined I'd been to battle it out, I was outnumbered. No amount of resolve could help me now. An awful sinking feeling came over me as I was dragged back, back, back into the center of the crowd. Metal clanged against metal by the steps. I could hear the panicked voices of the police as they shouted at them to get off me. *Too late.* They were too late. I thought of how I would die as three sets of hands held my legs down. My funeral would be so pitifully small. More hands joined in to force me into submission as I kicked and clawed in a useless attempt to fight them off. I would be buried next to Grams, at least. I looked up to find a wooden post, at least four inches wide, hovering above my face as it prepared to strike. Which one of my family members would move into the house? My eyes squeezed shut as I flung my arms up to shield myself, but…

The pain didn't come.

Nothing happened.

The crowd's ear-splitting cries dulled around me as the oddest feeling of weightlessness flooded through my limbs.

Was I dead? Passed out from the blow?

I lowered my hands and cracked an eye open to find the clear expanse of gray sky rushing past my vision. Eyes-bulging, I looked to the side to find that my body was ten feet above the crowd and moving steadily up towards the flat rooftop of the station. Flying. I was fucking *flying*. I turned to look at my other side, immediately smashing my nose into the hard chest of a man. A shriek of pure terror escaped my lips, causing the sensation to finally return to my limbs. The man… Angel? Was cradling me in his lithe arms like an overgrown baby. I looked up again, only to be met with the most beautiful set of eyes I'd ever seen. A curtain of thick, heavy lashes rimmed his hooded green gaze. No, he couldn't be an angel — no matter how beautiful his eyes were. Something behind them seemed dead, like I was face-to-face with a shark. A *real* shark, not at all like the ones Lucky used to imagine were in the pool. This was a predator ten times more vicious than all those Switchback Baptist idiots combined. What do they say? *Out of the frying pan…*

He laughed and finally broke our little staring contest to look skyward. I winced as I realized he was probably laughing *at me*. I knew it was stupid to feel embarrassed when I was literally being flown around by a monster, but I couldn't help it. Despite his cold eyes, he was still so oddly captivating to me, and I knew I must've been so… *Georgia*, to him. Of course, he thought it was funny I'd be staring at him so hard. He was clearly better than me in every way. His laugh had told me that he thought as much. We glided to a gentle stop on the roof, where he expertly flipped me out of his embrace and back onto my feet.

"You *can* stand, can't you?" He asked with one muscular arm still wrapped beneath both of mine.

He smelled of fresh-cracked black pepper and cloyingly sweet figs. The exhilarating smell was something I never wanted to forget. I committed it to memory — already thinking about all the ways I could replicate it in my workshop.

I immediately stepped out of his arms as blood rushed to the tops of my ears. What the hell was I even thinking? I'd almost died and now I was thinking about perfume recipes? My priorities were really out of whack. I cleared my throat awkwardly and straightened out my wet, ruined clothes. They'd nearly been torn to pieces in all the commotion.

"I'm fine," I huffed as I gathered up my tangled locks and threw them into a bun. My heart was still beating furiously, but I was, at least, grateful I could breathe again. "What the *hell* was that?"

Apparently, my escape had only infuriated the crowd even more. Rocks, and branches, and snowballs were now being hurled towards the roof at us. The projectiles pinged off the metal siding of the roof like a hailstorm. Thankfully, none of those morons seemed to have good aim. After a moment, I dared to peek at the scene below — careful to give the edge a wide berth. Slowly losing interest in my escape, they'd turned their attention back to the station. They pawed at the metal barriers around the front entrance again — seemingly trying to bullrush the already straining line of officers who'd remained there to protect the building. Maybe they hadn't lost interest in me, after all. They were probably trying to find an alternate route to the roof so they could finish the job. I shuddered, pulling my mangled clothes tighter against me.

I glanced back at the man again. *My savior… I guess.* My eyes rounded as my mind caught up. I recognized him now. Although I was on the shorter side, he completely towered over me. He was assessing me in that lazy, familiar way — eyes trailing over my body until finally landing back on mine. He was handsome, but in an unexpected way. His sly face held high, winged cheekbones, and unusual features that made it impossible to gauge his expression. To put it politely, he just *looked* untrustworthy, but… He'd saved me. Despite how unsettling he was, I figured I shouldn't be too quick to judge. Just because someone *looks* evil doesn't mean they are, right?

"You seemed like you needed help." His voice was the dry crackle of pine logs thrown onto fire. Smooth and warm as a summer's night, with a soft-spoken and pleasant huskiness that was completely out of sorts with his frigid exterior. Still, the urge to lean in closer to hear him was overwhelming. I wasn't sure what I'd been expecting, but it sure as hell hadn't been *this*. The man could make a dictionary sound good. *A mystery.* I decided he was a mystery.

"Sure… But how the *hell* did you do that?" I asked.

He brushed his sandy hair back and chuckled again. It fell in a choppy curtain down to his earlobes and swished faintly against his blue, orb-like earrings. There was a single snow-white piece in the front that almost made it seem like he'd grayed early.

Did Vampires even get gray hair?

"Don't play with me, Georgia."

I was frozen to the spot, unable to blink, unable to speak as one of his fingers snaked out to my chin. He took a deep shuddering breath as he pulled back, making sure to meet my gaze as he licked the blood from his honey-hued finger. I was horrified and weirdly turned on all at once. I couldn't seem to help myself, though. Something about him drew me in.

"Wha — How do you — What are you —"

Before I could humiliate myself any further, I was thankfully cut off by the piercing squeal of metal as the door to the roof was forced open.

"There you two are," Celine drawled. "Well, come inside, won't you?"

The man extended a palm. "After you."

Once inside the station, our fake-nice secretary, Tammy, took it upon herself to tend to my cuts and scrapes. She was probably doing it just to see me squirm. Or, to win brownie points with the Chief. I could never tell with her. Although I'd insisted I could handle it on my own, Tammy had forced me into a chair and begun daubing my chin with alcohol. I hissed as the cotton pressed into my raw skin, and I thought I saw Tammy trying to hide a smile beneath her curled helmet of red hair. She was clearly enjoying this. She'd wanted to see me squirm, then. *Bitch.*

The officers who hadn't been on riot duty out front had all been ushered into the conference room with us. They were clustered together uncomfortably at the back edge of the long table. Another group of plainclothes officers and a few suits I didn't recognize, probably all from Elkheart, were sandwiched in the middle near Garcia. Still, despite the crowded conditions of the room, they all sat a healthy distance from the other half of the table, which only held two lonely seats filled by Celine Bissonnette and her male companion.

"Glad to see you in one piece, Beretta," Garcia joked. "How's about you use the back door next time, though?"

I merely scowled at him and folded my arms across my chest.

Garcia reached below the table and lifted my beat-up backpack from the carpet. "We got this for you."

Completely unaware that I'd even been missing it, my eyes widened in shock, but I still didn't thank him. After all, it hadn't been him or any of the officers who'd gotten off their ass to rescue me. Even though we were on the second floor and far away from the front entrance, I could still hear the muffled screams of the crowd below. How long would it take them to finally get tired?

The last of our party, a slight, round woman in thick glasses carrying a messy stack of papers and a hard-shell suitcase, bustled through the door in a tizzy. Her short, spiky hair was as ruffled as her smart pink pantsuit.

"Hope I'm not too late," she panted, hurriedly taking a seat beside me and flipping open the case to reveal a stenotype machine. Without another word, she organized her papers and powered it up, only giving Garcia a curt nod when she was ready.

"I wanna start today by saying that what we discuss here *must* remain confidential," Chief Garcia began. "Our case would be severely compromised if this information gets out. So, under *no circumstance* must *any* part of this meeting be leaked or revealed to the public or the press. If I even hear *one* word of it got out from any of you, I'll have you arrested on sight."

There was a brief round of murmured agreement from everyone.

Garcia cleared his throat as the court-reporter shoved the stack of papers in front of him. "Thanks, Grace. Ahem — Alright. These are the facts of the case. At sixteen-hundred hours on the night of eight October on three-eight-seven Adelaide Road, the body of

Mrs. Francine Jessops was found with one six-inch laceration, two inches in diameter across her jugular, two seven-inch lacerations down the backs of her thighs, both four inches in diameter, and two puncture wounds of equidistant placement on the inside of her left thigh."

Hearing her death described so clinically, so matter-of-factly, made my skin crawl all over again.

"Now, it's our belief that the perp is a Vampire. Our coroner, Mr. Marks, was *very* clear about this," Garcia paused to give Celine a challenging stare. "Because, along with the injuries, and the puncture wounds, Jessops' body was completely drained of blood."

Celine's black eyes revealed nothing at the accusation.

He continued, "Due to the puncture marks and the lacerations being jagged in nature, this left Mr. Marks with only two conclusions — One, that, *though highly unlikely*, this uneven pattern would be similar to what one might expect from an animal attack, or two, that due to the wounds and draining of blood, the cause of death could be attributed to a Vampire attack."

"Has your coroner—" Celine said in that easy, confident way of hers. "*Mr. Marks*, ever *seen* a Vampire attack?"

A balding man in a cheap tweed suit near the end of the table fiddled with his tie, eyes bouncing back and forth between Garcia and Celine like he was unsure of whether to speak up.

"Does that matter? The puncture wounds are evidence enough." Garcia narrowed his steely eyes. "An animal would've dragged her off somewhere to eat her. We found no sign of that."

Having already sniffed out the bald man's fear, Celine's black eyes fell on him. She raised a brow. "Mr. Marks, I presume?"

"Ye-Yes."

"Well?"

"Well, no, ma'am. I-I've never actually *seen* a—"

"That's all, Mr. Marks, Thank you."

Mr. Marks was as white as a sheet when he sagged back into his chair.

"If Mr. Marks has never *seen* nor examined the body of someone who has been attacked by a Vampire, how can you be so sure that it *is* a Vampire you are searching for, Chief Garcia?"

His face balled up like a fistful of paper. "The puncture—"

"And how can *anyone* feel safe in Switchback unless another, more *expert* opinion is brought in to investigate this case?"

Garcia opened his mouth again to speak, this time nearly boiling over with fury.

Unbothered, Celine continued, "If this attack *isn't* the work of a Vampire, but a human, isn't it safe to say that it would be *your* neck on the line, Chief Garcia?" She gave him a toothy smirk that was more hungry than pleasant. "And we wouldn't want anything happening to *your* neck, now would we, *Chief Garcia*?"

Garcia's ochre skin deepened to a reddish-purple hue as the cords of thick neck went taut. "*ENOUGH!*"

Celine, nor her mysterious companion, even flinched at the outburst. In fact, it had only made Celine's smile stretch even wider across her elegant mouth.

"I've already told you that if you don't have a warrant signed by the—"

"By the Governor? I must be forgetting my head," she purred as she held out her palm towards the man beside her.

In a flash, too quick to catch, he'd produced a packet of papers and set them gracefully into her waiting hand. Celine murmured her thanks and slid the packet at full force down the table. My eyes rounded as they crested to a perfect stop at the edge of Garcia's pronounced belly.

"Warrants signed by the Governor for both the overdose case and this murder. We'll begin our investigation tomorrow."

Not even bothering to open the envelope, Garcia's fists slammed down hard across the table, causing the entire room to flinch. "Not without one of my officers there to watch you! How can we trust that you're not lying about the attack to cover your ass? You Supernatural scum will probably find a way to—"

"That's fine," Celine announced, to everyone's surprise. "A *liaison* of sorts would be perfect in helping both of our sides share information. Don't you agree, Chief Garcia? I think that it's best if we can work together on this."

Garcia sat back with a huff and folded his arms across his middle. It was so silent that the only sound to be heard was the *tick, tick, ticking* of the clock above the doorway.

"A liaison?" Garcia clarified, finally realizing he would be forced to concede to the ice queen.

"As it stands now, our sides clearly cannot work together in a civil manner. A liaison from your side would ensure that your… *Interests* and the integrity of your case is fully protected while our side would gain the necessary access to the findings in your investigation. A liaison would make it so that we may both find a quick and *honest* resolution to these cases."

"We wouldn't have to communicate directly? We could do it through this… *Liaison*?"

"If that's what you wish. The liaison can act as both of our sides go-between so that we never have to interact directly."

Garcia looked towards the other officers, who were already nodding in agreement. Apparently, everyone liked the thought of never having to talk to the Supernatural's again if it could be helped.

"Very well… But I won't have your team providing baseless, anecdotal evidence. We won't accept your findings unless your investigation is conducted just like ours currently is. No exceptions. No Supernatural funny business. Only *factual* evidence that you can back up with *real* science. If you do end up solving this, we've gotta be able to corroborate it ourselves."

"Fine. We'll play by your rules, Chief Garcia."

He merely grunted in response.

"May we pick?" Celine asked, carefully straightening the cuffs of her pert white pantsuit.

Today, she'd picked a slightly more risqué version of her typically snowy uniform. The form-fitting blazer and pants were the same as the first time I'd seen her, only with a bit of lace poking out of her sleeves. Today, though, she wore no shirt beneath it. Her voluptuous bare chest spilled out over the edges of the ultra-low collar; her modesty only preserved by the starched edges of her lapels.

The cautious glint returned to Garcia's eyes, as if he were wrestling with himself. She'd clearly won this battle today, and I'd say it wasn't in his favor to keep embarrassing himself by fighting with her.

Coming to the same conclusion I had, he finally nodded. Celine clapped her hands together in delight before her intense eyes flashed to me. I immediately looked over my shoulders to see if someone else was behind me.

"You."

"Me?" I asked, still giving the rest of the room a confused once-over.

Garcia laughed, an ugly sound that grated against my ears. "Fucking perfect. I shoulda figured. You sure do know how to pick 'em, Ms. Bissonnette."

"Rafe will come to collect you tomorrow."

Before I could ask where and how and what time *Rafe* would be coming to get me, the two Vampires had already swept out of the room.

Chapter Eight
Citadel

I got to the station early the next morning — deciding to use the back entrance as Garcia had suggested to avoid being pummeled by the protestors again. They'd camped out on the front lawn of the station — creating a dirty little city of tarps and tents that reminded me of Skid Row in Los Angeles. The mere fact that Garcia had allowed it told me everything I needed to know. He supported these violent protests. He actually sided with these homicidal psychopaths and their anti-Supernatural movement.

I'd only made it two steps into the building before I noticed that every single eye was turned on *me*. The marble lobby was like a shopping mall full of mannequins. I straightened my back and kept my chin held high as I wove through them all.

"Traitor," one officer hissed, too low to even determine whose mouth it had come from.

"Supernatural *slut*."

"*Vamp tramp*."

I paused before Tammy's desk at the front and looked around the room again, only to be met with unabashed stares of hatred and disgust. There wasn't one friendly face in the crowd. I didn't even need to turn back to Tammy to know that she was probably wearing the same vicious expression. I supposed she was done being fake then. Whatever. It was kind of nice not having to pretend anymore.

"She picked *me*," my voice echoed around the lobby as I threw my hands up in frustration. "Any of you could be in my place right now! Remember that!"

My words fell flat, though. Not even one of them seemed like they'd even heard me.

"Back to work!" Garcia commanded from the balcony that overlooked the foyer. When they *still* didn't move, his palms slapped against the railing like a thunderclap. "*NOW!*"

As if his shouting had been the magic spell to break their trance, they scattered until it was only me and Tammy left standing.

"My office, Beretta," Garcia called, before turning on one heel and stalking away.

When I'd made it up to the Chief's impressive corner office, I found myself hovering in the doorway, just staring at him. Although it hadn't seemed optional, I was already thinking of all the ways I could still escape. I wasn't in the mood to hear *anything* he had to say right now.

"Sit," he barked, still scribbling away at the papers on his desk.

I finally entered and took a cautious seat on one of his armchairs. His luxuriously appointed office made mine look even worse than I'd thought. My office was shoved in a dusty back corner of the basement where no one ever came, but I preferred it that way. I'd never had the need or desire to come up here before either, but now I was almost regretting that decision. If I'd known that *this* was how the other half of the office was living, well... I would've filed a complaint about my little basement hovel a long time ago.

"Lotta the guys aren't happy about this, Beretta. If you take this job with them, you'd better expect to get a lot of shit."

"Are you trying to say I have a choice?"

Garcia's pen stilled in his meaty hands. "I don't know."

"The Governor signed the warrants *herself*. Someone would've had to do it either way, so how is it *my fault* that I was chosen for the job, huh? And how come *you* can't keep your officers in check? Aren't you supposed to be the boss around here, or is that only when you feel like it?"

"Maybe it's because I don't want to. Have you ever thought about that? *Maybe* it's because I don't think the Supernatural's have *any* right to be interfering with *our* investigation. Maybe it's because I don't think *you* of all people should be helping them do it!"

"*Me*, of all people?"

"Oh, come on. Everyone knows you've been in support of their bullshit from day one. You're clearly biased, and we can all see it."

"Well, *forgive me* for having basic human decency."

"Don't you get it? You're missing the whole point! You talk about *basic human decency* but they're not even human!"

"Just because *they're* not human doesn't mean that *we* don't have to be."

The shrill ring of Garcia's phone sliced through the tense air between us.

Garcia wordlessly picked up, only nodding at the voice on the other end before slamming it back on the receiver. "He's here to pick you up."

Thankful for the quick save, I sprung to my feet.

"Beretta!"

I cast a glance over my shoulder to find him waving two hefty folders at me. I sighed and trudged back over to rip them from his hands.

The wrinkles along Garcia's forehead deepened, creasing with worry and something else... *Fear?* I couldn't tell.

"Don't screw this up."

I ignored him as I tucked the folders into my bag and headed back down the hallway. I nearly tripped over the first stair as I heard Garcia shout *yet again*, "Don't let them fool you, Beretta! Our perp is a Vampire!"

Rafe was waiting for me in the lobby with his hands folded behind his back, coolly examining his new surroundings. His finely tailored suit, complete with the triple triangle pin on his lapel, was as midnight black as Celine's Rolls Royce, and I couldn't help but notice how it hugged his tall, trim body in all the right ways.

He turned to assess me from top to bottom with the same amount of indifference that he'd given to the lobby.

"Good morning," he said at last.

The look immediately made me regret my decision to dress so casually. Not sure of what I'd be doing today, I'd chosen straight-legged jeans, combat boots, another black turtleneck, and a ruby-red blazer.

"Morning."

I felt a sudden burning sensation along the back of my neck and turned to find Tammy's awful red hair poking above her desk. I didn't know why she even bothered to hide. She was clearly staring at us. Her eyes rounded at our attention, but she didn't move an inch.

Rafe leaned in close to me, and a shudder rippled through me as his cool breath caressed the shell of my ear. "We're being watched."

"Let's get out of here."

I stuck my tongue out at Tammy as we passed, meeting her gaze as I threaded an arm through Rafe's, who'd jogged up beside me. It was a risky move on my part. I barely knew the man, and I was already treating him like a prop. I didn't care, though. I *wanted* Tammy to see. If everyone was going to talk about me anyways, why not give them a little material? Tammy looked like she was about to say something, but Rafe immediately checked her before she could speak — faux-jumping towards the desk with a warning hiss that sounded more animal than man. I giggled as she squealed in horror and quickly shrunk back down.

The Rolls Royce was already alive and purring with anticipation when we'd made it outside.

I gave Rafe a grateful look. "Thanks for that, by the way."

He ducked his chin in acknowledgement as he held the door open, and I climbed inside.

It was an effort not to marvel at the glossy interior and starlit roof. Compared to this car, my old girl might as well belong in the scrapyard.

"So, why me?" I asked.

Rafe's eyes didn't leave the road as he tapped on the huge console screen and started playing music. The rich, ominous sounds of violins filled the cabin, followed by a haunting chorus of voices singing mournfully in Latin. "You know this?"

I stared out of the heavily tinted window, barely able to see where we were going as the shops and restaurants blurred together.

"Lacrimosa. Mozart's Requiem. It's one of me and my dad's favorites. He says we can't play it in the restaurant, though — too gloomy."

Rafe laughed — a sweet husky sound that almost would've seemed like genuine amusement had it ever reached his shark-like eyes. I drank in his callous features, the honied skin, dishwater hair, and wide, expressionless lips that made it hard to tell what emotion was about to cross them.

My breath hitched as he caught my eyes, then laughed again. I glanced away and pretended to focus on the blurry scenery before he could catch my blush, too.

"Your parents own a restaurant?"

"You never answered my question," I huffed, reaching forward to lower the volume. The chorus had risen to a fever pitch as the prophetic voices crested towards the finale.

"I forgot you humans have sensitive ears."

I glared at him as he continued.

"A question for a question, then."

I pulled my bag against my chest tighter, feeling wary of this game.

"You stood up for us. At the repair shop. Celine likes your guts."

I knew it was just an expression, but a Vampire liking my *guts* seemed a little too on the nose for me right now. Still, though, a compliment from Celine? I could've died right then, because I didn't think my life could get any better than this.

"It was the right thing to do," I murmured.

On the outside, I was totally playing it cool, but on the inside, I was doing cartwheels. It felt like getting a Nobel Peace Prize or something. Celine was literally my idol, and the way she kept standing up to Garcia? That alone was enough to make my toes curl.

"I admire that about you, too," he said. "Anyway, it's my turn. What kind of restaurant do your parents own?"

I scoffed at the question. It just seemed so... *Mundane* compared to all the things I wanted to know about him, and Celine, and the Triad.

"It's an Italian restaurant and bakery... I think we passed it already," I looked out the window again, but we were still moving too fast to see much of anything. "My dad runs the restaurant part downstairs, and my mom runs the bakery up top. With all these new people coming into town, it's been busy lately."

"Are you Italian?"

I held up a finger, waggling it back and forth. "Not so fast, it's my turn now."

He growled in annoyance, but I ignored him as I tried to think of another question. There were so many that I had to mentally arrange them from order of most to least importance before I spoke again.

"How did you fly the other day?"

Rafe slapped his palm against the steering wheel. "I didn't *fly*, Georgia. I jumped. It probably seemed like we were flying to you because of how high and far I can go."

The answer only prompted a million more questions to spring up in my mind, but Rafe returned my earlier gesture and waved a finger — effectively cutting me off.

"Are you Italian?"

"Originally. What? You couldn't tell?"

"I'm not one to assume. That was another question though, so it's my turn again."

I cursed below my breath. He was tricky, alright.

"Before we all came into contact, Celine and I did some research on your department... Supernatural's always like to know what kind of situation we'll be walking into."

I nodded in understanding. I supposed it *was* smart, considering how many people would love to see the Supernatural's slaughtered and strung up by their toes in the town square.

"You can tell when people are lying."

I narrowed my eyes as I faced him. Of course, they'd found out. I wasn't sure how I felt about them knowing.

"*How* can you tell, Georgia?"

I wasn't sure how to answer him. Besides Charlie and my family, I'd never told anyone *how* it worked before. I'd never *allowed* myself to tell anyone. Even if I could, I'd always been too afraid of what people would think of me if they knew the full truth. He was a Supernatural, though. He was used to strange things... *To strange people like me.*

"I don't know, it's just something I've always been able to do. Everyone thinks I'm naturally perceptive, but... That's not entirely true. I don't know how to explain it, but I can *smell* when someone is lying."

The words slipped from my tongue before I could even think about the consequences they might have. Being able to finally tell someone, *anyone*, about this secret I'd harbored for so long felt freeing. And telling it to someone who could actually relate for once? I'd never felt more *seen* in my entire life. How had he gotten to me so fast? One little smile and I was suddenly an open book? God, why the hell was I so stupid? I should've lied or pretended it really *was* some weird Sherlock Holmes shit. Now he had leverage over me and I'd handed it to him on a silver platter.

"Smell… Interesting. I can see that it hasn't made you very popular around here."

"No," I said, feeling decidedly more tight-lipped than I'd been just moments ago. I still had to be careful. Even if he was just being friendly, he was still a mystery to me, and I didn't know his true motives yet.

"I understand the feeling, Georgia. More than you know."

"Why would someone inject themselves with Vampire blood if it's lethal?" I quickly inserted the question before he had another chance to trick me again.

The leather and wood of the steering wheel groaned audibly as Rafe's grip tightened. *Sensitive subject.*

"They call it Saph on the streets."

His grimace had revealed the sharp points of his incisors, immediately making me shrink back against the door. The realization that I was stuck in this car, *stuck* so very close to him and those *teeth*, suddenly made me very afraid. If he wanted to attack me now, there would be nothing I could do to get away.

"The Saph dealers are con men. Most times, they sell a variety of animal blood mixed with drugs under the guise of the real thing. When people inject it, they *think* they're feeling something different — it's a placebo effect. To answer your question, though, most people believe that we're lying about how deadly it is. The non-believers think that Supernatural blood, *especially* Vampire blood, can give them powers — enhanced cognitive and physical abilities that surpass human nature, but it's not true. They trick themselves into believing that shit."

I was frozen by the words. I knew what he was talking about, I'd read the same things about it online with Charlie, but…

"The blood my brother and his girlfriend injected was real."

His answering nod was as hollow as the feeling in my bones. "Yes, it was. Which is why it killed them — or, in your brother's case, *nearly*."

Dropping our game, I leaned into the middle console — desperation and morbid curiosity now consuming my every thought. "So, the real stuff, the real Saph, *does* kill humans? That's not some lie or big conspiracy theory?"

"No, it's not a lie. It's lethal. The body composition of a Supernatural is completely toxic to humans. Well, *mostly*... But it's only the dead Saph that kills."

My tongue felt as thick as if I'd swallowed a spoonful of glue. "Dead Saph?"

What did he mean, *mostly*? What happened to *all* Supernatural blood or fluid or whatever being toxic?

A range of emotion flickered across Rafe's face, too fast to catch, as he fought some internal battle. He almost seemed to be deciding on whether my hidden talent would work on him. I wondered that, too — if my ability worked on Vampires. I'd never had the opportunity to find out until now.

"Supernatural blood or body fluid is always lethal for humans to consume. The only exception to the rule is Vampire blood. If a human consumes Saph that hasn't been directly and *willingly* given from the vein of a Vampire, they will die... Which is why it's odd that your brother survived. I've never heard of a human surviving an injection of dead Vampire blood, especially considering the amount he took." He shook his head, now lost in thought. "I suppose he got help at the right time. Modern medicine has come a long—"

"So, humans *can* drink Vampire blood and live? What happens when a human drinks it from the vein?"

No wonder people injected the stuff then. Somewhere along the line, another human must've gotten the same information he was giving me right now. It must've gotten all twisted around though, like that telephone game everyone played in elementary school.

His cold, unreadable mask settled back into place as he shrugged. "Yes, they can, and it depends on what happens. My turn, that's three questions you've asked."

I grimaced, having almost forgotten our game.

"If your parents own a restaurant, why don't you work for them instead of the police?"

"It's not my dream. Besides, I can help more people working for the police than I can making pasta for our customers."

"Your brothers work for them, though?"

"Sometimes. Lucky saved up enough to get his repair shop, and Nico is gonna try to open his own gym in a few years. My parents don't care what they do, though. They only care about me taking over the business once they retire. It's bullshit."

"It would be a stable job." He reached out a hand towards me, as if he was going to brush back a stray piece of my hair but stopped short and cleared his throat. "And probably much better than having to deal with all those nasty comments from your coworkers for the rest of your life. You'd be the boss if you took it over, you know. No one insults the boss."

"Thanks, *Dad*, but I'm good. My parents have always tried to force that future on me, but I don't wanna live in Switchback forever. When I save up enough, I want to move away — someplace big where nobody knows me, or what I can do. Somewhere no one thinks I'm a freak."

"Do you *really* think you're a freak, Georgia?"

My nails scratched against the armrest as I curled my hands into fists. Of course, I thought I was a freak, but I'd never let *him* know that. He probably thought I was just some stupid, weak human and was going to laugh with all his Supernatural friends later about all the stupid, weak shit I'd said.

"I'm done playing this game."

"Fine, we're here anyway."

I hadn't noticed we'd nearly rolled to a stop until I saw the set of massive iron gates appear before us. The metallic bars were set between a towering concrete archway that connected to matching walls. They were at least twelve-feet in height and half as thick — sprawling out in either direction as far as the eye could see. Rafe flipped open a hidden compartment near the steering wheel and pressed a button, causing the gates to shudder and groan as they were forced open.

My eyes flashed to the clock as I tried to determine how long it had taken us to get there. We'd only been traveling for fifteen minutes, but somehow, it had felt much, *much* longer than that.

The Triad headquarters was called the "Citadel". It was located twenty miles from Switchback at an old military test site that the federal government had given them permission to use and renovate as they saw fit. I'd lived in Switchback my whole life, but only gone out here once. I could still remember the days when parents told their children that it was radioactive to scare them into staying away. Of course, when my parents had told me that, I'd smelled the lie, but still... I'd never had the urge to explore the place myself, until my brothers had taken me out on a drive to look at it before all the renovations started. Back then, though, it had been an old pile of rubble set on an empty field of dirt. I was curious to see what had changed. I'd always pictured the Citadel as being a big, spooky castle with gargoyles and gun turrets.

Rafe rolled down the smooth road much more slowly now. He was probably afraid Celine would have his head for driving so crazy earlier. At first, there was nothing but hard, flat earth covered in snow, though as we came up the small hill, I saw that the bowl-like expanse of the mountains was still visible on the horizon — offering a nice break from all the empty, white monotony. The Citadel wasn't exactly the haunted castle I'd imagined, but it was *certainly* a fortress. Since the Triad had taken up residence there, two more walls and gates had been constructed on the interior of the property. The walls gently curved inwards, sort of like the Triad had designed this place to look like a bullseye from the sky. We passed through the additional rings of gates in silence. This time, there were security checks being conducted by unsmiling guards who carried massive guns and growling rottweilers. I determined that by the way we'd come, there was only one way in and out of the place. Perfect for security, but decidedly *less* perfect for taking away the creep factor.

The Citadel was overwhelmingly pale — the windowless buildings were as colorless and drained of life as the immortals who worked there. Most of the squat, boring structures on "campus", as Rafe had called it, were already encased in a layer of ice as the early Wyoming winter firmly stood her ground. White boxes set on top of a white landscape. Even if it hadn't been the center of the modern Supernatural world, it still would've felt eerie.

Rafe directed the car down the salted road towards one of the larger structures on campus, pressing another button as we got closer. I braced myself on the handle above my head as the earth began to rumble and shake. A section of road had opened in front of the hood like a dark, hungry mouth. Rafe ignored my reaction as he drove into the shadowy cavern and sealed us into our tomb with another flick of his wrist. The subterranean space instantly flickered to life to reveal a massive underground parking lot. It looked normal enough, except for the fact that it was absolutely filled with rows upon rows of luxurious cars and trucks. The whole place looked like a billionaire's playground. Rafe slid into an empty spot at the front marked "*Lamia Primis*", near the doors of an elevator.

I swung my bag over my shoulders as I got out to examine the engraved placard. Its marble surface and gilded lettering reminded me of a headstone in a mausoleum.

My fingers lightly traced over the letters. "What does this mean?"

"They're the titles," he said, pointing at two matching placards down the wall to the left. "Of our leaders, the Council of Three."

"*Daeva Primis*" was above a sky-blue McLaren Speedtail. The ultra-fast, *ultra-expensive* sports car was so little it almost looked like a toy. The last placard read, "*Sorgin Primis*" — the car parked in front of that one, a Lamborghini Urus. I let my fingers glide across its pristine white surface, marveling more at the car than the sign in front of it. I'd always wanted a Urus. It was Lamborghini's version of an SUV — sleek, beautiful, and spacious, but with the torque and horsepower of a vehicle half its size. After growing up with Lucky and his non-stop chatter about automobiles, the obsession had eventually rubbed off on me. By the time I was twelve, he'd practically made me into a walking encyclopedia full of useless car facts. In fact, these days, the only way to keep him interested long enough to continue a conversation was to bring up something about cars.

The thought of Lucky made me blanch. I fished my phone from my pocket to check it, only breathing out once I found no new notifications. Charlie would finally be back from the farm to watch Lucky this afternoon, so I wouldn't have to keep freaking out about him being alone for much longer. But the thought of cars had made me realize something... Something *important*. Maybe we'd been going about this situation the entirely wrong way. Maybe, if we wanted Lucky to talk again, we had to bring up something that he was *actually willing* to talk about.

I gestured to the cars. "Can I take a picture of these?"

"If your camera works, sure."

I ignored the jab about my cracked-to-hell phone and snapped a few photos, hopeful that *this* might finally be the key to get Lucky talking again.

"So, what exactly do those titles mean?" I asked, joining him by the elevator. "Is Celine the… *Lamia Primis*?"

Rafe chuckled as the elevator whooshed open with a ding. If the inside of the elevator was any indication of how the headquarters looked, I knew I'd been right about under-dressing today. The entire space was made of a jade green marble and trimmed with golden features that were so shiny I had a feeling that they must've been *real*.

Rafe dug a heavy-looking black card from his pocket and pressed it against a circular pad on the wall. At first, I was confused because there were no buttons, but the doors slid shut at Rafe's touch and he announced "fifth floor" out loud. *Voice-activated elevator, wow.*

"Celine isn't Lamia Primis, by the way," he said.

"So, why did we park there? Wasn't that her car we were in?"

Rafe's hooded eyes flashed towards me. Their magnificent color was only amplified by the matching walls around us. "She and her wife share a car. Better for the environment, you know."

"Not that a Rolls is particularly environmentally friendly."

"No, I suppose it isn't," he replied with a toothy grin that immediately set me back on edge. "But one is better than two."

"So, her wife is Lamia Primis then?"

"You'll meet them all soon enough."

The doors whooshed open again to reveal an even more opulent lobby. The airy space was minimalist, yet cozy. The lack of windows and natural light were made up for by a balmy glow that poured out from the ceiling. It was the oddest light fixture I'd ever seen. Though the ceiling was wholly black and made of sleek metal bars set in a striped pattern, a hidden light flooded from within it. A large desk made of heather-gray stone sat in the center of the room before a sitting area of kidney-bean sofas. The turquoise material of them looked like velvet — a plush invitation to come and relax. Every wall in the space was made of a creamy, suede-hued wood and the marble floors were fashioned of that same jade green that covered the elevator. It looked more like a posh hotel than the evil lair I'd been expecting from the outside.

An impossibly tall black woman in a dark green dress was manning the desk with a smile across her plum lips. She was wearing a triangular necklace like Rafe's pin and had one of the most beautiful faces I'd ever seen. Rafe inclined his head towards her as we passed, and, at the sight of him, a flirtatious sparkle lit up her dark eyes.

"Hello," I said, stopping at the desk. Something about her had made me want to come closer. I wasn't usually social like this, but this woman was irresistible.

"Hello, Georgia." Her high voice was as sweet as rose petals.

If I hadn't been already, I was now rooted to the spot — completely entranced by her exquisite beauty and alluring voice.

"Georgia!" Rafe barked as he retraced his steps and took hold of my elbow to jerk me away.

"It's nice to finally meet you," the woman said.

Her voice had taken on a musical quality, and my heart pounded in time to the captivating beat of it. Though she'd stopped speaking, I could still hear its warbling loveliness swimming through the air.

Stay, stay, stay, it seemed to beg through every beat in my chest.

I struggled against Rafe's grasp as I tried to get back to the woman, but he was too strong.

Bastard. I didn't know what all the rush was about. I wanted to talk to her. I *had* to talk to her.

Rafe dragged me to the end of the room and made a right where a hallway branched off towards a singular door. Its ancient, painstakingly carved surface was filled with images of odd creatures and fierce warriors locked in combat on some bloody battlefield. The rubber soles of my boots squeaked in protest as Rafe pulled me towards it. The magical door was like something I'd only ever seen in fairy tales, but I didn't care about *it,* or whatever it led to. I wanted to go back to that woman at the front. Why would I waste my time with a smelly old door when that gorgeous creature was in the lobby all alone?

When we'd finally made it, he released me.

I rubbed the sore spot on my arm. "What was that all about?"

"Scylla is Fae. You should be more careful, Georgia. She's a siren." He turned to the wall and smacked a palm against it.

I flinched and he added a bit more gently, "You could've been hurt."

"Hurt?"

He raked his fingers through his hair, causing the white piece of it to fall over his eyes. "There are some of us here, like the ones in your office, that aren't particularly *fond* of the idea of having humans around."

"And you think they'd hurt me?"

"Maybe not physically, but there are other ways — worse ways — *invisible ways* to hurt you."

"Wouldn't that be against the law?"

"Sure, but are you saying that none of your people wouldn't break the law to hurt *us*?"

I chewed on the words, knowing he was right, but not wanting to admit it.

His shoulders slouched. "Just... Stay close to me, okay?"

Still feeling like I was being pulled towards the woman, I glanced back down the hall. "Okay."

We turned back towards the hefty antique door in unison. A black iron knocker sat proudly in the center, but that was it. I examined the door again and realized that there was no knob on the outside. Rafe grabbed hold of the hefty loop that hung from the creature's mouth and banged out two precise knocks. I gasped as the creature, a chimera of sorts by the contrasting mix of features, blinked and shuddered to life. Though its mouth did not move, I could still hear the words as it spoke to us.

"Raphaël," the creature said in a low, gravelly voice. "How many times must I remind you? You need not knock as hard. I'm old and frail, you know."

Rafe dropped into a low bow. "My apologies, Pix."

Pix's metal eyes, full of life and intelligence, slid to me as its panther-like nose sniffed the air. "A human? Is she dinner, or a plaything?"

"*She* is Georgia," I said, copying Rafe's bow before adding. "And she is *neither*."

"Do let me give her a riddle, Raphaël." Pix's raspy voice was filled with an odd, child-like excitement that made my hair stand on end. "It's been centuries since I've even *seen* a human, let alone tested one."

Rafe straightened, and I followed suit to find Pix's iron gaze was still locked on me. It took everything I had to keep from flinching as I stared back into those unnerving metal eyes.

"Perhaps another time, Pix. We've got important business to attend to today."

"You're not as fun as you used to be."

"Just let us through, Pix," Rafe snapped, losing his patience.

Pix grumbled, but the door jolted open without another word of protest.

"Thank you," Rafe said as he pushed past — careful to avoid Pix's needle-like mouth.

Once I was sure we were out of Pix's earshot, I asked, "What *was* that?"

"That was Pix. He used to guard treasure on Argos Island for the Witches."

My feet stuck to the ground at his words. "Argos Island?"

He'd made it about ten steps ahead before realizing I'd stopped moving.

He turned around with an exasperated huff and slung his hands on his hips. "If you keep stopping like this, I'm going to have to throw you over my shoulder and carry you... And you *don't* want to make me carry you, Georgia."

"Like Argos Island, Greece? The mythical place with the Minotaur and the labyrinth?"

"It's *not* mythical. It's a real place, with a real Minotaur and real danger. Witches used to live there a long, *long* time ago. Seriously, come on. I don't have time to give you a history lesson right now."

I swallowed hard as I thought about what he'd said earlier. Even though I felt like it, I needed to remember that I *wasn't* safe here. It was going to be hard to keep that in mind because being here made me feel like I'd stepped straight into a goddamn fairytale.

I jogged up beside him as we came to another set of doors, this time made of frosted glass. "Where are we—"

He shushed me as he pulled them open to reveal another wood-paneled room. The space contained a generously stocked bar area with leather stools and another circular sitting area sunken into the jade floor. A bulbous fireplace dangled from the ceiling above the eggplant-hued couches in the conversation pit where four people were already seated. They were chatting quietly amongst each other and delicately sipping from crystalline glasses as they waited for our arrival.

Celine stood first, her pale bob swishing as she traipsed up the small set of stairs to greet us. She wore her usual uniform of white with the gold Triad pin on her lapel, though this time the suit was a skirted version that showed off her long, pale legs.

"Georgia! Let's get you a drink before we make introductions, yes?"

Celine quickly flitted around the bar with superhuman speed, nearly blurring before my eyes. It was the near twin to the heather-gray desk in the lobby, only with the slightly more informal addition of a cherry-wood countertop. Within seconds, an aromatic mug of what seemed to be Celine's high-brow version of a Moscow mule was thrust into my hands and we were being corralled back into the jewel-toned pit.

Our trio sat across from the others, whom I could only assume were the elusive Council of Three. With Celine as their spokeswoman, the Council had never seen the need to make a public appearance themselves, and I could totally see why. Something about them seemed wholly... *Other* — compared to the Supernatural's I'd met so far. Although they all looked different on the outside, the sheer power that pulsed from them was exactly the same. It was overwhelming, and even *more* potent than Celine's terrifying aura.

I took a large gulp of my drink to hide the shudder of fear that rippled through me.

"Georgia," the small woman in the middle spoke first. She had a youthful, fresh-faced appearance with cinnamon-hued skin and commanding features that seemed to speak of South Asian origins. She wore flowing crimson robes and a delicate gold crown atop her black hair that held the Triad's logo in its center.

"I am Lamia Primis, leader of the Vampires. You may call me Mia, for short."

Though Mia only seemed to be about eighteen, her smoky voice revealed that she was somehow much, *much* older than that.

I nodded, feeling a bit more relaxed as the strong drink blanketed my terror. So, *this* was Celine's wife. I imagined that the two of them together made quite the power couple.

The man in the dark purple robes and matching crown to her right spoke next, introducing himself as the Sorgin Primis — Triad leader of the Witches. He was the eldest of the three — upper-sixties with long, graying hair styled in thick dreadlocks that fell around the sides of his severe, lion-like countenance. His skin was as dark as a starless night, but his poreless complexion had a glow to it, like it was being lit from within.

"You may address me as Gin," he instructed.

So, *Gin* was the owner of my dream car. If I wasn't so stressed out, I might've been tempted to ask if he'd let me take it out for a drive later.

"If you'd like," he answered my unasked question with a vibrant laugh that made it seem like we were old friends.

Before I could remember my manners, my mouth popped open in shock. I snapped it shut with a blush as Gin laughed again.

"You must be careful with your thoughts around here, young one. You never know who might be listening."

The last to introduce herself was the Triad leader of the Fae, the Daeva Primis — Dee. She also wore a crown and flowing robes, though in a soft blue color. Dee appeared only a bit older than me, maybe around thirty. Her fine-boned face was heart-shaped and surrounded by a waterfall of red hair that fell to her slim waist. Like the Fae woman Scylla, she was stunning. Apparently, as I was learning, the Fae were even more beautiful than the Vampires. In fact, I imagined that her appearance could've even brought the great Leonardo DaVinci to tears.

"They used to have a fling," Gin announced with a knowing smile. "Turns out old Leo was a bit too arrogant for our Dee. Isn't that right?"

Damn. I needed to be more careful about where I let my mind wander. A fling with Leonardo DaVinci, though... *That* was interesting. How old would that make her? Six hundred? Or was she maybe even older than that?

Dee let loose a peal of silvery laughter. "Oh yes, what a pompous ass he was!"

"Our lifespans are much longer than humans," Gin said, *again* tapping into my thoughts. "Although Witches and Fae are not immortal like Vampires, we do age far more slowly than humans. I'm nearly two-hundred and ten myself."

I struggled to keep my thoughts at bay, not wanting to reveal anything else to the man.

I'm already embarrassed enough as it is, I grumbled internally.

"Don't be embarrassed, dear," Gin soothed. "You don't know it yet, but there *is* a way even a human such as yourself can learn to shield your thoughts. I can teach you sometime, if you'd like?"

"Can all Witches read minds?"

His glowing orange eyes crinkled up with amusement. The Marking. There it was — those strange Witch eyes. They weren't as terrifying as I'd imagined, though. Like his radiant complexion, they seemed to shine from within — but only softly.

"No, no. My mind-reading has come along with great practice. It's a difficult skill only a few Witches like myself can master. Though, once learned, it's even more difficult to turn off, so I do hope you'll forgive me for the intrusion."

"Oh, uh… Y-yes, of course."

"Your ability," Gin said curiously. "Can we test it? Rafe seems to believe you can *smell* lies, but I wonder if it works on Supernatural's."

"I can."

It felt so odd to be discussing it so openly with people, I'd never done that before. Their expressions were not those of hostility or fear, though… Just curiosity. I guess it only made sense that they wouldn't think that I was a freak, considering all the crazy things they could probably do. I supposed it didn't matter how I felt about exposing my secret, because there was no choice but to comply now. The cat was already out of the bag.

Gin looked to the other leaders, then nodded.

"I was born in Liberia," Gin said first.

I narrowed my eyes, trying to follow along.

"I love cats," Mia went next.

Lie. I could immediately smell the rotten scent of it in the air.

"My favorite color is pink," Dee smiled.

"Which one of us is—" Mia began to ask, but I cut her off.

"You. You don't love cats."

Gin clapped his hands together in delight. "Marvelous! Another, another!"

"I like to—" Dee started, but Mia held up a palm.

"Enough."

Dee pouted and folded her arms.

Well, it was at least good to know that my ability extended to the Supernatural's. I felt some comfort knowing that they, at least, couldn't lie to me.

"I understand your brother was involved in the overdose case," Mia cocked her head and leaned forward on both elbows. "Did you bring the police files with you?"

I gulped, suddenly feeling very aware that I was related to the person who'd "desecrated" Vampire blood, as they would put it. I reached for my bag to retrieve the files and passed them to Mia.

"It should be in there somewhere. Those were all the ones Chief Garcia gave me."

Mia nodded absentmindedly as her slender fingers flicked deftly through the stack.

"Do you have any suspects?" Dee asked as she peered over Mia's shoulder.

"No, we —"

"Not *we*, dear," Gin interrupted. "We already know what the police think, but we want to know what *you* think."

"About which case?"

Why did they want to know what I thought? No one *ever* wanted my opinion on anything unless it had to do with an interrogation.

"Both," Mia said as she passed the files to Gin.

My eyes flashed towards Celine and Rafe for help. "Both?" When I realized neither were going to throw me a line, I cleared my throat and started again. "What do you mean *both?*"

Gin rubbed a hand along his clean-shaven jawline — looking lost in thought as he took his turn reading through the papers. "Your brother and his girlfriend were the key players in the overdose case, but what we'd like to know is who their supplier was. There's a possibility that they may be linked to both. It's exceedingly rare that two crimes involving Supernatural's would happen so close together, don't you agree?"

I shrugged. I hadn't even considered the possibility yet. One was a murder, and one was an overdose. Even though someone *had* died in both cases, I couldn't see how they could be connected.

"My brother won't speak to us… So, we really don't know where, or how, or even why he got the Saph in the first place."

"Perhaps I could read his mind," Gin mused aloud, still flipping through the pages.

"Oh, get off it, Gin," Mia snickered. "The press would have a field day with that one."

"Can't you see it now?" Dee joined into her laughter, splaying her hands out dramatically as if she were reading a headline. "Witch violates human overdose victim's mind!"

"He's no victim," Gin clipped, but his hardened expression turned soft as he caught my stare. "I'm sorry, Georgia. I didn't mean to be so insensitive."

"You don't have to apologize. Lucky should've never been around that stuff. He brought it on himself." Although saying it felt like a betrayal to my brother, I knew it was the truth. He had taken that shit on purpose.

"We can't use any of our powers to solve this case," Celine chimed in. "Our relationship with humans is tenuous enough as it is. Mia's right, if we used our powers to solve it, they'd never believe that we conducted an honest investigation. Besides, Chief Garcia made us swear to it."

Mia's brown eyes locked on Celine. Love and pride at her partner flashed within their depths, and I felt an immediate pang of jealousy. I knew it was stupid to feel that way, but... I'd never had anyone look at me like that before — not ever.

"Even if we could, they would think we were lying," Mia agreed.

"But isn't that why I'm here?" I challenged. "To make sure that you're *not* lying?"

Gin sighed as he reorganized the folder and set it back down beside him. "They're right, Georgia. Even with you here, the humans may say we're trying to cover up anything that could make *us* look guilty. We can use your skills, of course, but we must tread carefully with our own."

I scooted forward to the edge of my seat. "But if you can read my brother's mind, shouldn't we use it to find out who his dealer is? What if this happens to someone else before—"

"There is *another* possibility... One that would not *directly* involve our powers." Gin's sunset eyes darted back and forth between his colleagues as if he were listening to a private discussion. I supposed he probably *was* doing just that — tuning into Mia's and Dee's thoughts.

"It seems that we're in disagreement for now," Gin finally sighed after a long moment. "Let's move onto the other case, shall we? We can always circle back."

The women nodded, though Mia was a bit stiffer than Dee.

"So, who do *you* think could've done this, Georgia?" Gin asked again.

I went with the first answer that popped into my head — knowing that Gin had, no doubt, already heard it before the name even left my lips.

"Josh Peters."

Chapter Nine
Lesson

"What makes you suspect him?" Mia asked coolly.

I shrugged.

There were *so* many things that made me suspect him that I couldn't pick just *one*.

"How long do you have? Josh Peters was the first to blame Mrs. Jessops for everything that happened at his construction site. There were three separate instances of theft on the property, but the last time…"

"There was vandalism," Gin finished for me. "And Josh's behavior was much more erratic when he came to the station to report it." He got up and took the two short steps across the space to stand before me and extended his palms. "May I?"

I hesitated a moment before I unlaced my clammy fingers and placed them in his warm, dry ones. Rafe had said that I wasn't safe here, but surely a Triad leader wouldn't hurt me, *right?*

"I can read passing thoughts, but for whatever reason, yours seem to be a bit more difficult for me. If I'm going to see a memory, I believe it'll require *physical touch*," he explained.

His eyes flicked back and forth across his closed lids. "Your mind is like smoke."

"Wha—"

"Just think of that memory for me, Georgia. Focus on it."

As I waited, I couldn't help but notice that he was even more cat-like up close. His features were all angles, pointed and sharp, and probably vicious when he needed them to be. He sucked in a sharp breath as he dropped my hands and retreated to his seat.

"Josh Peters was acting like he wanted her dead," Gin told the others. "He was angry, on the verge of violence when he came to Georgia last. He was out for blood."

"He's the only one I can think of that would want to hurt her," I added.

Gin clucked his tongue. "That's not entirely true, now is it, dear?"

My nose wrinkled up in confusion. What the hell had he seen in my mind that I hadn't?

"Mrs. Jessops wasn't well-liked. Many accused her of being a Witch. Though she wasn't gifted with the *true* ability, that didn't stop people from spreading rumors she was," Gin flashed me an apologetic look. "Sorry, dear. Sometimes my powers get away from me. The Switchback Baptist Church leader, Leslie Rathmore, should also be considered a person of interest. He celebrated Mrs. Jessops' death, and it would seem that he *may* have some stake in making it appear like Supernatural's are to blame — perhaps, for both crimes."

My eyes rounded. *That's right.* I didn't know how I hadn't seen it sooner. Leslie's sole mission in life was to wipe out the Supernatural's, so it made sense why he might want to frame them for murder. If a Vampire was found responsible for Mrs. Jessops' attack, well... It would be national news. No, it would be *world* news! People who were already on the fence about the Great Integration would be swayed to *his* side. There would be riots all over the place, just like the ones in town. Any progress the Triad had made in gaining rights and protections would be walked back. Maybe Leslie even thought that the outrage would be enough to get some of them hunted down and killed — the rest eventually forced back into hiding. As for him? He would probably come out of the whole thing as the celebrity he already pretended to be.

But...

"What makes you all so certain that a Vampire wasn't behind the murders?" I looked towards Mia for the answer.

"That's a silly question, Georgia. Didn't you see the attack?"

I flushed, immediately feeling stupid for even asking.

"Be easy, Mia," Dee warned. "She's never seen a Vampire attack before."

"Apologies. We've had our suspicions ever since seeing that photo of Mrs. Jessops in the news, but... Seeing these full reports now has made it obvious that someone is trying very hard to frame one of us."

"But *how* is it obvious?" I asked.

"There was too much blood," Rafe's husky voice answered beside me.

I stiffened, having nearly forgotten he was even there.

"A waste," Celine purred. "A Vampire would never cause so much waste."

A waste of blood. That's what she'd meant. The grisly images of Mrs. Jessops' blood splashed across the living room popped into my head again. *So much blood.* Too much. On the walls, on the floor, on her dress. My stomach churned as I tried to push the memory back — back into that deep, hidden place in my mind where it belonged.

I swallowed hard. "And the puncture wounds?"

"Sloppy," Mia criticized. "Perfectly spaced *circles,* of all things. Our teeth are not *circular.* They're about the same as yours — as any human's, Georgia. If you bit your arm right now, that's almost what a true bite from any Vampire would look like."

"Can't we explain that to the police, though? The—" I paused as a chill rippled over my skin. "*Waste* of blood? The incorrect bite mark pattern?"

Mia laughed — a cold and cruel noise that reminded me of her *true* age. "We can, but they would never believe us anyway."

This was absurd! It felt like there were *so* many things they could do to solve this case, but instead they wanted to sit around and twiddle their thumbs. My fist came down hard on the couch. "So, how do you propose we solve this, then? We can't use your powers. We can't tell them the evidence is all wrong. What the hell *can* we do?"

"We can find the person or *persons* responsible and bring them to justice, the *right* way," Celine said as she reached out to cup the fist I still had buried in the cushion. Her skin felt cool, almost reptilian.

"How?"

"We look into the suspects," Gin offered. "Question *your* suspects and see if that gets us anywhere. We investigate the crime scenes ourselves; do everything that human investigators would do. No shortcuts, no powers — just as we've promised."

"Wouldn't it be easier if you *did* use your powers, though?" I asked hopefully, still unable to get the idea out of my head. Everything would be so much easier if they were willing to bend the goddamn rules for a second. "What if you used your powers — Secretly, of course, and worked backwards to find the evidence to support it? No one would even have to know."

I didn't see the issue with it. For Christ's sake, the cops didn't care when I did my little sniffing thing, so why would it be a big deal if we used the Supernatural's powers to our advantage here? I shook my head. No, that wasn't completely true, was it? The cops didn't know about my lie-sniffing thing — Not really. It was more of a don't ask, don't tell situation. But, still… There had to be a loophole like mine. Was there really *no* technicality we could use? There *had* to be. Why wasn't anyone even trying?

Dee rubbed her temples like she was about to have a migraine. "No, Georgia. That's final. It's already a risk having you here. We're letting a *human* be privy to our private discussions. It's completely unorthodox! We can't take any more chances like that. Gin is right, we need to be smart about this and play along with the human's rules."

"Fine," I huffed, feeling anything *but* fine with the answer.

"It's settled then," Celine clapped.

I jumped a bit. The booming sound her palms made was no less shocking than the first time I'd heard it.

"Rafe, how about you take Georgia on a tour around campus to get her acquainted, and then we pick this back up tomorrow?" Celine suggested. "You two are going to be partners now, so you should take a little time to get to know each other. In the meantime, I can get some of the others to start a preliminary investigation on Mr. Peters and Mr. Rathmore."

Partners? I would never admit it to Rafe, but I was honestly thrilled by the idea. I'd never been given so much responsibility at the station, and it felt about damn time *someone* took me seriously — Even if that *someone* was a Supernatural.

"Excellent idea," Gin agreed. "Stop by my place before taking her back, though, Rafe. I wouldn't want Georgia to leave without getting to take the Urus for a ride first."

"Want to run yet?" Rafe asked when we were finally alone.

"No. Not yet."

He scooped up my empty glass and headed towards the bar. "Another drink then?"

I followed him and sat atop one of the comfortable stools, then rested my chin between my palms to watch him. He was so tall, one would expect a bit of clumsiness in his movements, but... There was only fluid grace and agility in his lithe limbs. The simple act of making a drink was totally transformed by the way he moved. Each motion was as elegant and precise as if he'd rehearsed it all a thousand times before.

I took a slow sip of my drink when he'd finished. "Do you live here?"

Rafe gave me one of those rare, genuine smiles as he moved around the bar and sat down. "We can, if we wish. It's certainly safer than being on our own."

I struggled against the desire to lean into him, to breathe in his intoxicating scent.

"But do *you* live here?"

"Yes."

"Where?" I looked around the room as if the door to an apartment was going to magically appear. In this place, I wouldn't have been shocked if it did.

"The residences are on another side of campus. I can show you, if you'd like?"

I nodded eagerly. I wasn't sure why I was suddenly so curious, but I *had* to know how they lived. Did Vampires sleep in coffins? By the look of the windowless building I was in, it was highly likely, but... No, that had to be wrong. I knew they could be in sunlight; I'd already seen them out and about during the day myself. It was truly remarkable how much information the Triad had managed to keep out of the press. I was in their secret lair, and I still felt like I knew absolutely jack-shit about these people.

"Why aren't there windows in here?" I blurted.

"Safety precaution."

Hmm, that's not what I'd been expecting.

"Um... Rafe? I know you said you didn't have time for a history lesson, but I'm starting to think I need one."

Rafe's expression remained bland. He was probably thinking about all the things he would rather do than teach a stupid human about Supernatural history. I couldn't care less. I was positive that this would be my only chance to get as much information about the Supernatural's as I could without having to be sneaky about it. Dee had practically said it herself, they all felt weird about letting a human be "privy" to their lives.

"There's a reason we keep the details about our races from the media, Georgia."

I gave him a wry grin. "Safety precaution?"

His eyes slid to mine, and despite my lame attempt at a joke, there was no humor in his expression — not even the polite, pitying kind. Damn it, was I messing this up already?

"Yes. We can't have our weaknesses made public. Those who would like to hurt us could use the information as a weapon against us — like those cannibals from the early days. But I suppose if you're going to be working with us, there are *some* things you should know."

I was already giddy with excitement when I swiveled to face him. It was all so surreal. Being *here*, learning all their secrets, finally getting some answers to the questions I'd be wondering for years.

"Well? What exactly *do* you want to know, Georgia?"

"Okay, um... For starters, what's up with the whole sun thing?"

Even though I was completely serious, he laughed like I'd just told him the funniest joke in the world — the loud, shoulder-shaking, knee-slapping kind of laughter that instantly made my face go all hot. Yep, I was *definitely* messing this up.

"A myth. Honestly, this would be easier if I told you what *is* real and what's a myth. Most of the stuff people believe about us is pure fantasy."

I nodded, silently urging him to go on. I didn't trust myself not to say something stupid again.

"Everything about Vampires that you *think* you know is probably a lie. We don't need coffins, we don't get burned by the sun or holy objects, and we don't need to feed as much as you've probably imagined."

My mind instantly went to all those images of Vampires in movies ripping people's throats out. *Feed*. The word made me shiver. Such a small, insignificant word for such a horribly gruesome act.

"How often *do* you... um... *feed*, then?"

"Once every six weeks, maybe. Our species has only survived undetected for so long because most of us drink animal blood."

Most of us. Despite myself, I couldn't help but think of Mrs. Jessops' broken body again. Why couldn't I have stuck with the horror movie montage I'd been picturing earlier? The real-life version was so much worse.

He lazily swirled his glass and took a sip. "That's a fact I'm sure you already know, though. The government would've never allowed our Integration had they believed we Vampires fed exclusively on human blood. Of course, there are exceptions to the rule, but the Triad has maintained their distance from those outliers — the ones who have chosen to remain as drifters and rogues rather than change their diet. The rogues are offered no sanctuary or protection here."

I jerked my chin towards his glass, trying to stay away from the blood topic for now. "But you can drink other things, too."

"Yes, and we can eat regular food. In fact, I enjoy it almost as much."

"You're immortal, though, right?"

"Technically."

"What do you mean, *technically*?"

"Vampires can withstand a lot of damage. We heal very rapidly. We're stronger and faster than humans, more resilient with better reflexes and senses, but if we... If we're blown up or decapitated, or anything else as serious as that, we *can* die."

"What about the whole stake through the heart thing?"

He shook his head.

"So, you're strong, fast, and *sort of* immortal?"

A nod.

"What about the Witches and the Fae? What can they do? I know they're not immortal, but why do they live so long?" The questions spilled out rapidly, like a crack in a dam that had finally burst open. So much for keeping my cool.

To his credit, Rafe didn't seem *too* annoyed by my interrogation... *Yet.*

"The lifespan of a Witch can be anywhere from two to four hundred years. Their magic prevents them from aging as fast as humans, but they still age... *Eventually.* The Fae can live far beyond that, though — perhaps one or two thousand years. The "why" is more complicated, but, in essence, it all comes down to their biology. I'm sorry I can't be more specific. It's hard to explain without showing you the difference between our cells in a lab."

All this talk about lifespans was making me feel very, *very* small. Compared to their lives, we humans were only a blip on the radar of their existence.

"What about powers?" I asked, changing the subject before the existential dread could fully set in.

"Witches can do lots of things. Reading minds, searching memories, telekinesis, portaling, flying, healing, creating objects from nothing but the matter around them — all of it depends on the Witch and their source of power."

"Can Gin do all of those things?"

"And more. Some Fae can fly as well, but most of their abilities are reliant on nature."

"Mind-control is *not* nature," I grumbled, thinking back to what Scylla had done to me earlier.

His expression was soft as he leaned forward and plucked a stray hair from my blazer. He twirled it around thoughtfully before letting it flutter to the floor. "It's *human nature*."

I watched him — again feeling myself being pulled towards him like a magnet.

He caught my stare and cleared his throat. "There are several types of Fae, though. Like Witches, their powers depend on the type they are, but they're much more limited in terms of strength. Scylla is a siren, so she only has control over water and hypnosis. Others are windsurfers, or fire-sprites, or even Dryads who speak with plants and animals. Eventually, once we're integrated into human society, our plan is to use our powers for good — to help humans. For now, though, that future is a very long way away."

I nodded. It felt justifying to know that they *did* think it was a good idea after all — to use their powers to help humans in the areas we fell short. I guess the timing was wrong, though. If people could ever find it in them to tolerate the Supernatural's long enough to work with them, the world would seriously be a much better place.

"So, what kind of Fae is Dee?"

"Dee is a Sidhe Fae. The Sidhe are the most powerful of their kind. Dee can fly and portal, speak any language — human or otherwise, and manipulate light and emotions. The light manipulation comes in handy more often than you'd think. It can be used for invisibility or even a weapon to blind an opponent if she chooses."

I glanced around the room suspiciously. What if Dee was still here now, using her powers of invisibility to spy on our conversation? Should I be more careful about what I was saying? This could all been a test to see if I was trustworthy.

"So, uh… Do they all look the same?" I tried to pick my words carefully. I didn't want to offend Dee if she really was listening. In all honesty, what I'd wanted to ask was, "Do some of them look like monsters with hooves and horns?" But that felt a little rude.

"They all *appear* to be human, if that's what you mean. All Fae, no matter the subtype, can produce glamours — like a mask that makes you see only what they wish you to see. Some Witches have that ability, but something about their magic won't allow them to conceal their glowing eyes, even colored contacts are burned away by their powers... Which is why it was harder for them to hide than us Vampires or the Fae," Rafe answered, now moving to stand. "Let's get on with this tour, shall we?"

I nodded, still thinking about his answer. Some of them *definitely* looked like monsters with hooves and horns, they just used their magic to cover it up.

Rafe led me back through the lobby towards the elevators where I avoided eye contact with the beautiful but dangerous Scylla.

"This building is used mainly for Triad business," he explained as we drove back out through the weird, garage cave-mouth thing. "Like a city hall."

"So, if the Supernatural's have a problem, they come here?"

He nodded, looking faintly appreciative that I was finally catching on.

"There are over five thousand residents currently living on campus," he continued as he directed us through the maze of pale buildings towards the outer edge. "Although we're technically united, we still have separate living quarters." He pointed at one structure, nearly indistinguishable from the others save for the large carving on the side that read "F1".

"That one is a Fae building," he explained as he gestured to a few more that surrounded it. "As well as all of those."

There were six buildings in total for each Supernatural species, all perfectly square and spaced out in their own distinct areas.

"Why are they separate?"

"It's easier that way. Our species are all very different from one another. All of us have different ideas and beliefs about the world, so we're separated to avoid potential conflict when those differences come to a head."

Snow was drifting down from the sky again. In a few hours, I knew it would completely cover the boxy buildings until they merely looked like a landscape of rolling white hills.

"If you're all so different, what made you want to join forces?"

"When the CIA's data breach occurred, the humans essentially forced us out of the shadows. Our species all came to an agreement that it would be best to stand together rather than be divided alone."

I shifted my eyes towards him to soak in every inch of his honey-hued profile. It was hard not to get lost in all his strange beauty. I still didn't think he was drop-dead gorgeous, not exactly, but... He had this confident presence about him that quietly demanded attention.

"What was it like before then?"

"Each of our species were ruled independently. We mainly tried to stay out of each other's way until the leaders, the Council of Three as you know them now, came to an agreement to unite our peoples — safety in numbers and all that."

"So, what do people do around here for fun? Or work?" I wondered aloud as we rolled up to the "V4" building and Rafe popped open another hidden garage mouth.

"Some do the same jobs as we did before the Great Integration, while a few others have been contracted to work for the Triad." His arm snaked around the back of my seat as he put the car in reverse and backed into a spot.

I tried not to gasp at the sight of the powerful muscles flexed beneath his suit.

"I know some Witches have online shops selling astrology readings and spells and little charms," he was saying.

Ugh, what the hell was wrong with me? I blinked rapidly as I tried to focus on his words instead of his arms. "They can make a living from selling that stuff?"

"You're forgetting about how *long* we live, Georgia. A lot of us have already accumulated enough wealth to live off of for ten lifetimes. Besides, we don't really *need* jobs now, since your government pays for all our housing and expenses."

"What about you?"

"What about me?"

"Why do you have a job?"

"A sense of duty — and, perhaps, a bit of curiosity," he replied cryptically as he shut the car off and stepped out. "As for fun, well, most of us do the same things that humans do. What do you do for fun, Georgia?"

"You're changing the subject, Rafe," I countered as I followed him towards another elevator.

"No hobbies? Shame. With your ability, I thought you'd be less dull than the other humans."

"I'm not *dull*. I make perfumes sometimes," I shot back, instantly regretting the admission. Why the hell would I tell him that? He certainly didn't need any more ammunition to remind me of how weird I was.

He stepped closer to me, and I shivered as the tip of his nose brushed against my hair. "Are you wearing one of them now?" His voice turned dark and thick, and, if I hadn't known any better... *Seductive*.

I retreated a step back, only to find myself trapped between the elevator doors and Rafe's tall, muscular body. He lifted his arms around my sides and laid his palms flat against the doors to pin me to the spot. My heart raced wildly in my chest, audibly thudding against my ribcage with each fierce beat. Was he going to kiss me or bite me? I almost didn't care. I couldn't think straight when I was so close to him, to those lips.

"What are you thinking, Georgia?" He bent down to nuzzle against my hair again.

I was thinking that I needed to download a dating app and get some action immediately because I was being absolutely feral for no reason. Granted, I hadn't gone on a date in who knows when but, Jesus... *Have a little composure, Georgia.*

Apparently, my sex-drive and my self-respect were *not* the best of friends right now. His ghost-like touch had been enough to set my entire body ablaze. "Am I scaring you?" His lips were against my ear now, filling it with the irresistible sound of his raspy voice. That invisible cord connecting us tugged on me again, making me want to get closer, to press myself against him.

The elevator dinged and slid open, nearly causing me to tumble backwards and fall flat on my ass. Rafe's laugh was low and mocking as I regained my balance and stepped inside.

"You're not funny," I growled.

He slid the black card from his pocket and pressed it against the scanner before giving the elevator another floor command.

"I know, but I think *you* are, Georgia." His deep voice was back to normal now — all that strange, lovely seductiveness had vanished without a trace.

"Why?"

"You're not afraid of us. It's rare, and I don't know... I like that about you."

The luxurious V4 building was the near twin to the Triad's main office — clean lines, recessed lighting, polished green marble, and cozy wood paneling. The only difference being the rows and rows of doors that branched off in either direction when we exited into the hall. Rafe walked to one of the simple doors on the very end and pressed his card against the handle. It gave a little beep and clicked open to reveal a surprisingly spacious apartment.

The floors and walls of the entryway were coated in white marble, and gilded oil paintings, as large as my entire body, were hung below spotlights on either side. They all looked *very* old and *very* expensive.

"Are you coming?" Rafe called from another room.

I must've been staring at one of his paintings longer than I'd thought. It was an exquisite rendition of a beach landscape with enough detail to be an actual photograph. It might've even been beautiful, had it not been for its foggy backdrop and too-still waters. The effect made the whole thing feel somber and full of unexplainable grief.

"Did you paint these?" I asked, following the sound of Rafe's voice to an airy kitchen and living room space.

"Some of them," he said distractedly, as he searched through the fridge. "Do you want anything?"

Like the entryway, the professional kitchen was all marble and stainless steel, with an island that was big enough to be a king-sized bed. The living room was set below the dining area, down two small stairs. They led to a massive, pillowy couch made of taupe suede, and three surrounding walls were shelved and filled to the brim with books.

I immediately floated towards his collection, completely forgetting about his question. The books a person had in their home could tell you a lot about them, much more than they could ever possibly tell you themselves. My fingers traced along the weathered, but still well-preserved spines of Thoreau, Austin, Hemingway, Angelou, and Twain. Despite their semi-used appearance, I knew these books were probably for show. I knew this, because I had the same books in my home, just like Charlie had them in his. Anyone with a library always had the classics, but a real bibliophile like me knew that his *actual* collection, the books that he *really* enjoyed, had to be somewhere right around... Yes, there.

Julio Cortázar, Su Tong, James Joyce, Joanna Russ, and Ralph Ellison. The author's books were nestled into a back corner, hidden away from view. Compared to the first editions on his shelves, these books were barely hanging on by a thread. Apparently, his tastes leaned towards the controversial and avant-garde side of things. Each of the authors had a unique style that had caused much debate and frustration for readers and critics alike.

"Strange," I whispered, gently tapping over each of the spines. The confusing collection of novels hadn't given me any of the insight I'd been expecting. They were just as mysterious as the man who owned them.

"Do you enjoy reading?" Rafe asked, only a hair's breadth away from my ear.

I yelped — startled by how quickly, *and quietly*, he'd appeared behind me.

"It seems *you* certainly do," I scoffed, still trying to catch my breath. He'd nearly given me a heart attack.

"You found my favorites," he noted as he took a step forward and reached across me to pull the Cortázar book from the shelf. "Have you read this one?"

I peered at the spine to see what he was holding — *Hopscotch*.
"I've been meaning to."

"Sad story. A tragedy, really. I wouldn't waste your time," he replied, thoughtfully thumbing through its contents. "In the fifties, Julio Cortázar moved to Paris, where he met Mia. This book was written *ten years* later, after their fling. It was supposed to be a sort of requiem to their love, though I'm positive she was far less serious about the relationship than he was."

"That's still nice in its own way. He must've been a real romantic."

Rafe shook his head, making the unruly white piece of his hair fall into his eyes once more. I wanted to reach out, to brush that piece back to where it belonged, but I didn't let myself. A minor victory, considering how close I'd been to jumping his bones ten minutes ago.

"Humans and Vampires can never *truly* be in love, as Cortázar would have you believe."

The familiar, cold sneer had taken shape on his lips again. I still couldn't tell if he was doing it on purpose, or if that was just the way he always appeared, but... Whoever came up with the term "resting bitch face", must've been thinking about him.

"They always end up heartbroken, like how poor Cortázar was heartbroken when Mia moved on to Celine. Ten years later and he *still* wasn't over it... I got the book as a joke, to laugh at how silly and pathetic he was, but..." He gave the book an appreciative pout before putting it away. "I have to admit, the man did have a way with words."

"You knew Mia in the fifties?"

Rafe walked over to the couch and patted the space next to him. I obliged and found myself instantly sinking into its soft, fuzzy depths.

"I've known Mia for a long time. I knew Mia before..."

"Before what?" I asked when I realized he wasn't going to explain any further.

"Before I was a Vampire."

"You weren't *born* a Vampire?"

He blinked rapidly as if to clear his vision and sat up straight. "Of course not."

I gave him an exasperated look that said, "*How am I supposed to know?! You're the expert.*"

"Some Vampires are *made*, not born. Most, in fact."

"What? *How?* I thought being a Vampire was a genetic defect. That's what the Triad has always said. All the Supernatural's are *supposed* to be born."

His expression hardened, like knew he'd said too much.

"What about the Witches and Fae? They're born, right?"

"Yes, born."

"So, *where* were you from?"

The news was a revelation to me. *Made*. Rafe was *made* into a Vampire. But... *How?* I tried to remember what he'd said about humans not dying when Vampire blood was given *willingly* from the vein. He'd said *it depends* on what would happen. Maybe he'd been trying to tell me that all along. Maybe, he was saying that humans *could* become Vampires that way. I was shocked, but deep-down I also felt kind of stupid for buying into the whole "genetic defect" thing the Triad had pushed for so long. It had never made that much sense to me, considering nearly every single fantasy book I'd ever read.

"France, but I grew up in the Basque Country." There was a glimmer of melancholy creasing his expression now. "It's an old region between the western tip of Pyrenees mountains and the Bay of Biscay." When he figured out that the look on my face meant I wasn't very good at world geography, he added, "In the middle of France and Spain."

Basque... That must be where his odd, slight accent had come from. At times it was almost impossible to hear, but... When he'd started speaking about his homeland, it brushed against the words like an intimate caress.

"The painting in the hall..."

"Yes, that was the beach I could see from my bedroom window as a child."

The painting was *so* sad, though. *Why* was it so sad?

"*When* are you from?"

"1610," he said hollowly, as if he were worlds away again — transported back to that place and time so long ago when that sad beach was his bedroom view. "I was born in 1582, and then reborn in 1610."

I, too, was lost in thought — thinking about all the things he must've seen, all the places he must've been in his unfathomably long life. *Made*. He was *made* into a Vampire. I wasn't even sure what to think of the information yet. All I could do was think of Lucky. Was that what my brother had been trying to do when he overdosed? Was he really trying to become a Vampire? *Why would he ever want that kind of life?*

I wanted to ask him so many other things, but considering his earlier reaction in the car, it was probably best to steer clear of the touchier subjects for now. I felt like I would have to earn his trust for *those* answers.

"How did you meet Mia?"

"She found me."

I leaned an elbow on the back of the couch and rubbed my neck. Everything was a mind-game with Rafe — one where I had to make all the right moves so he wouldn't shut down. So, I waited for him to explain what he meant. I was learning that, like me, he clearly didn't like being pushed.

"She found me *on purpose*. It was all part of some revenge plot against my father."

"Wait, what? Who was your father? What did he do to her?"

"Pierre de L'Ancre," he hissed, as if the words tasted like poison. "He was an infamous Witch hunter back in that time. He terrorized the Basque region, killed women and children… Over six hundred *innocents*, based on nothing more than pure speculation."

"So, *Mia* found you?"

"She did."

"But why would *she* want to find *you*? She's a Vampire, not a Witch. I thought your species stayed out of each other's way."

I couldn't see why something like that would even involve her. She didn't seem like the vigilante superhero type.

"She was close with some Witches at the time, and Pierre's trials were becoming a threat to *all* the Supernatural's — their way of life. Pierre was getting too close to discovering the real Witches, so she took it upon herself and put an end to everything once and for all."

"By… *Turning you?*"

"Originally, I was only supposed to be her leverage. Pierre was a powerful man, and powerful men like him are often quite paranoid."

"Heavy is the head that wears the crown, I guess."

"Heavy indeed. With his line of work, and his *beliefs*… He was so afraid of *Witches*," he made air quotes around the word. "That he was constantly surrounded by guards, even in his sleep. She couldn't take him out without someone else seeing."

"So, what? The plan was to kidnap you until he called off all the Witch trials?"

"I suppose. But Mia didn't know that he only thought of me as his bastard son. My mother left me in a basket on his doorstep after I was born. She couldn't raise me herself, but sometimes I wish he'd left me there to die. Once I was old enough, I rejected his way of life, his goals and ambitions for me... So, he made me become his slave, for lack of a better term."

"His *slave*? What did he make you do?"

"He took me everywhere for the sole purpose of serving him. Mia saw this, saw how I lived in rags and chains while my father feasted on gold platters and slept on feather beds... She took pity on me. She promised me a better life, a *happier* life, full of luxury, travel, and freedom... On one condition."

"You had to kill him."

"I had to kill him, and then pretend to kill myself so that no one would come looking for me."

"How do you just *pretend* to kill yourself?"

"Like I said, Vampires can withstand a lot of damage. It wasn't difficult to make them believe I was dead. After I killed him and hung myself in his chambers... The guards did the rest. They threw my coffin into the sea like they did with all traitors to the crown, and Mia came along in a ship to pick me up."

Holy shit. If it hadn't been for my ability, I would've thought the whole thing was a lie.

I let out a low whistle. "I'm never going to call my parents unfair ever again."

"I think that's why I feel such a connection to you, Georgia. When you told me that running your parent's restaurant wasn't your dream, well... I understood because, in a way, I went through the same thing with my father. I never wanted to be like him — never wanted the future he'd so carefully laid out for me."

It was strange to hear him say that he felt like he could relate to me. Sometimes I felt like we actually *could* get along too, but other times... Well, other times it felt like he was annoyed just at the sight of me. Nothing about him made sense.

"Yeah, but I think my situation is a little less serious than yours was."

"I suppose, but I still know what it's like to be pushed towards a life that you don't want."

I edged in closer to him. "What did you want to do instead?"

"I wanted to be a painter," he smirked. "Not a lot of money in art, though, right?"

"I don't think you'd ever have to worry about a paycheck… When you're as good as you are."

He ducked his head. "My father would've disagreed."

"So, when… After you were… After you were reborn, did you have to take on a completely different identity… Like a spy or something?"

He gave me another one of those genuine smiles that melted his cold exterior. When he looked like that, it was hard to remember why I didn't think he was sexy. "Sort of. We sailed for Greece after that, so I only had to change my name. The world was much, much bigger then."

"What was your name before?"

"Lourdes Raphaël de L'Ancre," he scoffed. "A girl's name — given to me by my father, of course. He tried to belittle me in every way he could, right from the start. I believe he thought it would be easier to control me if I was broken."

"Like a horse."

"Like a horse," he repeated.

"Pix called you Raphaël earlier."

"Pix is very old, and he knows a great deal of things that many of us would rather forget."

"So, you knew Pix back then, too?"

"Yes. I knew Pix long before I was called Rafe Fontaine"

"*Fontaine*. That's pretty. How'd you come up with that?"

"It was my mother's surname. It's the only thing I ever knew about her."

"Did you not try to go find her? After you'd been… *Reborn*?"

He flinched at my words. "I wanted to, but Mia said it would be too risky to return to a place where I might be recognized. It wouldn't have done me any good, though. A few hundred years later, when I was sure that anyone who could recognize me would be dead, I went back to our village in France and found out she'd died when I'd been about thirteen."

How awful. His life was like one of those tragic stories you only ever read about in books. He didn't seem to be asking for my pity, though. He was too proud for that, I knew, so I only gave him a small, tight-lipped smile.

He laughed a bit at the expression. "I feel like you know so much about me. You're so... *Disarming*, Georgia. Few people in my life know those things about me. May I ask you something now?"

I nodded. I supposed it *was* only fair, and besides, I was trying to get him to trust me, right?

"You said you make perfumes, yes?"

"When I can find the time."

"Did you make the one you're wearing now?"

I fidgeted nervously. I didn't like where this was going, but I gave him another nod.

"What was the inspiration, Georgia?"

I blanched as a sudden dread slithered across my scalp. There was no way in *hell* I could tell him that it was based on Celine... Or the fact that I couldn't seem to stop wearing it. He could've asked me any other question in the world, and I probably would've given him an answer, but this? I couldn't do it. I didn't care how much of his soul he'd just bared to me. The thought of telling him was almost too humiliating to think about. Here he was, some ancient, immortal being with an incredible history, and here I was, an obsessed, human fangirl who didn't have anything better to do with her free time besides making a perfume version of his boss. *No. Way.*

"Nothing in particular. Anyways... I think I probably need to get going," I lied. "It's getting pretty late."

Chapter Ten
Plan

We drove in silence as we headed back through the slushy roads on campus towards the "city hall" building. Rafe had seemed more than a bit put off by me ever since I'd avoided his perfume question. He couldn't know for certain that I'd lied, but the answer I'd given was undoubtedly lame. After we parked, he led me towards another, clearly more private, level where Gin's apartment was located.

Gin waved a dismissive hand at the man and ushered me inside. "Thank you, Rafe. That'll be all."

Though the layout was like Rafe's, Gin's space was worlds away from the posh, modern apartment I'd just been in. His choice of decor was more on the maximalist side of things. Every wall and surface was filled with some colorful piece of art or curious trinket. The entryway was covered with dark, floral wallpaper and rows of paintings in all shapes and sizes that had been arranged into a strange, puzzle-like pattern.

The kitchen and living area were even more chaotic. The wallpaper and art had continued into the space, but the clear focal point of the room was the huge post-modern couch. The expansive sofa was constructed of tubular teal pieces and topped with an army of bright yellow and pink pillows. Gin's walls were also shelved, but instead of books, they were filled with cases of animal skeletons, herbs in glass jars, candles, and a collection of crystals. Mismatched armchairs, animal pelt rugs, and odd side tables completed the already too-full space. I loved it. Something about the overwhelming frenzy of colors and shapes was comforting — cozy, even, once you got over the initial shock.

"Would you like something to drink?" Gin called from the kitchen.

"Water, please."

"We need to talk, Georgia," Gin said once we'd settled into his sofa.

I shifted uncomfortably in the mountain of pillows behind me. I'd been trying to readjust them for the past five minutes so that I could sit up straight when I talked to him.

"What about?"

"I want to help you. The others didn't agree with what you had to say, but I believe there's no other option. If your brother refuses to speak, then I'm afraid I *must* use my powers to see inside his mind."

Startled by his honesty, I grabbed his forearm. "Why?"

"You know we don't believe that these two cases happening around the same time can be chalked up to mere coincidence, and... I know you don't believe that either, Georgia."

I nearly asked *how* he knew that before remembering he'd taken a dip into my mind earlier — or was maybe even doing that now as we were speaking.

"Even though you may not realize it, subconsciously I know you think Mrs. Jessops' murder was connected to your brother's Saph overdose... Someone is clearly trying to frame the Supernatural's."

"Why would a human inject themselves with Saph?"

Gin immediately leaned back — his weary expression deepening the wrinkles around his eyes.

"*Please*. No one will give me a straight answer. Rafe said that people do it because they think it'll give them powers, but..." I paused, struggling to admit the next bit aloud — afraid that it would make it real, make it true if I said the words. "My brother is a drug addict. He has been for a while. He's always been careful, though — careful enough to hide his addiction from us, at least for a while until it gets really bad... It just seems so strange to me that he would take so much Saph and not know what it would do to him. He'd never take so much of something the first time around. I know him. I-I want to know if there was a possibility he thought he was going to become a Vampire."

Gin's dark hand reached out to grip my shoulder. "I know, Georgia. I've seen it myself."

Of course, he had. He'd had a front-row seat to all my memories. It was so odd that I had to keep reminding myself that he already knew me, knew my life, so well.

"So, you know that it was so out of character for him. I — It doesn't make sense to me."

"There are many things in life that we may never understand, dear. Especially when it comes to people closest to us. I believe you, Georgia. Your brother Nico brought up his concerns before the overdose, though, didn't he?"

"Yeah, he did."

"So, what do you believe?"

I didn't know what I believed. When Nico had brought up the issue to me, I'd assumed that it was *actual* drugs, not Vampire blood. It was a whole different ball game now.

Gin spoke for me, clearly reading my thoughts again. "Rafe told you that dead Saph kills humans, but you believe Lucky has used it before and accidentally got a batch of the real stuff."

"Rafe said that it depends on what happens when humans take Saph... I know dead Saph kills humans, but... What if he didn't know that? What if he thought that enough of it would turn him? Maybe he'd heard the same things I've heard — the stuff Rafe has said about it not killing humans. Maybe he thought he knew what he was doing but didn't know that the blood had to be from the vein. Maybe—"

"The behavior Nico described to you did not seem drug-induced to me," Gin interrupted. "It seemed to be the behavior of someone who was planning to move on."

"What do you mean, *move on*?"

"When someone is planning to end their life, many of the people closest to them don't see the signs because they seem happy in their final days — exhilarated, or perhaps overly optimistic about the decision they've made. Sometimes, this can also be misconstrued as drug use. The memory I saw — what Nico described, was very similar to those types of behaviors."

"Are you saying he *wanted* to die?"

"I don't believe that was the plan, dear. I believe his goal was to move on in *another* way."

Another way... There it was again. "Some Vampires are *made*, not born," Rafe's velvety voice floated across my mind. *Made, not born.*

"Correct," Gin confirmed.

"So, you *do* think he wanted to become a Vampire?"

"Yes. He may have been experimenting with Saph before — testing the waters before he came to the decision, but... Yes, I believe that may have been his intention."

"But he'd never gotten real Saph before... Until the last time. Do you think he could've paid someone for the real stuff somehow?" I shook my head. "No, that doesn't make sense. How would he have even known the other stuff wasn't real in the first place? Unless someone told him..."

"You must never repeat what I'm about to tell you, Georgia. You must swear it."

I nodded, but seeing the firm set of Gin's jaw, I said aloud, "I swear it."

"What Rafe told you was true. Some of them *are made* through the willing exchange of blood between a human and a Vampire. Many Vampires are... Protective — *fiercely* protective over their blood. The creation of a Vampire is not taken lightly, so when humans go in search of Saph, it's seen as an intense sign of disrespect. A Vampire approached by a human looking for Saph may even give them their own blood, knowing that once it has left the vein and been collected into a vial... It becomes deadly."

"Like revenge or something?"

"Exactly. Even so, Saph has become increasingly high in demand because of the rumors many of its users have spread. Dealers of the stuff profit highly on the sale, even though they substitute it for a mixture of common drugs and animal blood. The belief of what a drug will do to you is sometimes more powerful than the actual drug itself."

"The placebo effect," I replied, thinking back to what Rafe had said.

"If this dealer, the one who sold the real Saph to your brother, found out about their overdose — about Olivia's death, they may have been scared."

"Scared enough to frame a Vampire."

"Scared enough to make it seem like a Vampire that had it out for humans. With the overdose and then the attack, it does seem like they've tried to make the obvious suspect a rogue Vampire — probably in hopes of turning the attention away from themselves."

I rubbed at my eyes, feeling overwhelmed with all this new information. I almost didn't want to believe it, but... There was something about the confidence in the way Gin spoke that made it seem plausible, despite how outrageous it was all becoming.

"The dealer may have been paid very well by your brother, enough so that they could've sought out a Vampire and been given the real stuff — unaware of the consequences that an injection of real Saph would have."

"So, you think that if we find Lucky's dealer, then we find whoever killed Mrs. Jessops?"

Gin patted at one of his graying dreadlocks thoughtfully. "I do. It's the only thing that truly makes sense to me. The dealer would've wanted to redirect the attention away from the overdose and onto the murder so that he wouldn't be caught for it. Saph dealers receive the death penalty, you know. Even the first-time offenders."

My shoulders caved in on each other. "I don't think Josh Peters *or* Leslie Rathmore are Saph dealers, though. And your theory doesn't account for why Mrs. Jessops was attacked."

"She was disliked by many in Switchback, and considerably old for a human. She also lived alone in a nearly isolated location. Perhaps she was just the easiest target."

My jaw worked as I thought about all the possibilities.

"We should just see what I can glean from your brother, and, if I'm wrong, we can go back to your theory, hmm?" He suggested.

"And the others? What if they find out about this? How are we supposed to explain it if you're right?"

Gin's returning smile was wide, and toothy, and utterly terrifying. "They need not know, and if I *am* right, well... We'll say that your brother *told* you, yes?"

As we drove back, Gin explained his plan to use the Lamborghini as a dual-fold trick to get close to my brother while simultaneously throwing the others off our trail in case they got suspicious that Gin had paid me a visit. I felt like I should've known that he was up to something when he told Rafe to bring me back, but how could I? Gin's mind seemed to work ten steps ahead of anyone I'd ever known.

Just as I'd imagined, the car drove like a dream through the icy roads. It was powerful and sleek, yet somehow utterly silent. When we rolled up, I was relieved to see that Charlie's massive red truck was already parked in the yard. Boy, did I have a *lot* to tell him.

"Not *too* much, I hope," Gin chuckled good-naturedly beside me, though the look in his eyes was all warning.

My face went tight as I shut the car off and stepped outside. "No, not too much."

The wintery air was so sharp that I broke into a jog and climbed up the stairs to the house without bothering to see if Gin had followed. A blast of warmth greeted me as I entered, followed by the gentle sizzle and pop of something frying in the kitchen, and then the smell of greasy meat and French fries.

"I'm home!" I announced as I strolled into the completely empty living room.

My stomach dropped to my toes as panic coursed through my veins. I sprinted past the front door where Gin had let himself in and headed straight towards the kitchen. Relief washed over me as I saw Charlie carefully flipping pieces of fried chicken in Grams' cast-iron skillet, while Lucky silently watched from the table.

Charlie waved the pair of tongs over his shoulder to greet me. "Hey, G!"

I walked over to Lucky, sunk my fingers into his slightly damp hair, and playfully ruffled the inky strands. "I see someone finally took a shower."

His dark eyes were dead — unseeing, unfeeling as he stared straight through me.

"Hey, Luck. I've got a surprise for you."

Lucky didn't even blink.

"What is it, G?" Charlie asked as he retrieved the chicken from the pan and placed it on a paper-towel lined plate.

"There's a Lamborghini Urus outside. Don't you wanna see it, Luck?"

Lucky's full, chapped lips twitched up. He blinked — once, twice, before saying, "Urus?"

My heart pounded with excitement. Finally... *Finally*, something had broken through to him. I grasped his shoulders tight as I tried to lift him up to stand.

"Yes, it's a friend's," I replied, still struggling against his immovable weight. "How about we get you a jacket and some shoes on so we can take it for a spin?"

"Uh, G?" Charlie hissed as he set the steaming plate of food down. "Who's that man?"

I slapped a palm to my forehead as I remembered I hadn't even properly invited Gin inside.

"Gin! That's Gin."

Gin finally slinked in through the doorway with a grin. "Nice to meet you," he extended a hand towards Charlie. "I'm Gin."

"I'm—"

"Charlie Fairburn," Gin supplied.

It was an effort not to roll my eyes as I realized Gin had already infiltrated Charlie's mind. That man was a real menace with that power.

"You know my father?" Charlie took his hand back and wiped it on the lacy apron he was wearing. Seeing the old thing wrapped around his faded blue jeans made me giggle. The whole lumberjack thing he had going on did *not* mesh well with my Grams' outdated cooking gear.

Gin shook his head slightly, like he was too distracted by something else to explain how he'd known who Charlie was.

"He's one of the Triad leaders," I whispered to Charlie.

"What!?" Charlie blurted. His sudden outburst had been loud enough to make even Lucky jump in his seat.

Seizing the rare moment of clarity, I bent to meet Lucky's eyes. "Lucky, there's a Lamborghini outside, wanna go see it?"

Lucky's brown eyes were less fuzzy than before. It was as if he were finally aware enough to comprehend I was speaking to him.

"A Lamborghini? Hell yeah, I wanna see it."

I stiffened at how normal he sounded. It was almost unnatural to hear him speak like himself again, but I knew the moment would probably be short-lived, so I had to move fast. I grabbed his elbow again and hoisted him to his feet before practically shoving him out of the door. I swiped a puffy coat from the rack near the front and draped it over him, before bending down and wriggling his huge feet into a pair of slippers.

I ushered him over the porch and through the snow to where the magnificent car was waiting. "See? Isn't it awesome?"

"Wow!" Lucky gasped like a kid on Christmas morning. "I've never seen one of these things in real life. Can I take a look beneath the hood?"

The car's headlights flared to life in response to his question.

"Sure you can," Gin called out from the porch in an overly friendly tone. He treaded down the stairs towards Lucky to help him pop it open.

"Wow!" Lucky breathed.

"Gorgeous, isn't it?" Gin replied as he clapped a hand across the back of Lucky's neck where it lingered a bit too long to seem casual.

Charlie sidled up beside me. He was so fidgety I almost wanted to hold him still. I knew he was biting his tongue. He probably had about a thousand questions to ask me, but I was too busy to give him any answers right now. I watched Gin carefully, watched every movement of his body, and each twitch of his face as he delved into my brother's mind. His glowing eyes rounded ever so slightly before he released my brother with a nearly inaudible huff of breath. The sound was so low that I wouldn't have caught it myself if I hadn't been staring. Before I could even blink, though, a warm smile was right back on his lips like nothing had ever happened.

Something was wrong.

He extended the keys to Lucky. "Wanna drive it?"

Lucky's black brows flew to his hairline, but he snatched the keys up without another word and slid into the driver's seat.

"Be back soon!" Gin promised us as they shot off down the drive.

After grabbing a coat for myself, Charlie and I took a seat on the porch steps and waited for them to get back.

"What the hell is all of this about?" Charlie demanded. "You're all buddy-buddy with the Council of Three now?"

"Sort of. I got assigned to the case yesterday, but I haven't seen you so…"

"Well, you could've—" Charlie threw his hands up. "I don't know, *called me,* or something."

"I didn't think that it was *that* important, besides—"

"Uh, Earth to G! This is literally life-changing news, and I think that *life-changing news* deserves a simple phone call."

At a loss for words, I shrugged. I hadn't thought that he'd actually be upset about this. "I was going to tell you when I saw you today, Char."

Charlie chewed on his lip. He was clearly deciding whether he should keep arguing with me. "It's fine... I guess that it's whatever, considering I didn't call to tell you that I have a date tomorrow, either."

I slapped his arm. "How is *that* even the same thing? Charlie Fairburn going on a date is *not* earth-shattering news. You go out with plenty of girls *all* the time."

"Nooo. Not just *any* girl. The girl of my dreams."

I pressed a palm against my mouth and pretended to gag. "And *who*, exactly, is the girl of your dreams? I don't remember making any plans with you."

"Oh, shut up, G!"

I quirked a brow.

"I'm going out with Amelia Williams," he grinned.

"Who's Amelia Williams?"

"She's from Elkheart. She goes to college there. I think her major is sociology or something."

"Okay, and how did you meet Miss *Amelia Earhart?*"

"Oh my God. Stop," Charlie turned away from me as his face flushed. "You promise not to judge me?"

"Just tell me, Charlie."

He scuffed his shoe on the stairs, still unable to look at me. "I met her at Olivia's funeral. I know it sounds terrible, but they were best friends, and I don't know... We clicked, so I asked her on a date right then and there."

I laughed. Only Charlie Fairburn could manage to turn a funeral into his own personal dating show. "What's she like?"

When he turned back towards me, the loved-up expression on his face almost made me vomit for real.

"She's super pretty, and sweet. She'd got red hair and the nicest brown eyes — and she's like so smart, G. There's something about her! We've been texting ever since, and I don't know... It feels like she *knows* me or something. It's *so* crazy how well we get along."

"Alright, alright! That's *enough,* lover boy. I get the point."

"You know, she said she was taking that same class you took when you went to ECC."

"What class? I only took like... A hundred of them."

"Puh-lease! You know the one I'm talking about."

I frowned as I realized what he was referring to. "Oh, gross. Introduction to the Modern Occult?"

"Uh-huh, that's the one! What ever happened to that professor guy who taught it? Didn't you two date or something?"

I scowled at the question. "Briefly, but what happened was that he was a liar, and a cheat, and had a whole ass family — wife, kids, dog, the works."

"*Asshole.* Amelia said that guy is a total creep, too. I bet you two would get along pretty well. You already have that one thing in common!"

"Let's see how the first date goes, huh?" I was desperate to change the subject already. I wasn't sure how he'd managed to bring up *my* love life when we were supposed to be talking about *his*.

"I never did figure out how he managed to hide it from you, though."

Come to think of it, neither did I.

"I didn't ask him enough questions, I guess," I sighed. "Love makes people blind... Even me."

"So, what exactly is the Triad having you do, then?"

A soft breeze floated through the bare fingers of the trees as I looked out across the yard. "I'm not sure yet. I'm supposed to act as the liaison between Switchback PD and the Triad while they conduct their investigations."

"The overdose and the murder?"

I nodded back.

"Does anyone have any suspects yet? For the murder?"

"I do," I said as I turned towards him. His blue eyes seemed to shine even brighter against the stark, snowy backdrop. "But I can't say. We haven't even started investigating on this side yet. I think that's what I'll be doing tomorrow."

"Hmm, at least they're giving you something important to do now."

I leaned away, feeling slightly wounded. "Hey, my job was important *before* all of this, you know."

"You know what I meant, G. I know your job is important."

"Yeah, I know," I said after a long moment. I'd probably overreacted, but it was an easy thing to do when just about everyone I knew made my job seem insignificant. "Everyone hates me even more now, though. This morning when I got to the station, practically everyone in there was trying to set me on fire with their eyes. Even the Chief told me to watch my back. He said people weren't happy about me helping them."

"Aren't they the ones that assigned you as the... *Liaison,* or whatever?"

"No, I was picked... By Celine Bissonnette herself."

He let out a low whistle. "Damn, G. That's some serious shit right there."

"I know, tell me about it."

Charlie covered my small hand with his huge one. "Are you worried, though? About what people will think?"

I flipped my hand over to interlace our fingers together and gave him a squeeze. "You know me," I chuckled, but the noise came out far more strangled than I'd intended. "I don't care what people think."

"What about what they'll *do*?"

"Well, they already attacked me once, and I'm still here, aren't I?"

He stiffened. "*Who* attacked you!?"

"Woah, settle down, Cujo. I'm fine now."

"Who was it, Georgia?"

"Leslie Rathmore and his band of cronies. They've been camped out at the station ever since the news about Mrs. Jessops broke. They're protesting the Supernatural's — everyone thinks that they're behind it."

"Do you?"

"No. No, I don't. Not after everything I learned today."

"Well, then I guess I don't either. I trust your judgment, G. For as long as we've known each other," he gave me a smile. "And as much as I hate you for it sometimes, you've never been wrong about much."

Lucky and Gin pulled back into the driveway. My brother had a huge shit-eating grin plastered across his face as he stepped out of the car and said his goodbyes. I'd only made it back to the screen door before I heard it.

"Does the name Amelia mean anything to you?" Gin's voice drifted into my mind.

I stopped in my tracks and pressed a hand to my temple.

"Gin?" I thought.

"Hello, Georgia." I could almost hear the mischievous smile in his voice. "I'm almost out of range now, so please do hurry."

I blinked and turned on my heel to find the driveway completely empty. Gin had left minutes ago, and yet, there he was... *In my mind! Speaking to me!*

"I don't think I know an Amelia," I thought back before remembering my conversation with Charlie. "Except for Olivia's best friend. Why? What did you find?"

"Navigating Lucky's mind was like treading through the ocean at midnight during a storm," he replied cryptically. "Needless to say, it was frustrating. The only word I could even extract was "Amelia". It seemed like she was tied to the Saph in some way. It's hard to explain because you don't have the gift, but I think we should look into her, Georgia. It could be nothing, but... It could also be the key to solving this."

"Okay, I'll see what I can do tomorrow," I thought back before the voice, and Gin's presence, drifted away from my thoughts.

Chapter Eleven
Ghosted

I tossed and turned all night. I wanted to tell Charlie about what Gin had said about Amelia, but I also didn't want to ruin his date with her. If I brought it up, he might think I was being the jealous best friend or something. Besides, Gin wasn't *completely* sure she had anything to do with the overdose. It was probably nothing.

"What time are you going out with Amelia tonight?" I asked Charlie the next morning as I made a fresh pot of coffee.

Charlie's sleepy eyes instantly brightened at the question. "Six o'clock, so be back before then, okay? I don't wanna be late for our first date."

I hid my expression behind the streaming mug in my hand. No, I couldn't tell him. I hadn't seen him this excited about something in a long time, and I wouldn't ruin it before I even knew anything for sure. Innocent until proven guilty, right? There could be plenty of reasons Lucky was thinking about Amelia. After all, she *was* Olivia's best friend. Maybe he'd been thinking about reaching out to her or something. I had to worry about Josh and Leslie first. Hopefully, whoever the "others" Celine had mentioned would be done with their preliminary investigation by now so that Rafe and I could get started.

I moved to peek out of the window as I heard the soft rumble of tires on gravel. The inky vehicle was stark against the white horizon as it purred to a stop. Rafe exited the car wearing a distressed leather jacket over the top of a black turtleneck, trim black jeans, and polished combat boots. Ugh, he looked so good that I wanted to scream.

I set my mug down in a hurry, only realizing that I was still wearing my pajamas after I'd opened the door to greet him.

"Casual Friday?" Rafe teased as he swept past me.

My face went hot as I looked at my stained sweatpants and nearly see-through t-shirt. "Just wait in the kitchen. I'll be ready in fifteen."

I pounded up the stairs without another word, hurriedly combed my long hair up into a messy bun, and blindly threw on an outfit. When I was done, I took a step back to examine myself in the mirror. I cursed as I saw I'd somehow dressed myself in the near twin to Rafe's outfit. I ripped off the top half of it and replaced it with a color-block turtleneck and a cropped red puffer jacket. How embarrassing would it be if it seemed like I was trying to match with him or something?

Back downstairs, I was greeted by the sound of male laughter floating out from the kitchen. Charlie was sitting between Lucky and Rafe with his head thrown back in sheer delight at something one of them had said. But, knowing good and damn well that Lucky was probably back in his ghost-state, I knew that whatever had made Charlie laugh so hard had come from Rafe. *Since when was he so funny, anyway?*

"Where have you been hiding this one, G?" Charlie looked up as he wiped a hand across his eyes.

I leaned against the doorframe with my arms folded and scowled at them all. Rafe gave me a conspiratorial glance that I could tell was only meant for me, almost like we were sharing a secret. Despite myself, I blushed and ducked my head, pretending that the look hadn't just sent a shiver down my spine. I wasn't sure how he did it, but sometimes, he could make me feel like I was the only person in the world. All it took was one of *those* looks. It was intoxicating.

"Good luck with your date tonight," Rafe winked at Charlie as he rose to stand.

Wait... I'd been gone no less than *fifteen minutes* and they'd already talked about Charlie's date? What in the absolute *hell* was going on here?

I was still fuming as Rafe pulled off from the drive and headed towards town.

"Where are we going?" I grumbled.

"Charlie's pretty great for a human. Simple-minded, yes, but... In a loveable, down-to-earth way. I can see why you're best friends."

"You don't know anything about him. He's *not* simple-minded."

He clucked his tongue. "No need to get defensive, Georgia. I'm just making an observation."

"Where are we going?"

"The crime lab on campus. Switchback PD sent over their evidence this morning, so the others have some information to brief us on before we get to work."

Despite the nonchalant description Rafe had given to me about the lab, it was the most technologically sophisticated place I'd ever seen in my entire life. Located on one of the subterranean floors of the Triad's main office, the cutting-edge crime lab looked like it could've belonged in some big-budget T.V. show. The stark, windowless space was all computers, glass, and hefty pieces of machinery whose purpose I couldn't even begin to imagine. Blown-up images from the two scenes were projected on the futuristic glass walls along with random strings of letters and numbers that flashed along the sides too fast to catch what they spelled out.

"DNA sequences from our Supernatural database," Rafe explained. "We're trying to see if we can match the blood from the overdose to any Vampires in our system."

"I thought you said the attacks weren't done by a Supernatural."

"No, but it doesn't hurt to check who the blood came from — it may lead us to the dealer. Besides, Switchback PD will want to see that we've done a thorough investigation."

I nodded distractedly, still lost in thought, as I watched the strings of code filter across the glass. "So, what evidence did they send over?"

"Cell phone records, internet search histories, clothing, drug paraphernalia, blood and tissue samples, and then the toxicology and autopsy reports from both crime scenes. It'll be our job to sift through it all."

I took a step back to give him an incredulous look. "I've never done *anything* like that before! I wouldn't know where to even begin."

"It's a good thing we'll be here to help," an intimidating voice purred from behind us.

I whirled around to find the air shimmering behind us. I blinked wildly as the two figures slowly appeared. One of them, the man who had spoken first, was already grinning. I didn't know how much more of this I could take — every day I spent here added yet another fear to my already ridiculously long list. The grinning man was Asian, normal enough in size and height, and wore an all-black outfit like Rafe's. His age was impossible to guess since the stringy, damp pieces of his black hair hid much of his face, but... I almost couldn't focus on anything else after seeing his horrible eyes. Unblemished, milky whiteness filled his terrifying gaze from corner to corner. His eyes, combined with the wet hair, made him look like the ghost of a man who'd been drowned.

"Cheyenne Thrasher," he said, taking a step closer towards me. His voice was ancient, impossibly deep, and echoed like he was stuck at the bottom of a well. It was like hearing ten voices speak all at once. It was so awful, I almost thought he had to be pulling a prank on me... Except, no one else seemed to think his behavior was funny.

Instead of extending his hand, he circled me and sniffed at the air like a dog. A sudden wave of terror crashed down on me. Every fiber of my being seemed to scream at me, seemed to *beg* me to run away from the corpse-like being. How the hell were there Supernatural's like *him*? He was literally a demon. There was no other way to describe it. Maybe humans could learn to accept the pretty Fae, the Vampires, and even the Witches and their glowing eyes, but this? There was no way in hell that anyone could ever see him out at the grocery store and not run away with piss in their jeans.

"No need to scare her, Cheyenne," the woman chided next to him. Dressed in a white hijab that matched her spotless lab coat, she was around my age and height, with caramel skin, and pleasant, bird-like features.

She pushed past Cheyenne's circling to shake my hand. "Jaidon Covey." Something about the rapid-fire way she spoke made me think it had been a very long time since she'd left this lab.

"It's contracted," Cheyenne announced as he clasped his hands behind his back and finally moved away.

Jaidon paused and retracted her hand from mine mid-sentence to scratch at her chin. "Blockage?"

My eyes flashed to Rafe, who shrugged in response.

"Possibly," Cheyenne admitted. "Though it seems *intentional*."

"What are you talking about?" I interrupted, as I looked back and forth between the two.

"Nothing important, dear," Jaidon replied. "We're both Fae, but one of Cheyenne's powers is reading auras."

Well, there went my theory... Not *all* Fae were beautiful. Though it did make me wonder if I was seeing Cheyenne's glamour or his true Fae form. I would have to ask Rafe about it later.

"But there's something wrong with mine?"

Cheyenne's bottomless, snowy eyes flashed in warning as he glanced at Jaidon.

She waved a dismissive hand towards me. "Nothing to worry yourself about. You've been through so much emotional trauma that it may have caused a temporary blockage in your energies."

"But a blockage is a bad thing, right? How do I get rid of it? What's it going to do to me if I don't?"

"*Nothing*," Jaidon repeated. "Perhaps some meditation or grounding exercises will do, but nothing *bad* will happen to you. Cheyenne gets to know people by reading their auras, so not being able to see yours is frustrating for him."

I nodded, still not totally convinced.

"I understand we're to be briefed on your findings," Rafe interjected.

"It's a very *brief* briefing," Cheyenne drawled. "We couldn't find much to indicate that Josh Peters or Leslie Rathmore had anything to do with either of the crimes, despite having motive."

"We've decided to shift our focus on the physical evidence for now. Follow the money, as they say. Shall we begin?" Jaidon asked as she extended her arm towards the lab.

After donning a lab coat and tying my hair back into a more secure bun, I found myself sifting through *months* and *months* worth of Olivia and Lucky's texts — some that I would've rather *not* seen. Thankfully though, most of them were your average day-to-day conversations — planning dates and talking about how much they loved each other.

Yuck.

"Don't you find it odd how they *only* talk to each other?" Rafe asked beside me. We'd both been placed in front of the glass computer screens while Jaidon and Cheyenne conducted their more complex experiments on the physical evidence.

I rubbed my tired eyes. "Not really. Once they fell in love, they turned into the type of couple who blocked everyone else out."

It wasn't entirely true, though. I *did* find it weird that Olivia hardly even talked to her best friend, Amelia. I'd been hoping to find something, a cryptic hint or buried clue in their exchanges, but... *Nothing*. All I could even find linking the two together were a few lackluster messages and the odd phone call — each spanning less than five minutes a piece. Gin must've been seriously confused, because I couldn't uncover *anything* that would've implicated Amelia's involvement in all this. In fact, to anyone else, it would've looked like the girls were barely even acquainted.

Rafe's dark chuckle snapped me back to reality. "Seems more like an obsession than love."

"Like you would even know the meaning."

Rafe's emotionless features shifted into something more sincere. "I would."

Before I could ask what he meant by that, I was interrupted by Jaidon's squeal of excitement.

"Find something?" Rafe called as he lazily stretched out his long limbs.

"Dirt," Jaidon said as she waved a glass slide around victoriously.

I followed Rafe to where Jaidon sat hunched over a microscope, peering intently down the lens. "Look," she said as she inched over to let Rafe past.

"It's a black earth soil, perhaps a Mollisol?" Rafe asked.

Jaidon nodded. By the passionate fire now behind her brown eyes, I could only assume that she was a Fae with earth abilities. I'd never seen someone get so excited over a bit of mud.

"From an argillic horizon — pachic subgroup, from what I can tell," she gushed.

She might as well have been speaking a whole other language, because I hadn't understood a single word.

"It's very rich in nutrients," she explained, finally catching the confusion that must've been painted all over my face. "It holds a lot of water and organic materials."

"And that's…"

"Good!" She exclaimed with a bubbly laugh. "*Really* good. This soil was found at *both* crime scenes. I can narrow down the location of it based on the compounds and amoebas present in the water it's retained — kind of like a GPS."

I nodded. "So, if we find out where the soil is from…"

"We can find out who lives there, or I suppose, what's located there," Jaidon finished.

"It narrows the suspect pool down to that particular location," Cheyenne chimed in. Despite myself, I trembled again as his hellish voice raked a claw over my spine.

I shook my head in disbelief. "It's kind of insane that you can find all of that out through dirt."

"Mother nature can tell us lots of things," Jaidon shot back a bit defensively. "You've just got to know where to look."

I squinted at her. "Where did you look? For the soil, I mean. What did you find it on?"

"Between the treads of two pairs of shoes at your brother's garage, and in the fibers of Mrs. Jessops' carpet… The shoes were odd, though. One was a size six, and the others were size sevens."

I scanned the lab. "Can I see them?"

Jaidon retrieved the plastic bags from below her workstation — two pairs of black heels. I instantly relaxed, only then realizing that I'd secretly been afraid they were a pair of Lucky's. I really didn't want to find anything that would make me believe he was somehow involved in all of this even more than he already was.

"So, the two crimes really were connected, then?" I asked, after handing the bags back over.

The corners of Jaidon's lips tugged down. "We can't say for sure yet, but this is a link — yes."

"All it means for now is that Olivia and Mrs. Jessops, or their guests, have all visited the same place since the last time they cleaned," Cheyenne added.

"So, how long is this going to take?" I wasn't sure I was cut out for this crime stuff after all, I was too impatient for answers.

"A day or two, perhaps," Jaidon answered. "Depending on how long it'll take to run the analysis."

I checked my watch and stifled a groan. Six thirty on the dot. *Shit.* I hadn't even checked my phone, but I knew Charlie must've been blowing me up. I'd made him late for his first date with Amelia.

I quickly ripped my lab coat off and threw it on the floor. "I need you to take me home," I barked at Rafe.

Thanks to Rafe's insane driving, it only took us twelve minutes to get there. By the time we rolled up, though, my anxiety was so high I almost wanted to tear my skin off. Charlie had called and texted me so many times that my phone had frozen. I knew he must've been beyond furious, but I couldn't blame him. I'd been a shitty friend. I'd broken my promise and now I had to face the music.

Charlie had stomped outside, and onto the porch before Rafe had even put the car in park. His curls were combed back, and he was dressed in his best jeans, clean boots, and had even thrown on a button down. Yep, I was in some deep shit.

"See ya," I called to Rafe as I shut the door and walked up the snowy drive with my head hung low.

"Where the *hell* have you been, G? I literally told you *six*! Do you not even understand how important this is to me?" Charlie fumed.

"I'm *so* sorry, Char!"

Hot tears already swelled in my eyes. I was more embarrassed and frustrated at myself than I was sad for ruining things for Charlie. I knew he'd probably make a smooth recovery with Amelia; he *was* Charlie Fairburn after all, but... As for *our* relationship? I'd probably be in the doghouse for *months*. I really needed him right now, too. With all this craziness in my life lately, he was the last stable thing I had. I didn't want to lose that. I *couldn't* lose that.

"Well, I guess you got what you wanted!" He yelled as he threw his phone over the porch railing. I stared at the spot where it had landed in the snow with a muffled thud. "She hasn't texted me back for hours."

I paused halfway up the steps, my tears suddenly drying up. "Wait, *what?* Charlie, I'm only like forty-five minutes late. What do you mean she hasn't texted you back for *hours?*"

Charlie's scowl wobbled, then shattered completely. Tears streamed across his cheeks as his palms clapped against his face to cover them. I jogged back down the stairs and grabbed his phone from the snow.

"Did you get blown off? Is that what this is all about?"

"No!" He shouted defensively, snatching his phone back. "You're late, that's what this is about! If you hadn't been late, none of this would've even happened in the first place!"

"Wanna go inside and talk about it?"

He was still all red and blotchy from crying, but he finally nodded and followed me in. Once we were seated at the kitchen table with two mugs of hot chocolate laced with a healthy amount of whiskey, Charlie began to talk.

"We'd been talking all morning, but when I texted her at three," Charlie swallowed hard. "To see if she was still on for tonight, you know? She didn't respond."

"Was she acting weird at all? Like today? Or was it normal stuff before she ghosted?"

The skin around his eyes puckered as a singular tear splashed into his mug. "Normal stuff. I — I don't understand why it always has to be like this, you know? Whenever I actually have feelings for someone, they always do this to me! I just don't understand it."

I got up and wrapped my arms around Charlie's back, leaning into him as he cried. "It's not always gonna be like this, Char."

He stiffened, clearly not finding any comfort in the words. "How do you know, G? What if it is? What if I'm *meant* to be alone? My own dad doesn't even care about me, what makes you so sure anyone else would be different?" His tone was harsh, but I knew his anger had nothing to do with me anymore.

I wasn't sure what to say, though. It wasn't like I was the resident expert on relationships. Hell, I hadn't had a relationship in over two years and none of them had been anything to write home about. I took a seat and clasped my hands around his forearms. He tucked them into his chest and tried to pull away, but I held on tight as I waited for him to meet my eyes.

"Do you really think that you're meant to be alone, Charlie? If you're even asking yourself that question, I think the answer is no."

"Why?"

"I think that anyone who is *meant* to be alone would be happy about the idea. If you're sitting here upset and asking yourself that question—" I splayed my hands out. "I don't think that you're supposed to be alone. Fate is meant to be a happy thing, not something that makes you upset."

Charlie bent to wipe his wet eyes across his shoulders. "I don't know sometimes, G. It's just... With everything that's happened with my dad over the years, it's so easy to think that nobody's ever gonna love me."

I nodded understandingly. Charlie's mother had died in childbirth, and his father had never been around for long since then. Hell, I'd only ever met the man twice myself and we'd been best friends since third grade. His nannies were the closest thing he had to any real family.

"It's hard. Every time I finally force myself to be vulnerable," he nudged his phone with an elbow. "Something shitty like this ends up happening. I'm so sick of it, you know?"

Another nod. I *did* know. I knew all too well.

"Your dad handled everything in a shitty way, Char... But not everyone is going to do what he did to you. Not everyone is going to abandon you at the first sight of trouble."

"It seems like it though, G. My dad couldn't even stand to see me after my mother died. He'd rather be with his girlfriend of the month, partying it up on some yacht."

"I'm not trying to make excuses for him, Char... But I think her death was hard on him. He probably couldn't handle seeing you because you reminded him so much of her..." I pressed my palm on his cheek. Now wasn't the time to say the wrong thing. Charlie barely opened up to me about this stuff, and I didn't want to mess this up. "That doesn't mean he doesn't love you, though."

"How am I supposed to know that? He hasn't been around for more than three months since I was born."

My lips flattened into a tight line as I pulled back. "I don't know. But you can't let how he's treated you in the past affect all your other relationships in the future."

"Tell that to yourself," Charlie gave me a small smile.

"What do you mean?"

"I mean, that I've seen whatever is going on between you and Rafe. You're trying to act all cool, but it's *so* obvious."

"Nothing's going on, Char."

"Please," he snorted. "I saw how you looked at each other this morning, you clearly like him, and he *clearly* likes you."

I didn't reply.

"Exactly what I thought. I think he's a cool guy, G. You don't even have to worry about him thinking you're weird this time. He's a Vampire, for Christ's sake."

"I'm not scared he thinks I'm weird, Char. He already knows about the lie thing I can do."

"And? What's stopping you then?"

"Um, he's a freaking Vampire, Charlie!" I scoffed, before adding a bit more glumly. "Besides, he's already said that a human and a Vampire could never work out."

"Ah, whatever. The man is probably playing hard to get, too. I do it with girls all the time. Works like a fucking charm," he grinned. "Besides, when we were talking this morning, he kept on saying how interesting you were, and how much he liked being around you. He's like, *really* excited that you got picked to be his partner in all of this."

I rolled my eyes. I didn't want to be talking about this. I liked Rafe, but... I knew it would be better to keep things professional between us. Besides, he was so hot and cold with me that it was impossible to tell what he was feeling from one moment to the next. We were coworkers, and *maybe* friends, but... That was it. That had to be it. We were incompatible, down to a biological level. He'd laid it all out for me himself. Plain and simple. But if I was being honest with myself... It wasn't just plain and simple, was it? It was complicated and messy and way too much for me to think about right now.

Charlie's rough fingers found my chin to give it a playful nudge. "I'm sorry for yelling at you earlier, G."

I grabbed his fingers back and held them tight. "No, I'm sorry. I broke my promise. I said I'd be back at six and that's exactly what I should've done. You had every right."

"Probably shouldn't have thrown my phone in the snow, though. I think I broke it."

"Welcome to the club," I laughed, immediately feeling relieved we were back to our normal selves. "Should we put it in rice?"

Chapter Twelve
Return

When Rafe picked me up the next morning, we headed in a different direction — one that was all too familiar to me.

"Why are we going to Mrs. Jessops'?" I asked through the last remaining sips of my coffee.

"Jaidon and Cheyenne want us to collect another soil sample from the rug," he explained as we came to the trident branch in the road. "And to see if we can find it anywhere else. The rug could've been a fluke, seeing as how many shoes trampled over it during the initial investigation."

I nodded as I remembered the swarm of officers standing helplessly over Mrs. Jessops' lifeless body. "Why wouldn't they take that rug as evidence?"

I wanted to puke at the thought of having to go back into her house — let alone having to touch that blood-stained carpet. The grisly image was already burned into my memory like a brand, and I *really* hadn't planned on seeing it in person ever again.

He stroked the slight stubble on his jaw. "They collected samples from it. I guess they thought it was too big to bring in or something, I don't know. It's not like Switchback or Elkheart has the best procedures when it comes to these things."

I couldn't disagree with him there. Although Elkheart was slightly bigger, neither of our towns had ever had to deal with a murder of this caliber. Ill-equipped was putting it politely.

The most startling thing about returning to Mrs. Jessops' was the familiarity of the whole thing. Today, the wretched feeling that had filled my belly from before didn't come when pulled up to the cheery yellow cottage. In fact, nothing felt amiss at all. I half-expected to see Mrs. Jessops opening the front door to greet us with her warm smile as we exited the car.

The ivy growing along the trellis remained evergreen and bright against the snowy backdrop — the one sign of life through the bleakness of all this tragedy. The police tape around the front entrance had come loose and was now happily dancing in the breeze like birthday party decorations. I immediately tore it down and stuffed it into my jacket pocket. I didn't want yet another reminder that she was truly gone — that she wouldn't be there to offer me finger sandwiches, and tea, and old stories about my Grams.

Rafe shifted his weight. "Are you sure you're okay to go in? You can wait in the car if it's too much."

"I'm fine."

An official red seal was also taped along the crack of the door, signifying that nobody had been inside since that fateful day. I might've been shocked if I hadn't known that the police and just about everyone else in America had already made up their minds about what had happened here. No further investigation necessary — Mrs. Jessops was murdered by a Vampire, end of story.

As Rafe flicked out a nail and sliced through the tape seal, I thought back to what Josh Peters had said to me — *No one in this goddamn place seems to be able to solve an open-and-shut case!* Looks like he was wrong again. *No surprise there.* Even though they still didn't have a clear-cut suspect, Switchback PD had opened and shut Mrs. Jessops' case in a single day. Twenty-four whole hours. It was almost laughable how lazy they were.

Even though it sort of felt like I was being a traitor to humans, I couldn't pin it on a Vampire like the police had done and call it a day. With all the facts and information I'd gotten from the Triad, I couldn't help but to side with them. I *had* to keep digging. It was hard to believe that everyone else would be okay with our police doing such a piss-poor investigation. People believed what they wanted to, though, and if they wanted to believe the worst about the Triad, well... They would find a way to do it, even if they didn't have all the pieces to the puzzle.

We walked to the living room in silence. All of Mrs. Jessops' things had been packed away in big cardboard boxes marked "evidence". Only the big-ticket items, the furniture, and rugs, and tables, were still present in the emptied house. Black smears of blood still lined the walls, though they'd taken on a sort of artistic quality now. Blank spaces of the stone wall where her decor had been taken down and put away were neatly framed by the murderous strokes of blood-splatter, like a Jackson Pollock painting. It was an out-of-body experience for me. It felt almost like I'd dissociated or something. The scene should've hit me like a brick wall. I should've been re-traumatized or devastated, but… I felt nothing. I'd been through so much in such a short amount of time that I was just… Drained. Not feeling anything, being numb like this, made me want to run to the nearest church and beg for forgiveness. The guilt was unbearable. I should feel *something*. This woman had been like blood to me. I should be *feeling something*.

"Do you see what we meant, Georgia?" Rafe was asking.

I turned away from the wall and blinked up at him. "Huh?"

"About the waste."

I wasn't sure what to say to that, so I nodded and watched as he shifted the armchairs and couches off the stained rug below. Rafe worked quickly as he picked up the edges of the rug and rolled it in a tight log.

I got the feeling I should be doing something useful, so I quickly asked if he needed my help.

"Just hand me the bag." He didn't look up as he focused his attention to the deep grout lines in-between the stone floor.

I looked at the hefty duffel bag in my hand with surprise. The weight of it in my white-knuckled grip hadn't even registered until he'd reminded me. I passed him the bag and watched as he removed the items with clinical precision. Although I'd been around the Supernatural's for some time now, it was still hard to shake off the initial shock I felt at how they moved with such utter grace. Each flick of his wrist or tilt of his head seemed as purposeful and polished as some beautiful piece of choreography. As he worked a small vacuum along the stone floor, I wondered if the Supernatural's, or the Vampires in particular, even noticed how elegantly they moved anymore. If some Vampires were made and not born like Rafe, surely, they saw how oddly fluid their bodies moved compared to us mere mortals.

My curiosity finally won out as I waited for Rafe to finish vacuuming. "When you were made—" I stopped as his golden-green eyes flicked to mine. It was still hard to tell what was off-limits with him, but... I hoped *this* wouldn't be one of those things, because I really wanted an answer.

"When you were made, did your body change?"

He pinched the bridge of his nose.

Shit. What the hell, Georgia? What kind of question was that?

"It's just that... The way you all move is so..."

"Seriously?"

One of those off-limits things, then.

I scuffed my shoe over the jagged ridges in the stone below. I only dared to peek back up when I heard the scratchy sound of Rafe unfurling a large piece of plastic sheeting. He picked up the rug-log and carefully shook it out over the plastic before plopping it back down.

"Yes," he admitted as he circled the woven rug.

Coming to a stop, he crouched again and lifted the edges of it, meeting my eyes as he *ripped* through the material with his bare hands. The network of veins along the backs of his honey-brown hands throbbed with the effort. Something about the sight of it, of those powerful hands, made my stomach do backflips. The rug rasped in agony as he tore through more sections until it was all divided into neat, even squares. Colorful fiber, dried blood, and dirt flaked off from the pieces like snow as they landed on the plastic sheet.

"The change strengthens us," Rafe explained off-handedly as he reached into the duffel and pulled out a large evidence bag. "But you knew that already, didn't you?"

I remembered how he'd rescued me from that mob at the police station. "I think you've said that a few times, but... That's not what I meant."

"What did you mean, then?"

He meticulously folded up the plastic sheeting — careful not to spill even a grain of the material he'd collected.

"Never mind," I shrugged, wishing I hadn't even brought this up.

"If you're trying to ask if I look any different, the short answer is no. I've had nearly the same face and body for over four hundred years," he chuckled to himself as he zipped the black duffel and worked on moving the furniture back into place. "But I've told you all of this before, Georgia. Why are you asking me again?"

"I don't know, I was watching you work and wondering if you even notice it anymore."

"Notice what?"

"How differently you move — compared to humans, anyway."

"I do," his words came out cruel, like an insult.

I shrank back a step. I was a total idiot. Of course, they knew. How could they not? I'm sure humans looked so clumsy and weak to them. It was probably hard *not* to see it.

He stood, straightened his already immaculate coat, and slung the duffel over his shoulder. "The grace you're referring to comes with age, though — not by simply being turned into a Vampire."

"Age?"

He raked a hand through his sandy locks, revealing a rare flash of the bluish orb earrings he wore. "New strength and reflexes certainly help, but… Think about it like this, Georgia. Compared to the long life of a Vampire, humans are still practically in their infancy. Learning how to move, learning how your body works — those things come with age and practice."

I crossed my arms. "Shut up. So, you're telling me that you move like that *on purpose*?"

I should've known that was the case. It was so annoying to hear that he, and all the others, knew *exactly* how attractive they were. They'd *practiced* it.

His plush lips returned to their familiar sneer. "Of course, but… It's not entirely about what you think it's about, Georgia."

"If it's not about your *vanity* or whatever, then what's it about?"

"*Evolution.* No matter what the Triad would like to have the humans believe, Vampires *are* hunters at the end of the day. The way we move is supposed to be attractive — seductive, even. Think of it as a tool we use to lure in our prey," he grinned. "Everything we do, even down to the way we move, is based solely off our need to hunt. As we age, our… *Tools* for the hunt only get better and better."

"When you say hunt, do you mean hunting for…" My mouth dried up at the sight of his delicately pointed incisors. "*Human* prey?"

In one blink, his body blurred before my eyes and in another, he was standing inches away from my face. The duffel thudded against the toe of my combat boots as he dropped it. The bewitching smell of fresh-cracked pepper and over-ripe figs overwhelmed my senses. He cocked his head as he surveyed me, the gesture now predatory and animalistic. I was conflicted. The way he was looking at me had me scared shitless but, knowing that he most likely wouldn't eat me, it was also kind of turning me on. A crazed sort of passion shot through me as our breath mingled in the increasingly small space between us. He smiled again, but there was no warmth in the expression — only hunger. I felt that hunger, too. Perhaps I'd been feeling it all along. I couldn't be the only one noticing all this weird sexual tension between us, could I?

"Tell me, Georgia," his raspy voice went low and enticing. "Tell me, if you were my prey, would you not even be a *little* fascinated?"

Honestly, fuck him. He already knew the answer — knew that I would probably willingly go anywhere he wanted me to be, if not for the single fact that I was so fucking scared of getting rejected that I could barely even admit that shit to myself. Charlie was right. I thought I'd been keeping everything under wraps, but whatever I thought I'd been doing wasn't enough. It might as well be tattooed on my forehead. *"I have a big fat crush on you, Rafe! Please like me back!"* God, I was so embarrassed.

Still, I didn't want to give him the satisfaction. I had too much pride for that. I made a big show of sucking my teeth and raising my brows like I had to give the question some thought.

"No," I said finally as I pursed my lips. "No, I don't think so. I've done a lot of self-reflection when it comes to my choices in men, so I can't say that I'd *ever* be tempted by an asshole like you."

He barked out a laugh, and his green eyes scrunched at the sides with amusement. The cool pad of his thumb brushed over my cheek — just once, but the touch still sent a trail of fire licking across my skin. His hand moved from my face as he leaned in and braced himself on the walls beside me. It must've been his signature move, considering how he'd trapped me against the elevator that first day, and despite myself... I had to admit that it worked. Desire pooled in my belly and my greedy hands ached at my sides. I wanted to reach out and touch him. I wanted to explore every single inch of him. I wanted...

He ducked his head and pressed his soft lips against my ear. "Never ever? I'm not so sure about that, Georgia." The tips of his teeth grazed my skin as he nosed his way further into my hair and breathed in deep. "I'm jealous of you sometimes, you know."

"Why?" I rasped, still trying hard to keep my hands to myself.

"You're so hard to read. I can never tell where we stand with each other, and I'd love to have an ounce of your ability so that I could finally figure you out."

"Oh, please. *I'm* hard to read?"

Rafe pulled back to search my eyes. There was a sudden vulnerability in his expression, a vulnerability that I'd *never* seen there before. The look was so utterly disarming that I felt myself get lost for a moment as I stared back at him. Was he seriously saying that he *couldn't* tell I liked him? It was honestly a relief. I'd been this close to crossing a boundary that could change our whole dynamic forever. If he didn't feel the same way, it would be so fucking awkward if he knew I had a crush on him and then we still had to spend all this time together doing the investigation. Still, I couldn't help but feel a little disappointed. Even if it was for a moment, it felt good to finally have everything out in the open.

"You know I like you," he said quietly, interrupting my thoughts. "And I think you like me, too, but... I can't... Will you tell me, Georgia? I want to hear you say it, just once. If you don't, I'll stop this—"

"You said we could never work out," I tried to tease, but the words came out breathless. "Are you trying to say that you were wrong?"

I was definitely deflecting. I couldn't help myself. What if he was messing with me? What if I was like, "Okay, yeah, I *do* like you." And then, he laughed in my face or something? I wouldn't be able to show myself in public for at least an eternity.

"I'm wrong about lots of things," he said as one of his hands snaked out around my waist and pulled me into him. "Please tell me that this isn't one of them."

My trembling lips parted as he leaned into me and pressed a gentle kiss along my temple. The gesture was so intimate, so sensual, that the only thing holding me back now was my last shred of dignity... And the fact that we were standing against a wall that was covered in Mrs. Jessops' blood. I instantly sobered up as her mauled body flashed before my eyes. What the hell was wrong with me? I couldn't do this! *We* couldn't do this. Not here, not now, not ever. My crushing fear of rejection aside, what would a future even look like for us? I'd be all wrinkly and saggy in thirty years and then he'd dump me on my ass. *Hell no.* If I was already feeling this way about him, well... I knew *that* would be one heartbreak that I couldn't possibly survive.

I pressed both of my palms against his hard, muscular chest. "Enough, Rafe. Enough."

When he pulled back this time, I swore I saw a flash of hurt behind his eyes before the emotionless mask slid back into place. Still, it was more likely I'd just imagined it to make myself feel better.

He cocked his head. "Can you smell that?"

"What is it? Rejection?"

His jaw hardened as he stepped back and scanned the room.

"Wait. What's wrong?" I asked, realizing that he was being serious now.

He slung the bag back over his shoulder and I followed him out of the door towards the car — having to half-jog to even keep up with his long, powerful stride. Rafe haphazardly flung the bag into the car before he was on the move again.

"That smell," he called from behind his back. He'd broken into a run now. We were headed towards the back of the house and straight into the edge of the tree-lined forest.

"What smell?" I shouted through panting breaths. I knew he was trying to slow down for me, but even when he was holding himself back, he was too damned fast.

"It's coming from the forest."

We entered through the trees, rocketing through the densely packed trunks and leaping over piles of fallen brush and snow. It was darker in the forest. The gray winter sky barely even peeked through the canopy of branches overhead. I tried to keep up but, with my vision still adjusting to the dim light coupled with my clumsy feet, it was slow going. Rafe finally came to a stop at a small clearing and dropped to a crouch with his nose hovering above the icy ground like a bloodhound.

"Can you *please* tell me why you dragged me out here now?" I groaned as I pressed a hand to my ribs and leaned against a tree for support. I really needed to get in better shape.

Rafe waved me off as he furiously brushed away at the snow and rotting leaves that littered the ground. He pressed a fist against his mouth and stilled. I raked the back of my hand over my sweaty forehead and finally stood up straight to see what the hell he was doing. A pale, purple-hued hand covered in grime extended from the ground like it was reaching out for help. Even though I'd still not caught my breath, I let out a scream that was so blood-curdling even the birds peering at us on the branches overhead took flight.

Rafe jumped to his feet in an instant and clapped a palm over my mouth — only releasing me once he'd decided I was through making a scene. He grabbed me by the shoulders and shifted us so that his body was between me and the dead hand.

"Look at me," he commanded, though his voice was gentler now. His hands trailed up to cup the sides of my face. My limbs were still trembling violently, and I really wanted to scream again, but I forced myself to obey him, nonetheless.

"We've got to call Celine first. I want to get the Department of Supernatural Resources on this before the police can contaminate the scene again." As he spoke, his hands ran down my hair and back up again in long, soothing strokes.

When I nodded, he shrugged off his jacket and draped it over my shoulders. I pulled the black lapels into my fist and clutched it against the base of my throat gratefully.

"It'll be okay, Georgia," he reassured me before making the call to the others.

Twenty minutes later, we were met by Celine, Jaidon, Cheyenne, and some slight curly-haired boy in a three-piece charcoal suit who I'd never seen before. Even if his smart outfit hadn't been in complete contrast to his white-clad companions, the boy still would've stood out to me. His scarily pretty face was as pale as milk — the unblemished color only broken up by his red slash of a mouth and flat brown eyes. As they came closer, I saw he also had two crutches cradled around his elbows and forearms.

Rafe sidled up next to me at the spot I'd taken near the edge of the clearing as the rest of the group surveyed the scene. I couldn't seem to tear my eyes away from the boy, though. He was no older than fifteen at most, but he had a strangely sophisticated air about him, like a man twice his age.

"Christian Easterling," Rafe whispered. "Second-most powerful witch in the world — behind Gin, of course."

"I bet she thinks I'm too young," the boy laughed as he bent to lift the body's purpled fingers with some tweezer-like instrument. Although he spoke with a pleasant British accent, I decided that the child-like pitch of his voice was even more unnerving than his appearance. Christian's nose wrinkled as he glanced up at Cheyenne, who was silently hovering above his shoulder and looking very official in his white lab coat.

"Blockage?" Christian mused aloud.

"Something like that," Cheyenne said in his haunting, multi-layered voice.

I narrowed my eyes and let out a little grunt of annoyance. They were *definitely* talking about me again.

"How odd," he replied as he stood up to brush off his trousers. "How *very* odd."

"Shall we get started?" Celine asked as she turned her attention to Christian. She was wearing some ridiculously expensive white fur coat layered above a snowy pantsuit and towering heels that made me wonder how she hadn't broken an ankle on the way out here.

"So, who is he?" I whispered back to Rafe as I brushed off the thought of Celine's outrageous shoe choice.

"Our digger," Rafe said with a mischievous grin that told me I was about to be in for a show.

Right as Rafe had spoken, the rest of the group had simultaneously backed up to the edges of the circular tree-line — leaving only little Christian standing in the middle.

Rafe gave me a nudge with his elbow, "I'd close my eyes if I were you."

Not wanting to find out what would happen if I didn't, I squeezed them shut. A blinding flash of light burst from behind my lids, and my arm instinctively jerked up to cover my face. What in the holy hell was *that*? I almost didn't even *want* to know. A moment later, Rafe's fingers tugged my arm down, and I opened my eyes to find a horrifying beast where Christian Easterling had once stood.

Chapter Thirteen
Digger

The beast Christian Easterling had transformed into was, without a doubt, the *most* heinous thing I'd ever laid my eyes on. Like the chimera shape of the talking door knocker at the Citadel, Christian's new form was a mash-up of creatures — each more terrifying than the last. He stood as tall and broad as a prehistoric cave bear, nearly twelve feet, with powerful scaled legs that shook the ground as he turned toward us. His snake-like tongue flicked at the air as his vicious horse-shaped snout curled up into what seemed to be a grin. The ghastly smile only made me panic more as it revealed rows and rows of serrated teeth like a shark. One of his massive glowing eyes, now yellow-hued and slit down the middle, closed into a wink as he turned back around.

With one swipe of his curved, shovel-like claws, he gouged out a section of frozen earth at least three feet deep — carefully discarding it to the side, then repeating the motion again and again until the slender body of a woman was revealed. I was too shocked to even feel anything else at the sight of her body. Christian's claws retracted back into his gray-brown fur as he bent and ever-so-gently pawed away at the remaining soil that covered her. As he lifted the body from the grave, pieces of rotting flesh peeled away from her bones and fell back into the hole with a sickeningly wet, squelching sound. I covered my nose as the atrocious scent of her floated over the clearing.

"Eyes," Rafe said, giving me another nudge.

Again, I did as he said — this time making sure my palms covered my face, too. With another blinding flash of light, the little boy version of Christian was back in the clearing, as good as new. He brushed a hand over his suited shoulders, wiping at some imaginary dust before jerking his chin at the others. At his clear "go-ahead" signal, they stepped forward in unison and began their investigation.

Jaidon clicked open the metal briefcase she'd been carrying and pulled out sets of gloves and goggles for her companions. A thin collapsible rod flicked out from her palm as she tucked her hijab over the back of her lab coat and leaned forward to examine the chunks of flesh still in the grave.

"The jagged pattern on the flesh seems consistent with the last victim," she announced, using the tip of the metal rod to prod at the fallen pieces. "Puncture wounds on the inner thigh flesh."

"Same thing on the neck, and no missing organs," Cheyenne replied.

"Besides the obvious burial, the jagged tears and puncture wounds seem to be a clumsy attempt at recreating bite mark patterns," Christian noted as he circled the grave. "Though, they seem to be similar in size and shape to a bear... Or perhaps a wolf."

"Bears and wolves don't kill their prey in the same spot they eat, though," Celine chimed in. "And they wouldn't kill just for sport."

"The killer is trying to replicate the work of a species that *will* kill for sport," Christian announced.

"Vampires don't kill for sport, either" Rafe grumbled beside me.

The two of us had remained at our spot on the edge of the scene. I wasn't sure if he'd stayed beside me to make sure I didn't scream again, or if he'd stayed to make sure I was okay, but... I was grateful for the company, no matter his reasoning. With the grotesque stench of the body now fully permeating the air, I wasn't completely sure how much longer my stomach would hold out.

"No," Christian agreed. "They don't, but a human might believe that."

"Humans are the only creatures who kill just to kill," Cheyenne said, though his chilling tone immediately made me think *he* might be the exception.

I pressed the back of my sleeve against my nose. "Why bury her then?"

Catching the gesture, Rafe moved in an instant — producing a jar of Vicks from Jaidon's kit and instructing me to smear it beneath my nostrils. Although I could still faintly smell the decomposing body, the gel made it far less revolting than it had been a moment ago. I returned the jar and smiled at him in thanks.

"Very curious, indeed," Christian replied. "The patterns on both bodies seem to match, though it is odd that *this* body would receive a burial while the other was left in plain sight."

"Maybe they didn't want to get caught this time," I suggested.

"I doubt that," Rafe observed as he jerked his chin towards the stiff, mangled body.

I hadn't been able to bring myself to get a full look at her yet, but now, with the help of eucalyptus to soothe my nerves, I managed a peek. Pale and slender, the red-haired woman seemed to wear a jean skirt, brown knee-high boots, and a baby blue sweater before her death. Due to the vicious nature of her attack, though, the clothes, like her face and body, had been nearly shredded to pieces.

"Her hand was exposed when we found her," Rafe continued. "The killer *wanted* this body to be found."

"If this *is* all connected like you think, and this killer really *is* trying to frame a Vampire, how could they even know someone would find her out here? Why not leave the body somewhere more public where someone was *guaranteed* to find her? What if the hand was just a clumsy mistake?" I asked, turning my gaze away from the woman again. I'd had it up to here with all the death, *thank you very much*.

"I don't think it was," Cheyenne replied. "The only part of her left untouched was *that* hand — the one exposed above ground. After our investigations were officially joined, I'm sure they knew it would only be a matter of time until we found her. It was all over the news, and everyone knows that with tensions running so high between us that *we* would come back here to investigate on our own, and that *we* would be able to smell it. No. This was no mistake. Rafe is right. This killer *wanted* the body to be found, just like they wanted the *other one* to be found."

The other one. So cold, so clinical. A shiver skittered down my spine.

"You're sure that the person who killed Mrs. Jessops killed this woman, too?" I asked as I met Cheyenne's soulless white gaze. "Like one hundred percent positive?"

"Without a doubt. The murders are nearly identical."

"She was drained," Celine said as she pulled her fur tighter around her willowy frame. "I can smell about a gallon and a half of blood on her clothing and in the dirt. The person behind these attacks wants to make it look like the work of a Vampire, but..."

"They're a fledgling killer," Jaidon finished. "Someone who is hedging their bets. They still don't know what a true Vampire attack would look like, and they're hoping the police won't either."

"The police *don't* know," Celine replied disgustedly. "They're so ready to believe Vampires are behind these attacks that they've already made up their minds."

I interrupted, "I still don't understand why you can't explain that to them, though! Just show them what a Vampire attack *would* look like, and maybe they'll change their minds."

The group let out a collective rumble of laughter that instantly made me want to crawl into that hole beside the frozen woman.

Celine pressed a pointed nail below her eye, wiping at an imaginary tear. "So naïve, dear. How would you suggest we do that? Find a willing participant to attack? Ha! Besides, you saw how the idea went over at the station. If we showed them what a Vampire attack looked like now, they would think we're lying to them to protect our own, or even worse..."

"They would finally get to see that we really *are* the monsters they thought we were all along," Rafe said.

"But you *are* trying to protect your own, right?" I pressed, ignoring Rafe. "Not in *that* way, of course, but... If you can't prove to them that a Vampire wasn't behind these murders, then the actual killer gets to walk free. Who knows how many more times they'll kill if we can't stop them soon?"

"We will," Celine said. "All we've got to find is *one* clue, one shred of DNA that will prove us right. I know it seems frustrating to you, Georgia. Believe me when I say that it's frustrating for us as well, but... It's the only way."

"The only lead we have for now is that soil," Jaidon admitted. "Even with the killer being new to all of this, they're still smart.

They barely left a single trace of evidence at the last scene, and I'm betting that it'll be the same case for this one, too."

"Do you have a profile?" Celine asked, turning her attention to Christian.

Christian's boyish face scrunched up in concentration. "The killer is someone with anatomical knowledge. The wound patterns seem to be placed at random, which might initially suggest that it *wouldn't* be someone who has medical training or an interest in hunting, but... I don't believe that's true."

I narrowed my eyes, trying hard to follow his train of thought.

Christian lifted a crutch to gesture towards the body. "These were slow deaths; the wounds were all placed in areas that would prolong the victim's survival. The killer must've known that — must've *wanted* to see his victims suffer before they struck the final blow."

"No defensive wounds," Jaidon added. "The victim knew the killer — perhaps she even came out here willingly."

I thought back to Mrs. Jessops' cottage, how none of the furniture had been moved or broken. "There was no sign of forced entry at Mrs. Jessops', either" I said slowly. "It was so strange to me because of how violent the attack was... It was the first thing I noticed when I got there."

"They knew this killer well, then," Christian said, still eyeing the body so intensely that it seemed like he was expecting it to get up and talk. "These gashes are deep, suggesting a lot of force was used in the attack. I suspect this was personal to the killer somehow."

Rafe's lips curled back distastefully. "Passionate."

"Personal items?" Celine asked, now looking at Jaidon.

"None. No purse, or cell phone, or anything."

"She thought she didn't need them — that she'd be returning to wherever they came from," Christian said, lost in thought. "Cheyenne, are there any tracks leading towards here?"

The long, dark pieces of his hair fell across his face as he shook his head. "If there were, the snow would have covered them up by now."

"It's been snowing since the day they found Mrs. Jessops' body," I said hollowly.

"The decomposition of the victim seems to fit that timeline," Jaidon agreed. "This must've happened right after the last murder, though — when the soil would've been softer."

"Yes," Cheyenne drawled. "This was clearly premeditated. The blood in the grave suggests she was killed *after* it had been dug."

"She was killed in her own grave," I rasped. The thought was chilling. I couldn't help but imagine the fear this girl went through in her last moments. It was enough to make me want to cry. What kind of monster could do this? They had to be a monster, no one with any single shred of humanity in them could do something this depraved.

Now in full business-mode, Celine ignored my comment and instructed the others, "Take photos and collect some samples. We'll call Switchback once you've finished."

My eyes rounded with shock. "Wait, what about the body? If they see it like this, they might think that you've done something to tamper with the evidence."

Celine patted a hand over her pale blonde bob. "Christian will take care of it, dear."

Thirty minutes later, after the group had finished their investigation, Christian replaced the girl's body back into the ground as if none of it had ever happened. Somehow, he'd even smoothed the snow covering the grave so well, I almost wouldn't believe it had ever been disturbed if I hadn't been there to see it myself. Celine instructed Rafe and I to stay at the scene to call the station while they took their evidence back to the Triad's lab for processing. It felt shady, but I knew that what we were doing was for the greater good. Even with Switchback and Elkheart's police forces combined, there was no way in hell they stood a chance against a case like this. This was far and beyond the scope of their investigative power. I was grateful all over again for the Department of Supernatural Resources. They would solve this. They would get justice for this girl, for Mrs. Jessops, Olivia, and my brother. I knew they would.

Chief Garcia was more than a bit peeved to find a Vampire standing over the crime scene when they finally arrived, but to his credit, he'd decided to remain professional today.

"What were you doing out here, Beretta?" He demanded after pulling me off to the side. The scoop, thump sound of the dig team working in the background punctuated each of his bitter words like the beat of a death march.

"We were collecting evidence from Mrs. Jessops', and Rafe picked up on the scent."

Although the chilled air had all but frozen the tip of my nose off, Garcia had begun to sweat. He furiously unzipped his official-looking jacket with a huff and threw it to the ground.

"You're supposed to be our goddamn liaison, Beretta," he hissed, shoving a meaty finger between my eyes. "*You* are supposed to be communicating with *us* about *their* investigation."

I swatted his finger away and narrowed my eyes. "I don't see *you* giving me any information about *your* side of the investigation. And I'm not a goddamn spy, Chief. They aren't the enemy here. They want to find out whoever is doing this just as much as we do."

"I see they've brain-washed you already. Didn't take long."

My hand shot out to grab at the bracelet on my wrist. I twisted it, trying to count my breaths as a black fury clawed up my chest — begging to be set free.

"Do you have any more evidence?" I asked, shifting on my feet. Holding in my outburst had stretched my skin so tight it felt like I'd explode if he even looked at me wrong.

"No. There wasn't shit at the crime scene. No DNA, no fibers —" he threw up his hands in frustration. "We've got nothing but those wounds to go off of."

Despite what Celine and the others had drilled into me, I couldn't hold in the information any longer — they *had* to know what I knew.

"I don't think it was a Vampire, Chief."

Garcia turned purple — the veins at his temples bulging wildly.

"Listen," I pleaded, hating myself for having to resort to begging to get him to take me seriously.

His head dipped in a movement so slight it could barely even be considered a nod.

"Think about this for one moment — separate yourself from everything and think logically for me, okay? Why would a Vampire kill someone?"

"To eat them," he spat the words out like he was being forced at gunpoint.

"Right, but specifically…" I trailed off, trying to prompt his answer. If I was going to have any chance of getting him to believe me, I needed him to come to the conclusion himself.

"They kill for blood."

"And what was at Mrs. Jessops' crime scene?"

His steel-gray eyes narrowed suspiciously. "A lot of blood."

"Right, and how would it make sense for a Vampire to kill someone, and then just *leave* all that blood? Seems to me like it would be a big waste of food."

"I'll give you that one, Beretta. But that still doesn't explain the puncture wounds," he jerked a thumb back at the clearing where the dig team had just pulled the body from the ground. "And I'd bet my life on it that more puncture wounds are gonna be found in that body, too."

I deflated, already knowing full well that he was right.

Garcia's nostrils flared. "Your own brother is one of the victims here, Beretta. Why are you protecting them?"

I bit down on the inside of my cheek as I tried to hold my tongue. "I'm not trying to protect them, Chief. I'm trying to find the *real* person responsible for this so they can't do it again."

Garcia's face hardened to stone. We stared at each other for a long, tense moment before he finally said, "If there are puncture wounds on this body, I'm calling it another Vampire attack."

More rage coursed through my veins. The intense feeling blinded me, made my vision expand and tunnel rapidly. I'd never been so fucking mad in my entire life. In a moment of clarity, I finally understood how someone could rip those bodies apart like they had. I wanted to do the same thing to Garcia right now… Or worse.

"Is there a problem here?" Rafe's level, husky voice sliced through the haze of my anger.

"The only problem is Beretta's denial," the Chief told him.

"Perhaps she knows something you don't."

I blinked up at Rafe, slowly calming down as his oddly handsome face swam back into view.

Rafe's laugh was cold and cruel. It was the laugh of someone who knew they would always be better than you, no matter how hard you tried. "Have you not told him of our findings, Georgia?" he asked as he placed a steady hand around my freshly wounded wrist.

At the touch, a new kind of fire replaced my irritation. I quickly pulled away before that fire could spread, feeling slightly embarrassed at the renewed desire that coursed through my veins.

Time and place, Georgia. Time and place.

Garcia looked almost as humiliated as I felt, though I knew it was for a completely different reason. Rafe's awful, snobby laugh had clearly done exactly what he'd intended it to do.

"No, she hasn't," Garcia admitted, though his embarrassment had been quickly replaced by a false sort of bravado. The whole chest-puffing act he'd put on was about as transparent as a glass of water.

"We've managed to collect soil samples from the initial crime scene which our team of investigators believe they can use to trace back to the killer's location—" Rafe leveled his piercing green eyes at Garcia. He was so tall, he literally had to look down his nose at the other man. "Or a place where the killer has frequented — a job or a local hangout, perhaps."

Garcia mulled over the words for a long moment, like he hadn't managed to fully digest all of Rafe's big, scientific ideas. "Dirt is dirt, isn't it?"

Rafe shook his head, causing that longer white piece of his hair to fall across his forehead. The effortless style almost made him look like the Vampire version of Superman.

"No, dirt is not dirt," he shrugged as he gave Garcia *that look* that made it seem like he was his oldest and best friend. "Who would've thought, huh?"

Put at ease by Rafe's sudden friendliness, Garcia chuckled.

"From what I can gather," Rafe continued. "They say that dirt has a *specific* makeup that can be traced back to a *specific* area. If we can find the origin of the dirt, we can find the killer," he let out an uncharacteristically jovial laugh as he nudged Garcia with an elbow. "Or, at the very least, get one step closer to them."

Garcia nodded in understanding as his flushed skin returned to its usual cinnamon color. None of it fooled me, though. Rafe was still a jackass in my book — a jackass who had saved me from assaulting an officer, but a jackass, nonetheless. He'd used that same goddamned Vampire trick on Garcia that he'd been telling me about earlier. Garcia was his prey, and he'd talked him right into his trap without even breaking a sweat. Admittedly, it *was* a highly useful skill, but I still hated the fact that Rafe *knew* how very convincing he could be. It gave me that same uncomfortable, slimy feeling I got every time I saw one of those videos of a monkey petting a dog. The power dynamic was just *wrong* somehow.

"Could still be a Vampire, though, right?" Garcia asked, now wholly focused on Rafe.

"Could be, but we'll have to wait and see what the evidence tells us," He patted Garcia on the back. "We'll have Georgia convey the message when we know more. Trust me, Chief, whether or not it's a Vampire, we're all on the same side here. We want to find the killer so we can get everything back to normal around here."

Garcia made a little grunt of approval as he clapped his own hand over Rafe's shoulder. The stench of toxic masculinity in the air between them was almost as pungent as the dead body behind us.

"Sounds like a plan," Chief replied. "You know, it feels good to hear that not *everyone* at the Triad is against us."

Chapter Fourteen
Below

The latest body was quickly identified as Amelia Williams — Olivia's best friend, and the girl that Charlie had been supposed to take on a date. Chief Garcia had called me that morning to break the news, meaning that it was now up to me to tell Charlie before he found out from someone else.

"We're announcing it to the press today," Garcia clipped out. "Puncture wounds like the ones we found on Mrs. Jessops were present, so we're certain it's another Vampire attack. I've already informed Celine, but Beretta… Things are about to get very ugly for the Triad, so I would suggest you tell them to get moving on their investigation. We need to find this Vamp, and we need to do it fast."

I wanted to tell him how absolutely hypocritical he was being, but he hung up before I could get another word out. The Department of Supernatural Resources had been working overtime since the discovery of the body a few days ago, but besides the soil samples, we literally had nothing else to go on. Still, though, it was hard to understand how Garcia could hate the Supernatural's so much, and yet still be relying on them so heavily to do the brunt of the investigation work. The Switchback police were just standing around with their thumbs up their asses while we were over here busting our own.

I was still staring at my phone when Charlie came into the kitchen. How the hell was I supposed to break the news to him? I wasn't good at these things… I'd never *had* to be.

I supposed it was too late to be delicate, though. I needed to get it off my chest before he could figure out that I was hiding something from him.

"Amelia's dead," I blurted. "I'm so sorry."

Charlie's back was turned towards me when I spoke. He'd been about to make coffee, but at my words, the opened bag of grounds slipped from his fingers and spilled out across the yellow and green floor tiles. I didn't move, though. We were both frozen, barely even breathing as if someone had pressed pause on the moment.

"How do you know?" He hadn't turned around yet, but I could already tell there were tears in his eyes.

My hand found my inner thigh and squeezed tight around my jeans as I tried to force the words out. "The body that we found the other day... The one I told you about that was..." I trailed off, deciding against bringing up the fact that it had been entirely mutilated beyond recognition... *Again.* I felt so stupid for having even told him about it in the first place. *Why the hell had I done that?* I should've kept my stupid mouth shut for once.

"It was her, Char."

Charlie bristled — the muscles in his back going taut beneath his white t-shirt.

"No," he said the word like a prayer. "*No.*"

My boots crunched through the spilled coffee as I went to stand beside him.

"I'm sorry."

I knew he probably wouldn't be comforted by anything right now, but I reached out and placed a hand on his shoulder, anyway. Charlie flinched away from me as if he'd been burned. When his blue eyes finally met my own, they were as cold and hard as diamonds.

"I've got to go," he spat.

I followed him, half-running to the door where he'd already begun angrily thrusting his arms into a jacket. "Wait, Char!"

His expression made me stop short, though. He was staring at me like I was some kind of stranger. It hurt like hell to see him look at me like that. Not even in our worst moments had he ever seemed so... *Cold.*

"This is too much... Even for me. I can't stand by watching you follow them around like a little puppy dog and pretend like everything's still all cool between us, Georgia. Newsflash, it's *not* fucking cool. I'm done."

I took a step back, feeling as if he'd punched me in the gut again. "What? Charlie, I told you that I don't think that—"

"I don't *care* what you think," he growled. "Don't you see how stupid you're being? I didn't see it until now, but…"

How stupid *I* was being? Anger swelled up in my chest, altogether replacing the hurt I felt. "But what?"

"Don't you see what they've done? Your brother? Mrs. Jessops? They're supposed to be people you care about, but you're stuck so far up their asses you can't even see your precious Supernatural's are playing you like a fiddle. How many people have to turn up dead for you to realize that, huh? This isn't some cover-up or drug deal gone wrong! It's *murder*, and *you're* helping them get away with it. Vampires *have* to be the ones behind this shit! Wake up! Look at the goddamn facts!"

"What the *hell* are you talking about, Charlie? I thought you were on my side about this!"

He yanked the door open to leave. "Not anymore."

All I could do was watch as his truck spun out in the snow and zoomed down the drive. I wasn't sure how long I'd been standing there when the shrill ring of my phone jolted me back to reality.

"I'm five minutes away," Rafe informed me. "We've got a lead on the soil sample."

I hung up without another word and gathered my things. I felt like a zombie. Charlie's outburst had left me feeling so wounded and confused that I wasn't even sure what to think about it yet. Surely, he had said those things out of anger. He couldn't have *really* meant them… but telling myself that wasn't enough to take the bite out of his words. It had hit too hard, cut too deep. I sent a quick text to Nico to let him know I'd be gone for the day and asked if he could stop by to check on Lucky. That was a whole other situation that I didn't want to think about, either. I didn't know how long I'd have to be my brother's babysitter, but at the rate it was going now… It felt like it would be forever. He was still barely talking, and was sleeping most of the day, but… I guess I should've just been happy that he wasn't getting any worse.

"What's wrong?" Rafe asked as soon as I got into the car and buckled my seatbelt.

I trained my eyes on the floorboard, twisting my bracelet around my wrist. "Nothing, me and Charlie got into a fight."

Rafe reached across the armrest and took hold of my hands. "Why do you do that?"

"I don't know," I huffed as I let go of the bracelet, feeling another stone fall loose in my lap.

He only raised a brow at me.

I sighed again as I watched the stone roll to the floor mat. "Sometimes, I get these feelings — feelings that I can't control. They're intense, like I'm going to burst at the seams if I don't do something about them. The thing with the bracelet helps me calm down. Focusing on the pain makes me feel better."

"You're hurting yourself."

"Sometimes."

"I don't mean this in a rude way, but… Have you ever considered going to therapy? I know it may seem scary but talking to someone about these feelings might make you feel better. You could even talk to me, if you'd like?"

I pulled my hands from his. "I don't want to."

Rafe reached out again, his long arms easily crossing the distance between us as he replaced his grip. "I want you to know that you're not alone, Georgia. I'm here if you change your mind and want to talk, okay? It'll help more than you might think. It's not good to keep everything bottled up inside of you."

I stared at him for a long moment before finally nodding. I'd never considered that what I was doing was *actually* that bad. It was an anxious habit. Just something I had to live with, but… Seeing how worried Rafe looked now was making me realize I might really need to talk to someone.

"Thanks," I finally said.

Sensing that I was done talking about the subject for now, Rafe let out a little grunt and changed course. "Have you ever heard of the Haunt?"

"No."

"It's a club in Elkheart. We were able to trace the soil samples back to the area — the same thing with the dirt on the boots Amelia was wearing when we found her."

"What kind of club?"

I'd gone to college in Elkheart, but I didn't think I'd ever heard of the place. Considering I'd been a bit of a bar rat for most of my college career, it was weird. Back then, Charlie would come up almost every weekend to see me and go out for drinks.

"It's pretty exclusive. Underground, members-only type of place."

"Members-only?"

"It's a club where Supernatural's and humans go to mingle."

"There's *really* places like that?"

The beginning phases of the Great Integration were focused on the Supernatural's normalizing their presence in the world, establishing their rights, maybe even getting employed, but... A place where Supernatural's and humans could *mingle*? It was unheard of. That was the end goal, sure, but how was there *already* a place like that? It was so oddly fascinating, it almost made me forget about how awful I still felt from me and Charlie's fight.

"Seriously, Rafe, thank you," I whispered.

His mouth quirked into the ghost of a smile. "For what?"

"For giving me something *else* to think about today... And, for caring about me."

"Was the fight that bad, Georgia?"

"Yes. When I told Charlie about Amelia this morning, he lost it. I think they really hit it off. You know how they were supposed to go on a date the other day, and then she ghosted him?" I chuckled darkly. "I guess we know why she blew him off now."

"What do you mean, *lost it*?"

I rested an elbow on the center console and leaned my head against my palm. "He said he can't support me anymore. He thinks these murders are some Triad cover-up..."

"And you're helping us get away with it."

"I don't know why he'd change his mind like that. Sure, I get that he liked her and all, but... It was like a switch just flipped this morning. I've never seen him act like that."

"He must've been really serious about her then."

"Yeah, he was. He said it felt like they'd known each other forever."

"Well, he just found out about it today, so he may need some time to cool off. If he really was as into her as you say, I'm sure he's just trying to process everything."

My teeth sank into my bottom lip. "I don't know... Something about this whole thing is so weird, Rafe. I want to ask Charlie about it, but... He's not going to take any of my calls right now."

"What's weird?"

"Well, for starters, the timeline. Charlie said they've been texting since Olivia's funeral, but I don't even know how that's possible, since Jaidon said she'd been killed right after Mrs. Jessops."

The muscles along Rafe's square jaw flexed as he considered my words.

"Wait, this might make it easier." I rifled through the glove box until I found a napkin and pen, then drew out a rough sketch of a timeline.

"The coroner said that Mrs. Jessops died around here," I said, pointing to the start of the line. "Olivia's funeral was the day after that — when Charlie met Amelia. But Amelia had to have died some time very soon after that, maybe a day or so later...Which doesn't make sense, because she and Charlie have been texting for like... A week or more."

Rafe's golden-green eyes widened in realization. A moment later, he had Jaidon on the phone.

"Get her number from Switchback and put a tracer on it," Rafe instructed. "The killer has her phone."

"You think Charlie's been texting whoever killed Amelia?" I asked once he'd hung up.

"Yes. It makes sense, considering she didn't have any of her belongings. We need access to those messages, though, Georgia. They might give us another clue."

"I can try calling Charlie, but..."

I really didn't want to be the one to give him any more bad news. He already hated me for telling him about Amelia, so I wasn't sure how he'd react if I was *also* the one to tell him he'd never been talking to her at all.

"I can do it, if you'd like," Rafe offered.

I wanted to tell him yes, but I shook my head. "I think it might be better coming from someone else."

"From a human, you mean?"

My face bunched up. "Yes."

"Fine, if *you* can't talk to Charlie, then let Garcia know. We'll leave it to him to get us those texts," he said coolly, but there was a flash of something on his face that told me that it was anything *but* fine.

He almost seemed hurt — about what part, though, I couldn't say.

After calling Garcia, we spent the rest of the drive to Elkheart in silence. The Haunt was near the edge of town in an old run-down neighborhood I'd always tried to avoid in college. If the rumors around town were true, this place was nothing but trouble. At the sight of the neglected homes and ratty yards, I couldn't help but be reminded of the McKinney's place — they would've fit right in here. We finally rolled to a stop in front of a single-story home set further away from the others at the end of a cul-de-sac. Every single window was boarded up, and its crumbling brick walls were filled with years of overlapping graffiti. I crunched through the snow after Rafe as we rounded the house towards the backyard. A little black shed was hidden near the furthest edge of the yard where the dense tree line began. Something about the way Rafe moved so confidently towards the shed told me that it wasn't his first time visiting the Haunt.

"The club is inside *there*?" I hissed incredulously as Rafe rapped out three knocks on the deceptively sturdy door.

A moment later, the pounding thud of footsteps on dusty concrete greeted us from inside. After a brief metallic rattling noise, the door swung open to reveal a pasty middle-aged man with wire-rimmed glasses and a balding head. He looked like the textbook definition of a serial killer.

"Rafe Fontaine," he drawled familiarly.

"Steve," Rafe replied as he dipped his head in acknowledgement.

The man cocked his head as he tried to see past Rafe's shoulder to get a look at me. Rafe quickly side-stepped him, though — shielding my body from view.

"Where is he?" Rafe demanded.

"Come back later," Steve said dismissively, as he turned away.

Rafe yanked the man back, quick as a striking viper. His doughy face contorted in fear as he let loose a yelp.

"We don't open until eight," Steve pleaded, shrinking into himself.

"Usually," Rafe purred, as his large, vein-mapped hand tightened on Steve's arm. "But today, you're going to make an exception, aren't you?"

Steve's watery eyes swelled beneath his thick glasses as he looked back and forth between the shed and Rafe's pointed incisors. Rafe only had to raise an eyebrow in warning for him to start nodding.

"Y-Yes," Steve spluttered as Rafe released him. He massaged his arm, where bruises were already blossoming from Rafe's grip. "I can't promise he'll be happy to see you, though."

I tried not to gasp as I followed the men into the little space. It was wholly empty save for a set of concrete stairs that descended into a pit of darkness near the back wall. Steve closed the door behind us and chained the lock back into place before flicking on a light switch. A few work lamps connected by a lengthy orange cord had been strung up on the damp wall of the stairs. The overall construction work vibe of the place only seemed to confirm my suspicions that Steve was probably about to take us into his murder den. I probably should've been scared by the thought, but with Rafe beside me, all I could think about was how cool this place probably was at night.

Three flights of stairs led us to a riveted iron door so wide and thick that it looked like it belonged in a bank vault protecting precious gems and fat stacks of cash. Steve scooted past us and produced a weighty set of old-fashioned iron keys from his khakis. The door groaned loudly as it swung out to reveal the most normal bar I'd ever seen. Well, maybe not *normal*, but not at all what I'd expected. The Haunt was an opulent blend of crimson drapery, intimate velvet-lined booths, and moody artwork. The focal point of the dimly lit space was the huge, rectangular bar that sat in the center of the black parquet floor. An iron cage was perched atop the bar's roof-like structure and extended to the surprisingly tall ceiling above.

"It's for dancers," Rafe explained, catching my stare.

"Looks like a jail cell," I said.

"Only for people that piss me off," a loud, brassy voice, coated in a thick southern accent, called from a booth. Startled, I jumped backwards and knocked into Rafe. Before I could fall, though, his hands snaked out to steady me at the waist.

"Batten Danner," Rafe greeted the disembodied voice as I regained my balance.

I stepped from Rafe's arms and tugged at the hem of my sweater uncomfortably as Steve silently led us towards Batten's booth. He was a wiry man no older than thirty-five, tattooed from the neck down and dressed in a battered leather jacket with no shirt beneath, a mountain of gold jewelry, and jeans slung low across his prominent hip bones. Batten's curly blonde mullet framed his mischievous face and kohl-lined eyes, completing the look of the dirtbag boyfriend every girl from the eighties would've swooned over. Hell, who was I kidding? People were probably still swooning over the man to this day, myself included. He was sprawled out at the table with his arms slung lazily over the back of his seat and had an unlit cigarette hanging limply below his well-groomed mustache.

"Hey, traitor," Batten drawled, though his narrow hazel eyes were focused on my own. "Who have you brought with you?"

I took a cautious step forward from behind Rafe, but he flung out an arm to stop me. "None of your concern, Batten."

"You're in my territory now, Fontaine," Batten spat, as he traced a long finger up and down his chest. "Be a little more polite, will ya?"

"I-I told them t-that we were c-closed," Steve stuttered from behind us with his bald head ducked low. His creepy little presence was somehow made worse by all the sniveling.

Batten pulled the cigarette from his mouth and flicked it at the man dismissively. "Leave us."

"I need a list of your members, Batten," Rafe said once Steve had finally slithered away.

"No."

Rafe took a menacing step towards the booth. "You don't really have an option."

"Tell me, Fontaine," Batten said as his finger resumed its lazy exploration of his tattooed chest. "Do you *always* tell people what to do when you're in their home, or do you save that kind of treatment just for me?"

Rafe's mouth opened to reply, but Batten's ringed finger lifted to cut him off.

"It was a rhetorical question," Batten chuckled, before focusing his gaze back on me. "Come here, kitten."

My feet were moving before my brain could catch up. I stepped up into the booth and took a seat beside him — not close enough so that we touched, but near enough to smell the manly tobacco and leather scent of his skin.

He placed one of his fingers beneath my chin and tilted it back and forth to examine me. "Since when do you hang out with humans, Rafe? I thought you were too good."

Rafe slid into the booth beside me as a hiss of warning escaped his lips. He quickly draped a protective arm across my shoulders and pulled me into his chest.

"She's mine."

The words instantly made me come back down to earth. I tried to throw off Rafe's arm, but he held firm. "I'm not anybody's."

Batten laughed, amused. "What's your name, beautiful?"

Perhaps he was using one of those Vampire hunting tricks, or perhaps he naturally oozed sex appeal, but every time he looked at me, I wanted to rip my clothes off. It felt different from what I'd felt around Rafe, though. My attraction to him was like fire and electricity, where my attraction to Batten was like a big hit of some heady drug. I'd always been a sucker for bad boys, but... This felt different. Almost forced — like the thought of being with Batten had been planted in my head somehow.

"Georgia Beretta," I replied before Rafe could stop me again.

Rafe immediately tensed up behind me. "Enough, Batten. I know what you're trying to do." The harsh tone of his words rang with authority, but Batten still seemed unconcerned.

"Why do you need a list of my members?" Batten challenged.

Rafe's arm tightened around me again as he spoke. "Don't play dumb. I'm sure you've heard of the murders by now."

Batten's answering grin revealed a small red jewel on one of his pointed incisors. "Sure have, but what's that gotta do with *my* club?"

"Give me the goddamn list, Batten. I don't have time for your games."

Batten flapped a hand towards the exit. "And I don't have time for *your* disrespect. So, get the fuck out of my club, Fontaine."

"Georgia, go wait in the car," Rafe snarled as he locked his hands around my waist and pulled me from the booth.

"We need the list because we have evidence that links the killer back to your club," I blurted as I tried to get a grip on the table. Rafe had already managed to half-drag me from my seat before I spoke but stopped short at my confession. "We think that the killer, or whoever is behind these crimes, is a member of your club. Please, can you help us?"

"Human or Vampire?"

"Human," Rafe gritted out at the same time I said, "We'll need both lists, just in case."

Batten extended a hand out to beckon me closer. I gave Rafe an exasperated look that said, "*Please, just play along.*" He hesitated for another moment before finally releasing me. I slid back into the booth and Batten's cool palms found the sides of my face. He squished my cheeks together uncomfortably as he drew me in even closer to him.

"Do you know *why* humans *really* come here, Georgia?" he whispered.

I tried to shake my head, but his grip on me was too hard to do anything but stare back.

"They come here to flirt with danger. They come here, because they're bored with their pathetic little existence, and will do anything to feel alive again. They come here because they have a *death wish.*"

I opened my mouth to speak, but Batten's fingers pressed down even harder — the tips of his black painted nails digging into my skin. "If you think a Vampire is behind it, then those humans who were killed probably had it coming. If they came to my club, well… They *wanted* to die."

They wanted to die? What a fucking asshole.

My fist went flying — connecting squarely across the sculpted curve of Batten's jaw. Batten's eyes were wide as he released me to press a palm against the freshly reddened skin. I looked at my hand in disbelief. What the hell had I been thinking? Hitting a Vampire who could so *easily* squash me like a bug? It was *totally* out of line, even for me. Rafe's presence might've bolstered my confidence about being here, but now I wasn't so sure he could protect me *and* take on Batten at the same time. *Shit, shit, shit.* What had I done?

I winced at Batten's answering laugh — a low, belly-rumbling sound full of frenzied glee. My shock was quickly replaced by that simmering rage I was all too familiar with. People didn't come to his club to die; they came to have fun. No one should have to fear for their lives in a club. Especially at a club like Batten's. A club that's actively promoting a place for Supernatural's and humans to hang out. How the hell were we supposed to make any progress on the Great Integration if this was the kind of bullshit that business owners like Batten tolerated?

"I said *just in case*," I hissed. "I don't *actually* think that a Vampire is behind these attacks, but we need to cover all of our bases for the human police."

Batten blinked at me slowly, then turned his attention to Rafe. "I'll give you the list, Fontaine, but... Only because I like her."

A moment later, Steve had returned to our booth with a hefty stack of files for us to sift through. With Rafe's Vampiric speed, though, we looked through them all in a matter of minutes.

Rafe slid two of the pages towards me as he let out a low whistle. The files were set up similarly to a dating profile with a polaroid picture of the member paper-clipped to the edge, their basic information, and how often they came. I looked at the two papers Rafe had given me — Olivia Roth and Amelia Williams. My mouth fell open in shock, even though, deep-down, I felt like I should've known the girls would be regulars here. The crimes were just *too* obvious. The killer clearly knew the girls had ties to this place, which would make it *that much* easier to blame a Vampire for what had happened to them. Especially with the type of atmosphere Batten was out here encouraging. It was like he'd handed the killer a perfect alibi. A club where humans came to die. *Jesus H. Christ.* I was thankful that it was me and Rafe who'd come here first. If the human police had been here... Well, I'd be back to work in my shitty little basement office in no time because there would be no chance in hell we humans would ever trust the Supernatural's again after hearing shit like that — The law be damned.

"Do you know who these two hung out with when they came?" Rafe asked Batten, sliding the papers over to him.

"Yeah, these girls liked to party. They weren't coming here to hang out with Supernatural's, though. They came strictly for the Saph."

"I thought Saph was lethal," I murmured.

"Dead Saph," the men said in unison.

"No self-respecting Vampire would ever give a human blood from the vein," Batten continued. "But some humans that come here still claim to be Saph dealers. I know they sell that fake shit, but it's honestly a win-win if you think about it. The dealer's cash in, none of the humans who use ever know they're not getting the real thing, *and* they can be repeat customers since it's not poisonous."

"I'm sure it's a win for you, too. You take a cut of the profit, yeah?" Rafe asked.

Batten slouched into the booth and slung his arms behind his curls. "It's my club, isn't it? Why *wouldn't* I get a piece of the action? Humans will pay a thousand or more for just *one* vial of the stuff."

"Who are the dealers?" Rafe demanded.

"What do the dealers have to do with this?"

"One of your dealers might be behind these murders," I replied before Rafe could explode and piss off Batten again. "Our theory right now is a drug deal gone wrong type of thing. Someone gave Olivia real Saph, and she died. The other murders might be part of some plot to cover their tracks — kill anyone else who knew about them, throw in a few randoms, then blame it on Vampires so no one figures out it was them."

As convoluted as it all sounded, it was still the best theory we had. It was really the *only* theory we had if I was being honest. I just prayed Batten wouldn't try to dig too deep into it because I definitely wouldn't be able to explain it any better than that.

"There are a few small ones, but the main guy — the one they all answer to — goes by Lazarus," Batten admitted. "He's a real freak."

I leaned forward on the table. "A freak how?"

"He just is. If anyone knows what happened to those people, it would be him."

"Does he have a file?" I asked.

Batten nodded as Rafe furiously sifted through the pile once more.

He finally pulled out a profile and flipped it around to show us. "This him?"

At the sight of the man in the picture, a torrent of bile rose in the back of my throat. I slapped a hand across my mouth, but it was too late. I ducked my head beneath the table and threw up all over Batten's leather boots.

Chapter Fifteen
Old Flame

"What the hell was that?" Rafe demanded when we'd finally sped away from the Haunt.

Batten had only laughed again after my little episode, but Rafe had been so embarrassed that we'd practically run out of the place without another word.

"You don't know how dangerous he is, Georgia. You could've gotten yourself killed!"

I stared out of the window as I rubbed the back of my palm across my mouth. I'd probably vomited up the entire contents of my stomach, but I still felt like I could do it again.

"Well, I'm still alive, aren't I?" I grumbled.

"Batten's not a part of the Triad. He's a rogue Vampire. He doesn't abide by our laws — which, *may I remind you*, are the same laws that ensure *you* don't get eaten!"

"Whatever, Rafe. I can't help that I got sick. Besides, nothing happened, and you were right there to protect me, even if something had." I hoped the last bit sounded more confident than I'd really felt about the whole situation. In truth, I wasn't sure how strong Rafe was — or if he would've been able to get me out of there before Batten ripped me to shreds.

"I'm not even talking about that! I'm talking about you practically throwing yourself at Batten! You should've never gotten so close to him."

Throwing myself at Batten? Why the hell did he care all of a sudden? Sure, I might've been flirting a little when we first got there, but was Rafe off his rocker? I *clearly* despised Batten and everything he and his rancid little club stood for. I thought my punch had pretty much said it all.

A growl escaped my lips. "I can throw myself at whoever I want. And, yeah, maybe I think he's hot. So what? Are you jealous or something?"

"You *don't* think he's hot," he said flatly.

"You don't know *what* I think."

A long moment of silence followed my words. I knew I was being petty, but I didn't care. I wasn't anybody's to control, regardless if Rafe had claimed me as his back there or not. Why the hell had he even said that? *She's mine*. What a load of bull. He really didn't know me as well as I'd thought. I would never be a kept woman, not even for the sexiest man alive. It just wasn't me.

"I guess I should thank you," he murmured.

"For what?" I asked hoarsely, now feeling exhausted.

"For getting those member lists. I don't think I would've been able to get them if you hadn't been there."

I just nodded.

"And for punching him," he added with a mischievous grin.

Despite myself, I smiled back. "You never answered my question, Rafe. Were you feeling jealous back there, or what?" I stifled the urge to cringe. The question had come out way more seriously than I'd intended.

"Why did you get sick, Georgia?" Rafe finally asked. Apparently, he'd chosen to ignore me again.

Hmm, interesting. I didn't know what to do with the information, but I decided it meant he *was* most definitely jealous. That didn't matter now, though. There were bigger things I needed to handle first.

"I need you to take me to the college," I replied.

To Rafe's credit, he didn't even bother questioning me again until we'd made it to the small campus in Elkheart. He followed my directions as we snaked through the tan buildings and the late afternoon crowd of students who were milling about on the snowy quad.

I pointed at one of the half-full parking lots near Jefferson Hall. "You can park here. It's that building."

"Why are we here, Georgia?"

I gulped hard as I tried to fight back the sick feeling in my stomach that had never really gone away. "Lazarus is my ex-boyfriend."

If Rafe was shocked, he didn't show it. His face remained wholly neutral as we weaved through the crowd and up the curved set of stairs that led into the building. Although I'd not been back there in years, navigating the dingy halls of Jefferson came as naturally as breathing. I stopped when we got to the wooden door with a frosted glass windowpane that read "Dr. Dax Winston" in bold, black lettering.

My outstretched hand shook violently as I reached for the doorknob, but Rafe grabbed my wrist before I could touch it.

"You've got to tell me what's going on." His fingers flexed over my skin.

"Nothing. It's just... I haven't seen him since..."

"Messy breakup, huh?"

"You can say that again."

I heard the door click open behind me and turned to see Dax's face peeking out from the crack. He was a clean-cut man in his mid-forties; olive-skinned, with dark, floppy hair, rounded glasses, and a goatee that fit his pretentious hipster vibe perfectly.

"Georgia Beretta," he crowed, throwing open the door to let us in. His floral-patterned shirt was rolled up to the elbows to display his tattoos and accessorized with brown suspenders to hold up his tweed pants. "It's been too long."

"I'm here on business, Dax," I said, pulling my hand from Rafe's.

He laughed and beckoned us inside again. "I'm sure you are. Please, come in!"

I was hit by a wave of nostalgia as we entered his office. Nothing had changed since the last time I'd been here. It was filled with shelves of dog-eared books, potted succulents, odd trinkets, and mid-century modern furniture that screamed "young, cool, professor". It was no accident, of course. Like Rafe, everything Dax did was intentional — down to the very last fiber in his oriental rug. I'd been too blinded by my obsession with him to notice it when we were together, but now... Every little thing he did seemed *so* obvious. He was a sad middle-aged man who was trying *very, very* hard to relive his twenties.

"I'm glad to see you're dating again, Georgia," Dax said brightly as he took a seat behind his desk. "After what happened between us, I was a little worried that the... *Pain*, I put you through might stand in the way of your future happiness."

That self-important prick. My nostrils flared, but I held my tongue. He was worried that I'd be so heartbroken I'd never be happy again? If I had half of his confidence, my perfumes would be on every shelf in the world outselling Chanel No.5. I shifted uncomfortably on the embroidered stool before Dax's desk, unable to forget about all the times we'd stolen away to this very office for some extremely inappropriate one-on-one "tutoring" sessions. He was right, though, damn him. Dax *had* hurt me, but... I definitely wouldn't be the one to tell him that I *hadn't* been able to even *trust* a man since. He didn't deserve the satisfaction.

"Cut the shit, Dax," Rafe growled.

Suddenly, I was all too grateful I'd brought him here. There was nothing in the entire world that could rival how big or small Rafe could make you feel with just one look, one word — Not even Dax Winston had that type of power.

"We know about the Saph," Rafe deadpanned.

Dax tugged at his collar uncomfortably. "I don't know what you mean." The lie in his words instantly stunk up the room, and I bristled at the smell.

Sensing my sudden aggravation, Rafe glanced toward me, and I mouthed the word *"lie"* back to him.

Rafe leaned forward in his stool to press his elbows on Dax's desk. "You go by Lazarus, right?"

His eyes darted back and forth between me and Rafe, like he was already trying to figure out an escape plan.

"There's no use in lying now," Rafe crooned. "We know who you are."

"Georgia, please," Dax barked a laugh. "Tell your boyfriend that I'm not that kind of guy! I'd never do anything like that."

I raised my hands in innocence. "Sorry, can't."

Dax's lips flapped as his mind raced to come up with another excuse. Rafe rose from the seat — now towering over Dax with hate sizzling in his eyes. Dax pressed both of his palms on his desk as he moved to stand. He'd clearly decided that he *was* going to run away after all, but Rafe was quicker. His large hand locked around Dax's throat in an instant — thrusting him up against the wall behind the desk until Dax dangled by the tips of his shiny dress shoes. I quashed the urge to smile. I was really enjoying seeing him squirm.

"Did you sell Saph to Olivia Roth and Amelia Williams?" Rafe squeezed his hand around Dax's throat even tighter.

Dax's brown eyes bulged as his skin turned scarlet. A choking sound escaped his lips as he struggled for air, and Rafe loosened his grip just enough for the man to speak.

"I don't sell Saph," he gasped.

I shook my head at the lie and Rafe sighed disappointedly. He slammed him against the wall again — this time knocking Dax's head against it so hard that one of his abstract paintings crashed to the floor with a bang. Even though it was selfish to be thinking about all the sweet, sweet revenge I was getting on Dax right now, everything about this moment was glorious.

"The *truth* this time," Rafe purred.

Dax desperately clawed at the fingers around his throat. "I'm the supplier! Please, I'm just the supplier."

At my answering nod, Rafe grunted a noise of approval and set him back on his feet. Dax doubled over, clutching his stomach as he tried to fill his lungs with air again.

Rafe slapped a hand across his back as if the whole exchange had never even happened. "No more lies, okay? We'll know."

Dax collapsed back into his seat, still holding onto his throat. "I don't know their real names. We all use aliases."

"You'll have to introduce us then," Rafe said. "When's the next drop-off?"

"Ten o'clock tonight at the Haunt."

Rafe's smile was inhuman and wolfish as he replied, "Good, we'll be there."

Dax sank back into his seat, but Rafe held up a finger before he could get too comfortable. "A few more questions, Dax. Just answer yes or no, okay?"

Rafe looked towards me, and I nodded again, suddenly realizing what he was trying to do.

"Do you know Amelia Williams?"

"No."

True.

"Olivia Roth?"

"No."

True again.

"Have you ever murdered someone, or been the accomplice to a murder?"

"No."

True... I gave Rafe a disappointed frown. It seemed as if we'd both figured it out at the same time. Dax wasn't the one behind the murders. Another dead-end. It felt hopeless at this point. We had nothing to go off besides a few specks of dirt and Dax's good word that he'd introduce us to his "colleagues" later. I sure as hell didn't trust Dax to hold up his end of the bargain, but I reminded myself that Rafe had put the fear of God into him. Hopefully, that fear would be enough. Dax was a slimeball, but he wasn't an idiot. Running away wasn't an option when you had someone like Rafe hunting you down.

Rafe smoothed a hand over his black sweater and stood to leave. "We've got some shopping to do," he explained as he extended a hand to help me up. I tried to wipe the confusion off my face as he winked at Dax and said, "We'll be back at nine-thirty to pick you up, sweet-cheeks."

Before we'd made it all the way out, though, Rafe paused in the doorframe and turned around — having the same thought as I had. "Please don't make us come find you, Dax. It'll be *much* worse for you if you run."

"Do we really need to go shopping?" I grumbled after we'd made it back to the car. Sure, our leads were shaky at best right now, but that's exactly why we had to keep digging. How was I supposed to drop all of this and go hang out at the mall right now? There was no way he was being serious.

Rafe gave my casual sweater and jeans a long, hard look. "You can't wear that. We'll stand out."

I scowled at him. *He was actually being serious!*

"Well, what about you? We're basically matching, so by your own logic, you can't wear that either!"

"Yeah, I know. That's why we're going shopping."

"What do people even wear to the Haunt?" I muttered, still annoyed he'd dissed my outfit.

"A lot less than we've got on now," Rafe replied as we pulled up to the strip mall. "Think skimpy, rocker-chic."

"I don't want to."

An hour later though, skimpy rocker-chic was exactly what I found myself being dressed in. I poked my head out of the curtain nervously. Having already found his outfit, Rafe was waiting patiently for me on one of the tufted stools in the fitting room. Something about seeing him sitting there amongst all the racks of cheap, colorful clothing was hilarious. Catching sight of the leather and fishnets in Rafe's hands pushed me over the edge, though, and I instantly burst into laughter.

Rafe rolled his eyes but waved a hand towards me. "Come on, show me."

I blanched, almost forgetting that I probably looked even more ridiculous than he did. "I think I need to try on something else."

"This is the tenth outfit you've tried on! Just come out and show me, it can't be *that* bad."

Honestly, I admired his optimism. It *was* that bad, though. After all my failed attempts, he'd insisted that *he* pick out the outfit this time. I picked at the fabric along my midsection once more and swished the curtain open to show him the slinky black minidress. It's shiny, ruched material hugged my hips and thighs like a second skin and dipped so low in the front that I was tempted to keep a hand over my chest to keep from spilling out.

Rafe's face darkened as he took me in — the plush curves of his lips parting ever so slightly as he sucked in a breath. His gaze was singular and intense as it slid ever-so-slowly across the planes of my exposed skin. I awkwardly tugged at the ends of my black hair in a futile attempt to shield my breasts. The way he was looking at me now made me feel even more self-conscious than I had been a moment ago.

"Told you it was bad," I insisted, already retreating to the safety of the dressing room.

The clothes slid from Rafe's grasp as he stood and quickly closed the distance between us. His cool fingers wrapped around my forearm, gently tugging me back towards him.

"Turn," his voice quavered. He sounded almost as flustered as I felt.

I obeyed and gave him a small spin before looking back up at him to gauge his reaction. A rapid flicker of emotion danced across his features — too quick to decipher as his breathing turned ragged. His fingers were still wrapped around my arm as he leaned down and pressed his lips against my ear. I didn't try to escape him this time, though. I leaned into him, unable to resist the heady scent of his skin so close to mine.

He nuzzled his strong nose deeper into my hair. "It's perfect. You don't *know* how perfect it is."

"Tell me."

His hips ground against my own as he tugged me even closer to his muscled chest. I gasped at the contact, the familiar desire already licking across my skin.

"It's *so* perfect," he whispered. His voice was thick with a desperate sort of hunger that matched my own. "That I'm almost tempted to take you right here in this dressing room."

His words shot a wild dagger of electricity through my body. Something about the way he'd said it told me that this wasn't another one of his games. This was different from his morbid fascination about testing my fearlessness of Supernatural's. He *actually* meant it this time, and I realized that I *actually* wanted him to. Something about that, something about the realization that he wanted me, and I wanted him back, scared me even more than the fact he could probably snap my neck without even batting an eye. Charlie, damn him, had been right after all. I *did* like Rafe. I couldn't lie to myself any longer.

"You know how I feel about you, Georgia," he murmured.

"I don't."

He bit his lip, then pulled back as he lifted a strand of my hair and twirled it between his fingers. "What do you want me to say? That I'm obsessed with the way you speak your mind even when you know people won't agree with you? That even with how utterly vulnerable and human you are, you're still somehow stronger than *any* Supernatural I've ever come across? That I've thought about the smell of your hair and the feel of your skin on mine since the day we met? Georgia, you're intoxicating. I've never known someone like you before, and as much as you don't want to admit it… I know that you already know *exactly* the way I feel. I couldn't make it any more obvious."

I hesitated for a long moment, unsure of what to say. There were so many things I wanted to tell him, but… Some part of me was still having a hard time grappling with the idea that *he* could feel this way about *me*. He was so… *him*. And I was so… *Me*. I didn't want to question it, though. At least, not right now. Not in this moment. In this moment, it felt like everything was possible.

It felt like we could be together, a human and a Vampire. The thought sent another thrill sliding down my spine. I wanted him. I wanted him here and now and I didn't care how terribly embarrassing it sounded. I needed to feel him against me. God, I'd needed it for so long. I cast my eyes over his shoulder, trying to see if we were truly alone when... I caught sight of the clock hanging above the exit. *Shit*. To be continued, I guess.

"We should probably get going," I whispered, even though the way I'd said it made it clear that I wanted to do anything *but*.

He took a step away from me and collected his clothes from the floor. "Okay but know that we're not through with this discussion."

After getting my hair and makeup done at a booth in the mall, followed by a quick bite to eat at my favorite burger joint, we headed back to Jefferson Hall as promised.

"Can't *you* go in and get him?" I pleaded with Rafe. I felt absolutely ridiculous in my new outfit, and I really didn't want anyone else to see it if they didn't have to.

"If I have to go out in public like this," he gestured at his equally absurd getup. "Then so do you."

I groaned dramatically, but finding no other way around it, I eventually followed him back to Dax's office. Unlike me, Rafe had somehow made his outfit *work*. I honestly wasn't sure that there was anything he *couldn't* pull off. He'd gone with a style similar to Batten's — a studded leather jacket, low-rise jeans, combat boots, and lots of chunky jewelry. When I'd seen that he'd *also* decided on going shirtless, I almost had a heart attack. I didn't know how he expected me to focus on the investigation when he looked *that* good.

Jefferson Hall was dim and ghostly by this hour, even the janitors had packed up and gone home by now. The only noise in the eerily quiet building was the sound of our booted footsteps echoing down the empty hall. When we reached the third floor, I was relieved to see the warm glow of light shining through the frosted glass window of Dax's office.

Rafe entered through the door without even bothering to knock... Then *froze*. I slammed into his back, feeling my face crunch against his leather jacket.

"Hey!" I protested, about to rifle through my backpack for a compact to check my makeup, when I realized the office was empty.

Damn.

Not only was it empty, but it was *trashed*, too. Books were thrown from the shelves, papers littered the floor, drawers were opened and not shut back. It seemed as if Dax had grabbed all his shit and gotten the hell out of Dodge in a hurry.

Rafe's fists clenched and unclenched by his sides. "I should've known he would run."

I rubbed my palms together as I tried to think. Damn, I'd been wrong after all. He obviously hadn't been scared enough. Knowing Dax's weaselly little ass, he'd probably run away as soon as we'd left his office. There wasn't any time to track him down now, though. We had to come up with a different plan.

I slapped my forehead as a sudden realization dawned upon me. "Check his desk! Dax is so Type-A, he couldn't take a piss without writing it in his planner first."

Rafe rolled his shoulders back determinedly and rifled through his belongings as I watched from my perch on one of the stools. There was no use in even offering to help when I knew Rafe could, no doubt, do the job twice as fast without me.

"We need to find the name of whoever he was supposed to meet tonight," I said. "We can take it from there after that."

"I don't know why we didn't ask who he was supposed to meet earlier," Rafe replied distractedly. His fingers were moving through the contents of the desk with expert speed — so fast they nearly blurred into one another as they explored. "Such a stupid mistake."

I twisted the onyx bracelet around my wrist a few times. "We didn't think about it, I guess."

In all honesty, I'd been almost sure that Dax was too scared of Rafe to run.

Rafe snapped his fingers in response. "Got it!"

"What does it say?"

"Meet Dash — Ten o'clock at the Haunt."

I grinned to myself.

Gotcha motherfucker.

Chapter Sixteen
Clubbing

The Haunt was an entirely different world at night. Nothing about the abandoned house, or the old shed, seemed even mildly creepy in the darkness — which was, admittedly, a conundrum, seeing as how old, abandoned buildings usually seem even spookier when the sun goes down. But the soft thrum of music and excited crowd that was lined up in the yard definitely helped lower the creep factor by at least ten points.

Rafe used his impressive height to shoulder our way easily through the line, and we were up to the front in no time. I was grateful, because the skimpy dress I was wearing didn't do much to shield me from the frosted night air. Some people seemed angry as we passed, like they were about to say something, but at the sight of Rafe, they shut right up. No one wanted to try their luck against a six-foot-five Vampire, and I couldn't blame them. Even knowing Rafe as well as I did now, he was still intimidating as hell.

"Back again so soon?" Steve greeted us at the iron-doored entryway.

Rafe didn't say anything to the man, didn't even bother to give him a second glance as he pushed through to the bar. The Haunt was absolutely packed. Red lighting now flooded over the room to give it a sultry, mysterious vibe. I looked up towards the cage atop the bar, and sure enough, scantily clad dancers were inside, writhing in time to the obnoxiously loud music.

"Where are we going?" I shouted up at Rafe as we meandered through the crowd.

I grabbed onto one of his belt loops and hung on for dear life. This was *not* a place that I wanted to get lost in, considering how he'd practically admitted to it being a popular hangout for rogue Supernatural's. I was sure the federal government would've loved to shut this place down if they ever caught wind of its existence. Like Rafe had also said, rogue Supernatural's *weren't* protected by the Triad's laws, meaning they were fair game for the government to do with as they saw fit, assuming they could catch them, of course... But that also meant humans weren't protected from the rogues, either. For the first time in a long time, I felt like I had a solid reason (other than my own paranoia) to fear the Supernatural's.

"We need to find Batten," Rafe called back, still cutting our way through the jungle of tightly packed bodies.

Just then, a hand wrapped around my wrist and yanked me back so hard I almost thought my shoulder had been ripped clean out of the socket. A shriek of horror escaped my lips as I saw I'd also lost my grip on Rafe's jeans. He didn't even turn back, though. He must've thought I was still behind him. *Shit, shit, shit.* What the hell happened to his Vampiric super senses? Icy dread crept over me as I helplessly watched his tall form snaking through the crowd further and further away from me.

"Hey, kitten," a familiar voice nuzzled into my ear.

The thick southern drawl instantly made me relax, and I turned to find Batten's wily grin. Sure, he might've sucked big time, but it was still a huge relief to see a familiar face. "You scared me! And you made me lose Rafe. We were looking for you!"

Batten cupped a hand around his ear and leaned towards me. "Do what, babes? I can't hear you!"

I blew out my cheeks and grabbed the back of his neck, pulling him closer towards me. "We were looking for you!"

"Where's Rafe?" He yelled back.

I pinched the bridge of my nose. This conversation was going nowhere. Weren't Vampires supposed to have enhanced hearing, too? This stupid club must be like their kryptonite or something. I pulled on his neck again so that his ear was crushed on my lips. "Can we talk somewhere quieter?"

Batten's ringed fingers sank to my hips and spun me around. "I thought you'd never ask!"

He pushed me forward into the crowd, but unlike Rafe, the crowd was almost *excited* to move when they saw who was trying to push through. Batten was like a king maneuvering through his castle. People clamored and pawed at us as we passed, trying to say hello or offer us drinks. Even though I knew that the attention wasn't for me, being beside Batten kind of made me feel like a rockstar.

It only took us a few more moments to make our way towards one of the velvet booths at the back of the room. The thundering bass of the heady music was quieter there, still obnoxiously loud but, we could at least have a conversation without having to yell anymore. A pretty waitress in an outfit that was little more than dental floss and a potato chip flitted up as soon as we slid into our seats.

"Two mint juleps, and..." Batten trailed off, looking towards me for a suggestion.

"I'm fine!"

"You're not coming to my club without doing a shot with me."

I worried my hands in my lap and scanned the crowd for Rafe again. I'd totally lost him. With his height, I thought that would be impossible, but... I didn't see him anywhere.

"Georgia! Give me a shot to order," Batten demanded.

I pursed my lips and sank back into the booth defeatedly. "Limoncello?" I knew I shouldn't be drinking anything at all, but the stern set of Batten's jaw told me that he wouldn't let this go until I gave him an answer.

He gave the waitress a flirtatious wink. "What the lady said."

"I've got to find Rafe," I repeated once the waitress had scampered off behind the bar. "We were looking for you earlier."

Batten pressed a finger against my lips to silence me. "No business before pleasure, kitten. It's the only rule I live by."

I didn't need my ability to know he was telling the truth. Even if I hadn't known that he was a rogue Vampire, it would only take one look at him to tell he wasn't a man who followed the rules.

I pulled away from him and crossed my legs. "Fine."

He licked his lips as his eyes trailed across my body. "You look different tonight."

"Had to fit the part."

He arched his hips up and fished a gold cigarette case from his back pocket. "It's perfect, Georgia."

He extended it towards me, but I waved him off. "I'm good, thanks."

"Suit yourself."

Thankfully, I could see the waitress already walking back with our drinks. I could feel my panic rising with each second that Rafe wasn't by my side, and I knew he was probably freaking out, too. I bet he thought I was dead and drained in some ditch by now.

Batten blew out a long stream of smoke and raised one of the shot glasses towards me. "Cheers."

We clinked glasses, and I downed the sweet lemon liquor eagerly.

I wiped the back of my hand over my mouth. "Can we talk now?"

Batten rolled his hazel eyes and took another puff on his cigarette. "Are you always this bossy, kitten?"

"Can you get someone to find Rafe, please? Or can we go look? I lost him and I'm really worried."

Batten raised a hand over his head and snapped. I wasn't even sure that anyone could hear it over all the music, but nevertheless our waitress was back at the table in an instant.

Batten scooted towards the edge of the booth and leaned over to whisper something into her ear. She gave him a thumbs up before disappearing back into the fray.

"Happy now?" Batten asked as he slid back beside me. He'd gotten so close that the sides of our arms and thighs were pressed tight against each other.

I stiffened at the contact but gave him the brightest smile I could manage. "Thanks."

He stamped out his cigarette on the table. "Did you find Lazarus?"

"We did."

"And?"

"He didn't do it."

Batten made a little tsk-tsk noise. "Ah, too bad."

"We got another lead, though."

He pinched at the edge of his blonde mustache — curiosity curling his lips beneath it.

"Do you know who Dash is?" I continued. "Lazarus was supposed to meet him here tonight."

He sucked on his teeth for a moment as he racked his brain for an answer. "No, not personally. I've heard the name, though."

"I thought you took a cut of all the dealer's sales?"

"I do."

"Then how do you not know him personally?"

Batten laughed, the sound of it a steely, grating rumble. "Do you really think that *I personally* go around and collect money from *drug dealers*? Honestly, Georgia! What kind of man do you think I am?"

A seedy, rogue Vampire who probably wants to eat me. I didn't say that, though. Instead, I took a coy sip of my drink and gave a slight shrug.

"I'm above those kinds of things, kitten. The dealers go through Steve."

I scanned the crowd again, but still finding no sight of the waitress or Rafe, I turned back to face him. "You knew who Lazarus was, though."

Batten leaned back and tossed an arm over the booth behind my shoulders. "He's a bit more important than the others." His fingers moved on my bare shoulder, tracing slow circles over my skin.

"You knew him well enough to know that he was a freak," I said as I tried to ignore the way his touch was starting to make me feel. Jesus, something was seriously wrong with me.

"I've gotten complaints from my staff before."

"What kind of complaints?"

"Let's just say he's been intimate with a few of our girls before and pressured them to do some kinky shit that they weren't comfortable with."

Disgust rippled through me, but I *had* to know exactly what he'd done. "Kinky how?"

"Kinky as far as humans go," he smirked, revealing the pointed tips of his incisors and the small red jewel. "He wanted bloodplay."

I recoiled in shock. My heart felt like it had been ripped out of my chest and splattered against the wall. Dax had been a lot of things, but... A sick and twisted pervert? It was hard to imagine since he hadn't exactly been a freak in the sheets when we were together.

"What do you mean by *bloodplay*?" I croaked.

Batten's smile turned hungry as his tongue snaked out to trace across his bottom lip. He leaned into me, pulling on my arm so that I leaned into him, too. His fingers buried themselves into my hair as he spoke. "I can show you, if you'd like."

A shudder rippled through me, but it was fear now, not pleasure, that was making me feel this way. Batten, however, wasn't picking up on any of the signals that I was putting down. He nipped at my earlobe playfully, then slid his teeth downwards against the delicate skin of my neck. I was absolutely frozen. I couldn't move — couldn't think about anything other than the feeling of his razor-sharp teeth pressing into my thundering pulse. He lifted a hand to cup my jaw and forced my head to the side to expose even more of my neck to him.

"I want to taste you, Georgia," he whispered against me. His voice was as soft and enticing as the velvet we were sitting on. "You want it, too. You know you do."

His tongue flicked out to trace a pattern of hot swirls on my skin, right across that throbbing pulse-point before his lips slid up to join mine. His kiss felt like a promise — a promise that he intended to keep. It was then that I realized he would never let me go. Even if it wasn't right here or right now, I knew that someday he *would* taste my blood. I could feel it in that kiss, could feel that he would get what he wanted no matter what it took. And some small part of me... Might've wanted him to. What would it feel like to give myself to someone like that? Would it feel good? Would it hurt? If it had been Rafe who asked me, would I let him? *Rafe*. All I could think about now was Rafe doing this to me. Rafe's tongue and lips and... *Rafe*.

Somewhere along the way I'd closed my eyes, but at the thought of Rafe, my eyes snapped back open. I sprung away from Batten in an instant, breathing hard. What the hell *was* that? A sick, oily feeling had settled over my skin. I almost wanted to vomit on his boots again. Something was wrong.

Batten raised his hands in innocence as he laughed. "You're curious, Georgia. Very curious. I can see why our dear Rafe has taken such a shine to you."

I scowled at him as I finger-combed my rumpled hair. "What are you even talking about?"

"Your ability to resist our influence. It's an astounding feat for a human. If you were anyone else, I'd already be fang-deep in your neck by now."

"Rafe told me about that already. I get you can make yourself more attractive to your prey just by moving or whatever—"

Batten's answering guffaw of laughter silenced me. He slapped a hand across the table and wiped a tear from his eye with the other. "By the way we *move*? What kind of nonsense has Rafe been feeding you, Georgia?"

I turned away, hoping to hide my shame. I felt so stupid. He was clearly suggesting Rafe lied to me, but why the hell would I even trust a man like Batten? Besides, no one could lie to me. I would've known if Rafe had lied when he told me all of that. *I would've known.*

Batten was a rogue. He was untrustworthy and probably evil, but... That little voice inside of me insisted he was telling the truth. If he hadn't been, then why the hell was I feeling so ashamed right now?

"Sure, that's *one* hunting tactic we use, but Vampires have pheromones in our breath, too. If we get close enough to you, we can influence you to do *anything* we want — I believe you humans have referred to it as compulsion before in your little story books about us."

My embarrassment was quickly burned away by a blinding rage. All those times Rafe had cornered me, all those times I'd thought he could actually like me, could actually *want* me... He'd been trying to use his *compulsion* on me? He'd fucking *lied* to me! How the hell had he lied to me? Lust was clearly clouding my judgment, my senses. And now, here I was... Looking like a stupid, human fool! Was he using his compulsion to seduce me in the fitting room today? He must've been. I wanted him so badly I thought I'd explode. *How dare he!*

"Is it something you can turn on and off?" I demanded.

"Of course," Batten grinned before his brows raised at something behind my back. "Rafe, you dirty dog! I believe you and Georgia are going to have a *long* talk after tonight."

I whirled to see Rafe hovering near the edge of the booth. His honied skin was even more ashen than usual, but his stony expression betrayed nothing.

"Let's go, Georgia," he murmured as he extended a hand out towards me.

I slapped it away with a growl. I wasn't sure what I was thinking, but I paused before I got out of the booth. Whether it was me being petty, and hurt, and betrayed, I couldn't be sure, but I leaned back towards Batten and grabbed a handful of his blonde curls. His lips parted in shock and delight as I crushed a long, passionate kiss on his lips — making sure Rafe saw every tongue-filled second of it.

Batten was in hysterics by the time I pulled back and flipped Rafe off. A dangerous storm cloud had rolled across his expression, but I pretended not to notice as I shoved past him and made my way out of the club. I didn't turn back or even slow down until we'd reached the car. I was so pissed I couldn't even feel the burn of the cold night air. I was a fool. A stupid fool who'd fallen for every stupid trick in the book. What use was an ability to sniff out lies when you couldn't even tell when the person you liked lied to you? Having a relationship wasn't in the cards for me. I guess it never was. Every guy I'd ever fallen for had fucked me over. I didn't know why I thought a Vampire would be any better. In fact, he'd been the worst of them all! Did I ever really like him? How could I even know if my feelings towards him had been real? He'd been *hypnotizing* me from day one.

I reached for the door handle as Rafe crunched through the snow behind me but stopped as my anger got a second wind. "Where the *hell* have you been all night?" I demanded.

Rafe's fingers wove through his sandy locks frustratedly. "I found Dash." The cool, even tone of his voice was enough to make me explode all over again.

"Well, I guess I should've known you wouldn't be worried about me."

A twinge of hurt crossed his eyes before they flicked to the ground. "He's in the trunk."

His shocking admission was enough to make my rage dissipate for a moment.

"What?"

"He's in the trunk," he repeated as he moved to go around to the back of the car.

I joined him a minute later after he'd unlocked the trunk and thrown it open. Sure enough, there *was* a man lying there in the fetal position — bound, gagged, and blindfolded. The man wiggled and moaned a bit as he felt the fresh air from the outside hit his skin. At least he was alive.

"Are we in the fucking mafia or something now?" I hissed. "What were you thinking?"

"*I was thinking* that I didn't want this one to get away. He hasn't been here long, though. I came to find you again once I made sure he wasn't going anywhere."

I rubbed at my eyes to make sure I was seeing this right. There was no going back now, though, so instead of complaining, I accepted the situation as it was.

"That's Dash?" I jerked my chin at the man.

Rafe grimaced. "I think so, but I'm not *exactly* sure. As you can see, he hasn't been too cooperative."

My fists clenched and unclenched by my side as I tried to get a grip on my emotions. "What. Do. You. *Mean?* It either *is* or it *isn't!*"

Rafe didn't respond as he leaned down to lower the man's blindfold. "If you behave, I'll let you sit in the car with us," he told him.

The man's brown eyes bugged out of his skull, glittering with fear and recognition. He tried to wiggle free again, desperately shouting something I couldn't make out beneath the duct tape over his mouth.

"Guess that's a no, then," Rafe sighed, replacing the blindfold and slamming the trunk shut.

My hands shot to my hips as I raised an incredulous brow. "Where are you going to take him?"

"*We*," he corrected. " — are taking him to the Citadel for an interrogation."

Chapter Seventeen
Interrogation

I stared blankly at Josh Peters through the two-way mirror. He was hunched over a metal table with his face buried in his arms. The interrogation room was a stark concrete box, lit only by a few fluorescent lights, like a jail cell without the bars.

I couldn't help but feel satisfied to see Josh there. Even though Jaidon and Cheyenne said they hadn't found anything suspicious about him, I'd known it all along. I wanted to shout it from the rooftops! Josh Peters was scum of the earth — always had been, always would be. It felt only right that he'd be the man behind all this. Dax Winston was the supplier, and Josh *fucking* Peters was his dealer.

"Drink this," Celine murmured as she slid a Styrofoam cup of coffee between my fingers. Thankfully, she'd been able to find me a spare set of sweats emblazoned with the Triad's logo to change into when we'd arrived.

I bobbed my head in thanks.

Rafe stood a few feet away, stiff-backed and closemouthed. I hadn't spoken to him since getting into the car, but the tension that had settled between us now was even worse than the silence.

The door to the slender room clicked open with an electronic beep and Gin poked his head inside. "All done," he announced. "Mr. Peters won't remember a thing. He believes he came with Rafe and Georgia *willingly* after the Haunt."

"Thank you, Gin," Celine replied as she started for the door.

After Rafe's little performance, it had been unanimously decided that Celine should be the one doing the questioning. Like me, the others didn't think that Rafe could conduct a full interview with the man while maintaining his professionalism. To put it plainly, he was in some *deep* shit with the Council of Three — especially since it had forced Gin to break the rules and rewrite Josh's memories.

"Do you want to sit?" Rafe asked once we were alone.

I scowled at him as he slid a rolling office chair in my direction but took a seat despite how angry I still was.

"We need to talk," Rafe said as he slid across the room in his own chair to a spot beside me.

"Not now."

"Not now," he agreed.

Josh Peters' head sprung up from his arms as the door whooshed open behind him. The steady click-clack of Celine's towering pumps as she crossed the room was an intimidation method all on its own. Josh's normally clean-cut appearance was now worn and haggard. Crescents of shadow lined the skin beneath his eyes like bruises.

Celine shook his hand, then straightened her white pantsuit and sat.

"Mr. Peters, I'm Celine Bissonnette."

Josh's face contorted in anger. "I know who you are, bloodsucker."

"No need for hostility, Mr. Peters. I only want to ask you a few questions."

Josh nodded, but his scowl stayed firmly in place. "Whatever. I can't believe I even agreed to this shit."

"So, why were you at the Haunt tonight, Mr. Peters?"

Josh's eyes bounced around the room. "To get a drink."

"The truth, please."

"That *was* the truth."

Celine turned back to the two-way mirror as if she could see through it — knowing the Supernatural's, I wouldn't be shocked if she really could.

"Georgia, the buttons to your left," Rafe pointed at a metallic panel set near the mirror. "Use the top one for truth and the bottom one for a lie."

I edged in closer. "What does it do?"

"It sets off a green or red light. See them there, along the top of the wall? Usually, they'd be used for observers to signal to the interviewer to start or stop, but you can use them to let Celine know if he's telling the truth or not. You can do that, right? He doesn't have to be in the same room?"

I hesitated, then gave him a shrug as I pressed the bottom button. I could smell the first one was a lie, so... I guess we'd have to see. At my touch, a little red light flickered on near the door Celine had come in through. She grinned as she turned back towards Josh.

"Do you see that, Mr. Peters? There, behind you," she gestured to the light.

Josh shifted to look, then nodded.

"Good. And I assume you've already been acquainted with Ms. Georgia Beretta."

Another nod, though much tighter this time.

"She's watching us, Mr. Peters. If you tell another lie, she'll let me know."

A muscle feathered in Josh's jaw as he stared past Celine and into the mirror. This time, I knew for a fact he couldn't see through it, but... The way his eyes were burning a hole through it made it damn sure seem like he could.

"Fine," he growled.

"Why were you at the Haunt tonight, Mr. Peters?"

Josh's eyes returned to the table as he fiddled with his diamond-encrusted cufflinks. "To meet someone."

I pressed the button for the green light. So far, so good. The mirror and concrete separating us didn't seem to affect my ability in the slightest. Strange, but I didn't have the time or energy to question it now. All I cared about was getting Josh's confession. The sooner he was put behind bars, the better.

Celine scribbled something on the notepad she'd brought with her.

"Were you meeting Lazarus?"

"No."

My fingers found the red button instantly.

"Do you ever go by the name *Dash*?"

"Dash? Of course not."

Green button this time. If he wasn't Dash, then who the hell was?

"Who were you meeting tonight at the Haunt?"

"A drug supplier."

There was no denying that Josh Peters was good at this. He was saying just enough to answer the question, but nothing more. The flock of women he'd dated and dumped must've given him *a lot* of practice in avoiding confrontation.

"What kind of drugs does this supplier sell?"

Josh hesitated for a long moment as his tanned face drained of color.

"Saph."

Celine scribbled a bit more in her notebook.

He leaned across the table on his elbows in a half-stand as he tried to read her papers. "What are you writing?"

Celine tucked the journal to her chest. "Notes. Please remember that I'm asking the questions here, Mr. Peters."

Josh sat back in his chair with a huff and crossed his arms.

"Why were you meeting someone for Saph?"

"I take it."

I pressed the red light again.

"*Why* were you meeting someone for Saph, Mr. Peters?"

Josh's arms squeezed around his chest even more. "I was just picking it up."

"Who were you picking it up from?"

"Fine, it was Lazarus, okay? I was picking it up from Lazarus."

Green light.

"So, who is Dash?"

Without warning, Josh leaned forward and slammed his fists on the table. "I want my fucking lawyer!"

Celine only laughed. "You're not under arrest, Mr. Peters. In fact, you're free to leave any time you'd like."

Josh gave her a suspicious look, as if *she* were the one lying now. Though, if he'd been able to ask me, I would've pressed the green light for Celine.

"I'd advise against it, though. If you refuse to answer these questions, you may be prosecuted as an accessory," Celine continued.

"An accessory to what?"

"Murder, conspiracy, obstruction of justice, attempted distribution… There are quite a few things we can get you for, Mr. Peters. So, it would be in your best interest to cooperate."

Josh's leg bounced beneath the table. "If I work with you… Can I get immunity?"

"I'm sure we could work something out."

Josh lifted a hand to his mouth and chewed his nails. "Fine. Fine, I'll answer your questions, but I want it to go on record that I get *full* immunity from prosecution."

"I'm glad we could come to an understanding, Mr. Peters. Now please, who is Dash?"

I could smell the lie in *her* words this time, though. Josh Peters wouldn't be getting what he wanted. *Good.*

"Harrison Howard," he said at last.

My fingers trembled as I pressed the green light. *Harrison Howard?* How the hell did *he* get messed up in all of this? I thought back to the enormous ring on his fiancé's finger — of how confused I'd been about him being able to afford it. Suddenly, it clicked. He *hadn't* been able to afford it... Not by the salary he got from Josh's construction company, anyway. Drug-dealing was his side hustle, and apparently, a very lucrative one at that.

"Why were you there to meet Lazarus tonight?" Celine pressed. "According to Lazarus, he was scheduled to meet Dash — not you."

Josh spit a piece of his nail out on the table. "Dash hasn't answered his phone since eight-thirty. He'll usually call me to confirm the pickup, but when he didn't... I figured I had to go take care of business myself."

Green light.

"Ah, I see. You're the middleman, then?"

"Yes."

"How did this arrangement come about?"

Josh turned beet-red. "I needed money."

"I understand you own a successful construction company, are you not quite wealthy?"

Josh slowly shook his head, still refusing to meet Celine's eyes. "I had some debts I couldn't pay off. I like to gamble, and I'm usually good at it, but I've had some unlucky breaks the past few months. I thought I could make it back, but..."

"But?"

When Josh looked up, I could see his eyes were now red and brimming with tears. "I was down bad. My newest construction site kept getting stripped and, on top of my gambling debts, I *couldn't* make it up. I would've gone completely bankrupt if I didn't do something about it quick."

"So, you started selling drugs?"

"Yes."

Truth, all of this was truth... I was in complete shock. I knew Josh had told me that he didn't have the money to keep fixing his construction site after all the vandalism and theft, but... I'd never imagined it could be *this* bad.

"How did this arrangement come about, then? How are you connected to Lazarus and Dash?"

"I met Lazarus through some mutual friends we had in poker. I got drunk one night and told him about my situation, and he offered me a job. He told me that if I could find people to move his supply, I could take forty percent of the profits. It seemed like too good a deal to pass up, so I told him I'd do it. I got some men from my company, like Harrison, to push the stuff."

Still true.

"Do you know anything about the recent Saph overdose?"

Josh's expression darkened. "Yes, but I don't know how that could've happened."

"Why?"

"Lazarus... Erm — *Dax* — told me that the stuff he was giving us wasn't *real* Saph. He said the real stuff was dangerous, so we sold people a knock-off version. To my knowledge, it *was* safe, well, as safe as any other drug is... just deer blood and a few uppers to make people think it was legit. It was never supposed to be the real thing."

"But it *was* the real thing. How could that happen?"

Josh waved his hands. "I'm telling you; I don't know! I'm not the one who usually deals with this stuff. I have my guys pick it up and then I take a cut of the profit."

"You're saying you don't know anything, then?"

He shook his head.

Celine leaned in close to him. "Are you aware that Dax Winston has gone missing?"

"Wait what!?"

Celine leaned even closer and pressed a finger on the table. "Do you realize the position you're in right now, Mr. Peters?"

Josh's lips flapped open and closed as he fumbled for words.

"Do you know what this looks like? Olivia Roth and Lucky Beretta overdose from *your* supply of Saph," she raised a hand and ticked off the points on her fingers. "Then, Francine Jessops

— Whom you have had *documented* and public aggressions towards — is found dead from a staged Vampire attack. Next was Amelia Williams, a woman who also *regularly* purchased Saph from your dealers. Now, Dax Winston, *your supplier*, is missing."

Josh's face went slack. "And Harrison didn't show up tonight."

"Each one of these victims has a connection to *you*, Mr. Peters. Can you explain that?"

Josh opened his mouth to reply, but Celine slammed a fist on the table before he could speak. The metal dented beneath the impact of her fist with a violent boom that echoed through the space. Josh's brown eyes were as round as plates when he looked back up at her.

"Were you planning on getting out of the business after the overdose? *Killing* everyone who knew of your involvement, and then trying to cover your tracks by blaming it on Vampires?"

Josh was frozen in shock and fear. He scarcely even breathed as he stared back at Celine.

"Answer the question, Mr. Peters. Did Olivia's overdose trigger you to make sure that you'd never be implicated in her death? Were you offing everyone who *knew* about your role in this one-by-one?" She punctuated every word with a slam of her fist, and with each sickening thud, Josh shrunk further and further into himself.

"Well?" Celine demanded as her voice turned to a deadly calm.

Josh's lips trembled violently as tears began to stream down his face. "N-no. I didn't do it! I swear it wasn't me! None of it was me!"

I wanted to press the red light so badly, but I couldn't. Josh Peters, *damn him*, was telling the truth. He didn't kill any of those people.

At the sight of my answering green light, Celine grumbled and relaxed back into her seat.

"P-please," Josh blubbered. "You've got to find Dax and Harrison! I think they could be in trouble."

Celine stiffly gathered up her notebook and stood. "You're free to go."

Josh sprung from his chair. "No! No, please! You have to protect me! I have to stay here!"

Celine pivoted on one heel and narrowed her black eyes. "From what?"

Josh lurched forward, trying to grab hold of her, but Celine jumped further away from his reach. "From whoever is doing this to them! I could be next! Please, think about it! I could be next! If all the people being killed are connected through the Saph, then I'm probably their next target!"

"Fine," she huffed, and stalked out of the room without a second glance.

Josh Peters raced towards the door, but it whooshed shut before he could stop it from closing. His knees hit the concrete as he collapsed and pounded against it with both fists.

"You can't just leave me in here!"

But Celine was long gone by then, so there he stayed — crying on the floor in a pathetic, wallowing heap. I didn't feel sorry for him, though. He'd gotten his wish. He was safe for now. It was more than he deserved. He'd practically been the ringleader of all this shit. Even if it *hadn't* been direct, it still meant that he'd had a hand in Lucky and Olivia's overdose — and now he had to suffer the consequences.

Chapter Eighteen
Suspect

"We placed a tracker on Amelia's phone earlier," Jaidon said in that fast-paced way she always did when she was excited. "And then on Dax and Harrison's," she pointed to the high-tech glass screen of the computer towards a map.

She'd pulled it up to display a detailed view of Switchback and the surrounding areas as Celine, Rafe, Cheyenne, and I sat and listened to her presentation. After Josh's interrogation, we'd headed straight to the lab to see what Jaidon had found out from the tracers. Now, three glowing dots were flashing on the screen to signify the cell phones — each of them clustered together in almost the same area.

"From the information we've gathered, the last tower these phones *all* pinged was right around here — about a ten-mile radius," she traced her pointer finger along the screen to draw a circle. "Before it went dead, Amelia Williams' last interaction with the tower was the morning *after* her body was discovered."

Cheyenne's horrible white eyes locked on mine. "You were right, Georgia. Whoever killed her had her phone and was using it to text your friend like she was still alive."

I grimaced. Even though I'd already figured that out, I really hadn't wanted to be right, for Charlie's sake.

"What about the others?" Rafe asked beside me.

Jaidon cleared her throat and pointed at one of the dots. "Dax Winston's phone went dead around six o'clock, but it appears he was headed into Switchback at that time."

Six o'clock... Rafe and I had been shopping around six, meaning that he *had* left right after our little meeting. Why was he going into Switchback, though? It didn't make sense. If anything, I thought he would've run away somewhere that we *couldn't* find him — not right to where he knew we'd be...

"Can you pull his phone records?" I asked hopefully. "See who he might've been talking to?"

Jaidon frowned. "We tried. The phone companies won't release them without warrants. We don't have the time to go through a judge for all that. Even emergency warrants take forever."

"And it seems we don't have forever," Celine agreed.

We all nodded at that.

"Harrison's phone was here in Switchback, too," Jaidon continued. "It pinged the tower around ten tonight."

My eyes flashed to the clock. It was a little after midnight now...

"We've got to find them," I said. "*Now*, before something happens. You heard what Josh said."

"Yes," Celine agreed. "Call Switchback PD, and get them to start searching that location," she instructed Jaidon. "Georgia and Rafe will go there now, while I get the Council for back-up." Celine's black eyes hovered over Rafe with a sudden seriousness pinching her face. "Be careful with Georgia. This killer is dangerous, but we want him taken in alive, Rafe. Don't do anything reckless that could cast the Triad in a poor light."

Rafe grunted in response and placed a hand on my lower back to guide me out towards the garage. I shook off his touch and sped up my pace. Even though we had to work together, that didn't mean I wasn't still furious with him. Rafe pushed the midnight-hued Rolls through town so fast that I was almost tempted to rekindle my relationship with God.

"How are we supposed to search a ten-mile radius in time?" I shouted above the roaring throttle of the engine. "It's too much ground to cover! They could be anywhere... What if something bad happens before we can get to them?"

"We're not!"

"What the *hell* are you talking about?"

Rafe's golden-green eyes slid to mine. He looked pained, like he was trying to protect me from something.

"What? What aren't you telling me?"

"Did you look at where that ten-mile radius was?"

"Yeah?"

"Did you see what was *inside* that radius?"

I hit the dash with my fist. "Spit it the fuck out, Rafe!"

The pain in his expression shifted to pity. "*Your house*, Georgia."

My chest caved in as I realized exactly what he was implying. The killer was at my house… Or, at least, in the area. I immediately thought about the cloaked figure I'd seen the night Lucky ran away. *The killer.* Whoever had been standing over Grams' grave was the killer. I wanted to kick myself for not telling anyone about it. Why hadn't I mentioned it? The woods were dense around Grams' place. It would be the perfect spot for a killer to hide out! No one *ever* went into those woods! Grams always used to warn us that we'd never find our way back if we did. The ten-mile radius around the house, the area Jaidon had identified, would place Grams' house smack-dab in the center of it. It hadn't even clicked until Rafe said it.

"GO!" I roared. "Lucky's not safe! *Fucking GO!*"

Although Rafe's booted foot was already pressed to the floor as far as it could go, he nodded anyway.

"Georgia… I have to tell you something else."

I didn't reply; I was too lost in my own thoughts to even care. I shook my head in disbelief — slapping my palms against my cheeks and dragging them down.

"It has to be Leslie Rathmore," I said. "He has the motive! I know Jaidon and Cheyenne didn't think he was suspicious, but they were wrong about Josh, too. He hates Supernatural's! How could we have been so careless? We should've looked into him! We should've—"

"GEORGIA!" Rafe boomed so loud I jumped. He cleared his throat a bit awkwardly before speaking again. "Sorry, but you kept on going, and I didn't know how else to stop you."

I raised a brow and gave him an expression that said "*Well, you've got my attention now*".

"I have to tell you something else," he repeated. At my answering nod, he took a deep breath in, as if he were winding up for some long story, and blew it out shakily. "I stalked you. I stalked you and I'm sorry, but I couldn't help myself. I was trying to figure you out and — That's beside the point, but when I was at your house one night, I saw something weird. I didn't think anything of it until... Until tonight."

"What did you see?"

"I saw Lucky covered in dirt, running from the woods."

My mouth went dry. "It was you. *You* were the one in the cloak?"

"I'll explain later, now isn't the time..." He paused as he tried to reach out and grab my hand. I jerked back and retreated towards the door as far away from him as possible.

"Georgia, I don't think the killer is Leslie Rathmore."

"Fuck. You," I spat out with every single ounce of venom and hate I had. "What are you trying to say right now? That my brother—" My words failed me. I was so furious, I couldn't speak straight. "My brother, who can barely even get up off the couch to eat or take a piss, is some kind of mass murderer? Is that what you're *really* trying to say to me right now?" My voice had risen to a shriek, but I didn't care.

 How dare he! How fucking *dare* he! I couldn't even believe what was coming out of his mouth right now. Given some time, I *might've* been able to forgive him for using his Vampire compulsion bullshit on me, but *this?* This was unforgivable.

"I'm sorry. We'll see for ourselves in a second, anyway. We're here."

I tossed myself out of the car and slammed the door shut so hard that the windows rattled from the force of the impact.

"Stay behind me," Rafe said, moving in front of me as we approached the dimly lit house. Nico's truck was parked in the drive, which I immediately considered to be a good sign. Lucky couldn't possibly be the killer when he was being watched almost twenty-four hours a day. Rafe was insane! He had to be.

I growled at Rafe and flung his protective arm aside as I marched up the steps and into the house. A small fire was crackling in the hearth, illuminating the living room enough for me to see two long familiar figures sprawled out beneath blankets opposite each other on the couches.

"See," I hissed at Rafe. "Nothing amiss here. And now, we're wasting time when we could be out there—"

Rafe's palm sliced through the air as he shushed me. He made his way towards the couches and threw the blankets off one by one. Nico was dead asleep on the first couch. He didn't even bat an eye as the covers were ripped off him. A horrible, sickening dread crept over me as Rafe removed the second blanket. It was déjà vu all over again when I saw what was beneath — an artfully arranged assortment of pillows were pushed together in just the right size and shape as Lucky's body.

"Fuck!" I screamed, definitely loud enough to wake Nico up, but still, he didn't even stir. Scared now, I ran towards him and grabbed him by the shoulders to shake him awake. Nico's head lolled back as limply as a sack of flour on top of a scarecrow.

"What's wrong with him?" I asked, already feeling my eyes get wet. I placed my fingers over his pulse, and let my tears flow freely as I felt the steady beat of his heart.

Nico is alive. Nico is safe. Alive. Safe. I repeated the words over and over again in my head to calm back down.

Rafe reached for a glass on the coffee table and gave it a long sniff. "Eye drops. Someone's given him eye drops."

"What do eye drops have to do with anything?"

"Untraceable in a drug test, but powerful enough to knock you out for a few hours."

I nodded, suddenly realizing that I didn't care about that right now. "Okay, whatever. We've got to find Lucky. He could be in trouble! Can you check the house?"

I knew that with Rafe's Vampire speed, he'd be able to search the place much faster, so I hung near the couch beside Nico and smoothed the strands of his hair like our mother used to do when she read us a bedtime story.

"All clear," Rafe announced a moment later, after he'd returned to the living room. "Let's search outside."

I gave him a little grunt of approval, then looked at Nico one last time before following him out to the yard. We didn't have to search for long, though. As soon as we rounded the house to the backyard, I saw it. The light was on in my work shed. I hadn't been out there in *days;* there would be no other reason for it to be on unless…

"There," I pointed at the shed. "He has to be in there."

We sprinted across the snow-covered yard towards the little building. Pain stabbed icy needles into my lungs as I struggled to keep up with Rafe's long stride. He was holding back again, though. I knew he could go faster than he was, but he was holding back for me.

"Go!" I panted. "Just go!"

He clearly had no concept of what an emergency was. Although I supposed the gesture was nice, I didn't want him to wait for me. Not when my brother's life was on the line. Honestly, I had no clue what was going on in his stupid Vampire brain anymore.

Rafe ripped open the door to the shed — like, *actually* ripped it open. The metal squealed as it was cleaved from its hinges before Rafe tossed it aside — the heavy panel coasting through the air as easily as a paper airplane. Finally catching up, we both burst into the shed at the same time to find Lucky. He was standing over my workbench with his back facing the door. The lithe muscles of his back were shaking so hard, it immediately made me think he'd gotten hypothermia or something out here. Who knew how long he'd been outside in nothing but basketball shorts and a t-shirt? He *hadn't* gotten sick, though. I could see that as soon as he turned to face us.

He was like a completely different person. There was nothing kind or familiar about his expression. His olive skin was flushed and glistened with a fresh sheen of sweat. His normally chocolate brown eyes looked shiny and black as he took us in.

When he'd turned, I could also finally see that a man was laid out before him on my table. His dark skin was swollen and bloodied, but I knew who it was without even having to see his face. Harrison Howard. Bound, gagged, and laid out on my workbench like it was Lucky's own personal operating table.

Drip, drip, drip.

The sickening sound filled the silence that had settled between us.

Drip, drip, drip.

Harrison's blood had trickled onto the floor and collected in a dark pool beneath Lucky's bare feet.

There was a hunting knife in his hand, too — long and serrated with a wickedly curved blade made for the sole purpose of carving through flesh. Lucky took a step forward, shoulders hunched up like a dog who'd raised its hackles before it attacked. The sticky sound of his blood-covered feet slapping against the concrete was even more nauseating than the incessant dripping noise coming from Harrison's wounds.

I took a step towards him with my palms outraised.

"Georgia, don't," Rafe hissed.

Lucky's answering laugh was more than enough encouragement to listen to Rafe. It was a sinister, oily sound. A sickening, hate-filled noise that beat against my better senses and told me to run far, far away.

"Georgia, don't," Lucky mimicked back. He laughed again and took a step forward. The tip of his knife flashed out in his hand as he idly picked out dried blood from beneath his filthy nails. "Do you know how long I've planned this? Did you really think you could come here and stop me, G?"

He was off his fucking rocker. He literally sounded insane. I'd seen actors portraying serial killers in movies, but that was clearly no match for the real thing.

"Tell me!" Lucky roared with so much animosity that I jumped back into Rafe for protection. He giggled at the sight of me cowering behind the Vampire. Lucky was enjoying this. He *liked* scaring me. He was feeding off of it.

"He can't protect you, G," he crowed in a sing-song voice. "No one can protect you from me, not even a Vampire."

"What are you talking about, Luck?" I stumbled over the words.

Lucky dropped his face into one of his hands and shook his head. When he looked back up, a perfect handprint of blood was painted over his nose and cheeks.

"You're *so* silly, baby sister. I've gotta kill you now! I can't have you running your mouth about this, can I?" He shook his head, then looked to the side and whispered to himself, "No, I can't have that. Not when there's still work to be done."

"Why?" I asked, the word as hollow as my insides felt. "Why would you do this, Luck? Why would you kill all those innocent people?"

"They're *not* innocent! They did this! They *made* me do this! You know it's true, Georgia! You *know* it!" He snarled. Foamy spit dripped from his mouth like a rabid animal. "They killed my Olivia," his voice had gone shaky, the first sign that the Lucky I knew was still in there, still human. But it only took another moment for the psychotic grin to return. "So now... I kill *them*."

I wanted to stay strong, but I couldn't. Tears filled my eyes once more — splashing over my cheeks. "*Who* killed her, Lucky? You guys took drugs! It wasn't anyone's fault but your own!"

"You're wrong about that," Lucky's dead eyes widened with conviction. "It's *all* their faults. All of them. They all deserved to be punished. Just one more after this… Just Josh left."

Rafe spoke this time. "Explain it to us then. Make us understand, Lucky. Maybe we can help you if we understand."

Lucky snarled and tapped the edge of his knife against his temple knowingly. "LIAR! You're lying to me! Georgia's not the only one, you know. I can tell, too! Take your bracelet off, G! You'll see. You'll understand."

I wiped at my eyes furiously, but the tears wouldn't stop coming. "Lucky, are you on something?"

"You think I'm crazy, but I'm not! Take the bracelet off, Georgia! You'll see then." He lifted his arm. "See? You see this? I took mine off and I've never felt better."

Rafe ignored his rambling. "We have Josh Peters in custody at the Citadel. If you tell us *why* we should help you, we'll take you to him."

"You swear?"

"Swear," Rafe promised.

Lucky twirled his knife around and paced. "Olivia went out with Amelia a lot. Girl's nights, or something. They liked to party, but it was never enough for Amelia. She was always trying to up the ante. She eventually managed to drag Liv out to the Haunt — dangerous and wild, just how she liked it. After a while, it got boring for Amelia… So, one night, they bought *Saph* from this motherfucker," his knife flew out towards Harrison. "And ever since then, Olivia was hooked. She never even would've *tried* Saph if it hadn't been for Amelia."

"It wasn't *actually* Saph, though," I blurted.

"I know that," Lucky sneered. "And so did she. Someone at the club eventually told her, and she got this crazy idea in her head that she wanted to try the real thing."

"Who told her?" I pressed.

"I'm getting to it!"

I stared at him, feeling my throat go raw and dry. This wasn't happening. I wanted to pinch myself to wake up from whatever nightmare I'd been dropped into. How was any of this real? He'd been a goddamned zombie for weeks! How was he doing this right now?

He worked a hand over the tense cords of his neck. "Like I was saying... She got this crazy idea in her head that she wanted to try the *real* thing. We're both picky that way, we like our shit to be pure."

I didn't even dare breathe as I watched Lucky resume his idle pacing. He was horrifying. I didn't know who he'd become or how, but... It was like seeing my worst fears come to life.

"She wanted *both* of us to try it," he corrected himself. "She wanted both of us to try the pure stuff since the fake shit was so good. She did some research on her own, to see if the rumors were true about it being deadly to humans, but... She stumbled across some blog that said taking enough Saph could actually turn a human into a Vampire. That was a shock to us, lemme tell ya. We thought they were all born, but... Not everyone online seems to agree with that. So, tell me, what's the truth, bloodsucker? Born or made?"

Rafe only blinked back at him in response.

"Fuck getting high, we wanted to be together forever. We didn't know..." His voice cracked with emotion over the words.

"So, you paid Harrison enough money to get the real thing," Rafe finished, nodding his head like he finally understood.

"Yeah, exactly, but I didn't have the money right away. I knew Josh Peters was building that new refinery though, so I'd go out there and steal all his copper and sell it off until I'd saved up enough for the both of us."

"*You* were the one stealing from Josh?" I asked.

"You can't *seriously* be mad about that, Georgia," Lucky laughed. "That bastard has enough money to build ten refineries if he wanted."

"No, Lucky, he doesn't. He's bankrupt. The only reason he even started getting his boys to sell Saph was because he couldn't afford to keep replacing all those pipes you stole."

I couldn't believe that it had taken my brother turning into some insane murderer for me to defend Josh Peters. Well, actually... No, I *could* believe it. Josh was definitely still a bastard.

"Smells like a lie, little sister," Lucky sang.

I squinted at him, forcing myself to meet his eyes. They were so... *Off*, almost like they were glittering or something. He *had* to be on drugs right now, there was no other explanation.

"Fine, he was actually in debt from gambling, but that's beside the point," I finally admitted.

"Whatever. Anyway, when we got the money, we paid Harrison for the real thing, and he got it." His eyes flashed to the ground. "We didn't know it was fucking lethal. Those blogs said it wasn't! They said it was just a lie so we wouldn't try to kill you for it! I lived, though. Somehow, I lived so I *know* there's got to be a way to do it. You Vamp's will never let that little secret slip, will ya? *Are you made, huh?* How does it work? Tell me goddamnit! I deserve to know."

Even though I knew Lucky was seriously deranged, I couldn't stop my heart from aching for him. He'd lost the love of his life. It certainly didn't excuse everything he'd done after that, but... A loss *that* significant is bound to fuck you up in one way or another.

Figuring Rafe *wasn't* going to tell him though, Lucky continued. "Anyway, when I came to, I made a promise to myself that I'd kill every single person who'd had a hand in murdering my Olivia. I wanted to make them *pay* for what they'd done."

"Amelia introduced Olivia to Saph, Harrison is the one who gave her the real thing..." Rafe trailed off.

"Josh Peters was the one pushing his boys to sell that shit in Switchback," Lucky finished for him. "Don't shit where you eat, motherfucker."

"Don't shit where you eat," I repeated, shaking my head in disbelief. Of course, that was Lucky, too. How poetic.

"Dax Winston turned out to be the supplier, and I got his ass, too," Lucky declared proudly. "You know it was him that Harrison got the real shit from? Dax was banging some of those Vamps at the club, and one of them gave him their blood. If I could've figured out which one of those bitches did it, I would've gotten her, too."

Bloodplay. Shit... It all made sense now. Batten had said that the girls at the club were creeped out by Dax, but maybe... Maybe one of them had been so annoyed by him that she'd given him the real thing so he would leave her alone.

"What about Mrs. Jessops, Lucky? She was Grams' best friend, she—," I broke off as my throat constricted. Lucky had killed her.

He had been the one to rip her apart like that. She'd been like a second grandmother to him...

"Yeah," Lucky deadpanned. "Yeah, I didn't want to, but it was necessary."

"How?" I thrust out an accusatory finger towards him. "How was *that* necessary? I saw her body, Lucky! You tore her to shreds! How was *any* of that necessary?"

"I didn't want to, okay?" His voice wobbled. "I didn't want to. She saw me in the woods — saw the grave, and what I was going to do. I had to kill her. I had to kill her so that I could finish what I started."

"Why make it look like Vampires then, huh?" I spat. "Why not just frame Josh Peters, or Dax, or somebody if you hate them so much? Saph dealers get the death penalty, anyway."

"Yeah, but do you know how long people get to sit on death row? They don't get to keep on living while Olivia has to be dead," he said coldly. "They don't deserve to live, and neither do you sick Vampire fucks!"

Rafe's lips twitched up slightly, and I could tell he was struggling to contain a laugh. He could probably take Lucky down in a second and a half *tops*, and he knew it.

"If it hadn't been for the Vampires, Olivia would've never gotten into Saph in the first place! She'd still be alive *right now!* We'd still be together," a tear escaped his eye, and he wiped it away furiously. "Vampires were the ones to blame for all this shit, so I made sure everyone knew it."

A slow, mocking clap rang out behind us. The unmistakably loud sound ricocheted through the small space like a gunshot. "Amazing show, but that's quite enough now, Lucky," Celine purred.

I whirled to find her standing there with an army of bodies all lined up behind the broken doors of my workshop. The Council of Three, the Switchback police, even the news people and their cameras had all been there to hear Lucky's confession.

Lucky's scream was pure animalistic rage as he leapt for me. The last thing I saw before I hit the ground was his bloodied knife slashing down on top of me in a wide, menacing arc. My head banged against the concrete hard, but... I didn't pass out like I'd expected. Pain radiated down my forearm in hot, pulsing waves as my blood spilled out from the fresh gash. Stars burst behind my eyes as I lifted my head and saw Rafe had stopped him. His hands were on Lucky's blade. He'd twisted the knife around in his grip and pierced it hilt-deep into his belly. My head flopped back to the floor. *No, no, no.* None of this was supposed to happen. I prayed that I'd finally pass out — prayed that the next time I opened my eyes, all of this would be some horrible bad dream.

Rafe's handsome face swam into my vision. "Medic!"

I tried to raise my arm and wave him off, but I couldn't seem to move it. "Don't let him die," I croaked instead, each word feeling like a fresh knock to the skull. "Don't let him die."

Rafe gave me a curt nod as he reached his hands below me and scooped me into his arms. I leaned against his muscular chest and took in his familiar, cloying scent. Then, I leaned into the exhaustion and closed my eyes — tumbling back into the beckoning darkness.

Chapter Nineteen
Broken

"There you are," a rich, warm voice greeted me.

My eyes fluttered open at the sound. I tried to push against the bed behind me but stopped to hiss as fire cascaded through my arm. His hands were on me in an instant, gently grasping my shoulders to push me back down.

"Don't try to move now," he soothed.

My head lolled to the side as I tried to track the owner of that voice. Gin's distinct feline features swam into my vision, his orange eyes twinkling with that strange Witchy light.

"Where am I?" I asked. My head felt like it had been squashed in an iron clamp.

A second later, a cold glass was being pressed against my lips and I drank greedily — not even realizing how thirsty I was until the water had touched my tongue.

"You're home, Georgia," Gin smiled above me. "All is well."

I passed the glass back when I'd finished and collapsed into my pillows. Blue-gray light streamed into my bedroom from the window, but I couldn't tell if it was early morning or late evening. I wasn't even sure how long I'd been out. Gin set the glass on my side table and scooted in on my bed further so that we were sitting side by side. Well, *he* was sitting, and I was lying. My eyes felt heavy again, but I fought the urge to shut them as the memories came flooding back to me. A sudden surge of adrenaline raced through my veins, dulling the pain in my arm completely as I shot up straight with a gasp.

"Where's Lucky?" I demanded, turning my head about so fast that I almost gave myself whiplash. "Is he okay?"

Gin gently forced me back to the mattress again. "Georgia, dear, don't move. You'll rip your stitches if you're not careful."

"Huh?" I looked from him, then to my arm to find it was bandaged from wrist to elbow. He'd cut me. Lucky had cut me. Yes, I remember that now. But... Rafe had cut him. *Stabbed* him.

"Is he okay, Gin?" He still hadn't given me an answer. Did that mean something bad had happened? *Lucky.* My brother. My flesh, my blood. I didn't care what he did or who he'd become right now. I just wanted him to be alive.

Gin's touch was as light and comforting as my own mother's when he smoothed my hair back from my forehead. I'd been sweating, the strands of it felt damp and sticky against my skin.

"He's going to make it."

The tension in my muscles instantly melted away at his words. *He was okay. Thank God, he was okay.*

"I'm sorry," I blurted, already feeling my cheeks go hot. I wasn't sure what I was sorry for, but I meant it. I was embarrassed... Hurt... Confused. I was so many things at once it was hard to latch on to one particular emotion. My brother was the murderer, but I was the one who felt responsible for it somehow. He'd fooled me. It was so humiliating that he'd fooled me.

"It's not your fault, Georgia. He fooled us all."

I squeezed my eyes tight and shook my head back and forth like I could make it all go away. If I fell back asleep, maybe I could wake up tomorrow and none of this would've ever happened. It hadn't worked last night, but, hey; I was willing to try anything at this point. Where the hell was the Punk'd crew when you needed them? I was so desperate for someone to tell me that this new version of the world was fake. This couldn't possibly be my life now.

"*Georgia.* Georgia, this is our reality now. There's no running from it."

I knew he was right, but I didn't want to believe it. My brother was a murderer. I was the sister of a murderer. It was funny, though, how even that knowledge didn't change how I felt. Lucky was a murderer, and I hated him for it, but... I also still loved him. I'd always love him. The way I felt reminded me of an interview

I'd seen of Jeffrey Dahmer and his father after he'd gone to prison. Dahmer was a cannibal and a monster, but there was his father — right beside him in jail, as he described all his heinous crimes in gruesome detail. I remember thinking, *how can someone still love him after all of that?* How can his father just sit there, hear all of *that*, and *still* stick beside him? I was so perplexed by it then, but now I felt like I could relate. I understood how that feeling wouldn't vanish because someone you loved did something awful. That was perhaps the most confusing part about this whole thing. That's why I needed it to be fake. I couldn't stand the guilt of feeling love for someone that had selfishly taken away lives and memories from countless people and their families. Was I a bad person for loving him still? I certainly felt like I was.

"There were things at play that none of us could've predicted," Gin sighed.

I turned my head towards him. He was idly fiddling with one of his gray locs, staring off into the distance with glazed eyes.

"What?"

He fiddled with his earrings. "You were an enigma to me, Georgia. I couldn't figure you out until I heard what Lucky said."

"What did he say?"

He'd said a lot of things last night, but they all seemed to run together in my memory now — each word more delusional than the last.

Gin gave me a funny look. "About your bracelet, of course."

I stifled a groan as I twisted up to face him, and Gin carefully rearranged a few pillows behind me. My eyes flashed to my bandaged arm. It felt lighter, almost empty.

"Where's my bracelet?"

Gin fished something out of the pocket of his dark purple robes, then dangled the strand of shiny black stones in front of me. "Curious... Curious, that I'd never taken notice of it before."

"Why?"

Gin laid the bracelet flat across my belly. "Do you know what an Elysium stone is?"

I shook my head. What was he on about? Not that it mattered, I was too exhausted to play along. I needed to be alone. There were existential questions I needed to mull over.

"This isn't a game," he scolded me.

"Sorry. No, I don't know what an Elysium stone is."

"A meteor fell to earth near the Tunguska River in central Siberia over a hundred and fifty years ago," he began, his tone now scholarly. "A black jewel was found at its core and split into fifty-seven stones."

"Elysium stones?"

"Exactly. The stones were set into jewelry shortly after and marked for auction. Many collectors wanted to get their hands on the stones because of their rare origin, but before they could be sold, they vanished." Gin lightly traced the bracelet with a finger. "I hadn't even considered the possibility until…"

"Until what Lucky said?"

"Until what Lucky said. The jewels look like onyx at first glance, so the thought had never even crossed my mind."

"So, you're saying the bracelets our grandmother gave us were made of Elysium stones?"

"That's exactly what I'm saying," Gin affirmed.

"Am I rich or something now?"

"You certainly would be if you sold them. But that's not the point I'm trying to make."

"What *is* your point, then?"

"Elysium stones were not only rare for their origin, but for their properties as well. They act as protection — protection from Supernatural forces, both to the wearer and to any of whom she may come into contact with."

"Grams was trying to protect us from Supernatural's?" I scoffed. "No, she wouldn't. She wasn't prejudiced like Leslie Rathmore and his merry band of idiots."

"No, I suppose she wouldn't be," Gin chuckled. "I think she was trying to protect you and your brothers from *yourselves.*"

My face scrunched up in confusion and I opened my mouth to speak, but Gin beat me to it.

"You're a Witch, Georgia," he smiled. "Don't you see? I couldn't detect any magic on you… Any curses, or spells that would explain how you could resist magic so well because *the stones* blocked your powers, and mine. It's the reason I could never *fully* search your mind. The reason you could resist Vampiric compulsion. It's the reason you can detect lies. The reason Lucky could survive an injection of dead Saph. You have Witch blood in you."

A hard lump caught in the back of my throat. *No.* No, it wasn't possible. I wasn't a Witch! There was *no way* that I was a Witch. I didn't have the Marking — those weird glowy eyes.

"There is a way," Gin said softly. "Sometimes, Witches like you and your brothers are born into dormant bloodlines where the gene has remained recessive for generations. Your Grams might've realized this. It could be why she tried to protect you all."

I didn't say anything, I couldn't.

"When did she give you these?" He asked, picking the bracelet back up.

"I don't know. I was just a kid."

"She never told you how she came to possess them?"

"She said she found a pouch of stones in our attic when we were young. They were like an old family heirloom or something. She didn't know what else to do with them, so she had bracelets made for me and my brothers."

"I suppose it could've all been a strange coincidence. It's also possible that your ancestors knew of the recessive Witch gene in your bloodline and obtained the stones for their own protection. Whatever her reasoning was for giving you all these bracelets, even the Elysium stones couldn't block your abilities completely, Georgia. I see that they've fallen out of their setting over the years," he pointed at where my anxious habit had dislodged the stones. "And each time, it's made you *that* much more vulnerable to magic."

All I could do was blink at him. I was at a loss for words. I thought about all the times my ability had failed me. Were there more stones in my bracelet back then? I couldn't even remember when the first one had fallen out. Was that why Dax was able to lie to me about his marriage? Could it be the reason I'd never known that Mrs. Jessops had been lying to Grams? Or why Scylla's siren thing had almost worked on me?

"With these bracelets, there was no way to tell how strong your family's bloodline really was," he continued. "But I believe your theory is right. The fewer stones you had, the more your powers could come out, and the more you could be vulnerable to others' powers as well."

"Lucky took his bracelet off."

"He did. And that's what made him so dangerous. A Witch whose powers have been blocked for so long could easily be driven to madness if the blockage is suddenly removed. The combination of trauma Lucky has suffered mixed with his newfound abilities were a recipe for disaster."

He sighed and scratched his chin. "A Witch's magic is tied to their emotions. Without proper guidance, the flood of emotions one feels after a blockage is removed can easily turn volatile."

The famous temper, the "Beretta bomb". We all had it. Me, Nico, and Lucky were all born with the same awfully short fuse. It was what we'd always been known for.

"You're right. I believe your powers are all rooted in anger. That may be why you find it difficult to control your temper."

"Where is yours from?"

"Peace," he grinned. "I'm at my most powerful when I'm at peace."

"Makes sense." It was embarrassing to find out that my "Witchness" or whatever was rooted in such an ugly emotion.

"Anger isn't always ugly. Anger can be fire and passion and conviction — if you learn to control it properly, of course."

"What if I don't want to?"

"It's your choice, Georgia. It hasn't always been, but now that you're armed with this knowledge, the decision is all up to you." He reached across me to squeeze my uninjured hand. "Whatever you decide, I will be there for you."

"And Nico... Lucky?"

An emotion like regret tugged at the wrinkles on his brown face. "I've placed a permanent containment spell on Lucky's powers. He'll be at peace now; I've made sure of it."

"Containing his magic won't hurt him, will it?"

"No, it won't hurt him."

"Rafe told me that a Witch's magic can't conceal their eyes."

"In most cases, that's true. Though, with these Elysium stones, it *is* possible."

"Is that why you know so much about them?"

"Yes," he smiled. "With the ability to conceal our eyes, we Witches could live like normal human beings. That's why so many people wanted to get their hands on them in the first place."

"Lucky's eyes were shiny," I said flatly.

"So are yours right now."

He held a palm up to my face like a mirror. The air shuddered and rippled for a moment before a small compact was in his hand — showing me my reflection. I gasped aloud as I leaned forward and examined my softly lit eyes. They were still hazel, but had a soft, shimmery sort light behind them now.

I bit my lip. "So, if I decide to embrace being a Witch... What will I, ya know..."

"What will your abilities be?"

I nodded.

His palm flattened again, now moving over me so that it hovered above my face. His hand moved in a scanning motion as his eyes shut in concentration.

"You're not as powerful as your brother," he announced, retracting his hand and steepling his fingers in thought. "But with practice, I believe you could become an accomplished empath."

"What's that?"

"You're naturally intuitive. You and your brother share this, though you're much more connected to your intuition than he is... It's the reason your ability to detect lies was the first of your powers to break through the Elysium stones protections." He clucked his tongue as if remembering something else. "You have that bad habit of yours to thank for your abilities manifesting so early on."

At my incredulous expression, he pursed his lips and added, "Truly, it *is* a good thing. Had you been exposed to your powers all at once like your brother, well..."

"What can an empath do, though? Will I be able to read minds like you, or change into some kind of beast like Christian?"

"No, no, I'm afraid not. You, dear one, will only ever be able to tap into people's souls — their energies."

I'm not gonna lie, I was more than disappointed. It felt like such a lame power compared to what I'd seen the other Witches do. After all the shit I'd been through, I, *at least*, deserved the consolation prize of a cool power.

"It's not lame," Gin chastised. "It's a very practical skill you possess. To know another being completely is to control them. It can be very dangerous if you're not careful."

"I can only tell when someone is lying, though... *Sometimes*."

All those times my ability had failed me couldn't have all been because of the stones, could it? I knew they'd been blocking my powers and all, but still... If my intuition was as good as Gin was saying, I felt like I should've at least been able to tell *something* was off. I may have been a Witch, but I was almost positive I wasn't a very good one.

"For now, your powers may seem weak," he replied. "But, in time — if you choose, of course... You will be able to look at someone and feel their every emotion. You'll be able to surmise their every motivation before they've even said a word."

"But I won't be able to read their thoughts?"

"No, but sometimes our thoughts can betray us. Knowing someone's emotions is much more reliable than listening to someone's inner dialogue," he chuckled. "We all lie to ourselves from time to time, do we not?"

I considered for a moment. I supposed he was right, because I was slowly realizing that I'd been lying to myself all along for not even suspecting my brother — even right up to the end. Perhaps, if Gin had been able to read my emotions, my gut feeling about the situation... We might've been able to stop Lucky sooner.

"Wait, so why can't you read others' emotions if you're so powerful?" I asked.

The big grin across Gin's feline face only brightened. He seemed almost giddy to be answering my questions. "I can *now*," he laughed mischievously. "But like the Fae, we Witches are born with certain abilities that are unique to us and our source of power."

I narrowed my eyes in concentration as I tried to follow along.

"I'll give you an example," he laughed. "Christian's source of power is fear — He has mastered fear and bent it to his will to the point where he is able to literally transform into a nightmare. The beast you see is a culmination of his worst fears turned to flesh."

I sucked on my teeth as I worked everything out. "Not every powerful Witch can shape-shift then?"

"Precisely, Georgia."

"So, what can peace do?"

"As you already know, I can read minds and see memories but, I can also contain magic, mimic it, or absorb it for myself."

A lightbulb went off in my head. "That's why everyone thinks you're the most powerful Witch. You can *copy* their powers — *steal* them?"

"Peace is an exceedingly rare source of power, and the ability to copy other Witches' abilities is even rarer than that. I can copy you, or Christian, or whoever I'd like — if I come into contact with them."

"You said Lucky was more powerful than me, though," I hesitated as I tried to come up with the right question. "What would he have been able to do — if his powers weren't contained, I mean?"

"Did he play sports?"

I nodded.

"Anger lends abilities of enhanced strength, speed, and reflexes. Considering his... *Crimes*, Lucky could've gone on to become an excellent tracker. We call them Blood Witches."

A shudder rippled through me. *Blood Witch*. It sounded sinister.

"What's a Blood Witch?"

"Blood Witches are like hunters; they can track their prey with ease and then manipulate them into doing what they want — like a Vampire's compulsion."

Horror — pure, unadulterated horror — clawed at my skin. "No signs of struggle."

"He must've figured it out somehow or maybe even done it by accident, but yes, Georgia. His victims never struggled because he was using his influence to sedate them."

"But he drugged Nico with eye drops because his *influence*," I spat the word like a curse. "Wouldn't work because of the Elysium stones?"

A sad sort of light dimmed his orange eyes. "Yes. He might've figured that out after his powers didn't work, but it makes sense why he wouldn't want Nico to remove his own bracelet."

"In case he took it off him and Nico tried to use his own powers to defend himself."

He nodded.

"He said he could detect lies like me, though."

"He could. But that's where your powers stop and his begin. Lucky carries a *deep* well of rage within him, and if you possessed such darkness, you'd likely be able to command similar powers."

"Why would he want me to take my bracelet off, though? He couldn't have known that I wasn't as powerful as him..."

"Blood Witches can sense their opponents' strength," Gin sighed. "With your missing stones, I believe Lucky *was* able to size you up."

"What about Nico?" My voice wobbled with fear.

I relaxed slightly as Gin shook his head.

"Nico seems to be the weakest amongst you all. Even with his bracelet off, his abilities might only ever work half of the time — Even if he *were* trained, he would only be able to pick up on someone's emotions or detect a lie if it were made obvious."

"Good," I rubbed at my eyes. "Good."

Nico deserved to live a normal life. He didn't need to get messed up in all of this if he could help it.

A knock sounded at my door, and I stiffened. Gin patted my head lovingly. "Now, I believe it's high time you two have a chat," he said as he rose to open the door.

Before I could ask *who* he was referring to, Rafe swept into the room.

Chapter Twenty
High Time

I groaned and buried myself deeper within my blankets, as if I could hide from him — hide from the conversation that I'd been so desperately trying to avoid.

"Hi," Rafe said softly. "Can I sit?"

I narrowed my eyes at him but nodded. I had no other option considering how he'd cornered me at my most vulnerable. Rafe patted Gin on the back as he left and shut the door behind him. He took a seat near my middle, where the ghost of Gin's warm body was still pressing the covers down.

"I'm so sorry, Georgia," he blurted just as I'd whispered, "Thank you."

"For what?" We both asked in unison.

Despite myself, I laughed and waved my good hand at him. "You first."

His eyes darkened, turning them more brown and gold than their usual sparkly green. "I shouldn't have tried to use my compulsion on you," his slight accent rolled over the broken words. It seemed like it only came out when he was getting emotional about something. "I won't sit here and make excuses for myself."

"Good."

He finally looked up at me and let me see the hurt in his expression. This time was different, though. This time, his cool, emotionless mask never returned. "It was wrong — *Beyond* wrong."

"Why'd you do it then?" I demanded, unable to keep my own hurt hidden like he usually could. "Was it all some sick fucking game to you?"

Muscles feathered along his clenched jaw. "No, even though I know that's what it might look like."

I couldn't look at him any longer. I turned my head to the side and pretended to be fascinated with the ugly floral wallpaper. "What was it then?"

"Curiosity."

I squeezed my eyes shut as a sudden anger set fire to my blood. "Were you *curious* to see if you could get me to sleep with you?"

His fingers tugged at my good wrist. "Georgia, what? I would never do that."

"So, that time by the elevator," I yanked my hand back and tapped a finger to my chin. "Or, that time at Mrs. Jessops," I lifted the finger as if I'd just thought of an idea. "Oh, and we can't forget about that time in the fitting room!"

"Georgia, stop it! I wasn't using my compulsion on you then." He crumpled slightly. "Well, the first time, yes, I was… But I swear I didn't do it any of those other times."

I wanted to spit in his face for the admission, but I held myself back. I was better than that. "When did you do it, then? Because Batten seems to think you've *been* doing it for quite some time now. *In fact*, when he did it to me, it felt almost *exactly* like all those times. So, which one of you is lying?"

"Can't you figure that one out for yourself now?" He hissed, then caught himself. His eyes rounded in shock, as if he were just as surprised as I was that those words had come out of his mouth. He pounced for my hand again, but I snatched it to my chest before he could grab hold of me.

"Go to hell," I snapped.

"No, I didn't mean that! I'm sorry." He ducked his face into his palms. "I'm sorry."

"You know what? You're right! With my bracelet off, I might be able to tell when you're trying to compulse me now."

Rafe shook his head, then lifted it from his palms to face me. "I'm not lying. I've never lied to you, Georgia… Just avoided the full truth."

Avoided the full truth. Crafty bastard. He might as well have been a politician with the way he'd worded that answer.

"You're despicable."

"If you'd asked me *directly* if I'd been trying to use compulsion on you and I'd lied, you would've been able to tell... I'm not sure if Gin told you that part. He's been coming up with a lot of theories since we finally figured it out — theories about your strength and abilities now that he's getting to test them out for himself," his wide mouth settled into a sympathetic frown.

Gin *hadn't* told me that, but I'd kind of figured it out for myself already. With my bracelet on, my powers only seemed to work if the lie was direct. I just couldn't figure out that someone was hiding something unless they talked about it explicitly. With my powers still being so weak, I guess he was trying to tell me that part would stay the same. *Yet another disappointment.*

Whatever the case may be, I wasn't about to give Rafe the satisfaction. Who cares if my stupid powers were weak, anyway? I never *asked* to be a Witch! I never wanted to live with this... This *thing* — *this curse* that never really lets me get close to people.

"Yeah, I know," I sneered.

He frowned. "When I found out about your abilities, I was curious. For safety reasons, we keep tabs on all the Switchback residents, so I knew *of* you — knew that you hadn't been identified as Supernatural. I couldn't help myself, though. There was just something... *Intriguing* about you, like a puzzle that I needed to solve for myself. If you weren't a Supernatural, what *were* you?"

He was talking about me like some goddamned science project. I hated it. I hated feeling like this freak who'd never fit in anywhere. I'd been a weirdo my whole life. It felt like I was too human to fit in with the Supernatural's and too Supernatural to fit in with the humans. Admittedly, it was nice to finally have an answer to *why* I was the way I was, but still... It hurt to hear him say those things. Before they'd all figured out I was a Witch, he'd been testing me — playing around with my emotions, with my life, like I was some pathetic lab rat. Was that really all he thought of me as? Some fascinating experiment that once solved, he would cast aside to find his next project? My eyes stung at the thought. I should've listened to my brain instead of letting my big, dumb heart get in the way. I thought that everything I'd felt for him was real, but how could that be possible now, knowing what I knew?

I searched his face for the answer, feeling angry tears prick at my eyes. "Hmm. Wouldn't a puzzle be considered a game, though?" My voice wobbled at the end, and I silently cursed myself for it.

Rafe gave me a pleading look that dulled my rage in an instant. Fine, I'd let him say his piece — but then I'd get to say mine and I wasn't going to hold back or spare his feelings just because he gave me puppy-dog eyes. After everything he'd put me through, I knew he didn't even deserve my emotions, but the immature part of me wanted him to feel it. I wanted him to know how much he'd really hurt me. It might not change anything, but it would definitely make me feel better.

"I followed you to your house," he admitted. "I thought I might be able to find something that would give me some insight about you. It wasn't all for selfish reasons like you think, though. Before the investigation, it was *my job* to find other Supernatural's and bring them into the fold. The Triad wants as few rogues as possible."

Now he was trying to say he was *forced* into making me his little pet project? It was so rich I had to laugh. Did he think that was going to make me feel better or something? Ha! He didn't even want anything to do with me in the first place!

"So... What? You were trying to recruit me or something?" I spat.

"Maybe. I don't know what I was trying to do, okay? It's so *rare* that a Witch is born not knowing that they're a Witch. They always have the Marking. I didn't know *what* you were... I knew that you were different, and I needed to figure out why."

"If the Triad wants as few rogues as possible," I snapped back. "Then you're doing a shitty job at it. The Haunt is literally crawling with rogues, you said it yourself."

Rafe's shoulders slumped. "I know. Believe me, I know. But it's harder than you think to convince them to play by our rules. I was in some deep shit with the Council already, and I thought that if I could get just *one* new Supernatural to join the Triad, then I could get out of it. Or at least make it a little easier on myself."

Wow, he was really digging himself a hole. I was his scapegoat then. *Nice*. Real nice, Rafe. I glanced at my mummified arm, deciding against unleashing the violence biting at my fingertips. I wanted to scream and yell and throw things, but in my current state, that would probably do more damage to me than to him. Besides, there was something else about what he'd said that had piqued my interest.

"Because you couldn't convince the rogues to join? How is that your fault? If they don't want to, it's not like you can force them."

His fists balled into my sheets. "It *is* my fault. It's my fault, and now I'm paying for my mistakes."

"How?"

Rafe released the sheets and ran a hand through his sandy hair, frustratedly. "I didn't lie to you when I told you I worked for the Triad out of a sense of duty. The Triad formed long before the Great Integration was made public knowledge. I was amongst those who disagreed about our unification. I didn't think that we'd ever be truly accepted by humans. And, in a way, I was right. We still struggle every day to get basic rights and protections, not to mention the hostility we get from the humans who think we're abominations."

I understood what he meant. Countless sects of people like Leslie Rathmore and his followers had cropped up across the United States to protest the Great Integration when it all came out. Those who didn't want to eat them for their powers had threatened violence and bloodshed if their voices weren't heard. And, although they *hadn't* been... It had never seemed to slow them down or dull their conviction. They would never stop until every last Supernatural was dead or forced back into hiding.

"I led a group of rebels," Rafe whispered. "Now known as rogues, against the Triad. I fought them tooth and nail up until the very last second, but it wasn't enough. There were too few of us, and too many of them."

"Why did you join their side, then? Why not just keep being rogue?"

"They infiltrated a rogue plot and captured me. It was all too easy for them, considering how Mia had practically raised me. She was always two steps ahead of me. I'd really underestimated how well she knew me. After my capture, they made it very clear I only had two options — join them or die. I wish I could say I'd been braver, but..."

Was I seriously feeling bad for this guy right now? I pressed my lips into a tight line. "You did what you had to do."

"No. No, I did what a coward would do. I didn't stand up for what I believed in and now I'm their slave," he spat with a special kind of disgust I could tell was reserved only for himself. "Like how I was my father's slave. It's now my *duty to* find rogues and convince them to join us. Who better to convince them than their old leader? That's why Batten calls me a traitor."

"So, you thought I was a Witch? Even with my powers being contained by the Elysium stones?"

"I thought you *could've* been, but like I said, I was curious either way. When we started working together, I admit I tried to use my compulsion on you. I wanted to test your powers. I wanted to see if you could somehow be consciously blocking me," he lifted a fist to his mouth — like he didn't want to let the words out. "Do you remember the day I rescued you?"

"How could I forget?"

"On the roof, that was the first time I tried to compulse you."

"To do what?"

"When I licked that blood off your chin, I wanted you to feel repulsed. You weren't, though. I tried it again at the elevators, I wanted to see if I could make you... Well, for lack of better words, *hate me*."

I snorted impatiently. He'd honestly done the exact opposite.

"You wanted me to hate you? Why would you want that?"

He fiddled with his earrings, twisting them back and forth so that the clear blue surface of them danced in the light. "It would be the easiest thing to make you feel. It's much easier to produce than love, or admiration, or happiness. I thought that, if you *were* intentionally doing something to block me, that I could use that feeling to slip past your boundaries."

"The only thing that's made me *hate* you, Rafe — Is how you've tried to manipulate me."

"Yes, I know." He reached out a hand again, but this time I didn't pull away. He gave me a grateful look as I allowed his cool fingers to interlock with mine. "I stopped after that. I *swear* I didn't try it again. I would *never* compulse you to sleep with me, no matter how badly I want you."

His words sent a ripple of pleasure through me. *Damn him.* I was so torn. On one hand, I hated his guts and never wanted to see him again, but on the other... Well, on the other, let's just say

I wanted him to get up and lock the door right now so that we could finally have some much-needed privacy.

I shook my head to banish the steamy scenario from my thoughts. "What about Batten, though?"

He scowled at me but didn't remove his hand from mine. "What about Batten?"

My face flushed as I looked at our hands. His huge palm had swallowed mine completely whole. "Well, he tried to compulse me…"

His thumb began making lazy circles on the back of my palm. "I assure you that whatever you felt was mostly his influence, but… With your stones," He paused as storm clouds rolled over his features. "I don't know. It's hard to say how much of his compulsion affected you."

It's hard to say how much? I wanted to disappear. I wanted to shrivel up into a ball and *die*. I couldn't actually want *Batten*, could I? Admittedly, he did have this odd sex appeal about him, but surely, I was too smart to fall into such an obvious trap as his. I thought back on the moment. The feeling of Batten's teeth grazing ever so lightly across my skin, the fiery feeling in my belly that followed. I was grateful Rafe hadn't been there to witness it. I was too humiliated to even admit to myself that maybe some part of me, no matter how small… *Had* wanted Batten. That maybe, just maybe, what I felt wasn't *completely* because of his compulsion at all. I silently cursed myself for falling for the whole bad boy act. It was just so… Irresistible.

"Whatever," I muttered. I didn't want to think about it anymore — didn't want to think about what I would've done, what I would've let Batten do if we'd been alone for one more minute. I squeezed my eyes shut and exhaled, trying to wipe that thought away, too. It was probably just hormones and a few too many drinks… *Nothing more.*

"Georgia," Rafe breathed. "I like you so much. I don't understand how it happened, but… It did. You're my favorite person. I've been trying to tell you that for so long."

When I opened my eyes, his face was mere inches from my own. My heartbeat leapt into my throat. He leaned forward over the bed so that his body hovered above my own. Our breath mingled in the space between us, hot and full of longing. I desperately wanted to close that short distance between us, but I held back. His eyes wavered a moment before his plush, sensual lips found my forehead. Warmth bloomed in my chest as he placed a feather-light kiss across my skin and leaned back to look into my eyes. "I'm so sorry."

Before I could think about it, I pulled my hand from his and reached up to tangle it deep within his silky hair. It was even softer than I'd imagined. I tugged on his head, bringing him closer towards me. He hesitated for a moment, then gave me a look that said, *"Are you sure?"* I laughed at his cautious expression.

"What's wrong with you?" I giggled. "One minute you're talking about all the things you'd do to—"

He crushed his lips against mine, effectively silencing me and making me forget about words entirely. There was no beginning or end to the kiss, no telling where my lips stopped and his began. Every ounce of my being was focused solely on his touch, the feel of his full lips dancing with mine — nipping and teasing and gliding across my skin as if they'd been made to kiss me and only me. His hands hid in my hair and cupped my cheeks. Our tongues and teeth and lips wove together, greedily exploring each other until he finally pulled back, leaving me gasping. I wanted more. God, I wanted so much more. I tried to pull him into me again, but he only laughed and shook his head.

"I think you're forgetting about that very large cut on your arm, G."

I hissed with realization as fresh pain spiked through the wound. *How had Rafe even known?*

"It's bleeding," we both said in unison.

I threw my head back on the pillow and laughed. "I think you made me pop a stitch."

Rafe leaned away and pressed a hand over his heart in mock surprise. "Me? I think *you* did that all on your own, darling."

I laughed again. I don't think I'd ever seen him be playful like this… It was nice. Of course, though, the moment could only last for so long until reality came crashing back down.

"What happened to Harrison?" I sighed. "Dax?"

Rafe's frown was all I needed to know. Lucky had gotten to them before we could.

"Harrison was still alive when we got here," Rafe said. "But he'd lost too much blood by the time he reached the hospital."

I looked up at the ceiling, feeling my vision glaze over. Mrs. Jessops, Amelia Williams, Dax Winston, Harrison Howard... All of them were gone. All their futures and lives and hopes and dreams... Taken away by the tip of my brother's hunting knife.

"Your family is in the hospital with Lucky for now," Rafe continued carefully. "But Charlie's here... If you want to see him?"

My eyes snapped back to his. "What? Of course, I want to see him! Why didn't you tell me sooner?"

Rafe brushed another kiss over my forehead as he got up. "I was being selfish, I apologize."

I blushed and gave him a little smile — one he returned like we were sharing a secret. I supposed we were, in a way. I didn't know where the hell we were going, or if I could even think about putting a label on it right now, but... I knew I liked him. I couldn't deny that part of myself any longer. After all the hate and fear and anger... It felt good to be liked back for once. He didn't even think I was a freak for being able to sniff out lies, because he was kind of a freak himself. A Vampire and a Witch. God, thinking about myself as a Witch felt... Strange, but also right — like I finally knew my place in the world. I supposed that this meant I forgave him. How the hell had he done that? I was basically the world record champion of holding grudges and Rafe had come in and completely shattered that. It was scary falling for him. I felt hopeful and so utterly vulnerable all at the same time.

We'll just see what happens, I assured myself.

I didn't want to complicate it any more by obsessing over it.

We'll just see what happens.

Chapter Twenty-one
Aftermath

Charlie had already been crying before he even got to my room. I could tell because every time he cried, he got this red splotchy rash along his neck and forehead. Without saying anything, he flung himself on my bed and wrapped his arms around me. I groaned as his weight landed on my bad arm but didn't pull away. We sat there like that for a long moment before he sat back and looked at me.

"I'm so sorry, Georgia," he shuddered as a fresh sob wracked through his body. "I don't know what I was thinking. I—"

I moved my good hand up to push the curls away from his splotchy face. "It's okay, Char. It's okay."

A single tear escaped his eye as he lifted my hand to press it against his cheek. "I was so angry. I was saying stuff I didn't mean."

"I know, Charlie. I know, and you had every right to be angry. You were hurt," I laughed at myself. "You're acting like I haven't known you my whole life. We both do the same thing when we're hurt — me especially. You don't need to apologize."

"I really liked her, Georgia. I *thought* I really liked her... It seemed like we had so much in common, but it all makes sense now why I thought that."

"Yeah, it does. I'm sorry, Charlie. I never would've expected that—" I tucked my chin to my chest. It was my turn to cry now.

I was just so angry, and embarrassed, and most of all, *hurt* by what Lucky had done. I knew Gin said it was natural, expected even. His powers were unleashed so suddenly any Witch could've predicted the outcome, but... That still didn't excuse anything. It would *never* excuse all the heartache and pain he'd caused. It would certainly never bring back all those people he'd killed, either.

Muscles jumped beneath Charlie's skin. "Lucky was texting me the whole time, huh? Makes sense why I thought me and Amelia were so alike."

"Yes," I admitted, even though I didn't want to. "Yes, he was texting you."

"Why?"

When I finally looked back at him, his tears had dried up. There was nothing but pain on his handsome features now — raw, fresh pain and confusion.

"I don't know. I think he was trying to cover his tracks long enough to finish what he'd started."

He nodded, although I could tell he still didn't understand. I knew the feeling. I didn't think that I'd ever *really* understand myself.

"You're a Witch," he said.

"I guess I am."

"Are you okay with that?"

I blinked at him, not knowing if I even knew the answer to that yet. It felt right, but would being a Witch change me? Would Charlie still be my friend if I was a Supernatural? Would my own family even look at me the same? They hated the Supernatural's.

"I don't have to be," I said cautiously, trying to gauge his reaction. "Gin can take away my powers if I don't want to be."

"I'm okay with it," he replied as he dropped our hands to my lap and interlaced our fingers. "If you want to be a Witch, or even if you don't... I'll support your decision."

"Thank you," I whispered as I gave his hand a squeeze. I didn't think he'd ever know how relieved I was to hear him say that. I'd lost so much that I didn't know if I could stand anything else in my life changing right now.

"At least we know *why* you can tell when someone is lying now," he said.

"At least."

"Wait, your eyes are crazy right now, G."

"Yeah," I said, trying not to squeeze them shut as he analyzed them.

"You know they're calling you a hero? You're like famous now, girl."

"What?"

"For solving the case. For stopping Lucky like you did and working with Supernatural's. You and Rafe and the Department are like... All anyone can talk about."

"It wasn't *me* who stopped him, Char. I didn't even see what was right under my nose until it was too late. I'm not a hero — Rafe is. He's the one that realized before anyone else did."

"*Yeah, yeah.* You know how the news is, though. Everyone is saying you're some kind of pioneer for the Supernatural's integration. Nobody really knows that you're a Witch besides me and them, so you're like this great example of how humans and Supernatural's can actually work together." He dropped his voice into a conspiratorial whisper. "Plus, I heard some of them talking downstairs, G. I think the Supernatural's are gonna offer you a permanent position on their team."

"What!?"

"This whole thing has been like super good press for them, especially with a human working for them... I'm sure they wanna keep the ball rolling on this before all the hype dies down."

"I bet Garcia's been taking all the credit for making it happen," I muttered.

Charlie's huge smile was all the confirmation I needed.

"Are you gonna do it?" He paused before adding, "If they ask?"

I didn't know what I was going to do. I didn't care that it was sort of a half-truth on their part to not reveal that I wasn't *exactly* human, but... Did I want to work for the Department of Supernatural Resources forever? What would I even be doing?

Sure, I'd had a lot of fun with them, and they definitely treated me way better than any of my human coworkers had, but... At what cost? I'd been through more shit with the Department these past few weeks than I had been in my entire life! Still, though, I couldn't help but be reminded of Mrs. Jessops.

"In the end, we're the same, you and I. We're both supporters of the Supernatural's."

We *were* the same in the end, and I *did* want to support the Supernatural's in any way I could. If my being a part of their team could help move the Great Integration along, I knew that I would have to do it. I knew I *wanted* to do it. It may have been that old social worker in me that pulled me towards the decision, but I couldn't stand idly by and watch as this major social injustice played out. Who knew how long it would take them to finally get the rights and protections they deserved? Who knew how long it would take for humans to stop hating them? If there was something I could do to help, I wanted to.

"Yes," I announced at last. "Yes, I think that I'll do it."

Charlie's smile only got bigger. "Great, can you stand?"

A sudden knock at the door cut me off. *What the hell did I need to stand for?* What I *needed* was some sleep and maybe some of my dad's famous ravioli.

Celine poked her head in. "It's time. Put that bracelet back on."

Charlie nodded, clasped my bracelet back on, then helped me to my feet.

"Time for what?" I squeaked.

"Sorry, Georgia," Celine frowned. "Gin was eavesdropping."

I leaned into Charlie for support. "Wait, what is it time for?"

Everything was moving too fast.

She hurriedly waved us through the door. "Press conference."

I immediately pulled away from Charlie's arms and jumped back into the safety of my warm bed. "No, no, no! No, I can't."

Charlie quickly chased after me and hauled me back upright. "Georgia *hates* public speaking."

Celine flapped a hand towards the door again. "You won't have to speak then, okay? Just stand there and smile while we give the announcement."

Charlie stopped me from running away this time. His strong arm was locked tight around both of my shoulders as he guided me through the door and down the stairs.

I gestured wildly to my huge granny-style nightgown. "I'm not even dressed! I probably look like hell!"

"It'll be better for our narrative, anyway," Celine replied curtly. "You're a survivor, and the people want to see that."

"I don't *want* the people to see that!" I latched on to the banister and held on for dear life. Hell no! I wasn't going anywhere! *The people* could wait.

"The humans need to see that we're not the monsters here, Georgia. *They are*. One of *them* did this to you!" Celine beckoned us again from the bottom of the stairway. "We've got to address this and show the world that Supernatural's don't want to hurt humans. We've got to show them that all we want is peace and mutual respect between our species."

I immediately bristled at the insult. "You're forgetting that the *one* who did this to me was my brother! I'm not some prop you can use to—"

"Further our cause?" Celine drawled. "Is that not what you want, Georgia?"

I hesitated for a moment, and Charlie let me this time. "I do, but not like this. I'm *terrified* of speaking in public. Not to mention speaking in public while I look like dogshit."

Celine pursed her lips. "Can you change quickly?"

I looked at Charlie, then back at her. They were both staring at me hopefully. Seeing that there was no other option, I finally nodded. "Five minutes max."

She tapped her shiny wristwatch. "Very well. Five minutes."

I raced back up the stairs and threw on my best sweater (the bright red one with no holes), black jeans, and combat boots. My hair was a lost cause at this point, so I just ran a brush through it and swiped on some mascara. I was right, though. I really did look like hell, but there was no time to worry about fixing it now. I should've been more concerned about, well, *everything* happening right now, but the world was suddenly turning at light-speed. I didn't even have time to process what I was about to do.

Five minutes later, I was back downstairs as promised and walking into the blinding flash of at least three hundred news cameras. The press swarmed around the house like locusts.

As of today, the world would know me as Georgia Beretta, an official employee of the Department of Supernatural Resources, not the "human lie-detector", or the weird girl with one friend. I was just Georgia now, and it felt good.

Still, though, I would have to decide on whether or not I'd become a Witch. What would people think of me then? What would *I* think of me then? Sure, it might've felt right, but it was so scary to think about having to admit that.

It was hard to be sure of anything right now, but one thing was for certain... My life was about to get a whole lot weirder.

About the Author

Based in Atlanta, Georgia, new author Kyra Fullam is an avid reader and lover of all things fantasy and science fiction. When she's not devouring her latest find from the local bookstore, you can find her cooking, painting, hanging out with friends and her dog Craig, or furiously typing away at her latest novel.

Made in the USA
Columbia, SC
30 March 2025

55873428R00148